II

COMPANY

OF

WOLVES

CORY BARCLAY

Of Witches and Werewolves
Book II

www.CoryBarclay.com

First edition: September 2017

Cover art by Vaughan Mir (wyldraven.deviantart.com
Cover design by Mike Montemarano (mikemontemarano.com)

ISBN-13: 978-1975933777

ISBN-10: 197593377X

Please consider signing up to my newsletter for new release information and specials at www.CoryBarclay.com

This book is dedicated to all my friends who have supported me in following my dreams and have helped me get this far.

You guys rock.

To Malachi

Is it faaaaar !

Cazy Burk

ALSO BY CORY BARCLAY

OF WITCHES AND WEREWOLVES SERIES

Devil in the Countryside

Table of Contents

PART I

Wolves in the Herd

CHAPTER ONE

ROWAINE

1592 – The North Sea

Rowaine frowned as she stared at the picture on her lap. Her nails bit into the ruffled paper, her hands shaking.

"You need to stop worrying, Row. You will find him someday."

She looked over her shoulder at Dominic Baker, a handsome young man with fine features and a warm smile. She wasn't sure how he managed to keep looking so youthful and healthy. It was as if he hadn't aged a day since she'd met him three years before.

"Right now we need to focus on the task at hand, yes?"

Rowaine sighed, folding the picture into a small square. Standing from her bench, she stuffed the picture in her tunic, close to her heart. She walked to the gunwale of the ship, put her hands on the railing, and gazed out at the blue-black water of the North Sea as it gently lapped against the hull of the boat. The waves rocked the *Lion's Pride* in a soft rhythm, back and forth. Rowaine felt at peace. She always felt at peace out at sea.

She faced her friend. "I feel we might never get the chance to finish that task, Dom."

"Don't say that," Dominic said. "You know you have support."

Rowaine shook her head, her dark red curls bobbing from shoulder to shoulder. "I'm afraid it might not be enough."

"It has to be. If we keep going like this, we'll all end up at the bottom of the ocean, or worse, at the end of a noose. We have to do something. You're our best hope. People are counting on you, so stop sounding so dreary."

"What would you have me do? He's our captain, for God's

sake."

"Doesn't make him any less of a madman, Row."

Rowaine peered down at the wooden railing. "I know that," she muttered.

Dominic put a hand softly on her shoulder. "The men are waiting on you. When you're ready." He nodded at her with his infectious smile.

After he'd left, Rowaine watched the sun for a moment as it fell behind the horizon. She sighed, then turned to observe the ship.

A few men were still on deck, huddled in a circle, sharing stew and swapping stories. One man was bent over, shivering uncontrollably in a corner even though the day was still warm. Adrian Coswell, the first mate, was perched at the helm, resting his elbows on the wheel and grinning at the sturdy woman beside him, both deep in conversation. He'd rented her the last time the *Pride* went to port.

That was a long time ago. Rowaine had stopped counting the days since she last saw land.

She glanced toward the horizon, the sky growing darker by the minute. To her right, the ship's flag—a red lion's jaw biting into a gold coin—billowed in the wind. Rowaine gave it a firm salute before turning away and heading to the nearest stairwell, where she slowly made her way below deck.

In her small room, Rowaine viewed herself in a dirty mirror as she tied the front of her leather shirt together. Her eyes moved down the mirror to the two pistols hanging from the belt around her waist.

She wanted to look battle-ready.

She ran a hand over the top of her smooth, leather shirt, as if trying to flatten her breasts. Then, taking her dark red hair in both hands, she tied the curls into a ponytail before stuffing it beneath her shirt.

She wanted to look like one of the boys.

Finally, she strapped on her steel-toed boots and grabbed a

small pouch that jingled as she tucked it away in her tunic.

She wanted to look like she had money.

She blinked at herself in the mirror, furrowing her brow as she leaned closer, then wiped some crust from her long eyelashes. Nodding, she left the room.

The *Lion's Pride* had two common rooms. She squeezed by a few men in the narrow corridors as she made her way to the smaller room near the ship's aft. The men she passed were just waking, getting ready for their shifts to begin. She nodded at them; they returned the gesture. Footsteps pounded from above. Some shouting followed, likely from First Mate Coswell.

She took a deep breath and opened the door. A cloud of tobacco smoke immediately surrounded and smothered her.

"Close the damn door, girl, you're letting all the goods out!" a gruff voice complained.

Rowaine coughed and squinted through the cloud, trying to find the person. Her eyes landed on a man seated at a table. Daxton Wallace, the ship's carpenter, was a stout man with a shiny head and a mouth incapable of forming a smile, mostly because of the tobacco pipe permanently stuck between his lips.

Next to the smoky carpenter sat Jerome Penderwick, a middle-aged, English surgeon with beady eyes lost deep in his head. Unlike Mister Wallace, Mister Penderwick smiled often, but it did him quite a disservice since he had only four or five teeth on any given day. In fact, each time Rowaine saw him, it seemed that his teeth fluctuated, in both number and location.

Rowaine's eyes moved to Alfred Eckstein, the ship's main rigger. Younger than Daxton and Jerome, he had big, strong forearms and ears too big for his head.

Dominic Baker, the *Pride's* cabin boy, was the last of the men at the roundtable. He was responsible for relaying messages from the ship's captain to the rest of the mates. With a twinkle in his eye he patted the empty chair next to him.

Rowaine ducked from the cloud of smoke and sat. She took a moment to look at the faces around the table: Daxton puffed on his pipe; Jerome's beady eyes circled the room; Alfred sat patiently with his hands folded; Dominic drummed his fingers on his legs.

All eyes focused on Rowaine.

"Well," she said, "shall we begin?"

A moment of tense silence followed. Dominic shifted in his seat. Alfred pulled at one of his large ears.

Then Daxton started chuckling. Smoke shot from his nostrils. "By God, yes we shall!"

With a collective sigh, everyone sat back.

Daxton reached inside his shirt, producing a deck of cards that he slammed down on the table. Alfred stopped pulling his ear. He leaned forward and rubbed his hands together. "What's it today, gentlemen?" he asked, then eyed Rowaine. "And lady."

"M-mister Baker, you won last time. What do you s-say?" Jerome asked. The surgeon had a stutter.

"I say One-and-Thirty," Dominic said, leaning across the table and grabbing the deck.

All the men faced Rowaine.

She smiled. "One-and-Thirty it is."

Daxton Wallace drew his sword from its sheath and placed it in the center of the table. Jerome Penderwick gasped. All eyes glanced at Rowaine.

They'd been playing cards for hours. One-and-Thirty was a simple game, perfect for thickheaded seamen. The goal was to get as close to thirty-one as possible with cards of the same suit. Each player had three cards, discarding unwanted ones and replacing them. Aces were worth eleven; face cards ten.

Rowaine studied her hand: an Ace of Hearts, a King of Hearts, and a Three of Diamonds. A score of twenty-one. All but she and Daxton were out. She peeked over her cards at Daxton, whose scowl made him difficult to read.

Daxton glanced up from his cards, then nudged the sword on the table. "I'll wager my father's cutlass, my prized possession"—he paused, waiting for everyone to eagerly lean forward in suspense—"in return for one night with that sweet flower of yours."

Alfred chuckled. Dominic tilted his head down.

Jerome started to say, "That's g-g-gr—"

"Spit it out, amputator," Daxton urged.

"That's gross." Jerome loudly exhaled.

Rowaine was smiling. "Fair enough. I've always liked that sword. It'll look good on my wall. If this is what it's going to take to gain your support . . ."

"Row," Dominic started, "you don't have to . . ."

Rowaine lifted her palm to stop the cabin boy. "Quiet, Dom." Her eyes remained fixed on Daxton. "What's it going to be?"

Daxton furrowed his brow. He glimpsed at his cards, sighed, then refocused on Rowaine. He knocked the table with his fist. "Stand."

Rowaine mimicked him, then laid her cards out, face-up.

Daxton's frown became a rare smile. He showed his hand: three spades—a nine, eight, and five. Twenty-two.

Everyone at the table gasped, avoiding eye contact with Rowaine, except for Daxton.

Rowaine frowned, then shrugged. She began to untie the cords holding her leather shirt together. "Well," she said, "I'm a woman of my word."

As she undid the first cord, everyone's eyes widened, none more than Daxton's. Jerome stuttered, mumbling incoherently. Alfred had his chin in his palm, observing the event with quiet contemplation. Dominic appeared frightened.

As she started untying the second cord near the top of her breasts, she stopped. She looked at Daxton. "I get to bring my guns in the room though, Dax."

After a moment of silence, Daxton chuckled nervously and the tension left the smoke-filled room. Everyone, except Daxton, leaned back and exhaled.

The carpenter blushed. "Bah," he said, waving a hand at Rowaine. "I know you've got sweet Dominic all wrapped up in your loins." He leered at the handsome cabin boy next to Rowaine. "He may be younger and more handsome than me, but if you're ever needing the *real* thing, it's waiting right here for you." He stood from his chair and grabbed his crotch, making clear to Rowaine exactly where "it" was.

The card game continued for some time, until the discussion took a more serious, quieter tone. This meeting, after all, had been for more than just a game of cards.

Jerome Penderwick, the *Pride's* lone doctor and surgeon, was the first to spoil the fun.

"I don't know how much longer we can s-stay out at s-sea," he said. "My s-supplies are running dry, and I'm sick and . . . sick and . . . t-tired of the feverish and dying. More people will die, at a f-faster rate if we keep on." The other men all shifted in their seats. It took so long for him to speak his mind that they were all losing patience.

Daxton was the next one to speak. "I'm with the amputator. The captain is more interested in his reputation and wealth than with the well-being of his ship or crew. He's near ready to run the *Pride* into a watery grave if we don't port soon. I'm running out of wood fast. I can hardly make repairs to the ship and I've got termites eating away at everything."

"One thing's for sure," Dominic said, "the captain's hellbent on furthering his own reputation. But some of us have *families* to feed—"

"You don't," Alfred said, drawing an irksome stare from the cabin boy.

"Thank you for reminding me," Dominic said. "I'm trying to make a point."

Daxton pointed at Alfred. "I know you can agree with me. I've seen your storage."

The big-eared rigger nodded. "You're right, Dax. Our ropes are weak and brittle. Our flagpole is liable to fall at any moment. The ship is falling apart."

Jerome looked at Rowaine. "You're our navigator, Row. So s-s-steer us."

While Rowaine didn't control the wheel, she was the *Pride's* best pilot at sea, always pointing the ship in the right direction. She could tell when ships were approaching by a simple change of wind. They could be a hundred miles from shore and Rowaine could sense where land was based on the taste of the sea salt or the smell of the birdshit. No one on the *Lion's Pride* questioned her judgment when it came to all things nautical.

But the trajectory of their ship didn't need deciding. What needed deciding was the direction the *crew* needed to take.

All eyes turned back to Rowaine. "I know, gentlemen, that we're in dire straits. Our ship needs repairs. We need food. We need medicine. We need to unload these spoils and celebrate with our families."

She studied each face.

"And our captain is a madman."

An image of their last ship-boarding episode flashed through her mind. She remembered watching her captain slit the throats of the male slaves being transported, grinning the entire time. Then he'd moved on to the few women aboard, allowing the crew to have their way with them and taking the youngest one to his own cabin. Rowaine could still hear her screams echoing through the ship.

A sheen of sweat had formed on Rowaine's forehead.

"Are you okay, Row?" Dominic asked.

Rowaine cleared her throat. "What do you boys think is the best plan?"

"We've been over this," Alfred said, forming a steeple with his hands. "And we can't seem to agree."

"I say we hold a vote," said Dominic.

Daxton snarled. "You may be pretty, but you're a dumb pup, Dom. We won't win a vote—we don't have the numbers. What do you think the captain will do when he finds out? He'll either maroon us or feed us to the sharks."

"So mutiny is our only option?" Alfred asked.

"Sounds dangerous and b-bloody. I expect I'll be n-needing more medical supplies," Jerome said.

All eyes circled back to Rowaine, hungry for the leader to respond. She sighed, then began to speak just as a flurry of pounding feet sounded above deck. Rowaine examined the ceiling. Dust rained down, mixing with the smoke in the room.

Then came more footsteps. Then shouting. Finally, a bell rang out, followed by the booming words of the captain blasting above them:

"Get your arses to the deck, mates! There's a ship on the rise!"

*   *   *

Above and below deck the scene was sheer chaos.

Gunners took their stations behind the cannons. Jerome Penderwick fled to his surgery room, readying for the dismal bloodshed sure to come. Dominic held Rowaine's hand for a moment before running off to the ship's starboard while drawing a rifle. Daxton joined him. Alfred worked the rigging and sails with other seamen, struggling to position the *Pride* toward the oncoming ship.

Rowaine watched men run into each other, snarling and baring teeth, as they prepared for whatever was on the other side of the water. Glancing past the railing, she could make out the blue flag of the other boat flapping in the windy night sky.

Rowaine realized it was a trade galleon. She gave a sigh of relief, hoping that the boarding would go off without complications, though she knew that was unlikely given her captain's violent predisposition.

Her eyes moved to the bow of the *Pride*, near the steering wheel. Captain Henry Galager waved his saber in the air, screaming at the sky. He wore his signature Viking helmet—or what Rowaine assumed a Viking helmet looked like—complete with menacing horns. It had been a prize-piece from a ship raided years back. First Mate Adrian Coswell stood next to the captain, wearing his long overcoat and high boots, mimicking Captain Galager's gestures.

A stream of gunpowder smoke wafted into the sky from the other ship, followed a moment later by a booming thunderclap. Rowaine held her breath.

Two cannonballs landed harmlessly in the water, far from the *Pride*. A rolling wave broke on the ship's hull. The galleon was too far from range. Rowaine figured it was filled with simple tradesmen who wanted only to keep their distance from Galager's frightening leonine flag.

But Rowaine knew that firing on the *Pride* was a bad idea.

Captain Galager hooted and hollered and shouted, "Steer right for 'em, boys! We're having a night tonight! Sounds like they want a fight—so let's give it to 'em!"

Some of the crew raised their fists to the sky and cheered. Others stayed quiet, including Rowaine. She made her way toward the bow, drawing her pistols from her belt.

They cut through the waves, edging closer to the galleon. As they neared, Rowaine could see her original assumption was correct: The people aboard the galleon were terrified, some visibly shaking.

It didn't take long for the *Lion's Pride* to reach boarding distance to the tradeship. Captain Galager made sure his men didn't fire on the boat, lest they damage whatever goods there might be.

As they boarded with ropes and ladders, the tradesmen shivered and backpedaled from the approaching pirates.

Captain Galager was the first aboard, his heavy boots clanking on the ship's deck. He twirled his saber in his hand as he paced in front of the frightened crew.

"Where are you headed, fellow?" he asked the first man he reached.

From the deck of the *Pride*, Rowaine aimed her pistols in the general direction of the other ship. Then she flinched and her pistols were aimed at Captain Galager.

She had a clear shot at the back of his head. *I could end this now,* she thought, but shook the idea from her mind. If they were in the midst of battle, with bullets flying and swords swinging, it would be one thing, but this was a peaceful boarding. She didn't feel like dying quite yet, which would surely be the outcome if her guns were the only ones firing and the captain was the only target.

"W-we're going to Spain, sir," the frightened man said.

"What are you transporting?"

"Linens, my lord."

They must be headed for the English Channel. Poor bastards were so close.

"Where is your captain?" Captain Galager asked.

A man emerged from the crowd. He was calm, tall, and stiff, with a long mustache and a neat beret on his head. "I am the captain—"

Captain Galager speared the man in the neck before he

could finish his sentence. Galager twisted the sword. The man stuttered and coughed, the blood streaming down his chin. His eyes blinked a few times before he crumpled to the ground.

Everyone on the trade galleon gasped and cried out.

A few of the pirates from the *Lion's Pride* chuckled, but no one louder than First Mate Adrian Coswell, who let out a bellowing cackle.

"For firing on my ship," Captain Galager said. He watched the huddled crowd of tradesmen while stepping over the blood pooling near the dead man's head. "Speaking of, where is the man who actually pulled the trigger?"

The crowd parted. A man was brought to Galager, arms held by two other men. He kicked and screamed the entire way, tears streaming down his face.

The two men gave the culprit to Coswell as Galager pointed to his first mate with his bloody sword and said, "Set him on his knees."

Coswell pushed the weeping man down. The man wedged his hands together. "Please," he begged, "my lord, I was only following orders!" The man was more a boy.

"I know, son," the captain said in a low voice. He lifted his sword and sliced down into the boy's skull. The boy's crying stopped, he fell forward, his face landing on the deck with a thud.

Rowaine grimaced and closed her eyes. She could hear the maniacal laughter of First Mate Coswell echoing from the other ship.

"Cos," Galager said, wiping his bloody blade on the dead boy's shirt, "find the linens. The rest of you, back to the *Pride*."

"W-what about us, my lord?" asked a brave man from the trade boat.

The captain sighed. "How many lifeboats do you have?"

"One, sir."

"Well, I count about twenty of you," Galager said, pointing his sword at the heads on board. "So I guess it'll be a tight fit, eh?"

Panic erupted on the ship, the tradesmen pushing and shoving each other as they all raced toward the single lifeboat.

Galager stomped his boot on the deck. "Not until we're done getting your loot, you shits! I don't care what you pitiful rats do after that. But if you cause a ruckus while my men are working, I'll take your lifeboat and you can all *swim* to Spain!"

Everyone on the galleon stopped moving.

It didn't take long for the crew of the *Lion's Pride* to raid the tradeship. They were a skilled, experienced group, after all. They boarded the *Pride* with barrels full of fine silks and linens.

Within minutes the raid was over. Captain Galager returned to the bow of the *Pride* as the ship slowly rocked away from the galleon.

"Just remember," the captain said to the tradesmen as the *Pride* floated away, "Captain Galager spared your lives. Don't forget it, and don't forget to tell your friends!"

He broke out in laughter and spun away.

As the *Lion's Pride* departed with its booty, Rowaine could hear the screams and hollers and gunshots from the other ship's crew, now transformed into bloodthirsty beasts, killing and maiming one another in their desperation to find room aboard their small lifeboat.

Rowaine figured the night was over.

She couldn't have been more wrong.

After the raid, a celebration was the usual order of business. But this time things took a very different turn.

"A job well done, men, but I'm afraid our good fortune has been sullied by an . . . unfortunate discovery," Captain Galager announced. "It's come to my attention, mates, that we have . . ." he waved a hand in the air as he paced the bow of the ship, as if searching for the right word. When he turned back to the assembled group of about thirty, he said, "We have . . . *rebels* in our midst, boys."

A wave of murmurs and whispers swept through the gathered crowd.

With a furtive glance, Rowaine squeezed Dominic's hand, gulping loudly.

"Isn't that right, Cos?"

"That's right, sir," First Mate Coswell assured.

The captain held his cutlass out, point-first at the crowd, moving the blade from face to face, all eyes following its tip.

When it stopped, everyone turned.

To face Rowaine and Dominic.

Rowaine began to sweat. Thoughts raced through her head. *Who betrayed me?*

Quickly replaced with more immediate and horrid concerns.

"That's right, gents. We have a *mutiny* on our hands! And to imagine, it stems from our own lovely navigator . . . *Rowaine Donnelly!*"

"Damn bitch," one man shouted.

"Traitor!"

"Awful whore! Let's all have at her!"

Two men grabbed her arms. With a cry, her hand was ripped from Dominic's.

"Now, now, gentlemen"—Galager put a hand to his chest in mock pain—"surely, I am heartbroken. But I can't be that surprised, can I? That's what I get for being generous enough to bring a treacherous, diabolical . . . *she-devil* on board! Whatever her reasons—and be assured, I'll find them out soon enough—this cannot stand."

Rowaine gaped helplessly at the angry sneers from the filthy men. Her gaze locked onto Doctor Penderwick near the back of the crowd, his beady eyes closed, his head bent downward. She next saw Daxton's big, shiny head, his frown green and sickly.

As Dominic Baker was pulled away from Rowaine, he cried out.

"Bring the bitch here!" First Mate Coswell screamed.

The pirates cheered.

"Wait!" Captain Galager shouted.

Everyone quieted, a few heads tilting in confusion.

"That's too easy," the captain clarified. "I can hurt her all I want, but why not take what she loves most, first? Then I'll deal with the red-headed whore."

A cruel smirk grew on the captain's pocked face. His sword moved to Rowaine's left, and everyone's eyes again followed the blade. "Bring me that man she holds so dear!"

The sword pointed at Dominic.

"No!" Rowaine screamed. "He's done nothing!"

The crewmen laughed, grabbing Dominic by the arms and legs.

"Rowaine!" he cried, trying to reach out to touch her hand. He was pulled away and pushed to his knees in front of the captain.

"Sir," he pleaded, "why are you doing this? I'm your cabin boy! Your messenger!"

Captain Galager nodded calmly. "Yes, Mister Baker, which is why I'm so crushed that you didn't warn me of this treachery. So, let's go to my cabin, *boy*, and maybe you can earn your forgiveness."

Captain Galager grabbed Dominic's arm and yanked the young man to his feet. People snickered as the captain passed by the parting crowd, ambling down the stairs.

Rowaine felt tears trickle down her cheeks. She closed her eyes.

It didn't take long for the screams to begin below deck. First loud, then muffled. Half the crew cheered and laughed; the other half remained awkwardly silent, their heads bowed.

The image of the young girl from the past flashed through Rowaine's mind, memories of those tortuous shrieks from the captain's cabin drowning out Dominic's muffled screams. Rowaine clenched her jaw. Tears of sorrow became tears of hatred, tears of rage. She tightened her fists so hard she felt the blood seep from her nails and fingers.

A few minutes later, Captain Galager appeared, tightening his belt. He gave a large, fake yawn. Some of the crew chuckled.

He then pointed at Rowaine. "Now, bring the girl here," he said, his voice dark and menacing. "And take her guns away."

Rowaine stood stunned and petrified. Her tears had stopped, replaced by a stone-cold expression of fear and anger.

She was dragged below deck, to the abyss of the captain's room. Dominic was huddled in a corner, naked, his legs drawn to his chest, his face nestled between his knees.

Rowaine almost broke down as she eyed the bloody sheets

on the bed.

Captain Galager unbuckled his belt and threw it against the wall. With a cruel grin he motioned for Rowaine to get on the bed. He started to untie the cords of her leather shirt.

The screaming started. High-pitched, loud, and frequent. Many of the pirates chuckled and cheered, while the others didn't.

Five minutes later, the screams and cheers ceased. The boat grew quiet. Only the gentle sound of waves lapping against the ship's hull remained.

Footsteps sounded below deck. The crewmen started hooting.

Then the chatter abruptly stopped. Heads tilted in confusion.

Rowaine stood in the doorway.

Several crewmembers drew blades and guns.

But Daxton Wallace was too quick.

He, with his crew of carpenters behind him, was upon the vicious men in seconds, his father's sword inches from First Mate Coswell's neck.

Meanwhile, Alfred Eckstein had a gun pointed at the back of another man's head. He clicked the matchlock.

Coswell, praying to live another day, urged his crewmen not to make any hasty decisions.

Even the timid surgeon, Jerome Penderwick, had two pistols aimed at two different men.

The scene was almost absurd, the ship at a total standstill, guns and swords pointing in all directions. No one dared move a muscle until everyone figured out what was what.

Rowaine's right, bloody hand held a small knife. In her left was something else. She dropped it onto the deck. It landed with a grotesque plop.

"Your captain," she said, nudging her chin toward the bloody thing.

Captain's Galager's severed penis.

CHAPTER TWO

SYBIL

County of Norfolk, East Anglia, England

Sybil Nicolaus rested near the window of her small house, smiling as she watched her child roll on the ground. She leaned over and tickled him on the stomach, causing the toddler to belch and giggle. At two-and-a-half, Peter Sieghart was the pride of Sybil's life.

She peered up from Peter, out the window, to the flat, rural countryside of Norfolk County. The springtime grass fluttered from a light wind as far as her eyes could see. She watched a group of men painting a four-walled structure a little ways from her house. Her husband, Dieter Nicolaus, was one of the men, laying tile on the roof of the building.

The front door of her house creaked open and a young man strolled in. Of medium height with a wiry frame and shaggy hair, he wore a frown on his face.

"Is there a problem, Martin?" Sybil asked. "How are the cattle?"

Martin Achterberg was sixteen years old and Sybil's dear friend. Several years earlier, when just barely in his teens, he'd almost become her groom in an arranged marriage, though she now viewed him more like a younger brother. Sybil often wondered about her *real* younger brother, though she kept those thoughts to herself.

"A slight one, Beele," Martin said, rubbing the back of his neck. "The young calf is having trouble feeding from Lily. She might have a bad leg." Martin eyed the floor, likely worried he might be blamed for something he had no control over.

"Is there anything we can do?"

"I plan to splint her leg. Only time will tell, I'm afraid."

Sybil sighed. "Very well. Start on dinner, will you? I'm going to bring the men some refreshments."

Martin proceeded to the far end of the room where he started cutting potatoes. Without glancing up, he said, "I'd like to help at the church some day."

"We really need help with the livestock, Martin. They are just as important as Dieter's church."

Martin nodded glumly.

Once outside, Sybil breathed in deeply, letting the wind caress her face. She filled a bucket by the door with cool water, then headed down the dirt road to the structure.

Dieter was climbing down from the roof. Shirtless, his tanned skin glistened from the sweat of a long day's work. To Sybil, his lean arms seemed to grow more muscular each day from his work on the church.

"You look like quite a man, my love," Sybil said, handing him the bucket.

"I'm sorry for being indecent," Dieter said with a smirk.

Sybil laughed, running her hand through his short, brown beard. "Please, don't apologize. The women at court would be in an absolute tizzy if they saw you like this. You look quite . . . alluring."

Dieter wiped his forehead with his forearm, trying to hide his flushed cheeks. "I don't care about those women." He put his hands on his hips, took a few deep breaths, then turned to his church. "We're finally almost done with it," he said. "We should have the first layer of paint done by tomorrow. Then we'll put up the cross."

As they spoke, the other men kept working, hammering nails, positioning posts, and painting.

"I'm very glad for you," Sybil said. "It's a great accomplishment."

"Be glad for *us*, Beele. It's what you wanted too, yes? Aren't you still planning things?"

"I have some ideas."

Dieter cupped his mouth with his hands. "Grant, David, Leon, my wife has brought water."

The three workers let out sighs and grunts, then rushed over, voicing their thanks to Dieter's pretty wife while scooping up large spoonfuls of water.

"How are you boys?" Sybil asked. They were all neighbors, and had volunteered to help build the church without pay.

The Frenchman, Leon, spoke in a thick accent. "Very well, Madame Nicolaus. Claire will be thrilled to hear that our church is almost complete."

Sybil curtsied. "Give Claire my thanks for letting us use you, monsieur." She scanned the men's faces one by one. "Make sure you tell your families they are all invited to our feast once the church is finished."

With the sun setting, the three men thanked Dieter and Sybil and took their leave, walking back toward their houses and families. After they'd left, Sybil asked, "When do you hope to have first Mass?"

"This Sunday."

"That's in three days."

"That's why we're working extra time tomorrow."

"Martin says our calf is having problems feeding."

Dieter crossed his arms over his chest. "That's a shame."

As the couple spoke of household matters, a carriage rolled up the road toward them. In the year Sybil had been in Norfolk, she hadn't seen a single horse-drawn carriage in the countryside.

"That's an odd sight," she said.

Several yards from the church, the carriage stopped. A middle-aged man hopped out. He wore a purple vest and puffy shirt, looking nothing like the farmers Sybil had grown to know. His cheeks were high and pointed.

The man bowed. "Good day. I am Clarence Bailey, the reeve of this land." He spread his arms out wide, gesturing at the rural shire. "Though he's not with me now, I believe you've met my tax collector, Timothy Davis."

Dieter put a shirt over his head. "Yes, my lord. We're surprised—but pleased—to finally meet you. Mister Davis seems like a good man, and a fair taxman."

"Indeed." Reeve Bailey had sly eyes. "I apologize for not making your acquaintance earlier in the year. Times are busy. But

I had to come down when I heard you were building . . . *this*."
He eyed the church in a strange way. Sybil couldn't decide
whether he approved or not.

"Worry not, my lord," Dieter said. "You would be quite
welcome at Sunday's Mass for your generous hospitality—for
allowing us to live on your land."

The reeve beamed. "I would very much enjoy that, as would
my wife." He reached into his vest and pulled out a piece of
paper. Perusing the paper with scrunched eyebrows, he stopped
when he came to a certain line, exclaiming, "Ah, here it is. It says
in my docket that you two are from London." His eyes moved
quickly from Sybil's to Dieter's. "But you seem to have quite an
accent, sir."

Dieter hesitated for a moment. "Sybil and I originate from
Germany, my lord. We escaped persecutors and shipped over to
London."

"Ah, so you are Strangers!"

Dieter gave the reeve a sideways glance. "Excuse me, sir?"

Bailey coughed into his hand. "Twenty-five years ago,
Norfolk was a refuge for people fleeing Catholic oppression
from overseas. The refugees were mostly French Huguenots and
Belgian Walloons. They were called Elizabeth's Strangers, and
Norfolk became their haven."

"Ah," Dieter said, scratching his cheek.

The reeve smiled broadly. "So it seems you are a new
generation of Strangers! Quite good, sir, quite good. And how
did you fancy England's capital?"

"I didn't care for it," Sybil said, stepping in. In truth, she'd
hated London. The bustling hub of English urbanity reminded
her of her chaotic life in Germany, which she'd come to England
to escape.

"Excuse my wife's brash tone, my lord," Dieter said, holding
out his hand. Sybil gave him a nasty glare. "We were welcomed,
at first, by the lords and ladies of London. But we both felt
strangely out of place."

The place reminded me of the nobles and ballrooms in Bedburg, Sybil
thought, shaking her head. *And Johannes . . .*

"My wife was pregnant, you see, so we couldn't travel far.

Also, our stories across the channel seemed to thrill and enlighten the gentry in London. But that didn't last."

Reeve Bailey sighed. "It hardly ever does," he said. "You cannot stay flavorful to those folk for too long." His eyes dipped as a private thought passed.

"Quite true," Dieter replied. "After our son was a year old, we came here. Your community welcomed us with open arms, sir, and we're grateful for it." Dieter beheld the green country surrounding him. "Although I was quite baffled when I learned there wasn't a parish church in the region. And quite pleased when Timothy Davis allowed us to build one here, as I believe it will benefit the community."

The reeve tapped a finger to his lips. "It will increase revenue, as well," he said with a cunning grin. "I'm sure Mister Davis explained how taxation works with churches in the area?"

"Not completely . . . no. But I believe it will pay for itself in the services that we'll bring to the people."

"And you plan to preach Martin Luther's teachings?"

Dieter nodded. "Among other things, my lord."

Bailey raised an eyebrow. "Other things?"

Sybil stepped forward. "After my husband holds Mass each morning, I plan to start a grammar school. I want to teach the families' children to read and write, sir."

"Lovely," Reeve Bailey said quietly, as if pondering how he'd be compensated for Sybil's hopeful endeavor.

Sybil noticed the glint in Bailey's eye. She'd been close enough to nobles to know that greedy look when she saw it, but she remained quiet.

"Very good, then," Bailey said. "You can expect to see Mister Davis within the next few days, so please have your taxes ready upon his arrival."

"Absolutely," Dieter replied, nodding. "Thank you again for your hospitality."

Reeve Clarence Bailey gave one last curt nod before returning to his carriage and driving off.

"He seems a good enough man," Dieter said, watching the carriage roll down the road toward the last remnant of the setting sun.

With a scoff, Sybil cocked her head. "Don't be fooled, Dieter. We're only numbers to him. Did you not notice that he never even asked our names?"

Dieter sighed. "Don't be so sour, Beele. You have to learn to give people a chance."

Giving her husband a weak smile, Sybil said, "You're right. I'm sorry." But she wasn't, since she didn't agree with her husband, though she felt bad about lying to him.

He's still naïve, believing too much in the good of people.

It was part of what drew her to Dieter in the first place—the kindness in his heart.

But Sybil also knew it could be a fault. And bring misery. *Look at the people I knew . . . Johannes, a chauvinistic pig and rapist; Johannes' father; that damn noblewoman, Margreth; my* own *father.*

Sybil and Dieter hiked back to their house, arms draped around each other. The sky had turned the color of a fresh bruise. Sybil looked up and thought about her father. And her younger brother, Hugo. More painful memories.

Poor Hugo, she thought, clasping her hands together as she gave a silent prayer. *I hope you're alive, brother, and I hope I'll see you one day. Each day I wonder how you're doing . . . hoping you've found success . . . perhaps a woman . . . and whatever it is you've always wanted.*

How are you, dear brother, and where are you?

CHAPTER THREE

HUGO

Bedburg, Principality of Cologne, Germany

Hugo Griswold sat under a decrepit tin awning, staring at the gray sky. He listened to the perpetual *ting* of the rain as droplets slipped through the holes of the roof. He shuddered and stuck his arms in his torn tunic, trying to warm himself.

Squinting both ways down the alley, he wobbled to his feet and wandered into the rain, letting it drench his body. The downpour plastered his shaggy hair to his scalp. He couldn't remember the last time he'd had a proper bath, so he took advantage of the rainfall, despite its bone-chilling coldness.

It was midday in Bedburg, and the streets were quiet. He didn't have high hopes for a successful day.

Someone appeared beside him. Hugo jumped with a start. "Jesus, Kars, how did you sneak up on me like that?"

Not quite fifteen, Karstan Hase was a moderately overweight boy and six months Hugo's junior. He was also Hugo's best friend. Karstan had an affable smile with a wide gap between his two yellow front teeth. Despite his lot in life, he always managed to stay positive. "It's my talent," Karstan assured Hugo. He gestured over his shoulder with his chin. "How much longer you think we got in that place?"

Hugo shrugged. They'd been residing in an abandoned house for days, but they never stayed in one place too long. The roaming patrol in Bedburg made sure of that. "However long it takes for the rain to waterlog it, I suppose."

"Have you decided what you're getting Ava for her birthday?" Karstan asked, raising his arms to the sky to let the rain wash them.

"Not yet . . ."

Two more figures emerged from the small house and stood in the doorway beneath the awning. Severin Lutz, the oldest member, was the self-appointed leader of their little brigade. The other, Ava Hahn, was a slight fifteen-year-old with pretty features, fair skin, green eyes, and dark hair done in a tight bun on her head. In the short time he'd known Ava, Hugo had come to love her. Or, at least, what he imagined love felt like. His heart always skipped a beat whenever she was close. Right now was no different.

"All right you wretches, you ready to earn your daily bread?" Severin asked. Sixteen and slightly taller than both Hugo and Karstan, Severin was crude, bad-tempered, and had eyebrows that always pointed down, accentuating his meanness. Although Hugo reserved the word "hate" for a select few, he greatly disliked Severin.

"What's the plan?" Karstan asked.

Ava had her hands clasped in front of her dirty dress. "We were thinking of doing a Beggar Drop," she said quietly. Hugo grinned at her. Her face reddened.

Hugo believed Ava felt a mutual likeness for him, but he wasn't sure. Severin always seemed to be at arm's-length with the girl, which angered Hugo to no end.

"Sounds like a fantastic idea," Hugo said.

Severin scoffed. "Who's got Tanner Row, and who's got Priest Circle?"

Tanner Row was the name the gang gave to the southwestern slum, where the hide tanners and butcher shops were located. It was one section of Bedburg's larger southern district, a slum relegated to the needy, poor, and decrepit.

Priest Circle was just south of the town's church, where all the beggars lined up each day to scavenge food from hapless priests. It reminded Hugo of his sister, who used to tell him stories of giving out food. But that was a long time ago. Hugo had shut those memories from his mind and hated hearing about Priest Circle.

"I'll take Tanner Row with Ava," he said.

Severin shook his head. "I've got Ava, and we're taking

Tanner Row," he said with a smirk. "You get Priest Circle with the fat one."

Karstan wiped his forehead with his filthy arm. "Phew," he muttered, "Tanner Row smells like shit."

"You can't *get* Ava, Severin," Hugo said. "She isn't your property—"

Severin bared his teeth, ready to pounce, but Ava stepped between them, holding out her hands. "It's fine, Hue. I'll go with Sev."

Ava hated conflict, especially between the boys, though it was an everyday occurrence.

Hugo sighed, clenching his fists. He badly wanted to punch Severin in the jaw but obeyed Ava's wishes.

Putting his hand on Hugo's shoulder, Karstan leaned in and whispered, "The Circle might be better for us, Hue. Let's just get on with it. I bet you can find Ava something pretty on a day like this."

"You're only saying that because you hate Tanner Row," Hugo said, leaning back.

Karstan bobbed his head. "Partly true."

"Well come on then, you lazy sacks, we ain't making money sitting here. We'll meet back in two hours," Severin said.

With their "leader" having given his orders, the two teams dispersed.

As Hugo and Karstan walked down the alley, Hugo looked over his shoulder. Ava was watching him, smiling.

Hugo smiled back.

"I'll be the Beggar, you be the Taker," Karstan said. They'd reached their designated spot, a circular district with shambled buildings surrounding them. Rain pelted the many beggars hovering around the opening. Priest Circle was one of the worst slums in Bedburg. Only foreigners unfamiliar with the city would dare venture into such a place, with raving lunatics and needy souls the only other people in sight.

Fortunately for the predators, there were plenty of hapless

foreigners in Bedburg, regularly wandering through the Circle.

"You aren't fooling anyone as a beggar, Kars," Hugo said, gesturing at Karstan's body. "You look like you just finished a cake, then dunked yourself in a pond of syrup."

Karstan put his arms over his belly. "I take offense to that," he said, jutting his chin to the sky. He didn't really though. He never took offense to anything. "Just because I'm not a raggedy bag of bones like yourself doesn't mean I can't beg with the best of them."

Sighing, Hugo opened his mouth to say something.

"Besides," Karstan added, wiggling his fat fingers in front of Hugo, "these aren't exactly made to go perusing in pockets."

Hugo ran a hand through his wet hair. "Fine," he said, "I'll be the Taker. It's not like we're here to get pennies in that tin cup, anyway."

Kars rattled the cup in his hand, shaking the few pennies inside—pennies they'd put there. With a gap-toothed smile, he said, "Every penny counts, Hue."

"What's your story?" Hugo asked impatiently.

Karstan tapped his chin in thought. "I'm a simpleton, and my mother's dead?"

"I know that, Kars."

Karstan frowned. "Damn you, sir. I'm *blind*, and my mother *recently* died. I'm trying to pay for her funeral."

"Fair enough," Hugo said, patting his friend on the shoulder. As they both slipped out from the shadows, Hugo had suddenly developed a limp in his right leg. Karstan tried to mimic him.

"Don't limp the same way, you fool," Hugo whispered through the corner of his mouth.

"I don't know what else to do—"

"Act like you're blind!"

Karstan put his hands in front of him, waving them around like a cadaver searching for his lost gravesite. Hugo sighed, then placed one of Karstan's hands on his own shoulder. "I'll be your guide," he said.

They walked like that until they entered the Circle, surrounded by other lost, living corpses. Hugo watched a woman feed bits of soggy bread to two small children, and he felt a twinge of guilt.

An actual, suffering family, he thought, frowning. He quickly shook away the guilt, focusing instead on Ava, and what he would get her for her birthday.

Before long, several carriages and misguided foreigners began trickling their way. As one of the carriages slowed, homeless folk quickly besieged it. But Hugo and Karstan stayed clear of the action, instead zeroing in on a man and a woman in fine clothes and knee-high boots walking toward the Circle. As the couple apprehensively approached the area, the woman put her arm around the man, leaning closer to him as they passed the surrounded carriage.

Seated near the corner of a building, Karstan, with eyes closed, aimlessly rattled his tin cup as Hugo watched from the far end of the same building.

Karstan, ever the master beggar, somehow managed to lure the couple closer as they walked by.

"Oh, honey, he's merely a boy. Don't be so heartless," the woman said.

"He looks like he just ate an entire lamb, Bernadette," said the man, scowling.

"Mother is dead," Karstan mumbled, scrunching his face to make the rain look like tears. "I can't pay the undertaker."

"Jonathan, come now," the woman said, tilting her head to the side. They moved in closer, two steps from Karstan.

As the nobleman sighed, Hugo meandered toward them. Hiding his face, he reached into his left pocket, then came up to the man's right side and bumped him. "Oh!" he said, glancing up, "I'm so sorry, sir. Please forgive me."

Jonathan groaned, narrowing his eyes on Hugo. "Watch where you're walking, boy!"

"Jonathan, enough!" Bernadette cried. "Give me a coin."

Hugo moved on, hands in his pockets. As he rounded the corner, he heard the woman say, "Here you go, young man, for your mother's funeral. I'm so sorry for your loss."

Once out of sight, Hugo flipped the coin in his hand, smiling. It was an old trick, but rarely failed. Creating the proper number of distractions—the "blind" beggar, the demanding wife, a stranger's bump—easily masked Hugo's quick hand in and out of the unfortunate man's pocket.

And not only did he have a shiny silver coin to show for it, but something else he hadn't anticipated: A ring—a wedding band, in fact—with a green stone planted in the middle, surrounded by slivers of silver. *He wasn't wearing his wedding ring, so Bernadette was probably his mistress. So . . . Jonathan is an adulterer.* Thoughts like that helped Hugo rationalize his deeds. He was doing God's work, punishing the sinners. And suddenly he didn't feel so bad for robbing the man.

Over the next hour, Karstan and Hugo continued the same basic play, until the priests came down with loaves of bread, and the stragglers slowly wandered away."What'd you get?" Karstan asked excitedly as they returned to their dilapidated house.

Hugo showed him the silver coins and pieces of cloth. But not the ring, safely concealed in his pocket.

"Very nice," Karstan said. He furrowed his brow. "What's wrong?"

Struggling to keep the ring a secret, Hugo's face betrayed him. Karstan was his best and most trusted friend. Plus, Hugo wasn't past showing off a bit. So, after a moment's hesitation, he said, "I believe I've got Ava's birthday present."

"Oh?"

Hugo took out his prize.

"Ah!" Karstan said. "She'll love it. The stone matches her eyes."

The four thieves spent the night in their rundown, makeshift home, divvying their loot and feasting on a roasted chicken. They rarely spent their earnings on food since it was simple enough to steal. Because Severin had pilfered the night's meal, he laid claim to both legs.

When Karstan complained—as he often did when his portion of the meal wasn't largest—Severin smirked. "I took the risk breaking into that house, so I get the king's size. Plus, I'm the oldest."

Hugo sat in the dismal living room and picked at bits of meat. He hadn't made the ring he'd stolen part of the collective booty, which constituted a crime even among thieves. He kept it hidden in his pocket.

When he looked up, Ava was standing in the doorway, gazing out into the alley.

"How's it?" Karstan asked her, following Hugo's eyes to the young lady.

"Rain has stopped," she said, extending her hand into the cold night. She peered up at the sky. "Looks like it won't rain tomorrow, either."

Severin slapped his knee with a half-eaten chicken leg. "Great, that means we can do a Bird Coup."

"A witch is being executed tomorrow," Hugo pointed out. "The marketplace will be packed—"

"Perfect! It'll be ripe for the taking."

Hugo watched Severin's pointy eyebrows. "There will be too many eyes tomorrow, Sev. It's too dangerous."

Severin made a clicking sound with his tongue. "So . . . you're scared? Ah, look at the frightened kitten," he mocked in a high-pitched voice, swishing his chicken leg in the air. Then his face grew dark. "Let's have a vote then, eh? Raise your hand if you're *for* the Coup."

The room was silent. Then Severin raised one of his chicken legs. Karstan hesitated before raising his hand. Hugo narrowed his eyes on his friend, but Karstan wouldn't meet his glare. "Sorry, Hue. It's as good a time as any for a Coup—crowded market, sunny skies . . . and we got to eat."

Waving Karstan off, Hugo glanced at Ava in the doorway.

"I'm with Hue," she said. "We could use a day off. We made off with plenty today."

"That's rubbish!" Severin yelled. "We can never have too much. If we don't work, we starve." He raised his other chicken bone in the air. "This vote's for Danny."

Danny was the fifth member of their illustrious gang. He'd gone missing a few months prior and hadn't been seen since.

Severin glanced from face to face. Finally, he said, "Then it's settled. We're doing the run."

Hugo opened his mouth to argue, but Ava shook her head at him. He sighed, then joined her at the door as the others continued eating.

Reaching into his pocket, he pulled out the ring. "I-I got this for you today," he stammered, smiling nervously. "Happy birthday, Ava."

Her eyes lit up. And Hugo's heart pounded. "You remembered," she said, her eyes transfixed as she toyed with the ring in her palm.

Hugo tilted his head to the side. "Of course I did. How could I not?"

Ava beamed. Leaning toward him she planted a kiss on his cheek. "It's beautiful," she whispered.

"The stone matches your eyes," Hugo blushed, repeating the point Karstan had made earlier.

Greasy hands on their shoulders startled them. It was Severin, standing between them. "What's that you got there?" he asked, snatching the ring from Ava's hand and holding it up to the sky, making it sparkle. "Keeping things from the group now, are you? That's a no-no, Hue. Makes it seem like you don't *trust* us."

"Hey!" Hugo said, "give that back to her. It's a present."

"It's part of the group," Severin sneered, holding the ring higher than Hugo's hands could reach. He laughed at Hugo's futile attempts to grab it.

Ava frowned. She took no part in the boys' altercations.

Noticing her expression, Severin sighed, then finally relented. "Fine . . . the stone looks fake anyway," he said, letting the ring fall from his hand to the wet ground. Hugo quickly snatched it up, rubbing off the grime as Severin sauntered away.

The next morning the quartet gathered at the town's marketplace, an open-air bazaar where merchants hawked their wares. Today however, bystanders filled the area, waiting to watch the public execution set to begin shortly.

It was the third witch burning in less than a month. It

seemed that more and more witches were popping up every day. So common had they become, Hugo hadn't even bothered learning the name of this newest offender.

Instead, he sat on an overturned fruit crate, eating an apple and watching the crowd grow. A scaffold had been raised in the center of the marketplace. On it stood a wooden cross—man-sized. The town's bishop, Balthasar Schreib, stood next to the cross, waving his arms as he announced the multiple charges the witch faced.

All four thieves now occupied strategic locations along the perimeter of the marketplace. They waited patiently for rich stragglers to come riding or walking by.

The Bird Coup was a particular ploy requiring all four of them.

The Owl was the lookout, responsible for keeping an eye out for patrolmen or guards. At any sign of trouble, he'd give a *hoot*. He also was responsible for picking the mark, but was otherwise relatively free from harm or exposure. Today, Severin played the Owl.

The Falcon did the mugging, because he had the fastest wings—or in this case, hands. Hugo was the designated Falcon.

The Eagle was the decoy and, if necessary, the muscle, because he was the biggest and most flamboyant. Not surprisingly, Karstan always played the Eagle.

The final part was the Raven. This role was the trickiest and required the most skill since the Raven took the handoff from the Falcon. Ava played the Raven.

The set-up was straightforward: The Owl chose the target and kept watch. The Falcon dove in, snatching the goods, while the Eagle distracted the mark. The Falcon would then hand off the goods to the Raven, who'd disappear into the shadows.

And if anything went wrong, and a mark or bystander suspected foul play, it would be the Falcon they'd go after, who would innocently show he had nothing on his person.

The group had successfully pulled off the ploy countless times.

As Bishop Schreib finished off his grand proclamation, the crowd parted to make way for two guards who escorted the witch toward the scaffold and cross.

Which was the cue for the Bird Coup to start.

Sitting nonchalantly on a stack of flour bags, Severin nodded toward an incoming merchant. Seeing Severin's sign from across the market, Hugo bobbed his head, the sign that the target had been picked. The merchant carried a large purse over his shoulder, wore lavish clothes, held a smaller knapsack on his hip, and had a woman clinging to his arm. The perfect mark.

The woman will be my best advantage, Hugo thought, watching the rich lady almost melt into the laughing merchant. They were probably drunk, arriving right as the execution was set to begin. A few people stood between Hugo and the merchant, but all faced the scaffolding, their backs to Hugo.

Hugo's heart hammered. He was twenty paces from the merchant, trying to meld into the crowd. His eyes shifted from the scaffold, back to the merchant, then back again to the scaffold.

The screaming witch was being dragged through a row of onlookers. Hugo passed her with his head down.

When Hugo was fifteen paces away from the couple, Karstan calmly nudged in behind him, keeping a few paces back. Meanwhile, Ava remained out of sight. Hugo could literally hear his heart thumping as he closed within ten paces of the merchant.

Bells and whistles abruptly sounded in his head. He stuttered a step as a man walked up alongside the merchant. A man Hugo hadn't noticed—middle-aged, blond hair, stern face. Most telling, though he wasn't outfitted like a patrolman, he carried a sword at his waist.

He looks strangely familiar, Hugo thought. But with no warning from his Owl, there was no reason to scrap the plan, so Hugo quickened his pace.

When he was within five steps of the mark, he stopped sharply, pivoting to his side so Karstan could pass. Karstan bumped into Hugo, causing Hugo to stumble into the merchant.

"Oh my!" Karstan said, shoving Hugo out of the way and facing the merchant. "My apologies, sir," Karstan said as Hugo walked away with the merchant's knapsack.

The merchant growled in protest.

Appearing from the shadows, Ava passed by Hugo as he handed off the knapsack to her. Head down, she quickly disappeared into the crowd.

Hugo exhaled as he strolled away. His heart slowed.

Until he heard a yelp.

Spinning around with panic in his eyes, he scanned the faces of the crowd.

Someone was dragging Ava by the arm through a cluster of people. As she cried out, Hugo focused across the way to the flour-stack. Severin was gone.

Coward!

He could see Karstan trying desperately to shove people aside to get between Ava and her captor.

Which was when Hugo realized her captor was the same blond-haired man who'd been beside the merchant. As the man reached for Ava's chest, as if to grab her breasts, Ava screamed.

"Pervert!"

Undeterred, the man ripped open the front of Ava's shirt and out tumbled the merchant's knapsack, which he raised in the air.

By this time, several members of the crowd had turned from the execution to face the growing commotion between Ava and her captor. When the man raised the knapsack, they collectively gasped.

Karstan finally made his way to Ava and appeared ready to bull-rush her captor, just as the man drew his sword and leveled it at Karstan's throat. Karstan gulped and put his hands in the air.

"Back, thief," the man shouted, "she's coming with me!"

He then backed into the crowd, dragging Ava behind him with the knapsack over his shoulder. As he passed the intended mark, he handed the bag to the man. "Your purse, sir," he said.

"Ava!" Hugo shouted, reaching out but clutching air.

The last thing Hugo saw was Ava opening her bright green eyes, gazing through the crowd and locking onto him, her hands outstretched.

And then she was gone.

CHAPTER FOUR

GUSTAV

Gustav Koehler doubled over in his seat, his head in his hands. He groaned. His insides felt like a snake had coiled around a porcupine and couldn't untangle.

His carriage bumped along the shoddy dirt road, twisting his intestines even more.

Gustav glanced to his right, at the legs of his scribe, Hedda. He lifted his eyes, taking in the rest of Hedda's petite body. His pain momentarily subsided. Her face was buried in a book, her large, round spectacles almost reaching the tip of her small nose.

"How you can possibly read during this treacherous carriage ride is beyond me," he said, wincing at her.

"It was your idea to come here, Gustav," Hedda replied, her eyes never leaving her book. Her light hair bobbed on her shoulders with every bump of the carriage.

"It was my father's idea," Gustav reminded her.

Hedda put her book on her knees and watched his pained face. "You didn't *have* to come here. You could have stayed in Germany."

Gustav snorted. "Not if I'm to show my father I have what it takes to carry this family onward without him."

"You give him too much credit," Hedda said. "Do you think he really cares what you can or can't do?"

Gustav ignored her, instead turning left to watch the rolling green countryside out his window.

Hedda went back to her book.

"How far are we from Norfolk?" Gustav asked.

"I don't know, Gustav."

Silence followed.

Gustav took the opportunity to reach into his tunic, very

casually so as not to draw attention. He fumbled around until he felt the glass bottle. Then, after glancing to his right to make sure Hedda wasn't watching, took a quick shot of the laudanum tincture. Quickly, he stowed his secret potion back in his tunic.

Within seconds the warm sensation surrounded his head like a fluffy cloud, separating his mind from the outside world. His intestines smoothed out, the imaginary snake unwinding itself from its prickly prey. Again he groaned, but this time in satisfaction. His muscles relaxed; his mouth fell open. A bit of drool dribbled from his lips, which he wiped with the back of his hand.

Gustav closed his eyes and leaned his head back. "What are you reading?" he asked, eyes still shut.

"Paracelsus," Hedda said, "what *you* should be reading, if we have any hope of keeping these plants alive."

Gustav opened his eyes and followed Hedda's to the cart behind them. A blanket covered an assortment of plants, flowers, and herbs. He smiled. This menagerie of plants went everywhere with him—even across the seas from the Netherlands to England. His collection of medicinal plants, herbs, and spices was his prized possession. He considered himself somewhat of an amateur botanist and herbalist, and dreamed of one day sprinkling the world with his green gifts.

Gustav glanced over at Hedda's book cover perched on her lap. *The Doctrine of Signatures*—a reference book explaining the medicinal uses of some plants and their connection with the Creator.

"I've already read that one," Gustav said, "so you don't have to."

Ignoring him, Hedda picked up her book and continued reading.

Gently, Gustav placed his palm on Hedda's cold knee. He began rubbing the warm flesh behind her kneecap, before moving his thumb up her thigh.

"Come now, put the book down," he said. "We have time before we reach Norf-f-folk . . . " His mind was swirling in a euphoric haze from the laudanum, his speech slurred.

Hedda slapped his hand away. Gustav winced. "I don't like

you when you're like this," she said.

"Like what?" Gustav asked, kneading his hand and pouting.

"In a fog."

Hedda studied his glazed, rheumy eyes, then returned to her book. "We'll be at Norfolk shortly, Gustav. Try to clear your head and get ready for what you have to do."

A few hours later, they reached the rural community of Norfolk just as the sun was setting. As their carriage rolled by the farms and small houses, Gustav noticed a church on the horizon that wasn't quite finished. The only hint it was a church was the man standing on its roof erecting a white cross. Compared to the legion of bland houses and farms they passed, the stark-white church stood out like a beacon—the most memorable landmark they'd seen thus far.

The carriage continued on. Gustav directed the driver to the largest house in the vicinity, a two-story structure with a bit more flair than most of the other buildings. Clearly, the residence of someone important.

Gustav's brain had long since shaken off the effects of the laudanum, the cloudiness now replaced with a dull aching. His insides had begun hurting again, but he hid his discomfort.

Gustav stepped out of the carriage first. He was a tall man and had to duck down so as not to bump his head on the carriage roof. As he stretched his arms over his head, then grunted and yawned, Hedda stepped out. Under her arms, she held a different booklet than the one she'd been reading.

Gustav perused the green scenery. "Dull place," he said.

Hedda didn't reply.

A man came out from the large house. He was middle-aged and wore a ridiculous, frilly outfit with a puffy shirt. His face was gaunt yet cheerful, almost like it couldn't decide whether to be happy or suspicious.

"Hello, good sir," Gustav said, meeting the man halfway. He stuck out his hand and flashed a charming grin.

Eyeing Hedda, the man cleared his throat and hesitated.

Finally, he put out his hand and shook Gustav's hand. "Can I help you? I was just sitting down for supper."

"My apologies," Gustav said, "but are you the proprietor of this land?"

The man slowly nodded. "I am the reeve, yes. Clarence Bailey. And you are . . ."

"Gustav Koehler." He spoke his name as if expecting recognition. When none came, Gustav cleared his throat as Hedda sauntered up alongside him. Reaching into her booklet, she produced a sealed letter with a red stamp across it and handed it to Reeve Bailey.

"That letter is proof of who I am, Herr Bailey," Gustav announced. "My father owns these lands. So, in turn, you work for him."

The reeve looked baffled. Before opening the letter, he asked, "And your father is?"

"Read the letter, good sir," Gustav said, shivering. "Seems like it's to be a chilly night."

With narrowed eyes Clarence Bailey stared at the letter in his hands. A few seconds later he muttered, "Yes, yes, we'd better take this inside. I'll introduce you to my wife and child, and it so happens I was sitting down with my taxman, too. Tax season is upon us, after all."

"I am aware," Gustav said. He and Hedda followed the reeve inside the house.

They wandered through a living room and came to a large table where a young woman and child sat on one side and and an overweight man with puffy red cheeks sat at the head. The fat man's face reminded Gustav of a squirrel with nuts in his cheeks.

Clarence Bailey gestured to the man. "This is Timothy Davis, my tax-collector."

The plump man finished off the chicken leg he was eating before staggering up from his chair and holding out a greasy hand.

Gustav looked at the hand with disgust, not moving to shake it. "A pleasure," he said, feeling just the opposite.

Timothy Davis rubbed his hands on his trousers, then turned to Clarence. "Friends of yours, sir?"

"Er, no," Clarence said, clearing his throat. "This man claims to be the son of the owner of these lands."

"And what is he here for?" Timothy asked, as if Gustav weren't standing in the room.

"Yes, what *are* you here for, Herr Koehler?" Clarence echoed.

Gustav inspected the small room, leering at Clarence's young wife and child. He was somewhat taken aback by the selfish attitude of the reeve—not offering his weary guests any food after their long travel. Both men seemed tense, as if trying to hide something.

"In all honesty," Gustav began, "I am here to take over the tax routes of your man."

The reeve glanced at Timothy, whose fat cheeks jiggled about, flabbergasted. "What ever for?" Timothy mumbled with a full mouth. "I've never cheated a soul."

Hedda positioned her spectacles on her nose and thumbed through a page of her book. "Unfortunately, that's not what these numbers say."

"Who's that woman?" Timothy asked.

"My scribe and assistant," Gustav said, "and you'll refer to her as Frau Hedda."

"Just hold on here," Reeve Bailey said, "I'm sure we can get to the bottom of this amicably. Timothy, take this letter and confirm its legitimacy."

"But . . . I'm eating, sir," the taxman complained, blinking sadly at his half-eaten plate.

The reeve simply stared at the round man. Timothy whined, then snatched the letter. "Tomorrow I'm supposed to go on my routes to collect the taxes," he added.

"Oh?" Gustav said. "Well, since I can guarantee that you will find my letter authentic, I shall be taking over your duties."

"You can't simply barge in here and take over my assignment," Timothy said, his floppy cheeks turning red.

But Gustav was an imposing character, tall and stoic in front of the out-of-shape taxman. "I can, and I have," he said, "because this land belongs to my father. I am here to make sure everything goes smoothly from here on out. I would like to meet the people of this shire. I will also need a place to store my plants—wherever I'm staying will be fine."

"Your . . . plants, my lord?" Reeve Bailey asked.

"Yes, Herr Bailey. My plants. If you'll come outside with me, you'll see what I mean."

Gustav and Hedda led the way out, but not before Gustav dipped his eyes to the small woman and child at the table and said, "Excuse me, ladies," as politely as he could.

Outside, the carriage-driver was feeding the horses. Gustav walked to the back of the wheeled cart. He grabbed the blanket inside and dramatically flipped it off his herbs and spices. "These are my plants. Is there somewhere nearby I can stay, so that I might come here in the morning? I'm an early riser."

Clarence scratched his sunken cheeks. He motioned toward the flat horizon. "The closest farmstead over there has been vacant for a time. There is a small plot of land where your plants should fit nicely."

"Yes," Timothy added. "The couple who lived there weren't able to pay the proper taxes, so they were ousted." He smiled, clearly pleased with himself.

"Now, now, Herr Davis, there's no need for that," Clarence said, putting a hand on his taxman's shoulder. "I'm sure Herr Koehler doesn't plan on staying overly long. Correct, sir?"

"I'll stay as long as I need to," Gustav said flatly.

Timothy Davis grunted. He put his hands on his round belly and tucked the letter he held into the band of his trousers. "I'll see if I can verify the legitimacy of this letter, Clarence."

And with that, the fat man waddled off.

Once Timothy was gone, Clarence asked, "What is it you think my taxman has done, exactly? I've known him for years. He's as trustworthy as they come."

Gustav faced his scribe. "I'm here to audit your acreage's expenses and taxes, Herr Bailey. Believe me, if there's foul play afoot, Hedda will find it. She's the brightest auditor I know."

"And what brings you here, if I may ask?"

"I'm here on my father's bidding. Yours is not the only land I've come to check. So in that, you are right, I won't be making myself comfortable for too long."

Gustav could see the relief splayed across the reeve's face. It told him, once again, that something wasn't right. *Perhaps he's guilty of something more ominous than simple tax evasion.*

Bidding farewell to the reeve, Gustav told him he'd be back in the early morning hours, then climbed into the carriage with Hedda.

As the carriage rolled off toward the vacant plot of land across the way, Gustav took another swill from his bottle of laudanum. He glanced at Hedda, who squinted disapprovingly at him.

"Now I'm your auditor, Gustav?"

Gustav shrugged. "I had to call you *something*, my dear."

CHAPTER FIVE

ROWAINE

"**Y**es," Rowaine said, "I severed the captain's prick, then his throat. If anyone wants to join him, my knife is ready."

The tension on the *Lion's Pride* was as taut as stretched rope, ready to snap. Rowaine stood at the ship's helm, hands bloodied, eyes cast down at the crew. Half of them stared at her with daggers in their eyes, the other half held weapons aimed at the first half.

She gazed at the hardened faces. "I know I wasn't the only soul tired of his antics, his madness, his bloodthirst. Constantly ordering us to go where we did not agree. Enough was enough. Captain Galager is dead. All we can do is go forward from here. I'm angry I didn't slay him sooner. If I had, what happened to poor Dominic could have been prevented."

A few mutterings floated through the ranks of the men. With fire in his eyes, First Mate Adrian Coswell yelled out, "You're a traitor, you bitch. Who will lead us now?"

Daxton Wallace, his pistol pointed at the first mate's head, clicked the matchlock, then whacked Coswell over the head with the butt of the gun. "It's a bit obvious, isn't it, mate?"

"L-long live Captain Row!" Jerome Penderwick shouted from the starboard railing. For such a skittish surgeon, he showed an amazing amount of courage.

"Yes, long live Captain Row!" Alfred Eckstein echoed.

Half of the shipmates followed suit, while the rest stayed quiet.

"I was next in line for the captaincy!" Adrian Coswell screamed, rubbing the back of his bruised head.

Daxton laughed. "I don't think you're in any shape to be bargaining, fool."

I don't want this, Rowaine thought. But she knew it couldn't be helped. *The mutiny was my idea. Someone has to lead these sorry bastards.* She kept her gaze on the first mate, before abruptly turning her head, her red hair fluttering in the breeze. "How are our medical supplies, Doctor Penderwick?"

"D-dismal, my lady."

She turned to the rigger. "And our riggings, Mister Eckstein?"

"Soggy ropes and loose lines," the young man replied.

"Termites have gotten into our wood," Daxton said, loud enough for all to hear.

Rowaine held her arms out wide. "Don't you see, Mister Coswell? Henry Galager was leading us on a death march. Can't you see the struggles of the men?"

"Henry Galager was my captain," Adrian scowled.

"As he was mine," Rowaine said, "but not anymore. Believe me, I didn't plan on doing it like I did. But when I saw how he hurt Dominic, and what he was about to do to me—" she faced the floorboards and suddenly stopped speaking.

"You'll never be more than a usurper to—"

A loud crack interrupted the first mate. Coswell crumbled to the ground in a heap. Daxton leaned over him with his pistol raised into the air.

"Dax!" Rowaine shouted as faces surveyed the commotion.

The bald carpenter shrugged nonchalantly. "I was gettin' tired of his yammering."

Rowaine groaned. *I'm trying to bring us a sense of unity, and he threatens to divide us even more! He needs a talking-to.*

Although there would be no official vote, it was clear what the outcome of Captain Galager's death would bring. Having single-handedly spearheaded the mutiny, Rowaine became the de facto captain of the *Lion's Pride.*

Now I need to figure out what to do with the people who hate me . . . including Adrian Coswell.

"Bring Coswell to Doctor Penderwick, Dax," Rowaine ordered. "Make sure he's okay, Jerome."

The surgeon nodded, scrambling over to the carpenter and fallen first mate. Grabbing Adrian's arms, while Daxton took his legs, they carried him through the parting crowd to the stairs.

As they reached the hallway, Daxton gasped then stepped aside, forcing the small surgeon to follow him—they almost dropped Adrian in the process.

Dominic Baker stood in the doorway, head downcast, his tunic torn, hands at his side, fists clenched. His normally kind face was masked with pain, his mouth a mere slit, his eyes burning with rage.

As he limped ahead, the men quietly got out of his way. When the cabin boy stepped onto the bloody deck, he stared down at Captain Galager's severed penis.

Then he stomped hard, directly on target, a grotesque squelch sounding beneath his foot. With dead eyes aimed at Rowaine, he spun around and headed back downstairs.

As his footsteps faded, no one spoke.

Rowaine sat in the same room she'd been playing cards in just hours before. *Things have changed so quickly.* She felt dizzy, but tried to hide it by crossing her arms over her chest and pursing her lips. Daxton, Alfred, and Jerome stood solemnly in front of her.

"Where's Dom?" Rowaine asked.

"Locked in his room, Row . . . er, captain," Alfred said. "He refuses to come out."

Rowaine frowned. "Even though I asked him to be here?"

"Er . . . *especially* because of that, I'm assuming."

Rowaine understood. *He blames what happened to him on me. I would too, were it me.*

"We m-must go on w-without him," Jerome stuttered, nodding to himself.

"The amputator is right," Daxton said. "No offense, Row, but why do we need him here? He *was* just the cabin boy."

Rowaine shot Daxton an icy glare, forcing the big carpenter to find an interesting speck on the wall to stare at.

"Because I'm going to name him my first mate, Daxton."

The carpenter's shoulders slumped.

"Isn't Daxton the most able and senior of our group?"

Alfred asked.

"Yes, captain, s-should we really have s-such a youngster in charge?" Jerome added.

An hour into my captaincy and I'm already sowing discord. I'll need to change that. "I am the captain, boys. You said it yourselves." She faced the carpenter. "Don't worry, Daxton, you aren't forgotten, but I've made my decision. Dominic Baker is my first mate."

Daxton said nothing. For the first time in a while, his lips stayed still.

"With that being said," Rowaine continued, "we need to make our plans. I consider you three—and Dom—my cabinet. I'll be asking you for advice. Can I trust you in that?"

She eyed each man one by one. They all nodded firmly, although Daxton hesitated a beat.

"Our first plan of action needs to be docking the ship. We will return to port on the Dutch coast, unload our loot, and acquire more men."

"*More* men?" Alfred scoffed. "Is that necessary? We can hardly keep the men we have aboard content."

"We need to replace Captain Galager's loyalists with our own. I don't trust half those wretches. We'll simply trade them out."

"They won't like that, Row . . ." Daxton said, trailing off.

Rowaine narrowed her eyes. "I don't care what they like, Dax. That's why I have you three—to help make this work."

"Right," said Daxton. "But before any of that, we need to figure out what we're going to do with Coswell. We can't trust him, either."

In unison Alfred and Jerome both nodded.

"I know that," Rowaine said. "As long as he goes, the people loyal to Galager will go with him."

Daxton sneered, his mouth agape. "Let him *go*, Row? You can't be serious. You're asking for a counter-mutiny doin' that. What do you plan to do, simply let him wander off when we dock, free to assemble his own crew?"

Rowaine slowly exhaled. "We'll be out of port soon enough—"

"We'll need at least a week on land," Daxton argued, "which

gives him plenty of time to raise a ruckus. Not only that, but we'll have to come *back* to land at some point. Revenge will be the only thing on his mind—as I'm sure it is right now."

"Well, he's un-unc-unconscious right now, so I doubt he's thinking much of anything," Jerome quipped.

"What do you suppose we do, Dax?" Rowaine asked.

Daxton reached into his tunic and produced his pipe. "I figured it was pretty clear, Row. Adrian Coswell needs to die."

Rowaine was shaking her head before he even finished. "I won't have any more blood on my hands."

"That's fine," Daxton said. "I'd be happy to do it."

Rowaine sighed, raising her eyebrows and turning to Jerome and Alfred.

"I'm w-with Daxton, captain. Adrian Coswell is a major t-t-threat," Jerome said.

Rowaine was shocked to hear that from the usually peaceful surgeon.

Alfred spoke. "It's too messy. Row, er, the captain is right. We don't want to risk another mutiny by provoking the men who are loyal to Adrian's cause. I don't think we should kill him."

All eyes focused back on Rowaine.

She sighed. After a short moment, she said, "I'll be democratic about this and ask Dom his opinion."

"Good luck getting him out of his room," Alfred said.

"I'll worry about that," she said, then spun toward Daxton as he lit his pipe. "But you'll need to put that out, Dax."

"Why is that?"

"Because you're going to steer the boat to land."

Daxton gaped. As Rowaine stomped away, she heard the carpenter yell, "Don't worry, captain, I can steer and smoke at the same time!"

It was true that Rowaine wanted Dominic's opinion on what to do with Adrian Coswell, but there was more to discuss than that. She raced to his cabin and knocked softly on the door. "Dom, it's Row," she said, barely more than a whisper.

Silence.

After a moment, Rowaine knocked again, harder this time. "I need to speak with you, Dom. It's important."

More silence.

Rowaine sighed. "Look," she began, "I know you blame me for what happened—and I'll never forgive myself, believe me. I wish I'd blasted that bastard's head off before it came to this, maybe while he was strutting on that tradeship's prow. That would have saved us all a lot of—"

The door creaked open. Dominic's face appeared in the doorway, but he looked different. Gone was the kindness in his eyes and his soft features—replaced by hard angles and a clenched jaw.

"I don't blame you, Row," he said, stepping out of the way to let his captain in. He ambled to his bed and sat down on the hard cot, wincing.

Rowaine paced the room, ready to go into her spiel, but she stopped. Taking a deep breath, she sat on the chair opposite Dominic and asked softly, "Are you okay?"

"I don't want to discuss it," Dominic said, his head slouched. "Why are you here? What do you want?"

Rowaine's throat clenched and her heart sank to her stomach. Never before had Dominic spoken to her in such an abrupt, snappish way. She paused for a moment—her mind somersaulting—barely able to speak. Now she knew how Jerome Penderwick felt every day of his life.

Clearing her throat, she fought back tears so Dominic wouldn't see her weakness.

"I want to know what you fancy we should do with Adrian Coswell . . ." she finally said.

Certain what his response would be, Dominic surprised her.

"Let him go," he said.

Rowaine teetered back. "B-but, he was Captain Galager's right-hand man, Dom. He hates you—he hates *everyone*."

Dominic shook his head. "Too much blood. I've seen too much blood."

Rowaine started to speak again, but Dominic cut her off. "If you already know what you're going to do, Row, then why ask me? Do what you will. You have my answer."

Rowaine took another deep breath. Her heart began racing. She had a sudden desire to leave the room. Seeing her best friend this way was just too depressing. But she fought on. "I'm making you first mate," she announced.

Dominic just stared at the ground.

Rowaine craned her neck sideways. "Did you hear me, Dom? I said you are going to be my first mate." But her words sounded hollow. In fact, the whole room felt hollow and empty. As if Dominic's body was there but not his soul.

"I'll let you know if I accept," Dominic said softly.

Rowaine felt a flash of anger. "With respect, Dom, I am the captain of the *Lion's Pride* now. It isn't your decision to deny or accept. Now, can I trust you to do as ordered?"

Dominic nodded. "Of course," he muttered, "I wouldn't dare deny the command of my fearless leader—"

"Enough!" Rowaine growled. "You must stop this self-pity, Dom. I need you back!"

Dominic said nothing. The longer the silence lingered, the more Rowaine regretted her outburst. "I . . . I'm sorry," she finally said. "But I'm going to need your help. Please. You're the only one I truly trust."

Dominic's eyes finally found Rowaine's. Maybe it was his realization that he needed to stop wallowing, or Rowaine's words about trust, but finally, through tearful yet firm eyes, he said, "What is it you need, captain?"

"I need you to find out who spoke about our mutiny to Galager. Someone squealed. *That* is the person I want to kill, dammit, even more than Adrian Coswell. Someone betrayed our trust and I want you to find him. When we dock in the harbor, I imagine everyone will head for the taverns. That will be where you'll discover the traitor."

"I'll get to the bottom of it, Row, you have my word. Any suspects?"

"Besides you and me, three others knew about the mutiny. And they're all currently standing in the card-room."

CHAPTER SIX

SYBIL

Sybil sat in a pew near the back of the church, watching her husband survey the front of the room. Dieter ran his hands over the fresh wood of the back wall, then moved to the pulpit.

He seems at peace, she thought, *back where he belongs.*

Dieter's church was basically complete, though it still needed some interior work, such as the stained-glass windows, some statues, and paintings of the Virgin Mary and Jesus. But for now, simplicity would suffice.

Though Dieter would never be a ministered priest again, his current neighbors didn't need to know that. He was still the holiest man within thirty miles. People valued him.

The day before he'd confessed to Sybil his nervousness about giving a sermon. But there was no question he was glad to be part of a congregation again. He liked their new neighbors, and they liked the Nicolaus'.

"You'll do fine," Sybil reassured him. "The people here need hope—something to take their minds off their farming and their poor lot in life. And you can give them that hope."

Dieter kissed Sybil passionately, then asked, "Are you sure you want to teach those rambunctious children? Do you believe they'll listen to you?"

Sybil looked into his eyes. "Do you remember when we first met?"

Dieter grinned and blushed. "How could I forget? You were in a white gown, searching for the perfect apple."

"And what was I to do with those apples?"

"Feed the poor."

Sybil nodded. "We walked hand-in-hand through Bedburg's slums, serving the most destitute and needy. I've never felt more

IN THE COMPANY OF WOLVES

useful. And I want that back. You belong in a church, preaching, just like I belong with the children, helping. You taught me things that opened my mind, Dieter. I too wish to help unburden those around us—the young innocents—from the stresses surrounding them and their families. From taxes and farming and war. Just as you do."

With a single finger, Dieter caressed Sybil's soft cheek. "You'll do great, my love."

And so Sybil sat in the back pew, surrounded by a dozen neighbors and their children, watching Dieter prepare for the first day of his new life. She marveled at how different he looked compared with just three years earlier.

Claire, the French wife of Leon Durand, Dieter's construction helper, ran a hand across her pregnant belly. As she too watched Dieter, she seemed to be thinking the same thing as Sybil. She leaned over to Sybil and whispered, "Your husband is quite enticing, Beele. So . . . confident. You're a very lucky woman."

Sybil turned red. "Leon is a fine man as well, Claire. And your daughter is adorable," she added, speaking of Claire and Leon's first child, Bella, the twelve-year-old sitting next to Martin.

Martin and Bella were whispering to each other, but Sybil paid them no attention, instead admiring her husband, remembering how shy and pale and soft-spoken he once was. Now his chiseled and bronzed features from his labors in the sun cast an impressive, confident, and, yes, enticing image. It may have taken him time to find his place in life, but now he was a strong man with a commanding presence. A man whom people listened to.

Sybil smiled to herself. She wasn't sure if Dieter's transformation came from his departure from the Catholic priesthood, or from their difficult journey across the North Sea, or their frightening time and escape from Bedburg—or a combination of them all. But whatever it was, he was indeed a changed man, that much was clear.

Dieter lifted his worn copy of Martin Luther's *Ninety-Five Theses* from the pulpit, holding it high for all to see. Sybil had given him that leather-bound book, stolen from her father, and it had become Dieter's instrument of change.

"Martin Luther tells us," Dieter began, "that we can only achieve repentance by our practice of faith alone—not through our deeds." The small room drew silent as all eyes focused on the speaker at the pulpit.

"He once asked, 'Why does not the pope, whose wealth is greater than the wealth of the richest Crassus, build the basilica of St. Peter with his own money rather than with the money of poor believers?' We are the poor believers, my brothers and sisters. Our wealth, our farms, our buildings—they do not dictate our faith, nor do they form it."

Dieter set the book back on the pulpit and raised his arms wide. "As such, our building of this church was *not* a holy endeavor." He held up one finger. "But it gives us a place to practice our faith, to commune, to repent. *That* is holy."

Eyeing the three men who helped him build the church—Leon, David, and Grant—he continued. "This was a radical idea, one that was shunned by the Catholics. It still is, to this day. They called Martin Luther a heretic and a 'demon in the appearance of a man.' But I have learned, through my own studies, that Martin Luther was a man of resolve. A man of great piety. It is my hope that we may all learn from him."

Sybil glanced to her right, where Martin Achterberg sat whispering quietly with Claire's daughter. Though Bella was four years younger than Martin, and still a prepubescent girl, Sybil couldn't help but feel a surge of hope in her heart for Martin. He had been through so much: his love for Dorothea, who was then murdered in Bedburg; the failed arranged marriage with *her*, the bride-to-be, orchestrated by Martin's own father; the murder of his father; the burning of his mother as a witch; the crushing degradation he faced at the hands of Bishop Solomon; his months-long imprisonment.

Any lesser soul—especially one so young—would have long since given up hope, or become a shell. But Martin Achterberg was strong, and Sybil felt that Dieter's words spoke directly to him.

But of course Martin wasn't listening, his attention diverted to Claire's daughter.

Sybil frowned, wondering whether she'd be any better at keeping the attention of her listeners when it was her turn to begin teaching. And unlike Dieter, she had never been a teacher or a speaker. *Will I be any good at it?*

'You'll do great, my love,' she remembered Dieter telling her.

Soon, Dieter's sermon was finished. The congregation closed with a prayer. As the adults filed out, conversing with one another, the children stayed behind. They were now Sybil's charge.

Sybil faced Martin and said, "Will you be my assistant today, Martin? I could use your aid."

With wide eyes, the young shaggy-headed man looked at Sybil. "Me?" he asked, pointing at his chest. "What could I possibly do?"

"Yesterday you said you wanted to help."

Martin glanced at Bella. "But—"

"I would like to teach you your letters as well. Like these children." *If only to keep your distractions at bay!*

Martin wrinkled his forehead, inspecting the six children left behind in the room. He was a head taller than any of them, and a handful of years older. "I think I'm too old to learn my letters, Beele. Besides, I have Lily to attend to, and her lame calf."

"You can never be too old to learn to read and write, Martin. I'll have Dieter tend Lily and the babe. Come now, I want to help you, and you can help me."

Martin narrowed his eyes. "So . . . are you doing this for the children then, or for yourself?"

A good question, Sybil had to admit. But instead of answering, she grabbed Martin's arm and pulled him to the front of the room, to the pulpit, where they looked out at those little innocent, smiling faces.

Finally, Martin relented. "They're all waiting for you to say something, Beele," he whispered, nudging his chin toward the children.

Dieter had left his copy of the *Ninety-Five Theses* on the podium for Sybil to use in her teachings. It was the only book they owned—probably the only printed book in a thirty-mile radius, not including Timothy Davis' tax book.

It will have to suffice. Sybil rubbed her hand on the crinkled pages, a wave of sad memories washing over her, memories of her father and brother. Then Martin tugged her arm, returning her to the moment.

This might be more difficult than I anticipated . . .

Teaching proved easier than Sybil imagined. She discovered she had a knack for getting the kids to learn and already felt accomplished as her hour-long class let out.

She watched Martin run off with Bella, holding her small hand as the two exited the church.

From the back of the room, Dieter was walking toward her, clapping and grinning.

"Are you poking fun at me?" Sybil asked, faking a frown.

Dieter gave her a shocked look. "Me? No! I'm applauding your effort. You were a natural, Beele, as I knew you would be." He kissed her on the cheek. "The kids loved you," he whispered in her ear, the hairs on the back of her neck prickling.

"I hope I wasn't too harsh with them . . ." she whispered back, nestling her head in the crook of his shoulder.

"Not at all."

Someone in the room cleared his throat.

Dieter and Sybil jumped back from their embrace.

A tall, blond man stood at the back of the room. He had a smooth, handsome face and wore a perfectly-tailored, gorgeous gray outfit, unlike anything Sybil or Dieter had seen since arriving in the shire.

Clearly a nobleman.

The man had his hands behind his back. A petite woman with spectacles stood behind him, a large book in her hands.

The man leered down his nose at Sybil and Dieter. "You two must be the Nicolaus'," he said. The man stood a full head taller than Dieter.

Dieter narrowed his eyes, moving to stand in front of Sybil. "That's correct," Dieter replied. "I don't believe I've seen your face before. You are?"

The man held out a large gloved hand.

"No, Herr Nicolaus," the gentleman said, shaking Dieter's hand with such force that Dieter involuntarily winced. "You have not seen me before. My name is Gustav Koehler. This is my assistant, Hedda." The girl behind the man bowed slightly.

The man appeared to be waiting for his name to be recognized. But neither Dieter nor Sybil showed the slightest recognition. The gentleman parted his lips slightly, then sucked them together.

"How can we help you, Herr Koehler?" Dieter asked.

"Well, I came to admire this new church of yours." He gazed at the ceiling and the plain walls. "It's marvelous. I believe it's the only church in quite a distance."

"It is," Dieter said. "If you would like to join our Sunday Mass, I'm afraid you've just missed it. But we'll be having another next week."

"I'm not much of a religious man."

"A shame."

"Perhaps."

A tense silence ensued as the two men stared at each other. Sybil looked from face to face, while Hedda simply gazed through her large spectacles at the book she held.

Finally, Gustav broke the silence. "I am the new tax-collector for Reeve Bailey."

Dieter furrowed his brow. "Where's Timothy Davis? He's our usual man."

"Indisposed."

"Well, you're early."

"Early is a relative term, Herr Nicolaus. In fact, I am right on time. Tax season is upon us, and this church will be quite an addition. After all, it is built on my father's land."

"Your father's land?"

"Yes. This church is on our property."

"Who is your father?"

"That's not important, Herr Nicolaus."

"I disagree."

Gustav shrugged.

Dieter continued. "We received permission to build this church from Timothy Davis, and from the reeve himself. Where did you say the regular taxman was?"

"Indisposed."

"What does that mean?"

"I've taken his position. Temporarily. I don't believe he was being as truthful to the reeve—or to my father—as he claimed."

"He always seemed like an honest man to me."

"Not to me."

Dieter squinted into the taxman's steely blue eyes. Sybil could tell her husband didn't like him. She didn't either. In fact, he seemed completely out of place in this rural part of Norfolk. And he definitely wasn't English.

His name, his blond hair, the blue eyes, his height. Clearly this man was German.

A nauseating feeling rolled over Sybil, but she didn't know why. "Must we do this here, gentlemen, in a holy place?" she asked, trying to break the tension in the room.

"Your wife is quite right," Gustav said, keeping his eyes on Dieter the whole time. "This may not be the best venue for discussing these matters. But I will ask to see you. Hedda, when am I free?"

"See us where?" Dieter asked.

"Tomorrow night, sir," Hedda said, peeking from her book.

"At my home," Gustav said.

"Your home? You said you were only here temporarily."

"I am aware of what I said."

"Are you?"

"Yes. Please, if we could speak tomorrow night at my *temporary* home, Herr Nicolaus, I would be most obliged. It's the one behind Reeve Bailey's."

"I'll be there."

Gustav strutted away, his boots echoing off the newly-laid floorboards. When he got to the doorway, he turned. "And please, Herr Nicolaus," he said with a smile, "don't forget to bring your lovely wife."

CHAPTER SEVEN

HUGO

After wiping his grimy eyes, Hugo curled into a fetal position. He tossed and thrashed in his ragged cot, listening to the rain pelt on the tin roof overhead. Silver moonlight streamed into the room through a single window, blanketing the upper half of Hugo's body in murky light.

The jeweled ring he'd stolen for Ava lay next to his cot, on the ground, along with a few copper and silver pieces, some knickknacks, and a half eaten slice of hard bread. The moonlight lit the emerald ring as if it were on display at a jeweler's shop. He touched the ring, rolling it across the ground, watching the shadows dance on the dusty floor.

Then he cursed himself.

He'd forgotten to give the ring back to Ava before she was captured.

Images played in his head of Ava crying out for help, from *him* in particular. *What a way to spend her birthday—scared and alone.* He knew the feeling well, reflecting on his own time in jail.

A few feet away, his big friend Karstan snored soundly on his own undersized cot, legs spilling over the end of the bed. Severin was asleep as well, near the front door of the small room they called home.

Hugo frowned as he watched Severin sleep. *If that weasel had given us a warning, Ava might still be here right now.*

He closed his eyes. Red and green colors battled behind his lids. Before long, he drifted off, the image of a terrified Ava his last conscious thought.

He wasn't sure if it was a dream, but he felt something . . . someone . . . reach for Ava, grabbing her by the arm, then her fingers. The hand pulled her until he could see her no more.

Then in her place, a faint ruffle. Hugo's eyes shot open. Craning his neck, he saw a blur reaching out of the shadows, into the sliver of moonlight where his coins and ring lay.

A hand. Like a spider, slowly creeping toward its prey.

The hand closed around the ring and descended back into the darkness. Hugo's eyes widened.

He wasn't dreaming.

He rolled off his cot and reached out, snatching a wrist and tugging it forward.

Severin's ugly, hawkish face came into focus, utterly shocked as Hugo cried out and cocked his free hand back.

Severin tried to pull away, but too late.

Hugo's fist crashed into his face with a *thwack* and the taller boy reeled back against his cot.

Hugo let go of Severin's hand and the ring fell to the ground with a *ping*. As Severin's hands flew to his bruised face, Hugo leaped on top of him, grabbing around his neck with both hands and growling like a rabid animal. He squeezed Severin's throat with all his might until the taller boy's face turned purple.

Severin desperately tried to grab Hugo's arms, pulling back toward the front door, which swung open.

The two young men spilled onto the muddy alleyway outside, Severin on his back, Hugo still raging on top of him.

Hugo released Severin's neck, yelling, "You thieving wretch!" as he kicked him in the ribs, again and again, then in the face. Severin wheezed and curled into a ball, defeated and rain-drenched to the bone.

Panting and still crazed, Hugo stepped away and closed his eyes tightly. The greens and reds behind his eyelids were no longer fighting. The red had won. He turned back to Severin on the ground and raised his foot, ready to crush down on the boy's windpipe.

Then a great tendril wrapped around Hugo's waist like a python, lifting him off the ground.

"Hugo, stop!" Karstan shouted, pulling Hugo away. "You're going to kill him!"

"Let go of me, you bastard!" Hugo yelled, writhing and flailing his arms and legs. But Karstan held tight, his grip too strong.

The more Hugo struggled, the less he could breathe or move his limbs.

Karstan carried Hugo into the house, then threw him to the ground like a rag doll.

"He tried to steal Ava's ring while I slept!" Hugo screamed, red rage still in his eyes.

"We're all thieves here," Karstan said with a strange calmness. "That's no reason to kill him, Hue. Are you really that surprised?"

Hugo slowly crawled on hands and knees until he found the ring on the floor. He swept it up and held it with white knuckles.

Meanwhile, Karstan walked back outside to tend to Severin. Hugo gazed out the open front door, eyed Karstan helping a disheveled and bloodied Severin up off the ground, then crawled back to his bed and carefully placed the ring on his own little finger. Then he clenched that hand into a fist, closed his eyes, and imagined Ava's face smiling at him.

The rain stopped before dawn. As the inhabitants of Bedburg rose, the morning sun peeked through the gray clouds and showered the village with warmth.

By the time Hugo woke, Severin was gone and Karstan was up, humming to himself.

"Where'd he go?" Hugo asked.

"Out," Karstan said. "He didn't want to be here when you awoke."

Good, Hugo thought. *Maybe getting beaten half to death will make that snake think twice next time he tries laying hands on what's not his.*

"You showed him little mercy last night," Karstan said. "I had to stitch his forehead. He may never look the same."

"He won't be missing much—he was already ugly enough." Hugo leaped up from his cot, Ava's ring still wrapped around his little finger.

Karstan chuckled. "I'm pretty sure it would look better on Ava," he said, reminding Hugo he was still wearing it. Quickly,

61

Hugo slipped it off and put it in his pocket.

"I'm going to get Ava back," he said, his voice strong and steady, his eyes tense.

Karstan's chuckle faded. He studied Hugo, a perplexed look on his chubby face. "How do you plan to do that? Just traipse into the jailhouse and ask for the key?"

"Something like that," Hugo said. He rummaged through his stash of coins and accessories, grabbing something and pocketing it.

As Hugo moved for the front door, Karstan stopped him. "Wait, Hugo, honestly . . . what are you doing? Trying to get yourself killed?"

"I told you what I'm doing," he answered, determination written on his face. "Goodbye, Kars. I hope I see you again." Then he walked out the door, leaving Karstan reaching out for him, speechless.

Hugo breathed in the crisp air that always followed a storm. Weaving through trash-filled alleys, he made his way up the hill toward Priest Circle and Bedburg's church.

At this time of day, the area was relatively free of preachers and beggars since Mass had already let out and the poor had already been fed. *Which also means no more carriages will be riding through,* Hugo reckoned.

Making his way to the town square and marketplace, he passed through an alley, ignoring several straggling beggars. He pulled his half-eaten piece of bread from his pocket and bit into it. When he finished, he dusted his hands off on his dirty tunic and scanned the square.

The market was in full bloom. With the new sun came a new lease on life for the townsfolk. Tents and carts were spread out in ragged columns, merchants and farmers hocking their wares, while a plethora of shoppers rummaged around.

Nobles and peasants alike perused the goods.

Hugo turned as a loud commotion caught his attention. A farmer and old woman were scuffling. Shouts became shoves, until a town guard arrived to split them up.

For several minutes, Hugo kept his eyes on the guards circling the square in their gray-and-black liveries. Like bees buzzing near the hive, they scurried about making sure things stayed orderly.

Then Hugo narrowed his attention to a lavishly attired nobleman who was scrutinizing a merchant's stock of dresses. Two guards surrounded the aristocrat, insulating him from all who passed with a five-foot circle of protection.

Hugo didn't care who the nobleman was. He reached into his pocket, tossed something into his mouth, then headed toward the man.

Usually, Hugo had the requisite grace and subtlety while thieving to get away without being detected. By the time a mark realized his purse was gone, Hugo was already counting his winnings in an alley three blocks away.

This time, however, after passing the guards Hugo clumsily bumped into the nobleman, then didn't pull hard enough when attempting to dislodge the purse from the man's waistband.

"Hey!" the aristocrat cried, raising alarm. "Thief!"

Hugo made no move to dodge the guards. They quickly clenched his arms. "Not so fast, boy," one of them said. "You're not so good at this, eh?"

Hugo let himself be pulled along like a marionette.

"Ost, keep watch on Herr Clifton," the one guard said. "There might be more where this ruffian came from. I'm bringing him to Old Ulrich. Maybe he can set this delinquent straight."

Hugo sat in Bedburg's cold jailhouse, listening through the walls to a prisoner's choked screams echoing through the stale, damp jail. Hugo shuddered at the cries.

He wasn't a perfect judge of time, but he reckoned he'd been in the cell for most of the day. There were three other cells in the room besides his: one belonging to the screaming prisoner next to him, and two empty ones across the hall.

Since arriving at the jail, Hugo hadn't said a word, or complained, or raised a single racket. In fact, no one had even come to check on him. He felt his stomach groan in protest.

A large man finally appeared in front of his cell. He had big hands and old cuts on his hairy arms. He wore a dark apron covered with splotches of something even darker. This man had been sent to scare the bandit out of him. But if his job was to exorcise Hugo's thieving demons, it was going to take much more than a bloody apron or veiny arms to do it.

On the other hand, the jailer's face was downright terrifying: bald, shiny dome; small, black eyes devoid of hope; a large purple scar running down the side of his forehead and cheek; and a scowl unlike Hugo had ever seen.

I guess the city doesn't mind that the jailer looks more criminal than his resident prisoners. It doesn't matter what side of the cell we're on, as long as we're all kept from the public eye.

"So. You're the little thorn." The man had a deep, raspy voice.

"Thorn?"

The jailer leaned forward. "The thorn between the noblemen's toes."

Hugo shrugged.

"And a shoddy thief at that," he added.

Hugo stayed quiet.

The man craned his neck and squinted his beady eyes. The scar on his face seemed to move with his tilting head, staring right at Hugo.

"I know you from somewhere," the man whispered.

Hugo squirmed away from the purple scar, unnerved. "I doubt it," he said, lips barely moving. "I've never been here, and I doubt you've ever *left* here. So our paths haven't crossed."

The man put his hands on his hips. "You're lying. Let me know when you want to tell me where I know you from. I'll be next door, getting information." He smirked, pulling a three-inch nail from his pocket and leaving little doubt how he obtained information.

An excruciating hour later, the prisoner next door was silent, unconscious from the torture. Then Hugo heard footsteps, first growing louder, then stopping, and then fading back down the hall. As if the jailer had had second thoughts; first thinking he'd pay Hugo a visit, then changing his mind to let him stew a while longer.

Hugo heard a door slam on the far end of the hall.

Once he finally had peace and quiet, Hugo wasted no time. After making sure no one else was coming down the hallway, he reached in his mouth and pulled out the small metal pick he'd hidden there back in the alley. It had been hard to talk with the thing in his mouth, which was why he'd stayed mostly quiet.

He checked the lock on his cell. A simple bolt—not too strong, not too weak. Luckily, the lock's strength was irrelevant since only the finesse of the escape artist mattered.

Which Hugo most definitely was. He stuck the pick in the keyhole and played with it. Moments later, the lock clicked, then opened.

He pressed lightly on the bars. With a faint groan, the cell door opened. He tiptoed down the hall peering left and right. The terrifying jailer had gone to the left, through a door into a different room. So Hugo headed right, toward another wooden door.

He held his breath as he touched the door. His heart was pounding. *If someone's on the other side . . .* he didn't let himself finish the thought.

He gently pushed down on the door handle. It wasn't locked. He slowly opened it and poked his head out.

The hall was empty.

Short-staffed.

He came to a small room with two cells on each side. He crept past the first two. Both were empty.

He kept moving, his heart hammering.

In the third cell a man was staring into a corner, his back to Hugo.

Hugo moved on to the last cell, which was empty. Then he did a double-take.

A small form sat in the corner, nestled in the shadows, knees brought to chest, head between legs, dark hair cascading over the person's knees.

Hugo immediately recognized the shape and the pouting sounds the voice made.

"Ava?" he whispered.

The man in the cell behind Hugo ran to the bars. "You!" he shouted, "if you're getting her out, get me out, too!"

Hugo whirled on the man with an icy scowl, instantly quieting him. Then he rushed back to Ava's cell. "Ava, it's Hue!" he whispered louder.

At the sound of his voice, Ava slithered up from her knees. Her green eyes were dark and downcast. Her face wet with sweat, or tears. She obviously hadn't bathed since her capture the day before.

"Hue!" Dimples formed a smile. She pushed herself off the ground.

Hugo's heart filled with joy.

"Come on, let me out of here, dammit!" The man yelled from the other cell.

"Quiet, man, or we'll all be caught!" Hugo urged.

But the man wouldn't relent. Rattling the bars of his cage, he pushed and pulled as hard as he could.

Hugo used his pick in Ava's lock. He felt the click a few seconds later and threw open the cell door.

Ava rushed into his arms.

"Come on, we must hurry," Hugo whispered. He led Ava out through the first door, meanwhile leaving the remaining prisoner behind to shout obscenities.

The intimidating jailer—nearly twice Hugo's height and thrice his weight—stood in the middle of the hallway, blocking their way. A cruel grin formed on his face, slithering his scar toward his nose.

Hugo's eyes went wide.

"Run!" he shouted, while doing the only thing he could think of—rushing the jailer.

Being the Falcon, Hugo was quick and sprightly. He imagined he'd be able to pivot and dodge the big man's hands.

But the man wasn't as clumsy as he appeared.

With surprising speed, the jailer grabbed Hugo by the wrist. At the same time, Ava streaked past them both.

Glancing back at Hugo, much the way she'd done when first captured in the town square, her sad eyes creased with worry.

"Keep running, Ava! Go!" Hugo screamed.

Ava opened the final door. Hugo saw a flash of sunlight as it opened. He smiled as Ava vanished up the stairs, out of view, before his face hurtled toward the nearest jail cell bars.

The Raven was free!

With a violent smash, everything went black.

When he came to, his head ached and his mind buzzed. Frankly, after that head slam he vaguely remembered, he was surprised he woke at all.

Now, everything just hurt.

He was in a different cell, arms tied to a chair. Across from him sat the jailer, eyes drilling into him.

"You must be Old Ulrich," Hugo said.

The jailer frowned. "*Old* Ulrich? I may be ugly, but I'm not old. Who said that?"

"The guard who captured me."

Ulrich's frown grew. "I'll have to teach him the error of his ways. But you're first." He smiled.

Hugo shifted his weight. "If it's 'information' you want from me, I have none."

"You're just a stupid boy. What kind of information could you possibly have?"

"Exactly."

Ulrich stood and stepped in front of Hugo. He leaned down and stared at the boy. He was so close Hugo could taste whatever god-awful thing the man had had for lunch.

But to Hugo's surprise, Ulrich reached over and untied his arms.

"That was a . . . *courageous* thing you did back there," he said. "Rescuing your little friend. Stupid, but courageous."

He pronounced "courageous" as though a foreign word, one he'd never uttered before.

"I love her," Hugo said.

Ulrich scoffed. "I'm sure you've been told this before, but you have no idea what love is. Do you really believe that girl would have done the same for you?"

Hugo felt his cheeks grow hot. "I remember my father saying that to my sister, years back. But never to me."

Ulrich squinted. It was only then that Hugo realized the man had no eyebrows, which is what probably made his face so monstrous—besides the nasty scar.

"Your sister and father . . ." Ulrich said, tapping his chin. "Ah! That's how I know you. You're Peter Griswold's son."

Hugo reeled back. "How in God's name did you know that? Do I look like him?"

Ulrich pondered for a moment "Actually, you look nothing like him. But I've seen you before. That much I know."

Hugo put his hands in his lap. The silence dragged on for what seemed like hours, until Hugo said, "What happens now?"

Ulrich shrugged. "I guess I knock you around a bit, maybe slice off a finger or two so you can't go thieving again, then let you be on your way."

Hugo's heart caught in his chest.

"Or, I could dump your head in a bucket of cold water, rip off your fingernails, ask where the rest of your gang is holed up. Maybe I'd even get to hang you, eventually, if Bishop Schreib allows it." Ulrich eyed the ceiling as he rambled.

A bead of sweat dripped down Hugo's upper lip. He imagined being fingerless. Not a good image, he decided.

Ulrich chuckled, as if he read Hugo's thoughts. "How many of you are there?"

"Thieves . . . in Bedburg? Hundreds. Of my own crew? Five. Well, four—our friend Danny went missing some time ago."

Ulrich pinched the skin beneath his chin. "Daniel Granger?" he asked.

Hugo's eyes perked. "Yes! Have you seen him?"

Ulrich let out a sucking sound. "I hanged him."

Hugo cringed.

Another silence lingered in the stagnant room.

"I *am* sorry about your father," Ulrich said at last. "I don't think Peter Griswold was a bad man."

"What do you care?" Hugo said. "He was just another victim to you."

"True. But it's different when you know a man's innocent."

Hugo's eyes lifted. He felt the red rage pulse through him. "You knew he was innocent, but you killed him anyway?"

Ulrich lifted his arms. "Orders, son. Heinrich Franz and Bishop Solomon gave them. I followed them. I didn't like it anymore than you."

"I doubt that."

Ulrich sighed. "For what it's worth, I apologize for leaving you an orphan bastard. In a way, you remind me of me, when I was your age."

Hugo snorted. "You remind me of the Devil."

"Fair enough. I suppose I deserve that."

"And much worse."

"Actually, I've been in your position more than I care to count. I used to run with a gang, wreaking havoc wherever I went. I didn't have much choice. Same as you, I suspect. But that only brought me pain and grief. If I were you, I'd leave your vagrant cohorts and start a new life." He shrugged. "If I don't kill you first."

"A new life . . . like you? What happened, exactly, to turn you to the noble path of torture and execution?"

Ulrich grinned and winked. "I found God."

After a bit more talking, Ulrich closed the cell door to let Hugo sleep. Much to the boy's surprise, during their entire "meeting," Ulrich never touched him. In fact, they left on much friendlier terms than how they began.

Despite his tough talk of finger-slicing, nail-yanking, and hanging, Ulrich remained remarkably peaceful. He never even searched Hugo's person or stole the ring still in Hugo's pocket.

The next day, Hugo awoke cold and sore. He still had a lingering headache from being smashed against the jail cell.

Stumbling to his feet, he walked to the front of his cell and grabbed the bars. As he leaned forward to look out, he felt the bars move with him. Gently, he pushed a little harder and the cell door opened.

His eyes narrowed. *Would the jailer actually forget to lock my cell?*

Not likely . . .

Whatever the reason, it didn't take much coaxing for Hugo to take off down the hallway.

Proceeding cautiously, he called out as he walked. "Hello?"

But the hall was empty.

Definitely short-staffed . . .

He tiptoed through the first wooden door. It too was unlocked.

Entering the main lobby, he started up the stairs.

Less than sixty seconds later, he was free, walking down the road with the sun on his back, just another peasant out for a stroll on a lovely day.

So befuddled by his unexpected "escape," he actually began skipping. Then he reached in his pocket and clutched Ava's ring, smiling as he headed home.

To the slums, to his friends, to Ava.

He wondered how Severin would react to seeing him after being beaten nearly to death the previous night.

But he decided it didn't matter. There was only one person that mattered. And he desperately wanted to hold her as soon as possible. More than that. He wanted the two of them to have a life together.

Hugo stopped skipping when he got to the slums in the southern part of town. Walking briskly, he rounded the corner leading to the alley. The ramshackle place he called home came into view.

And, at that moment, it never looked better.

As he shoved open the front door, his heart was ready to burst.

The door swung on its hinges then bounced back. Hugo blinked, unsure what had just happened. The door had sprung back with such force, had he not put up his hand, it would have smashed into his face.

He pushed the door open again, slowly this time, then moved just inside the doorway for a better angle.

His fat friend Karstan was not on his cot. Instead, he was hunched over *Hugo's* cot.

"Kars what's going—"

As the full scene took shape, Hugo's stomach knotted and his mouth dropped open. The ring almost slid from his hand.

What Karstan was hunched over was . . . *Ava*. She was sitting on Hugo's cot and she and Karstan were locked in a deep embrace, lips touching.

Images of past betrayal instantly flooded Hugo's mind— Sybil promising to never leave him, to never forget him; his father's promises to always be around.

Promises never kept.

And now his best friend and the love of his life.

In his home. On his bed.

The ultimate betrayal.

Fighting back tears, Hugo stood stone-still.

"Hue, what are you doing—" Ava began, then saw the look on Hugo's face and stopped.

Karstan turned around. "It's not . . . Hue, it's not what it looks—"

But Hugo was already out the door.

Running.

From the only people he trusted.

Soon, he found himself back at the jailhouse, facing the big, terrible jailer.

"You were right," he said through tears, "I should have never gone back."

"And?" Ulrich said.

"I think I've learned what love is."

Ulrich chuckled. "And what, do you imagine, I can do about that?"

With a dark expression, Hugo stared into the man's eyes. "Teach me what you do."

CHAPTER EIGHT

GUSTAV

The sun shined on Gustav's back as he struck the soggy ground with his shovel. He grunted, put his foot on the lip of the shovel, and pushed down into the earth. When he'd dug a three-foot hole, he backed away to survey his work, running his forearm across his forehead, wiping away sweat.

Hedda struggled to drag a shrub to the hole. With gloved hands, she positioned the plant in place, then carefully packed the earth around it.

She clambered to her feet with a sigh. Gustav rested his arm on her shoulder, motioning at his makeshift arboretum. Yellow hibiscus flowered alongside purple lavender from Spain, violet foxglove and larkspur from Germany, and other brightly colored flora. "Nearly finished," he said, smiling.

Hedda removed his limp wrist from her shoulder as if it were a dead rat. "Why did we do all this if we're just going to be moving soon?" she asked.

"We don't know how long we'll be here, Hedda. I'd like to see what dies and what grows in this climate."

Hedda faced the sun. Squinting, she shielded her eyes. "We have another hour or two of sunlight, if you'd like to finish that last plot."

Gustav sighed at the only bit of empty soil remaining, a hole large enough for a small casket. "Maybe tomorrow," he said. "You go inside and get supper ready. I'll be there soon."

Hedda walked inside the place they called home as Gustav watched her leave. When she was gone, he rested the shovel against his leg, reached into his tunic for his bottle of laudanum and took a quick pull. The familiar sense of fuzzy euphoria enveloped him almost immediately. He followed Hedda into the house, setting his shovel against the open front door.

It was a small home—two rooms, a hearth, a kitchen—and had been vacant for some time. Entering the living area, Gustav's eyes focused on Hedda's backside as she set a pot of water on the stove to boil. The sight brought a pang of sharp lust. Grinning, he slithered behind her and rested a hand on her rear. Hedda's shoulders slumped. "You said to make food," she sighed, stirring the soup.

Gustav leaned in closer. "The food can wait," he whispered, nibbling the nape of her neck. "I'm hungry for something else."

It was always the same when Gustav was in one of his laudanum hazes. His body tingled as he ran his hand down her slender shoulder.

Hedda tried to move away from him, but Gustav growled, grabbing her by the waist and pulling her in closer.

"Stop, Gustav!"

But he would not. "Enough of that," he barked, forcing himself onto the much smaller woman.

Hedda sighed, resigned to her fate. She was his assistant, after all, and to him that meant he was *entitled*. She put down the spoon and mechanically began caressing his smooth face. Then, as he leaned in closer for another kiss, she stomped on his foot as hard as she could.

Gustav squealed, his eyes darkening, his playful grabbing becoming more vicious.

As Hedda tensed for what was to come next, there was a sudden knock on the door.

Hedda and Gustav froze, then turned toward the source of the knock. A large man, almost as wide as the doorframe, stood at the doorway, calmly staring back at them.

Gustav straightened. Hedda used the moment to her advantage, adjusting her spectacles, then storming from the kitchen and, without uttering a word, squeezing past the large man out the front door.

The man turned to watch her walk away. "I . . . hope I'm not disturbing anything," he said, then turned back to Gustav and smiled.

"She enjoys the gardens," Gustav said, smiling back. "What

are you doing here, Herr Davis?"

As he stepped inside, Timothy Davis' smile disappeared, replaced with a frown from his sagging jowls. "I'm here on word of your . . . *letter*," he said, speaking the last word as if he'd just stepped in a puddle of vomit.

Gustav stepped to the boiling pot on the stove as he spoke. "And? Isn't that news for Reeve Bailey?"

"Indeed, but I wanted to bring my findings to your attention, first. In good faith, you see." The fat man removed his floppy hat.

"If we're going to talk business," Gustav said, "I'll need to put a shirt on. Forgive me." He trudged past the taxman, into the separate room, appearing a moment later clothed in a brown, loose-fitting tunic. "Please," he said, gesturing to the table in the middle of the room. "I'm famished and was preparing to dine. Won't you join me?"

At that, the man was clearly conflicted—a war between brain and belly.

On one hand, Gustav thought, *he feels out of sorts—wants to say his peace and be gone. On the other hand, a man that size isn't likely to refuse a meal.*

Gustav stirred the pot then walked to the table. As he sat, he called out to Hedda, then gestured for Timothy to join him at the table.

"It does . . . smell lovely," Timothy said, sitting on the opposite side of the table.

"Good," Gustav said. "By the way, it's duck stew."

Hedda re-entered the house with a scowl. After sharing a brief look with Gustav, who nodded to her almost imperceptibly, she walked to the stove to serve dinner.

Gustav, meanwhile, turned his attention to his new dinner guest. "Now, what is it you wish to tell me?"

"I'm here on good faith—"

"You've already said that."

Timothy cleared his voice. "Then I'll get to it. This . . . *letter*," he started, pulling it out and shaking it in front of Gustav, "is made from Italian paper stock. But your father is from Germany, yes?" Without waiting for a response, he added, "Do they not have paper there?"

"Not as good as the Italians, I hear," Gustav replied, folding his hands on the table.

"Right. Well, this stamp, too, it just isn't right. The wax—"

Gustav's voice was low as he interrupted. "What are you trying to say, Herr Davis?"

Timothy folded his hands on the table, imitating Gustav. "This letter is a forgery, Herr Koehler—if that is your real name."

"You're calling my father a liar?"

"No. I'm calling *you* a liar."

Both men went quiet. As a ray of light shined through the window, Gustav could see the dust dancing in the air between himself and Timothy. He felt his mouth twitch, not sure whether his growing anger or the laudanum was to blame. The only sounds he heard were his heart pounding in his ears and Hedda pouring the soup in the kitchen. Several long moments passed before Timothy continued. "I don't know what you're doing here in Norfolk, sir, but it's not as your father's regent. And it's not as the owner of this land. And it certainly is not as a tax-collector."

Gustav unfolded his hands, scratched his chin, then casually leaned back. "What are we going to do about this, Herr Davis? Why haven't you gone running to your master?"

Timothy frowned. "I'd like to get this settled, so you will leave. I'll even offer you money if it means you'll leave with haste. This is a peaceful land of Strangers—people who've been victimized, who were accepted as refugees by the graciousness of Queen Elizabeth. We don't want trouble."

"You didn't answer my question, taxman."

"If I tell Clarence, he'll most certainly involve Norwich and the guards . . . possibly even soldiers. You could be arrested for forgery, fraud, and banditry. I'd rather get this taken care of quietly."

Hedda walked over, placed a bowl of stew in front of each man, and walked away.

"You're offering me payment to leave?" Gustav asked, putting his wooden spoon to the soup.

Timothy's face sagged as he tore into his stew and slurped it up. Gustav watched him eat.

"It's very good, dear," Timothy said to Hedda, not answering Gustav. Then, between slurps: "If I may ask, what is it you're doing here? Spying? Reconnaissance? Thievery?"

Gustav poked at a carrot bobbing in his stew. "You may ask, Herr Davis, but I am not inclined to answer."

Timothy finished his stew, then looked toward the kitchen. "Then I'll ask your ass . . . assistant." But Hedda was not there. Timothy's smile faded. His brow creased, lines formed on his forehead. He tilted his head, blinking uncontrollably. "W-what in God's . . . g-good graces . . ." He couldn't finish the words.

Gustav calmly took his first spoonful of food. "You should always watch how voraciously your guests are eating, Herr Davis. Not that it would matter in this case."

Timothy's eyes fluttered. "W-what's wrong with . . ." Drool ran from the corner of his mouth.

"You're losing function in your face, I believe," Gustav said nonchalantly. "Your heart's likely beating faster than a hornet's wings. As you grow dizzier, the numbness will move to your extremities."

"B-bast . . . bastard," Timothy croaked, hands going to his neck. His fingers moved aimlessly, like he couldn't feel what he was touching.

"Oleander from Portugal and aconite root from my home country," Gustav smiled. "Also known as wolfsbane." Gustav leaned back in his chair, watching Timothy suffer like a scientist gauging an experiment. "I considered using spotted hemlock or nightshade, both also from Germany, but those are too common and you may have recognized them."

Timothy was now sweating profusely. Gustav leaned forward to get a better view as the man started to keel over . . .

Thwack!

Gustav jumped out of his laudanum-haze as Timothy's face slammed into the table. The back of his head gushed blood. Hedda stood behind him holding the shovel—the one Gustav had left by the door after tending his lovely garden. With a thud, it fell to the ground. Hedda tilted her glasses up the bridge of her nose.

Gustav threw his arms up. "Dammit, woman, why'd you do that? I wanted to see what happened!"

"He was going from being alive to being dead. *That's* what was happening, Gustav," she said, walking away. "I simply hurried the process."

Hours later, Reeve Clarence Bailey appeared at Gustav's new home. He stepped off his carriage, admiring Gustav's plants and flowers. "Quite a collection you have there, Herr Koehler," he said as Gustav finished patting down a new plot of soil between two of his prized foxgloves from Germany. "I take it your tax rounds went without incident today?"

Gustav stood up and nodded. "The farmers are very understandable about the minor change, Herr Bailey," he said with a grunt.

The reeve scratched his balding head. "Er, is there any reason why you're gardening at night, sir? I would think the daylight would make the job easier."

Gustav shrugged. "Wanted to fill this last hole." He took a moment to wipe the sweat from his forehead. "Plus, it is much cooler this way."

"Right . . ." Clarence said, trailing off. He turned to leave, then spun back. "Say, sir, have you happened to see my tax-collector around these parts? He was supposed to be back hours ago."

"Who, Herr Bailey? *I'm* your taxman."

"Indeed," Clarence muttered, shuffling his feet. "I mean the other one. You met him last night—the one I sent running off. Timothy Davis was his name."

Gustav stuck the shovel in the ground, inches from his newly-filled plot. "Ah, right. Can't say I've seen Herr Davis, my lord. But I'll certainly let you know if he turns up."

CHAPTER NINE

ROWAINE

The *Lion's Pride* docked near Amsterdam on an explosively sunny day, tucked far away from all other trading vessels. At least forty ships filled the harbor, all with storage rights to be there. The *Pride* did not have those rights.

But Captain Rowaine and her crew were not interested in conducting trade. She had a mind to repair, relax, and reinvigorate. The crew was exhausted. They'd been scavenging at sea far too long.

Trade could wait.

Walking up the rickety wooden dock, she couldn't help but be awed by the enormity of the harbor. Ships and galleons and seafarers mingled together, rocking and bumping each other. The port was one of Europe's centermost trading depots, connecting outlying towns through Amsterdam's extensive waterways.

Still, she was surprised at the pace of Amsterdam's economic progress. She reckoned that by the turn of the century, it'd be the most important trading hub this side of the North Sea.

She yawned, stretching her arms as she made her way along the dock. Her two-dozen seamen, all stinking and ragged, followed.

She breathed in deeply. The salt, the birds, the buzz. It was enough to make a lesser person dizzy.

"Dom," Rowaine called out, "get the boys situated at Dolly's." A few approving grunts rang out. "First round's on me."

Several cheers followed while others stayed silent. There'd been a telltale awkwardness on board the *Pride* since Rowaine had taken command. Half the crew still didn't trust, or like, her.

And she knew it.

I'll have to win them over with my . . . feminine wiles, she joked to herself. *I don't need them to like me, just respect me, and to know I'll be a good leader.* After all, she'd always been the tomboy, not giving any quarter. *Captain Galager's fate should be proof of that.*

"Dom?" Rowaine called again, turning her head. He was nowhere in sight.

"He's near the back, Row." Daxton came up beside her, running a hand over his shaved head. "I'll get the boys settled."

"Thank you," she said, eyeing the thick-armed carpenter.

Could it be him—the most talkative and supportive of my little entourage? Could he be the traitor?

The question hadn't left her mind since Captain Galager had met his fate. Someone had given her up, gotten Dominic hurt. She would never forgive that wretch, but it wasn't easy hiding her thoughts with everyone constantly pestering her. She'd attempted to implore Dominic to be her hideaway investigator, but he'd been despondent since his incident, and not exactly the most reliable detective.

She tried to let the thoughts of vengeance and turncoats drift from her mind. As she and her crew strutted into the bustling city, everyone cleared a path.

Not long ago, she'd been begging for scraps, eager to make a name for herself. Now she was the captain of a notorious gang of pirates.

Not exactly the illustrious profession she'd dreamed of, but it certainly fit her nature. If people wouldn't give her what she wanted, fine. She'd take it. Things were different now. The richest merchant wouldn't dare disrupt her lunch.

Fear outweighs money. And I carry both.

A few passersby hailed Rowaine as she strolled by. She was well-known in this place, but now carried a new air. She sensed it, as did all those around her. She tried to think of a word.

Magnetic. That's what it was. She was *magnetic.*

That's how I'll build my new company, she thought. *The promise of money, respect, dignity . . . the people will listen to that. My job is just finding the right people.*

They passed a dozen shops and markets, but Rowaine had

her sights set on Dolly's, her favorite tavern and brothel. Captain Galager had been a part-owner. *Guess that makes* me *part-owner now.*

A favored destination for both vagabonds and the hard-nosed, there wasn't a better recruitment office in all of Amsterdam. Her face lit up as the tavern appeared in the distance.

Dolly's was a two-story affair, a perfect balance of depravity and self-indulgence. The place had the best whores in town and the ale was always frosty.

Rowaine felt her mouth water before she even pushed through the creaky double-doors.

Rising cheers erupted as she entered. Her crew pushed past, taking seats, reuniting with lost friends, brothers, and wenches. A few crewmen grabbed the nearest women they could find and dragged them upstairs.

Unfortunately, one of the girls so grabbed wasn't one of Dolly's workers, and a scuffle broke out between the pirate and the girl's husband. It ended quickly when the pirate smashed the man's own beer mug over his head and took the girl.

"This isn't the place to bring a suitor," muttered Alfred, standing beside Rowaine.

Rowaine searched the smoky tavern with half-lidded eyes. The person she was looking for wasn't there. She frowned, thinking, *Maybe upstairs . . .*

Before she could go, Daxton shoved a mug of ale in her hand and shouted, "Beat you to it! Got the whole bar a round!"

A bit of beer splashed on Rowaine's leather shirt. She wiped it off, took the beer, and stared daggers at Daxton.

"Don't worry," he said, putting an arm around his captain. "I used your money!"

Jerome Penderwick sauntered by with a girl on his arm, flashing his best three- or four-toothed grin.

Half the tavern patrons left when Rowaine and her crew took over the place. Dolly herself came downstairs to welcome her guests. She was a large woman with a tight corset shoving her breasts up to her neck. Her two chins wobbled, and entirely too much makeup mucked up her eyes.

"Look who's here to steal all my business," Dolly grinned.

"Technically, it's my business I'm stealing," Rowaine replied.

After a short pause, Dolly's face broke into a smile. "Get over here, you cold bitch," she said, wrapping both arms around Rowaine. She leaned into her ear. "I hear you're captain now. Slit the bastard's manhood off, did you now?"

Word travels fast.

Dolly held Rowaine at arm's-length, eyeing her head to toe. In a feigned weep, she said, "My little waif, all grown up."

Rowaine turned toward the far corner of the room. There sat Dominic, alone at a table, staring at his untouched beer mug.

"He did his damage," Rowaine said.

Looking to see what she was talking about, Dolly frowned. "I won't ask what happened to the poor boy, but I'm sure you could always warm his bones." Rowaine reeled back, surprised. "Oh!" Dolly said. "And speaking of warming bones, I've got a surprise for you. Hold on, let me get it."

She dashed off, climbing the stairs as quickly as her heavy dress and stubby legs would allow.

Rowaine got up, grabbed her mug, and walked to Dominic's table. She sat, putting her hand on his shoulder, but remaining quiet. Several long moments later, she whispered, "Come now, Dom, I'm sure one of these girls can lighten your mood." She gestured to the wide bar. There certainly seemed to be more wenches around than usual. *Perhaps someone tipped Dolly off that I'd be arriving with my crew . . .*

She chugged her beer.

"They've already tried," Dominic said, motioning with his chin to two girls at the next table. He tapped his mug, looking up at Rowaine. "I saw Adrian Coswell talking to Mister Penderwick a minute ago."

Rowaine nearly choked mid-drink. "Our surgeon? Where? I just saw him go upstairs with a pretty thing on his arm."

Dominic shook his head. "Coswell stopped him at the foot of the stairs. The girl ran up without him."

"Are you sure?"

"You told me to report anything suspicious. I think that warrants a report."

"No, no, you've done good, Dom. Thank you," Rowaine tried to sound as mild and sweet as possible. Dom had been so frail lately, it tugged at her heart. She ran a hand down his back.

"Ah, look here, the lovesick duo," Daxton called out, coming to sit at their table. Alfred joined him. They plopped down on the bench across from Rowaine and Dominic, shaking the table in the process.

Before Rowaine had a chance to explain, a voice called out: "Here, here!"

Rowaine recognized it immediately. Her lungs jumped to her throat as she swiveled to find its source.

A woman sitting at Dolly's side grinned back. About a head shorter than Rowaine, she had brown hair, a wiry frame, and an amber face. Rowaine jumped up to greet her.

The two embraced. A few eyes glanced their way.

Rowaine brought the girl back to her table, holding her out like she'd won a prize.

"Who's that? Your sister?" Daxton asked, taking a gulp of ale.

Rowaine's eyes narrowed. She slapped the girl's rear, brought her in close, and kissed her hard on the lips.

Daxton's beer shot from his mouth and dribbled down his beard. After recovering from his coughing fit, he could only stare, glancing from Rowaine to the girl.

For once, he was at a loss for words.

Finally regaining some composure, he stammered, "I . . . did not . . . expect that. Sorry."

Rowaine's smile broadened. "This is Mia," she announced proudly.

Rubbing the back of his head, Daxton said, "I've known you for over a year. How have I never known you were . . . that way?"

Rowaine put her hands on her hips. "How many women do you recall being onboard the *Pride*, exactly?"

"Good point," Daxton responded. He pointed to Dominic. "So you and the cabin boy weren't . . ." he let his sentence trail off.

"Did I ruin your dreams, Dax?"

Daxton thought about that. Then he smiled. "Actually, you might have made them better."

He raised his mug and loudly finished off the beer. As the liquid dribbled down his chin he grinned foolishly, exclaiming, "Here, here, captain! Always full of surprises!"

"What do you have for me, love?" Rowaine asked Mia. They finally had the table to themselves. They'd been at Dolly's for hours. Many of the men had long since passed out or given in to their fantasies. Among those still remaining, fights were breaking out. At the far end of the bar, several others were playing music.

Rowaine had her arms stretched out on the table, holding Mia's hands.

"I have nothing on the person in your picture," Mia said. She shook her head and frowned. "I haven't seen him. This place is too damn big, Row—too many people."

"I know. It's okay, I'll find him. What else? My crew is here for a week while we fix the *Pride*."

Mia looked over her shoulder, then leaned in close. "There's a wool merchant leaving in a week—small boat, huge load. They're trying to leave under the cover of darkness, I hear, since they have no backup."

"Perfect timing," Rowaine said, holding up Mia's hands and lightly kissing them. "I knew I could count on you. Oh, there's something else I need from you."

"Name it," Mia said, eyes alert.

Rowaine told Mia about the mutiny against Captain Galager, what had happened to Dominic, and her own new station in life. Mia wasn't surprised—she expected great things from Rowaine. But she was surprised to hear that the field of possible traitors had been narrowed to three of Rowaine's closest advisers.

"Keep an eye out for me, will you?" Rowaine said. "I expect the culprit will be talking to Adrian Coswell, Galager's first mate. Know what he looks like?"

"That weasel?" Mia scoffed. "You should have killed him and dumped his wretched body at sea, Row."

"So I've been told."

"It isn't smart keeping him alive. One more person you have to watch out for. I'll keep an eye out—hopefully I'll find something for you. But it will have to wait a while. At least an hour or two. You see, I'm a bit preoccupied at the moment."

Rowaine furrowed her brow. "With what?"

Mia batted her eyes, then gave Rowaine a salacious grin. She nodded her head toward the stairs at the far end of the room.

With no further words needed, the two women stepped around a passed-out drunk, then proceeded hand-in-hand up the staircase.

CHAPTER TEN

SYBIL

Playing with her thread and distaff, Claire looked up at Sybil. "Do you have any idea what he wants?" The two mothers sat on chairs outside Claire's house, watching Martin and Bella running across the grass enjoying the sunlight.

Martin seems so young and innocent when he's around her, Sybil thought. *If that girl knew the horrors he'd been through . . . if anyone here knew . . .*

"Beele?"

Sybil snapped out of her daze. "Pardon me. What does who want?"

Claire smiled, dimples forming on her young face. "Are you sure I'm the only one here who's pregnant?" She grinned. "You've been so faraway all day."

Sybil shuffled her feet, embarrassed. "I'm not sure what Herr Koehler wants. He didn't invite you and Leon to dinner?"

Claire shook her head. "I don't suspect he invited any of the farmers. Only you and Dieter."

"That's odd. I suppose it's got something to do with the church. I'm afraid that place may end up causing more trouble than it's worth."

"Nonsense," Claire said, "you and Dieter have been a godsend to us all. The church, too. I know working on it gave Leon something to do all day."

Sybil considered the sweeping green countryside before her, spanning all the way to the horizon. *Boredom,* she thought. *'Idle hands are the devil's plaything.'* She thought she'd read that in the Bible, but couldn't be sure.

Her thoughts wandered to more exciting times: The thrill and danger of sneaking away to meet Dieter in the dead of night.

But that was a different life, she reminded herself. *One that almost got Dieter, Martin, and I killed.*

And that made her think of her son Peter. And how there would be no Peter at all if her time years ago in that cold jail cell had turned out as it nearly had.

She forced her thoughts back to the present. She watched Peter try to catch Bella and Martin, only to wobble in the grass, then fall flat on his rump.

The mothers giggled.

"I hope little Rose can be friends with Peter," Claire said, rubbing her belly.

"Rose? What if it's a boy?"

"It's a girl," Claire said, shaking her head. "I can feel it. Come, put your hand here. She's kicking."

Sybil hesitated, then softly touched Claire's bulging stomach.

"Oh my!" Sybil exclaimed, "you're right!"

In truth, she hadn't felt a thing. But it didn't do to steal away her friend's excitement like that. She smiled at Claire, who still watched Martin and Bella in the distance. "I wouldn't worry," Sybil said. "Rose and Peter will be great friends."

Nighttime brought a cold chill that swept in from the west. Sybil bundled herself in a wool coat and laid Peter in his little bed. She spoke to Martin. "Are you sure you can handle everything here? If Peter gets antsy, there's a fresh bottle of Lily's milk outside."

Martin put a hand on her shoulder. "Don't worry, Beele. We'll be fine. I've done this before."

"If anything out of the ordinary happens, you know where to go?" Sybil told him.

Martin bobbed his head.

"Right," Sybil said. "We'll be back in a couple hours, if that. I'm not too keen on staying out."

Through the window, Sybil noticed a carriage coming to a stop outside the house.

"I've been sent to escort Dieter and Sybil Nicolaus to Herr Gustav Koehler's abode," the driver yelled into the night.

Sybil kissed Peter on the forehead. Hesitating, she eyed Martin one last time, then she and Dieter left the house and stepped into the carriage.

Once the coach was on its way, Dieter asked, "Do you remember the last time we were in a carriage?"

Sybil stroked her chin, nodding. "When we were getting carted off to jail in Bedburg."

Dieter stared out the window at the darkness, a faraway look overtaking him. "I built this church here . . . because—"

"I know, my love," Sybil said, putting a hand on his knee. "You long for your calling—I saw it in your eyes at Mass. You belong on the pulpit."

Dieter sighed. "I just pray things won't be the same here as they were in Bedburg."

If only we could be so lucky, Sybil thought. But not wanting to dishearten her husband, she simply said, "They won't."

Sybil watched Dieter for long while. She felt that, deep inside, there was a part of him missing what they'd left in Bedburg—the sermonizing in front of a legion of supporters, the gardens, helping the poor. Much as she missed the sneaking around and nightly rendezvous. *How could he not? He was an important man in Bedburg. And surely the reason why he built the church here in the first place—he missed his calling.*

Sybil could only hope Dieter would leave the past alone. That he could be happy in the present. With what they both now had. *We might be in a strange new land, but not* every*thing has changed. We have much to lose, even more than what we had in Bedburg.*

Peter.

Each other.

"Is everything all right?" Dieter asked.

She hadn't realized she'd been staring at Dieter the whole time, almost through him.

She blushed. "Y-yes, everything's fine. I was just wondering what Gustav might want to talk to us about."

"I suppose we'll find out soon enough."

*   *   *

87

When they arrived, Gustav took Dieter and Sybil on a short tour of his gardens. As they zigzagged through the cloister, they'd occasionally stop, taking in the vibrant colors and arrangements.

Along the way, Gustav rattled off the names of the various species, then explained his goals with the transplants.

"The toxicology of these plants," he told them, "is what especially draws my interest—what they can offer science and medicine." Cradling a purple, bell-shaped flower, he added, "And I also like using spices and such from my own garden."

Dieter nodded. "You do have quite a collection. I used to have some of my own, such as that violet hibiscus, a time ago."

"Did you?" Gustav asked, eyebrows arching. He seemed much cheerier than when they'd first met.

Sybil walked behind the two men while Hedda lurked a few steps behind, her big book under her arm.

Dieter eyed another plant. Biting down on his lip, he spoke casually. "Being a man of science, what is your take on religion, Herr Koehler?"

Gustav grinned at Dieter. "I try to stay away from religion and politics whenever I can, Father Nicolaus."

Somehow I doubt that. Sybil still didn't trust the man. *He didn't invite us here to marvel at his floral arrangements and spices.* There was a darkness about Gustav Koehler that she couldn't quite put her finger on.

Gustav mock shivered. "Shall we head inside? Getting a bit chilly. I'm sure our dinner is ready. Yes, Hedda?"

The secretary nodded. "We have duck soup tonight, and a spiced chicken."

"Excellent," Gustav replied, bending his neck at an odd angle and eliciting a sharp crack.

Inside, a fire flickered on a wall-hearth next to the table. It was a quaint house, about the size of Dieter and Sybil's, but empty of most normal amenities. Where the land surrounding Gustav's home was lush and vibrant, the inside was starkly barren.

Staring at Gustav, Sybil couldn't help but wonder if this empty home and lush garden somehow served as a metaphor for Gustav's life.

Gustav pulled a seat out from the table for Sybil, as Hedda escaped to the kitchen to prepare the soup.

When everyone was seated, he said, "Though I try to avoid talking of religion, especially with a priest present, I suppose you understand that is why I've called you here."

"You're referring to my church," Dieter stated.

"Quite. I understand you received permission to build it from Reeve Bailey and Timothy Davis."

"Yes," Dieter said. "And speaking of Herr Davis, when will our regular taxman take his routes?"

"I couldn't say." Gustav raised a finger. "But, your church, sir, is a more expensive endeavor than your parishioners might know."

"Meaning?"

Gustav cleared his throat and pulled a piece of parchment from his tunic. "The laws in Norwich—the same laws which dictate the land belonging to the Strangers—require a double subsidy to pay for the parish priest and the land tax for the church."

Dieter craned his neck. "I don't ask for money from the people. They struggle enough as it is."

"Even so," Gustav continued, unfolding the parchment in front of him, "it is a requirement. If your church is to be officiated as a place of worship for the Lutherans here, the tax must be paid. And I don't know how the people—or you—will afford it."

Hedda brought a tray holding three bowls of soup from the kitchen.

"Thank you, my dear," Gustav said, briefly touching Hedda's elbow.

Sybil watched with half-lidded eyes at the exchange. *She seems more of a servant than an assistant.*

"Can this wait?" Dieter asked suddenly. He was squinting at the soup, breathing it in. "Can we do this another time?" He had a strange look in his eyes.

Gustav glanced up from his soup, spoon halfway to his mouth. "What was that?"

"I can agree to help the people with the taxes, if it will make your father content."

Sybil was ready to start eating, but now she peeked at Dieter with uncertainty. Dieter widened his eyes for a quick moment, fast enough so that Sybil was the only one who noticed.

"What's the problem, Herr Nicolaus? Does the soup not suit you?" Hedda asked from the kitchen.

"No, no, I'm sure it's fantastic," Dieter said, "it's just that our son, he's . . . ill, and I feel ashamed for eating now while he is left alone. Sybil and I must take your leave, Herr Koehler."

Gustav dropped his spoon on the table with a clang, wiping his mouth with the back of his hand. "This is most unordinary, Herr Nicolaus." His voice was flat, the cheeriness gone.

"We can reschedule for tomorrow, if you'd like," Dieter said, rising from his seat. Quickly, he grabbed Sybil by the arm, hard, lifting her to her feet.

Gustav sighed, shrugging. "If you're trying to escape your duties, sir, I do not appreciate it. Neither will my father."

"It's nothing like that." Dieter and Sybil were already halfway to the door. Sybil glanced back at Gustav, who still sat at the table, hands forming a steeple as he watched them.

"Have a safe trip home," Gustav said, spite in his voice. "I'll have Hedda reschedule our appointment."

Dieter stormed out of the house, into the night.

Sybil followed, but heard Gustav say, "I'll be seeing you two soon, I'm sure."

"What in God's name was that, Dieter?" They were safely away in the carriage, heading home.

"Something wasn't right, Beele." Dieter's voice was edgy, his eyes darting as he looked out his window toward the sky and back toward Gustav's farmstead.

"He seemed much nicer than when we first met him," Sybil said.

Dieter leaned close to her. "That was his plan. You don't understand." He lowered his voice to a harsh whisper. "He was trying to poison us!"

Sybil's eyes bulged. "Why would he do that? And how do you know?"

"That man isn't who he says he is. I'm sure of it. And I could smell it in the soup. When we were walking through the gardens I recognized some of those plants. The ones he didn't name. I saw wolfsbane, deadly nightshade, spotted hemlock!"

"Why would the man try to kill us if he's trying to get taxes from us?" she scoffed. "You're not making sense."

Dieter breathed heavily. "If we're dead, our land and our church go back to the landowner—his father. Perhaps he wants the church—I don't know. But we have to go."

"Go *where*, Dieter? You must calm down."

"Away from here! We have to leave Norfolk."

Alarmed, Sybil said, "Absolutely not. We have Claire and Leon and the congregation. I'm supposed to help Claire with her baby, and teach those children, and you're supposed to give Mass. We have obligations here, Dieter."

"I'm sorry, my love."

The frustration overwhelmed Sybil. "We can't let this man get the better of us. Not so soon! Why don't you report him, if what you think is true?"

"No one would believe us, Beele. He has the law on his side. Didn't you hear him?"

They reached their home on the outskirts of the flat farmland. It was eerily quiet as they jumped out of the carriage into the windy night.

As they entered their home, their worst fears were realized.

Sybil gasped. Dieter groaned.

Martin and their son were gone.

CHAPTER ELEVEN

HUGO

The torturer and his apprentice stood in a jail cell, across from a prisoner who sat upright on a cold chair. The man's eyes were bloodshot and weary.

Ulrich pointed at the prisoner. "What is that called, boy?"

Hugo glanced at the object on the prisoner and gulped.

A double-sided, metal pronged instrument stretched from the prisoner's exposed breastbone to his throat. The prong resembled a fork but with sharper points, like a horned devil. It was attached so that every time the man's head dropped forward from fatigue, the points stabbed into his throat, causing him to jolt awake in pain.

Simple, yet exquisitely cruel.

"A Heretic's fork," Hugo said.

"And what does it do?"

"It forces the man to stay awake."

"And why would we force the man to stay awake?"

Hugo paused for a moment. He tugged at his chin, then faced Ulrich. "So he'll give a tired confession?"

Ulrich rocked back on his chair. "Good. Let's see how it works, shall we? Just listen." The prisoner moaned and flinched when Ulrich ambled to him. Ulrich patted the man's head, leaned over him, and undid the straps of the fork, pulling the apparatus away.

The man gasped.

Ulrich slapped the man lightly across the face. "Are you with us, Sturl?"

The two pinpricks on the lower half of Sturl's neck trickled with blood. Apparently he'd tried to sleep.

He looked up at Ulrich, his eyes glazed, wild, angry.

"Where were we?" Ulrich began. Calmly, he sat across from the prisoner, resting one leg over the other. "If you tell me what I want to know, no more fork."

"Burn in Hell, punisher," the man's voice like sandpaper, his lips cracking as he spoke. Tiny rivulets of blood continued trickling down the man's chest.

Ulrich smiled cruelly, the scar on his face moving with his mouth. "I'm sure I will. Now, the archbishop of Trier, what was his name, Sturl?"

Sturl shrugged. "I don't know the archbishop of Trier."

Trier was one of the seven electorates of the Holy Roman Empire, located south of Cologne.

"Ah," Ulrich said, raising his index finger. "Johann von Schönenberg. That was his name. So, Archbishop Schönenberg wants more inquisitors for his witch-hunt." Ulrich turned to Hugo. "Since Trier is having a bit of a witch problem lately— dozens of people have been killed already, I hear. The place is ripe for the killing. It would be a good place for an executioner, I suspect . . ." he trailed off.

Sturl coughed and spat a wad of blood and phlegm on the ground near Ulrich's feet.

"In fact," Ulrich continued, "Archbishop Schönenberg of Trier doesn't have enough inquisitors for all the witches he's trying to kill. Enter Sturl here"—he waved his hand at the prisoner—"who has come to Bedburg to recruit."

Sturl licked his parched lips. "I was sent by Archbishop Ernst of Cologne."

Ulrich sighed. "So you've been saying. The problem is . . . I don't believe you. Why would Archbishop Ernst help Archbishop Schönenberg? Why would Cologne come to Trier's aid?"

"Ask him yourself," Sturl growled.

Ulrich stood and crossed his arms. "This isn't working." He turned and left the cell. A moment later he returned with another contraption: two bands of iron, held together by a large screw.

Ulrich sat, placed the device in front of Sturl, then shoved one of the prisoner's thumbs between the two bands. Ulrich turned to Hugo. "Do you remember the name of this one?"

This one was easy. "A thumbscrew," Hugo answered.

Sturl groaned.

Ulrich nodded. He put his hand at the top of the screw and began rotating it, forcing the top band down until it pressed against Sturl's thumb. "Last chance, Sturl," Ulrich said.

The prisoner looked like he was ready to weep. Instead, he steeled himself, gritting his teeth and sucking in his cheeks.

Ulrich tightened the band one more measure. A loud crack signaled Sturl's thumb had been crushed. The prisoner wailed in agony.

Hugo flinched, then recoiled. Blood was seeping through the prisoner's shattered thumbnail onto the floor.

Ulrich unfastened the band. Sturl moaned, breathing in short gasps.

"Shall we try again?" Ulrich calmly asked. "Was it Archbishop Schönenberg of Trier who sent you here?"

Sturl rapidly shook his head.

Ulrich removed Sturl's hand from the device, grabbed his other hand, and jammed his thumb between the iron bands.

Slick with blood, the screw made a squealing sound as Ulrich turned it. But just before the bands pressed together, the prisoner shouted, "Okay, okay! Please, stop this! No more!"

Ulrich looked at the man with his browless eyes, trying his best to unnerve the prisoner with his gaze. "Well?"

"Archbishop Schönenberg sent me from Trier to Cologne. He and Archbishop Ernst are acquaintances, I s-suppose."

"So why are you here—in Bedburg—then?" Ulrich asked.

"Because Schönenberg wants Jesuits, and the bishop of Bedburg is one of the most notorious Jesuits in the land—he's the man who uncovered the Werewolf of Bedburg, after all."

Balthasar Schreib did not *uncover the werewolf,* Hugo thought. *My father was no monster.*

Ulrich gave Sturl another look, as if to say, *Continue.*

Sturl did. "Everyone knows Bishop Schreib used to be Archbishop Ernst's ear, when he was still in Cologne."

"You were sent from Trier, to Cologne, to here," Ulrich said, pointing his finger in the air three times. "But Archbishop

Schönenberg of Trier doesn't want it to look like he's asking for help. He wants Archbishop Ernst and Cologne to simply *offer* their aid."

Sturl nodded. "Schönenberg is stubborn. He wants to look powerful. I suspect he wants his electorate to be more dominant than the Cologne electorate. He'll appear weak if he has to ask for help . . ."

Ulrich smiled and undid the band from Sturl's thumb. "Well, his secret is out."

Sturl's eyes bulged. "P-please, I told you what you want. Don't betray my secret. Schönenberg will kill me."

Ulrich's face darkened. "I wouldn't worry about that," he said, quickly leading Hugo out of the room by his shoulder.

"Where are we going?" Hugo asked, trying to keep up with the punisher.

"To find the new inquisitors Sturl was talking about, and to report to Bishop Schreib."

Hugo peeked over his shoulder. "And what will happen to Sturl?"

Ulrich shrugged. "It's up to the bishop, but I suppose I'll have to slit his throat and toss him in the Erft River."

Hugo's mouth fell open. "B-but he told you what you wanted to know!"

"Yes," Ulrich said, "but didn't you also hear him complain about his 'secret' getting out? Killing him is the only sure way of stopping that."

Hugo wanted to say more, but what more could be said? *Here I was thinking we were the ones trying to* find *the murderers,* N*ot become* them.

They came to Bedburg's church. The lush gardens on either side danced in the wind. The stained-glass doors mesmerized Hugo with their reds, greens, and blues.

Ulrich lightly cuffed Hugo on the side of the head. "Enough staring," he said, pushing open the doors.

The nave inside was empty, save for two folks sitting at

separate pews, heads bowed, and a homely woman sweeping by the pulpit near a gray statue of Christ.

Ulrich approached the woman. "Sister Salome," he said with a curt nod. The woman held a long frown. Hugo soon realized this was her regular expression.

"Punisher," she said with slight disgust, standing her broom upright.

"I must speak with the bishop."

"Why don't you go to the keep?" she said, her tone bitter. "He seems to be there as much as here."

Ulrich opened his mouth to say something, then simply shouldered past her instead. "I don't have time for this. I know Balthasar is here. Mass just let out."

Hurrying behind Ulrich like a dog, Hugo could tell the torturer and nun had a history—and not a pleasant one, he guessed.

Sister Salome shuffled behind Hugo, putting a hand on his arm. "Boy, let the brute speak with the bishop alone. Their discussion is no place for you."

Hugo creased his brow, pulling his arm away.

"The boy comes with me," Ulrich said over his shoulder.

"He's in a meeting," Salome protested, walking past Ulrich, trying to get to the door at the end of the hallway first.

"I was hoping so," Ulrich said, moving the nun aside and knocking hard on the door.

Hugo heard voices coming from the other side. But none offered Ulrich entry, so the torturer let himself in, pushing hard on the door and shoving his way inside.

As Hugo followed Ulrich in, he gazed around the large circular chamber. Shimmering rays of light, in all colors of the rainbow, poured through the many stained-glass windows, casting an almost angelic haze across the room. A large oak desk stood at the front. Hugo had never seen a desk that big. And an equally large man, round-faced and jovial, sat behind it.

In front of the desk, with their backs to Ulrich and Hugo, sat two other men, who both turned quickly at the sound of the door crashing open.

"E-excuse me, father," Sister Salome exclaimed, dashing into the room. "He wouldn't be stopped."

"I have good news, bishop." Ulrich exclaimed, spreading his arms out like some war-ravaged general greeting his loyal soldiers.

The round man at the desk stumbled to his feet, grabbing his walking-stick leaning nearby. "Excuse me, brothers," he said to the two men sitting in front of his desk. Taking the hint, the two immediately got up and left the room, not looking at Ulrich or Hugo as they passed.

Nevertheless, Ulrich gave them his best torturer's smile.

When the door closed, Bishop Balthasar Schreib sighed. "What do you have for me, my son? And who is that?" he asked, wrinkling his face at Hugo.

"Runaway boy I found. Took him in."

"What do you plan to do with him? Send him to an orphanage?"

"Not sure yet. Guess we'll see how good he learns. I've been bored in that stinking jailhouse, so I could use the company."

Bishop Schreib chortled. "Are you growing sentimental, my friend? It's so unlike you."

Ulrich drew back like he'd been struck. "The man you had me arrest will be dead by sundown."

"That's better," Schreib said. "Can we talk in front of this boy? I'd hate for him to end up in the same predicament as your prisoner."

"Yes, we can talk in front of him." He nodded, eyeing the boy. "He'll be helping me get rid of the body."

Hugo's eyes widened. *That was never discussed . . .*

Ulrich moved on, saying, "Sturl was sent by Archbishop Schönenberg, as you suspected, father. It seems a storm of shit is raining down on Trier. People are turning up quite crispy throughout the principality."

"Ah," the bishop said, limping to a table next to his desk and pouring himself a cup of something. "Wine, torturer?"

Ulrich shook his head. "I don't drink. You know that. But the boy can."

The bishop chuckled, holding out the cup. Hugo trotted over and took it. The wine was warm and bitter, almost making

Hugo cough.

"Does it taste like the blood of Christ, boy?" Ulrich asked.

The bishop glared at the torturer. "So the man was sent from Trier to Cologne, and from Cologne to here?"

Ulrich nodded.

Bishop Schreib poured another cup for himself, then took a sip as he stared out the green-and-red window. "I wonder why Ernst would keep that from me . . . I'm like a brother to him."

"Well, he's giving you work. Maybe he just wants to keep his neck clear of any sharp blades. I doubt he wants a repeat of Bedburg." Then, thumbing over his shoulder, "And those men?"

Balthasar tapped his tinny cup. "That was the inquisitor and his assistant. Stalwart members of the Society. They should do nicely in Trier."

"Trier's a long ways from here," Ulrich said.

"Not so far, Ulrich. Why? I see that glint in your eye."

"I have a proposition for you, father."

Balthasar set down his cup. "I'm assuming you won't leave until you offer your services."

Ulrich smiled again, the scar slithering to his chin. "You know me too well, bishop."

"Where are we going now?" Hugo asked, dodging and weaving around smelly, drunken men smelling of beer, shit and mud, to keep up with Ulrich's quick pace.

They'd left the church and immediately headed toward the southern slums, a place Hugo knew well. As they neared Tanner Row, the smell of beggars and filth was replaced by the stench of rawhide and rotting meat. This was the slum adjacent to Hugo's old home, one of his favorite haunts for poaching unsuspecting marks.

"All the drifters and vagrants down here . . . you must feel at home, boy." Ulrich scowled, pushing his way past two stumbling men. His voice went low. "I know I do . . ."

They stomped through the mud, passing the taverns, brothels, and tanners, until they made their way to a large, open-spaced district that Hugo had always avoided, mainly because no one worth robbing ever frequented the area.

A group of men were huddled in a tight circle, shoulder-to-shoulder, jeering and cheering, hands clenched into tight fists, all gawking at the same spectacle.

Hugo heard repeated rings of steel on steel, singing out like squawking birds.

Ulrich made his way to the loud circle. Hugo stood behind him, peering around on his tiptoes to see what was happening.

Two men were at battle. One with a half-helm on his head, tufts of dirty blond hair sticking out from underneath; the other wore a chainshirt, vambraces on his arms, and a wide full-helmet covering his entire face.

The combatant in the half-helm wore the ragtag leather garb of a mercenary. Hugo could see the man's jaw locked tight, heavy breathing blowing from underneath the helmet.

The men circled each other, gauging the other's footwork. The man with the blond hair and half-helm had open holes in his helmet, allowing his piercing blue eyes an unobstructed view. The man with the full-helm had simple slits in his mask, partly obscuring his view but completely protecting his face.

Each man held, double-gripped, a crude longsword.

The blond man, his weapon held high with the blade aimed to the sky, grunted then dashed forward, striking out as quickly as Hugo's hands moved during a pilfering.

The full-helm fighter staggered to the left, swinging his blade down on top of the blond man's blade. He swept his weapon along the edge of Half-helm's, trying to take off his opponent's head.

Half-helm ducked as the blade swept overhead, nearly connecting with his face.

The people in the circle gasped. Hugo's eyes moved from man to man, unable to look away for even an instant for fear of missing the imminent mayhem.

Half-helm, the quicker of the two, danced back, shuffling his feet and pacing left to right.

When Full-helm's head tilted down, to gauge his opponent's feet, Half-helm struck, lunging and catching Full-helm on the wrist—but only bouncing off the metal vambrace.

Full-helm grunted, then cocked back and punched out with his gauntlet, striking Half-helm square in the face.

Half-helm stumbled back, dazed. Full-helm raised his blade high, moved two steps forward and brought his blade down fast and hard for the killing blow.

The crowd collectively cried out.

But Half-helm ducked at the last moment, bringing his sword around in a low, one-handed sweep, hitting Full-helm's protected knees. He jumped back as Full-helm twisted, roared, pivoted. He raised up his weapon. Half-helm brought his down.

There was a tremendous *clang* as the blades met.

Half-helm riposted, digging his back foot into the ground. He leveled his sword then hammered down, Full-helm just barely able to check it with his own blade in time.

But Half-helm now had the momentum, fluid in motion, dancing to the symphony of crackling steel and sparkling crescendos. He continued his onslaught of offensive slashes, his blade swinging down over and over, Full-helm clearly on the defensive.

Finally, the pressure was too much. Full-helm buckled, his back leg slipped, he lost footing and went to a knee.

Half-helm circled the man, still swinging, wild and wolf-like yet precise as a hunting falcon.

Full-helm was no match. He couldn't move fast enough, couldn't get his sword to his side quick enough, and Half-helm struck him in the shoulder, drawing blood.

Full-helm grunted and fell to his side, dropping his weapon and clutching his shoulder. He reached out for the blade but Half-helm, standing over him, stepped on its handle and Full-helm's hand with it. The crunch of bones was unnerving.

Half-helm held the point of his blade at Full-helm's throat.

Some in the crowd cheered and jumped in the air, pumping fists. Others simply stormed away, the battle over.

Coins were handed out to the bettors. The circle dispersed, the working men going in different directions, the entertainment for the night finished.

Hugo let his breath go.

Ulrich walked to the man in the full helmet. The man was still rolling on the ground, no one coming to his aid.

Ulrich kicked him in the stomach, then stepped to the victor. The fighter took off his helmet, his blond hair sticking raggedly to his forehead and scalp. Ulrich patted him hard on the shoulder. Then the two men embraced.

Hugo stayed back. He saw their mouths move, but couldn't hear the words. He looked down at the man in the chainshirt and full helmet. Broken and defeated, he breathed in ragged gasps.

Hugo bent down, eyes moving over the injured man. His eyes moved past the blood seeping from the man's shoulder, down to the steel of his longsword. Hugo ran his finger over its cold, flat edge, then wrapped his hand firmly around its hilt.

I want to learn to use this, too, he thought, wide-eyed.

A moment later, he laid the weapon back down and looked up, trying to refocus his mind from its bloodlust. His eyes moved to the man Ulrich was still talking with, the victor of the sword fight. He knew that man.

Ulrich was pointing in his direction, and the fighter's blue eyes honed in on Hugo.

Ulrich brought the man over. "Boy, I want to introduce you to Tomas Reiner."

"Yes," Hugo said, his eyes getting smaller. "We've met."

"Have we?" Tomas cocked his head.

Ulrich scratched his chin. "He's going to teach you to fight proper, and he's agreed to let you tag along with him, at my behest."

"Tag along where?" Hugo asked.

"I'll let you two get reacquainted," Ulrich said, ignoring Hugo's question. "Bring him back to the jailhouse when you're done with him, Tomas."

Hugo wasn't listening—the voices drowned away. All he could remember was two-and-a-half years ago. When the blond man before him had taken him from his home, from his safety, from his family, and paraded him in front of his father.

The man who had locked Hugo away in the jail cell next to the doomed Werewolf of Bedburg.

CHAPTER TWELVE

GUSTAV

Gustav took the key from the pocket of his tunic and slipped it in the keyhole. The box made a sharp clicking noise as it creaked open. Besides clothing, his plants, some money, and his laudanum, the oak box was the only real possession he'd brought with him to Norfolk.

The pistol rested inside a fuzzy red slotted compartment. He ran his hand over the muzzle, then gripped the wooden handle.

"This was my brother's," he whispered to no one.

Hedda was standing behind him, in the detached room off the main den. "What are you doing, Gustav?" she asked.

He turned to her, gun cradled in both hands. Hedda was pretty. Her spectacles too big for her head, her short hair in a tight curl, her button nose. Gustav fought the laudanum lust and shivered. "Those two left for a reason," he said. "They know something."

Two men entered the room, both dressed in dark leather, knives dangling from their belts, muskets strapped to their backs. They could have been twins, despite one having dark hair and the other fair.

Both soldiers saluted Gustav. "We searched the house and surrounding land," the fair-headed one said. "The child was not present."

"I expected as much," Gustav said. He'd sent the men to inspect Dieter and Sybil's house while the couple was busy dining at Gustav's. He hadn't expected Dieter and Sybil to leave early—or leave at all, really.

"We made our escape when we saw the suspects returning home," the soldier continued.

"Did they see you?"

The man shook his head. "I advise we head back in the morning. We'll have a greater chance of success when there's light."

"Nonsense," Gustav said. "It'll be too late then."

"Too late for what, Gustav?" Hedda asked. Both soldiers glanced at her.

"They must have suspected something, or they wouldn't have left early. I don't know what you did to set them off, my dear, but we'll have to talk about this later." Gustav's frown twisted into a smirk. Pictures played in his head: Hedda bent over his knee, dress hiked up, receiving her spanking, crying out, spectacles flying off her face. He felt his body tingle.

"Me?" Hedda said, scoffing. "If anything, it was your constant gaze that raised suspicion. They hardly noticed me."

"Nonetheless," Gustav said, "if we wait 'til morning, they'll be gone. You won't be sleeping yet, boys. We go back."

The men sighed, softly, so as not to anger their master. They hadn't had the luxury of a carriage to bring them to Sybil and Dieter's estate, and it was a long trek by foot.

"Hedda, you stay here. I'll deal with you when I return." Gustav reached into the red-layered box, found five bullets nestled in the cushioning, and loaded his gun. Tucking it in his waistband, he led the soldiers to his carriage and proceeded into the night.

Fifty minutes later, Gustav and the men pulled up to Dieter and Sybil's house. Stepping out of the coach, the brisk wind warmed Gustav's face. He stormed inside, the soldiers following. His eyes darted around the cozy interior. The soldiers weren't lying. The boy was not present.

"Damn," Gustav said. He'd hoped Dieter and Sybil would still be home, but alas, they too were gone.

He walked over to the small bed. It was fit for a toddler, pillared by four planks of thin wood. Feeling his blood start to boil, he kicked the thing over. His insides gave a twist. He groaned and reached inside his tunic for his laudanum, taking a quick pull before stowing it away.

He moved to the kitchen area. He could smell the earthy stench of boiling potatoes.

"They probably arranged this, so we wouldn't suspect they'd been gone long," the dark-haired soldier opined. "Quite clever."

Gustav put his hand against the boiling pot, then pushed. It crashed to the floor, water and potatoes splashing across a wide area, steam billowing up.

"Now we search the surrounding houses," Gustav said, turning to leave.

"That'll raise suspicion from the reeve, my lord. He might not like that."

"I don't care what he likes. We won't lose these bastards."

They left the dwelling. Gustav peered out into the darkness. He saw smoke rising in the distance, from the nearest home.

He stalked across the property toward the neighbor's place, trampling rye and barley along the way.

When he reached the front door, he pulled out his pistol. Taking their cue, both soldiers unslung their muskets from their shoulders.

Gustav kicked in the door. It exploded into the adjoining wall, splintering one of its hinges.

A man and woman lay in bed, clothes flung haphazardly on the floor beside them. Their heads shot up as the door crashed open. The man leaped from the bed, naked, to protect his wife. He started to reach for something but thought better of it when he felt the muzzle of Gustav's gun touch his face.

"No," Gustav said, "we won't have any of that."

"Who the hell . . ." the man started. "Wait . . . you're the new taxman. What in God's name are you doing here?"

Gustav didn't recognize the man in the dark. He probably wouldn't have recognized him in the light, either, due to the laudanum melting his brain and slowly destroying his memory.

"What is your name?" he asked.

"David," the man answered. "And Reeve Bailey will hear about this, sir!"

"What is your wife's name, David?"

"I'm not his wife," the woman said, sheets pulled to her

neck.

So threatening her may not work, Gustav thought. He walked to the bed. David started to move with him, but one of Gustav's soldiers stopped him.

Or maybe I can.

"If you don't want your mistress' brains splattering your walls, you'll tell me what I want to know. Maybe we can even have your wife come clean up this mess."

The woman cried out and began weeping into the sheets.

"Jesus, man," David said, holding his palms up in surrender. "Say your piece and get out!"

"What is your relationship with Dieter and Sybil Nicolaus?"

David scrunched his face. "My neighbors? Er, well, I helped Dieter build his church."

"Where are they?"

David's body trembled. "At home, I'd think. Though how in God's name should I know?"

Gustav nodded. One of the soldiers slammed the butt of his musket into the side of David's head. The naked man collapsed to the ground. His mistress howled.

Gustav leaned over David. "Where would they go in case of emergencies, David?" Gustav's eyes were red and glassy.

Rubbing his head, David groaned. "I-I don't know."

Gustav cocked the matchlock on his pistol, aiming it at the woman on the bed. She cried out again.

David held out his palms. "Okay, okay! They'd most likely go to Leon and Claire Durand's. They seem close."

Gustav tucked the gun into his pants. "Where can I find Leon and Claire Durand?"

"Their house is a mile south."

"Good man," Gustav said. He exited the house quickly, his two lackeys close behind.

This time when he burst through the door, a cacophony of shouts and shrieks told Gustav he'd likely found what he'd been looking for. Holding his gun on the closest person, the young man appeared to be about sixteen—and definitely not Dieter. But his two soldiers had better luck, pointing their muskets at the couple huddled in the corner.

Dieter and Sybil.

Sybil was cradling her baby against her chest.

Gustav counted seven people total in the small home. Besides Sybil, Dieter, and their child, there was Leon, Claire, and their daughter, plus the young man currently looking down the barrel of Gustav's pistol.

"Aha!" Gustav grinned. "Easy now," he said to the wiry youth. "I don't want to have to put bits of your skull on the pretty girl behind you. What's your name, boy?"

"Martin."

"And the girl?"

"Leave her alone!" Claire shouted from the back of the room. It was quite obvious, even in the darkened room, that Claire was with child, her belly practically bursting at the seams.

"Shut up, woman!" Gustav growled. His eyes went wild. Pregnant or not, he would do whatever it took to get what he wanted. He turned back to Martin. The young man had stepped closer to Gustav.

That won't do.

Gustav whipped his gun around, smashing Martin across the head. The boy dropped like a rock. He wouldn't be getting back up anytime soon. The young girl rushed to his aid, kneeling.

"What do you want with us, you brute?" Dieter stepped in the line of one of the soldier's muskets. Pushing the gun aside, he moved away from Sybil.

Gustav cleared his throat. "Dieter Nicolaus and Sybil Griswold, I am here to arrest you."

Everyone's eyebrows raised in unison.

"Griswold?" Claire asked.

"It's my maiden name," Sybil said. She tilted her head. "Who are you, Herr Koehler?"

Gustav ignored her question. "Yes, it is your maiden name. You are the daughter of Peter Griswold." He faced Claire. "Have you heard *that* name, madame?"

In a thick accent, Leon said, "It sounds familiar."

Gustav pointed at Sybil. "This woman is the daughter of the Werewolf of Bedburg."

All eyes went to Sybil.

He reached into his tunic, but instead of his bottle of laudanum, he held a necklace. A wooden cross with fractured edges.

Sybil yelped, her hand going to her mouth.

"So you recognize *this*, witch?" Gustav clenched his teeth, dangling the cross amulet in front of Sybil's face. "My name is Gustav Koehler von Bergheim."

Sybil paused. "Bergheim . . ." she said under her breath.

Gustav placed the necklace over his head so it hung from his neck. "My father is Ludwig von Bergheim. My elder brother was Johannes von Bergheim—now deceased."

Dieter took a step back as Gustav's eyes narrowed on him.

Gustav grasped the cross against his chest. "And *this* was the murder weapon that took my brother's life." He pointed past Sybil, past Claire and Leon, straight at Dieter Nicolaus.

"And you, you . . . *hellion*, are his killer! I have come to this cesspool to take you and your wife away. So you can both be properly tried and executed. I am here to bring you back to Germany."

Leon and Claire stared at Dieter and Sybil. "What he's saying can't be true, can it?"

"Oh, it is!" Gustav yelled, aiming his pistol at Dieter and his wife. "These two heretics you're protecting have been lying to you, Herr Durand. They are murderers and fugitives from Bedburg. They didn't escape Germany to flee oppression, sir. They left to escape their *justified destiny*." Spittle flew from his curled mouth.

"Dieter?" Leon begged.

Dieter's head sank. "It's true," he muttered. "This man's brother hurt Sybil. In a rage, I killed him." He looked up with wet eyes. "But I'm not that person anymore, Leon."

"You will always be that person, you wretch," Gustav said.

"We are still your friends, Leon, you must know that. I love this place, the people—much like I once loved my homeland."

"You must be held accountable for your actions," Gustav

said. Clenching the cross tighter, he stared at Leon. "Not only are they murderers and fugitives, Herr Durand, but they're also *Catholics*. They have no right preaching the words of Martin Luther to your people. They are frauds!"

"I was converted more than two years ago," Dieter tried to explain. "I have every right to give Mass, just as my wife has every right to teach the children."

Gustav smirked. "If that is the case, then you will be owed monies from the same people you teach. So you hurt the very people you say you are trying to help. Norwich law states that subsidies for churches must come from the landowners' pockets."

Dieter opened his mouth to protest, but the words would not come. Shame had chased the anger from his face. "I . . . I'm sorry, Leon, Claire, Bella. I'm sorry that Sybil and I have been a nuisance. But you must believe me—everything we've done here was done without expectation or reward. We only wished to be part of a conventional community again." He lowered his head. "That is all."

"Ah!" Gustav exclaimed. "You hoped the past would never catch you. That was your real goal. I've heard it again and again." Gustav nudged his chin toward Dieter and Sybil. "Guards, take them."

Dieter put his hands in the air. "We will go peacefully," he said. "Just please don't hurt this family."

Tears trickled down Sybil's cheeks. "My baby," she said, as one of the soldiers grabbed her arm. "What do I do with Peter?"

Gustav shrugged. "That's not my problem. If you want him to rot in a cell with you, by all means, bring him along."

Dieter wrapped his arms around Sybil, then kissed Peter on the forehead. He turned back to Gustav. "You're heartless," he spat, eyes narrow.

"Is that the same look you gave my brother before stabbing him in the skull over and over, priest?"

"I'll take him," Claire cried out, rushing to take Peter from her friend's arms. "I'm sorry, Beele. I'll make sure he's safe. I promise with all my heart."

Sybil held her breath and bobbed her head. She couldn't

speak. Sniffling, she kissed her baby, then handed her to Claire in his wrapped blanket.

As Sybil and Dieter were led from the house, Martin began to wake, groggy and groaning.

Hands tied behind their backs, the two were escorted into the carriage. The scene reminded Dieter of their first arrest, years ago in Bedburg.

"Let's move," Gustav said, climbing into the carriage.

As they departed, Claire Durand came running out, her hands supporting her giant belly.

"We'll come with help, Beele!" she cried out. "I promise! Don't give up hope!"

Gustav craned his neck as the coach rolled away. "Do that, you harlot, and we'll be back. For your daughter and newborn."

CHAPTER THIRTEEN

ROWAINE

Rowaine lay sideways on the bed with her elbow bent, her head resting on her hand. With quiet content she watched Mia dress at the end of the bed. Mia was thin but toned from years of exercise in Dolly's bedrooms. Despite her frame, she was ample in all the right places. She was one of Dolly's best earners.

Rowaine sniggered as Mia grunted and struggled to bring her pants to her waist. She latched a belt and rummaged the ground for a shirt. She bent over, to Rowaine's delight, and Rowaine scooted like a crab to the edge of the bed and wrapped her legs around Mia's waist, pulling her close.

Mia yelped and chuckled, running her hands across Rowaine's feet. "Don't you have things to do?" she asked, pulling Rowaine's toes. "People to lead?"

They'd been locked away in Dolly's best chamber for half the week, only leaving their room for the occasional meal, or when Rowaine had business to attend to.

"Come with me," Rowaine whispered in Mia's ear.

"You know I can't do that," Mia said. "I have no place on a boat. It makes me feel trapped—"

"You don't feel trapped here? Stalking these rooms, pleasing the snide bastards who walk in, day in, day out?"

Mia frowned. "That's not fair, Row. The bloody business you do is not for me."

"I will protect you. I am the captain, you know. You don't have to work here anymore—or anywhere, for that matter."

Mia pushed Rowaine's legs away and put her hands on her hips.

Rowaine leaned forward and ran a finger up Mia's leg. "Please?" she asked.

Mia shivered. She inched backward. "No, no, no. I told you, Row. Papa isn't doing well. I have to take care of him. When he's finally gone, maybe then I'll have the courage. But right now, I'm staying here. Our situation works—I can keep an eye on your enterprises here."

Hearing the finality in Mia's voice, Rowaine leaned back in the bed, propping her arms for support and sticking out her lower lip like a sad puppy. Her red hair fell across her face.

"Why are you looking at me like that?" Mia asked.

"Because I want you."

"You have me."

Rowaine sighed. Glancing down, she said softly, "And so does every other man in Amsterdam . . ."

Mia flinched. She clenched her teeth and strode to the bed, flexing her fists.

"I . . . I'm sorry, Mia," Rowaine said, shaking her hands. "I don't know why I said that. I didn't mean it."

Mia stormed out of the room, slamming the door on her way.

"Wait, don't . . . go," Rowaine said to the empty room. She sat on the side of the bed, searching for her clothes. "Stupid, *stupid*," she muttered to herself.

But Mia was right about one thing. Rowaine did have things to do.

She walked down the hall, stopping in front of a door with a chair wedged underneath the knob so it couldn't be opened. Moving the chair away, she opened the door.

Inside the small room Doctor Jerome Penderwick sat at the edge of the bed, his hands folded on his lap. He lifted his head as Rowaine walked in.

"C-captain," he said in a dreary voice. "Can I p-please leave? You can't k-keep me imprisoned forever."

"Wrong, surgeon," Rowaine said, stepping toward the small man. She grabbed his hair and lifted his head, forcing him to look at her. "I'll keep you stowed here until you tell me what I want to know."

Jerome swatted Rowaine's hand away. "I can t-tell you what you want to hear, b-b-b"—he took a deep breath—"but it would be a lie."

Rowaine slapped him hard across the face. The surgeon yelped, then looked away. Rowaine wasn't sure why she hit him—maybe to take her anger out after her outburst at Mia—but it didn't make her feel any better.

A moment passed. Finally the doctor said, "Are you mad, w-woman?"

"Yes, I am *mad*, Jerome." She bent down, eye-level with the surgeon. His mouth stank, his lips were cracked. He licked his gums, his tongue going over grooves where teeth should be.

"Why were you speaking with Adrian Coswell?" Rowaine asked. "Why did you betray me?"

"I did no s-s-such thing!"

S-words were the worst for him to pronounce.

Pointing her finger inches from his face, she yelled, "Stop lying! I have eyes telling me they saw you speaking with Galager's first mate."

"Your eyes are blind," Jerome said. "I s-s-supported your mutiny, Row. Captain. What would I gain by betraying you?"

"That's what I'm trying to find out."

"I simply wanted to s-speak to Coswell about s-s-s—"

Rowaine finished his answer for him. "Supplies." She stood to her full height. "Yes, I know. So you keep saying."

Jerome shrugged, as if to say, *What more do you want from me?*

There was a knock on the door.

Daxton Wallace stood in the doorway, glancing back and forth from Rowaine to Jerome with a furrowed brow.

"Is there something you need, Dax?" Rowaine asked, trying to snap him to attention.

Daxton stayed quiet for a moment, then shook his head. "Oh, yes," he remembered. "I've brought the men here—the ones that want to join us."

"And you vouch for them?"

Daxton grunted, which Rowaine took to mean yes.

"Very well," she said. "Anything else?"

Daxton stared down at his hands. "Um, well, wouldn't you like to see 'em, captain? Say a few words?"

"I trust your judgment, Dax."

"Right, right, but I'm sure they'd like to see *you*, Row. You'll be leading them to sea for weeks, possibly months. You can't blame them for being curious, wanting to see what they're getting into."

Rowaine groaned. "*Fine.* I'll be down shortly."

Daxton gave a curt nod and shuffled away, closing the door behind him.

The men were huddled together at the foot of the steps, awaiting their captain. Daxton stood in front of them. They were a ragtag bunch, some farmers, some working men, some barely men at all.

Daxton introduced each man to Rowaine, who forgot them almost immediately. She had too much on her mind.

She glanced over to the bar, where Dominic sat, alone as usual, staring at his mug of beer.

Meanwhile, Daxton rattled on. "This is Charlie." The young man had shaggy orange hair and freckles that dotted his face like a plague.

Daxton put his hand on Charlie's shoulder. "Says he's good with a rig and line."

Without looking over, Rowaine commented, "We already have a capable rigger," her eyes remaining fixed on Dominic. Daxton introduced another new crewman but the words floated by Rowaine like a leaf in the wind.

Suddenly she darted her eyes around the room. "Where is he?" she began.

"Didn't you hear, Row? Er, captain?" Daxton said.

Rowaine looked at him. "Hear what?"

Daxton took Rowaine's arm and led her away from the group of newcomers. When they'd rounded a corner, he leaned close to her. "While you were sealed away in your room these past few days, Coswell took off. Took about ten men with him. I think he was scared of your . . . retribution. Probably learned about your witch-hunt. That's why I've brought all these new boys . . ."

"Adrian Coswell left?" *Damn. I should have killed him while I had the chance. Next time I'll listen to my advisors.*

Daxton eyed the ground.

"What is it, Dax? Spit it out." When Daxton stayed quiet, she rolled her eyes and said, "I promise I won't strangle the messenger. This shyness is unbecoming of you, Dax."

"Well . . ." he began. He cleared his throat. "Alfred Eckstein went with him."

Rowaine cringed. "Our rigger?"

Daxton nodded.

"Why . . ." she began, but trailed off. The implication finally hit her. "That goddamn weasel," she growled.

"That's what *I* said. It's why I looked so confused when I saw you interrogating Jerome. I assumed you knew."

Rowaine shook her head. She'd been wrong. Alfred was the traitor, not Jerome.

That young, dumb fool. No . . . I'm the fool. The least talkative of my inner group, always observing, hardly speaking. I should have seen it.

"So, would you like to reintroduce yourself to the new guys?" Daxton asked.

"Like I said, Dax, I trust you. I have to speak with Dominic."

She walked away quickly.

She sat next to Dominic at the bar, ordering herself a beer. She turned toward him. His fair, handsome face showed no emotion. She placed her hand on his shoulder. He flinched.

Quickly, she removed her hand and recoiled. "How are you holding up, Dom?" she asked softly.

"I'm sorry, Row." For the first time in days, Dominic made eye contact. He looked exhausted, new wrinkles creasing the space between his eyes and temples.

Surprised, Rowaine leaned back. She hadn't expected those words from him. "Sorry for what, Dom? Nothing you did was your fault."

"I'm sorry for being so weak. I'm sorry for being such a

degenerate. I'm . . . just sorry." His eyes filled with tears.

Rowaine smiled. "It's okay." She turned to her beer and took a sip. Setting the mug down gently, she said, "Do you remember when I first found you?"

A hint of a smile appeared on Dominic's face.

"You were just a pup, running errands for thieves. A mess, really, but oh how you've grown, Dominic." She squeezed his shoulder softly. "I tried to take care of you, groom you. I never wanted to see you hurt again. If anything, I've failed *you*, Dom. *I'm* the one who should be sorry."

Before she could continue, Dominic wrapped her in a tight embrace, snuggling his head against her bosom.

With an open mouth she hesitated, then put her arms around him. It was like coddling a child. After all he'd been through, it was no wonder he acted like one.

"I'll make the people who hurt you pay," Rowaine whispered.

"You already have, Row. There's nothing more you can do."

As the *Lion's Pride* prepared to leave, Rowaine stood at the helm scanning the bustling docks for Mia. And there she was, in the center of the crowd, waving goodbye. It had taken Mia three days to forgive Rowaine for her misguided lashing-out. But last night, their final night in port, the two had spent the night together and all was forgiven.

Mia knew Rowaine didn't mean to hurt her. The captain was simply used to getting what she wanted.

Rowaine knew she'd overstayed her welcome in Amsterdam. It was time to hit the sea with her crew. Everyone was rested and hungry for action. And now their sights were already set on one particular ship, a very sneaky one, but one that promised a good haul.

It was a clear day as the *Pride* floated away. Rowaine blew Mia a final kiss as the dock grew smaller and the rowing crew's grunts grew louder.

Rowaine turned her attention to her shipmates. The ones

who weren't rowing stood at the ready, alert, prepared to bloom the sail once they hit the open water.

"We move fast, we move hard," Rowaine ordered. "For those who don't know me—I am Captain Rowaine Donnelly. There are traders in these waters who are begging to be taken. So we take them. Do we all agree, mates?"

The crew pumped their fists skyward, cheering their captain on.

With a grin on her face, Rowaine gripped the well-worn wood of the polished wheel with both hands.

I'm ready to lead.

Eyeing the horizon with the wind in her face, she radiated a level of confidence unlike anything she'd ever known.

It may have taken me twenty-four years to get here, but I was born for this.

CHAPTER FOURTEEN

SYBIL

Sybil watched Dieter praying on his knees, hands clasped together. He sat in the corner of the room, speaking inwardly, mouthing out his prayers with closed eyes.

She shook her head. *He's struck with fear, more than I've ever seen.* Her tears had dried up. She'd wept for most of the first three days locked inside Gustav's house. But now her tears were spent. She was dejected and faint. She worried she'd never see her son again. She'd lost all track of time, trapped in an empty room—four wooden walls, a cold floor, and a bucket.

The room smelled rank and fetid. They hadn't bathed. They'd been given barely enough food to live, once or twice a day—she couldn't really tell how often.

How quickly your senses betray you when they're stifled and stripped away, she thought. *Is it day or night? When have I eaten last?*

She could only hope that Peter and Martin fared better than she and Dieter.

"What are you praying for?" she asked Dieter, her voice cracking. She hadn't spoken in hours; words were slow to come. Her tongue felt like leather stuck to the roof of her mouth.

"Or should I say, *who* are you praying for, Dieter?"

Dieter opened his eyes and turned to his wife. "I'm hoping God will forgive me. I was foolish to think I could escape my past . . . the things I've done." He looked away. "But I don't know if He's listening anymore."

"Are you listening to *yourself?*" Sybil said, more severely than she'd intended.

Dieter tilted his head. "Pardon?"

"Before I first met with Johannes von Bergheim, I remember my father telling me to stop being so selfish and thinking only of myself. He told me to think of my family—of the greater good that would go with marrying a man like him."

Dieter narrowed his eyes, confused.

"Perhaps you should heed his advice," Sybil said, her voice rising. "We may never see our *child* again, Dieter, and you can only think of God?"

She knew her anger was displaced, but it was all she could do to stop herself from dry heaving or becoming hysterical.

Dieter's pained brows creased the corners of his eyes. "I'm—I'm sorry. You're right, of course, my dear. It's just that this . . . helplessness is crippling."

He's right about that. This fear is worse than death. She leaned back against the smooth wall. "I'd say this madness is more painful than any physical torture."

"Indeed," Dieter said, thinking how he'd been physically tortured before, in a room not too different from the one here. "But we will see our child again, my dear. And Martin. I promise."

Sybil scoffed. "You know how I hate that word. Don't guarantee promises you can't keep." She'd made her own promise like that over two years back, to her younger brother, and she hadn't seen Hugo since. She'd never forgiven herself for that.

But at the moment she had more pressing concerns. *Where will this man take us? How will we get there? How can I see my child again?*

As the hours passed, their feelings of utter helplessness intensified.

The click of the door awakened her. She didn't know how long she'd been asleep. Gustav appeared in the doorway.

"You two are proving to be much more of a problem than I'd anticipated," he said.

Sybil heard voices behind him. Rushed. Urgent. One she recognized as Hedda's.

"The boats aren't ready," she heard Hedda say, though she remained out of sight. "But we don't have much time here, Gustav."

Gustav replied under his breath, then faced Dieter and Sybil with a scowl.

"What's going on?" Dieter asked.

Gustav stepped into the room, closing the door behind him. "Your friends are causing a ruckus, priest. That's what's going on." He sighed. "They've been at our door for nearly two days, refusing to go to work or home, until you are released."

"Who?" Dieter asked.

Gustav threw up his hands. "God only knows. The *farmers*, priest. Your friends! Nearly ten people outside. You two aren't making this easy."

"And will you let us go?" Dieter asked.

The man actually laughed at that, short and cruel. "Of course not. I merely have to hurry my plans. Though you might cost me my plants." He frowned, looking wild and tense.

"Your plants?"

"I may not be able to bring them with us."

"Poor man," Dieter said.

"Where are you taking us?" Sybil asked.

Gustav ignored her, focusing instead on Dieter. He spoke through gritted teeth. "Burn in Hell, priest. I know you will once my father's done with you."

Dieter raised a brow. "You're not man enough to deal with us yourself?"

Impatiently, Gustav huffed. "If only I could." He reached into his tunic for his dark bottle. He swigged the liquid, then threw a thin leg-bone of dark meat into the room. It hit the floor with a thud. "Eat. We may be leaving soon."

And then he was gone. Sybil heard the lock click into place. She crawled to the door, putting her ear against it. She felt like a young girl again, trying to eavesdrop on her father.

" . . . we'll have a full peasant revolt on our hands before long," she heard Hedda say. They must have been in the room next door—Sybil could hear them clearly.

"Say one thing about those two—the farmers love them," Hedda continued.

Sybil pictured Leon and Bella standing outside, he with a pitchfork, she holding her pregnant belly, demanding liberty. The image was almost funny if the situation weren't so dire.

"And the harbor?" she heard Gustav ask.

"We aren't ready yet . . ." Hedda's voice trailed off as she likely walked into a different room.

Sybil turned to Dieter. He was eating small bites from the mystery meat. "You shouldn't give them the satisfaction," she said. "How do you know that's not poisoned, too?"

"We must eat if we're going to try and escape, my dear. Besides, we'd be dead already if he wanted it."

"Escape?"

Dieter leaned forward. "For Peter. Do we have any other choice?"

The hours dragged on. Every so often they'd hear commotion beyond the walls, outside. Sybil recognized some of the voices: Leon, Grant, David. Dieter's church helpers protesting their support.

"I wonder where Reeve Bailey is hiding during all this," Sybil said.

Dieter started to respond, then his eyes shot to the opening door.

Gustav jumped into the room, knife drawn. "Up, both of you," he ordered, waving the weapon in the air. He seemed agitated, eyes more crazed than usual.

Whatever concoction he's drinking is clearly ravaging his brain.

Both prisoners stood as ordered, Gustav grabbing Sybil by the arm. She yelped.

Dieter started to lunge but stopped when Gustav's knife pressed against his throat.

"None of that," Gustav growled, eyes glistening. He tensed his jaw and gnashed his teeth. To Sybil, he looked to be a man possessed. And very frightening.

"Where are we going?" Sybil asked again, and again was ignored. Gustav yanked her out of the room. Dieter followed.

Once outside their room, the dark-haired soldier—musket drawn—stepped in behind Dieter and nudged him forward while Gustav pulled Sybil along. They were led to the back of the house, then out through the back door.

As the cool night air jolted their senses, Sybil and Dieter anticipated a throng of friends to appear in the night. But all they heard were the lonely sounds of crickets chirping.

Where are all our friends and supporters? Did they forget to surround the whole house?

Despite the chill, the change was invigorating after spending countless hours in that stifling room.

Dieter repeated Sybil's earlier question: "Where are you taking us, Gustav?"

"Shut your mouth," Gustav whispered, spittle flying out. Though it may have seemed trivial at the moment, for some reason it bothered Sybil even more that Gustav only responded to the man of the family.

They made their way over fields. No one spoke.

Finally, they came to a carriage hidden in the darkness, two black horses snorting at their arrival.

They were forced inside, the fair-haired soldier driving. They circled the perimeter of Gustav's estate to avoid any lingering protesters. And as they passed by Gustav's plants, Sybil could make out several tents and campfires surrounding the house.

She grumbled. *By the time they realize the house is empty, it'll be far too late.*

As they plodded along in the darkness, Sybil recognized the terrain. Instead of traveling *away* from the Norfolk countryside, they were heading deeper into the fields.

Before long, they came to Dieter and Sybil's house, and then Dieter's white church, shining like a lighthouse atop a seaward island.

Gustav stopped the carriage at the church. He snapped his fingers at the guard. "Do you have it?"

The soldier handed Gustav a bucket and a wooden stick.

"What are we doing here?" Dieter asked.

Gustav smiled. The moon streaked through the carriage window, basking half his face in a savage way. "Something I've wanted to do since I arrived here." He stepped out of the carriage.

Dieter started to follow but was halted by the muzzle of the

121

soldier's musket.

Minutes later, tears poured down Dieter's face as his church went up in flames. The carriage rolled off.

Through the carriage window Dieter watched the orange-white flames and thick black smoke billow into the sky.

His beacon of hope reduced to a doorway to Hell.

Sybil also watched, transfixed, as the rafters and roof tiles crumbled into smoldering gray ash.

The last thing to fall, like a blasphemous reminder, was the white cross that Dieter had jubilantly erected just days earlier.

As it toppled and collapsed into the flames, so too did the hopes and dreams of a proud and honest man.

CHAPTER FIFTEEN

HUGO

Hugo stumbled to the side, unbalanced, nearly falling over. His ears rang as he set his feet and gritted his teeth. Tomas stood in front of him, sword comfortably poised—like he'd done this all his life.

Hugo had wanted to learn swordcraft. And for the last week that's what he'd been doing. Tomas Reiner was his teacher—a harsh critic. But everyday Hugo learned more and he could tell his efforts were paying off. Muscles in his hands and arms that he hadn't known existed no longer ached each morning.

Hugo rushed at Tomas, sword gripped in both hands. He yelled and sliced down at his teacher. Tomas made an odd flick of his wrist and Hugo's sword flew from his grip, clanging to the ground.

They used real steel.

When Hugo had asked why they weren't training with wooden swords, Tomas' response was curt: "You won't learn anything if your biggest punishment for failure is a tap on the wrist. No one you find in the real world will be using wooden swords, so we won't either. I'm not here to teach you a romantic fantasy, Hugo. Swords are bloody and cruel and deadly. Killing is ugly. And defending yourself from *being* killed equally so."

And Hugo had the new scars to prove that. He'd already suffered cuts on his arms and legs, though he considered himself lucky that that was all the punishment he'd received. Tomas could have done much worse.

At first Hugo complained, believing Tomas a reckless man. And maybe he was, but his advice was strong and his words held more weight when reinforced by two and a half feet of gleaming steel.

Hugo stood wide-eyed, staring down the cutting edge of Tomas' blade at his neck. All he could do was hold his breath and freeze.

"You're too eager," Tomas said, pointing his sword to the ground. "And too . . . polite. Swordcraft is either a brawl or a dance. It can be brutal or it can be beautiful. What you're doing is, unfortunately, neither."

Hugo closed his eyes and exhaled, trying to control his frustration. Tomas often spoke this way—eloquent, but not exactly helpful or encouraging.

"Is that what you have to say to me? Or do you have some kind of critique?" Hugo asked.

Tomas stared at Hugo for a long moment. "By being eager, you open yourself up to danger. You leave yourself vulnerable, unprotected. You tell me your next move before finishing your last one. You're an easy read."

Hugo quashed his first instinct—to object. He was smart enough to know that swordcraft was more than physical. It also required training the mind. And a big part of that was learning patience.

Too eager, too quick, not defensive enough, Hugo thought, trying to absorb Tomas' remarks.

"It's like playing chess," Tomas explained. "If you try to check the king before you're in position, you're likely to lose your queen—or your head."

That was another thing Hugo noticed about Tomas' sword-teaching traits. He used every analogy imaginable—wrestling, dancing, chess.

"Pick up your sword and come at me again," Tomas said before Hugo could finish his thought.

The ringing in Hugo's ears subsided. He cracked his knuckles, then bent down and picked up his sword. By the time he looked up, Tomas already had his sword at his throat. Again.

"Don't ever turn your back on your opponent," Tomas said, frowning.

"You told me to pick up the sword!" Hugo whined.

"Don't ever trust your opponent. Not even me."

God be damned. Hugo sighed. He stepped back, loosened his

grip on the sword, and tossed the blade from hand to hand. *Be more unpredictable, be more savage, less polite.*

Hugo circled his opponent. Tomas remained impossibly still, gazing out the corner of his eye. When Hugo rushed in from his flank, Tomas sidestepped, bringing his sword down on Hugo's, ready to knock it flat.

But Hugo's sword wasn't where Tomas expected it to be. The boy had moved at the last moment. Rather than lunge, he swung his sword high.

There was a brief pause in Tomas' eyes. Hugo smirked. Tomas backpedaled. Hugo hammered down at Tomas' sword, trying to get past the man's defenses.

Tomas kept retreating, then suddenly flicked his wrist.

But this time Hugo was ready. He'd expected it, learning from his earlier mistake. He let Tomas roll his wrist outward, as Hugo stepped forward, close enough to hear Tomas breathing. Then, putting a foot behind Tomas' ankle, he pushed him with his free hand.

Tomas' eyes faltered and widened. He realized he was falling, tripping over Hugo's foot. He managed to catch himself, but in the process Hugo was already moving to his side. He had his blade at Tomas' waist, edge-forward.

They both stopped moving and, as far as Hugo could tell, breathing.

A long moment passed.

As the wind rustled his hair, Tomas clapped his hands. "There we are," he said. "That's the kind of heartlessness I'm talking—"

Hugo finished Tomas' sentence for him. He pushed again, with both hands this time, and Tomas lurched over Hugo's foot and fell on his back.

Tomas snorted at him from the ground, his mouth open in a silent gasp. "You rogue!"

Hugo was smiling. "Don't ever trust your opponent," he said.

After one week of practice, it was Hugo's first victory against his teacher.

*   *   *

As the sun fell behind the horizon, Hugo realized how exhausted he was. In fact, nothing he knew of sucked the energy from him the way swordfighting did. And with his adrenaline now depleted, rest was all he could think about.

Unfortunately, that's just when Ulrich decided to make his appearance.

Addressing both him and Tomas, Ulrich wiggled his fingers. "You two, follow me."

Obediently, they followed Ulrich toward Bedburg Castle.

"How's the boy with a blade?" Ulrich asked Tomas as they strode side-by-side, as if Hugo wasn't there, three steps behind.

Flipping his blond hair from his shoulders, Tomas smiled. "I think I'm too good of an instructor."

Ulrich chuckled. "Is that right?"

Tomas nodded. "He definitely shows promise."

Without looking back at Hugo, Ulrich said, "Then you must be something special, boy, because I've never heard this man say that about any of his students." Neither Tomas nor Ulrich could see Hugo's smile, stretching ear to ear.

Tomas snorted, turning toward Hugo. "Don't get ahead of yourself, boy. And wipe that smirk off your face. Remember, your eagerness will surely get you killed. I offered no compliment—only the observation that I haven't yet beaten the vagrant out of you."

Hugo chuckled to himself. He could tell Tomas was still irritated about being played by his own trick.

The trio made their way up a winding hill, passing a church where several people were huddled.

A voice called out, "Jailman, over here!"

Ulrich looked perplexed as two men approached. One, about Hugo's age, and nearly as thin; the other, a soldier with facial scars, tufts of salt-and-pepper hair at his temples, and a thick, unkempt beard reaching his chest.

"I told you to meet me at the castle," Ulrich barked at the older man.

The soldier said, "I reckoned we'd cut you off, give your old legs a bit of a rest. Plus, I wanted to hear the bishop speak."

"How was he?" Tomas asked.

The man hesitated, then said, "Still full of piss."

Ulrich smirked. He moved over so Hugo was no longer hidden. "I nearly forgot. This is the boy I told you about—"

"The one you took for a son?"

"Easy there," Ulrich said with a frown. "Hugo, this is Arne," he said, gesturing to the younger boy. "And this"—pointing to the soldier—"is Grayson."

Considering the color of the old man's beard and temples, Grayson seemed an apt name to Hugo. Then he turned to the boy, studying him.

"Arne is the best tracker we have," Ulrich added. "He has a nose stronger than a hound's, ears bigger than a bat's, and eyes wider than an owl's."

The mention of an owl instantly brought back memories of Ava. When she was taken away, before she'd betrayed him. It had been Severin—playing the role of the "Owl"—who had failed to play his part, causing Ava's capture.

The young boy interrupted his thoughts.

"Is there something the matter with you?" Arne asked, his voice much deeper than his small frame suggested.

Realizing he was scowling, Hugo shook off his expression. "No, no, my apologies. It's a pleasure to meet you both."

Grayson grunted. "I'm sure."

"These men will make the rest of your company," Ulrich said. "So you'd better get to know each other."

"Our *company?*" Hugo asked. "Company for what?"

Ulrich put a hand on the boy's shoulder. "You're going with them to Trier, boy. As guards for those slippery inquisitors."

"I'm an *escort* now?" Hugo said, crossing his arms over his chest. "I didn't agree to that."

Ulrich smiled, the shadows playing tricks with his scar. "You said you wanted to learn to do what I do? Well, here you go. There will be adventure and good pay. All the things a boy your age should enjoy."

"You're not coming with us?"

"No, son. I am content here. Besides, if I came, who would

be Bedburg's executioner? Just because Trier may need more executioners and inquisitors doesn't mean I can abandon my post. There are still plenty of people *here* I need to make dead."

As the group dispersed, planning to meet bright and early the next morning, Tomas spoke to Ulrich. "There's one more I'd like to bring along. Make it an even five of us."

Ulrich frowned, staring at his friend. "Five isn't even, Tom."

"You know what I meant, dammit."

"Who is it?"

"My nephew, my sister's son. I promised her I'd help him get out of his transient life. Like you've done for young Hugo here." Tomas gestured behind him, to Hugo, who was struggling to keep pace with the taller men. "He's in a bit of trouble right now, in fact. I fear he might end up dead—probably by your hand—if I don't help her."

"Who?"

"My sister!"

"Oh," Ulrich said. "What's wrong with him? Can you trust him?"

"He got caught stealing something, I heard. I told my sister I'd help, but she'd have to let me do it my way."

"Is that why we're heading to the slums?" Ulrich asked.

Tomas stopped walking, allowing Hugo to catch up. "I'd like Hugo to get a try at him in the ring. I deem the boy ready."

Ulrich shook his head. "In only a week?"

By the time they reached the edge of the southern slums, all traces of daylight were gone. Hugo's heart started racing. *I've never fought in the dark before,* he thought, running his hand over the rough hilt of the sword hanging at his waist.

The crowd had already gathered at the square. Hugo groaned. *They talk of bettering people—getting them out of their former lives—but then bring us to this . . . vagabond justice, archaic and violent.*

Several people in the circle held torches. As Hugo was pushed through to the center, the orange light of the torch flames danced shadows across the ring.

He sighed, drawing his blade, preparing for the worst.

The other side of the circle opened—a silhouette was shoved through.

Hugo almost dropped his sword in shock.

Across from him stood Severin—his nemesis and former leader of his gang, the coward who Hugo blamed for getting Ava captured, the man he'd almost killed once already—less than ten feet from him, a nasty scar now adorning his forehead.

The crowd hooted and hollered. People began passing coins around, judging the combatants by their appearance. Because Severin was taller, a bit older, and had a hawkish face, Hugo assumed most of the money favored his opponent.

A brooding rage swelled within Hugo, quickly consuming him. But he understood that his anger really wasn't directed at Severin. After all, Severin had never done anything out of character. He had always been consistent in playing his part: the jealous, angry, bullying fool. Yes, he'd tried to steal the ring Hugo had stolen for Ava, but that should have been expected. Making life miserable for Hugo was just Severin being Severin.

No, Hugo's rage was traceable to what Severin *reminded* him of—the whole chapter of memories during that period in Hugo's life. Flashbacks flooded his memory of Ava and Karstan kissing; of the miserable, pathetic existence they all led; of their little troop gallivanting through Bedburg, carefree; and the shock and fear when that whole lifestyle came crashing down on them.

And now Hugo was staring at the ringleader of that entire debacle.

Hugo's sword was out of its scabbard before his brain could react.

At first, Severin looked scared. But his hawkish features softened once he recognized his opponent. He narrowed his eyes, offering a concentrated stare. A man in the crowd shoved a sword into his arms. He took hold of it, then awkwardly lowered it to his side.

With white knuckles, Hugo gripped his weapon tightly, his jaw tensing.

"Perhaps they know each other," Ulrich murmured from behind.

Then all sounds faded away. Hugo felt the pulsing behind his ears.

He leaped forward.

You're too eager.

Severin barely had time to react, jerking his sword up at the last moment, eyes bulging, trying to block Hugo's onslaught.

Hugo rushed into him, point-first. Severin managed to slap his sword away. Hugo reeled back, preparing to swing again as Severin began taking cautious steps backward in retreat. But hands from the crowd propelled him forward, pushing him back into the middle of the ring.

Hugo prowled around Severin like an angry wolf protecting its cub. He swiped his sword a few times to test Severin's reaction, but the taller boy was clearly lost with a sword in his hand.

Hugo charged again, howling.

Cheers erupted from the crowd.

At the last moment, Severin somehow managed to stick his blade out. Hugo ran shoulder-first into the point. Searing pain shot through Hugo's body, instantly replacing rage with momentary shock.

Severin took the opportunity to reach his arm back, ready to stab Hugo again.

Fighting through the pain, Hugo growled, dropped his sword and smacked away Severin's blade as it whooshed in.

Hugo was now inches from Severin's body.

Swordcraft is either a brawl or a dance.

There was no time for dancing.

Hugo wrapped his arms around Severin, pushing the taller boy back while planting his foot behind Severin's ankle just like he'd done to Tomas.

Severin crashed hard on his back, crying out for help. Hugo jumped on him, punching him in the face repeatedly.

The first strike froze Severin in panic, allowing a clear second shot which exploded his nose in a cloudy mist of blood. By the third strike, Severin's eyes had rolled back.

The fourth . . .

Hugo couldn't move his arm. Something held it back. He

IN THE COMPANY OF WOLVES

snarled, trying to free it, desperately wanting to finish the job his former friend Karstan had stopped him from completing the last time he'd had the chance.

This time Severin had to die, pummeled to death as savagely as possible.

But it was not to be.

"Save that anger," said a low voice.

Hugo twisted his head. It was Tomas.

"I can't let you kill him," Tomas whispered, as the crowd booed and jeered at the sudden intrusion.

"He's my sister's son," Tomas said, pulling Hugo off the beaten young man.

"And besides, he's coming with us."

CHAPTER SIXTEEN

GUSTAV

Leaving the blazing monument in their wake, they'd spirited away by moonlight. Gustav's carriage bounced along the uneven roadways through the night, maintaining a steady gait.

Gustav did not regret razing Dieter's church. A self-described man of science, he saw religion—and followers of Christ in particular—as sheep at best, or wolves in sheep's clothing at worst.

And while the church could have been a great source of income for him, he wrote off the fiery inferno as a necessary loss.

Anything that will help destroy these two devils is worth doing, he thought.

Gustav's eyes drifted to his two captives seated across from him. Sybil was staring out the window, likely wondering where they were headed. Dieter, however, gazed straight ahead at nothing, the depth of his sadness etched in the lines on his face, clearly visible even in the darkness.

After a while, Gustav figured it was time to tell the two what was to come. "We're going to Yarmouth," he said. "It's a coastal town between the River Yare and the North Sea."

Neither Dieter nor Sybil responded. They all rode in silence for several more minutes. Finally, Dieter spoke. "And from there?"

Gustav ignored Dieter's question. "It's a more ancient town than Norwich, in fact." He cleared his throat. "And from there, we set sail for the Dutch coast."

Knowing it was pointless to object, Dieter simply stared out at the passing landscape.

Hedda turned to Gustav. "Given our premature arrival,

Kevan and Paul say we may have to spend a night in Yarmouth since our boat might not be ready." Kevan and Paul were the two soldiers outside on the driver's bench.

"It's no matter," Gustav said, "I doubt anyone will follow us that far." He faced Dieter again. "Once you no longer offer them a service, you'll find your friends will quickly forget you."

"That's not true," Sybil said, turning to Gustav for the first time all night.

"Oh, dear, so beautiful and naïve. I hope I haven't angered that pretty face—we wouldn't want it tainted by early wrinkles." Gustav smirked, then grew serious. "Those people have families and lives of their own. You suppose they can afford to venture out thirty miles from home, for a futile rescue attempt? They couldn't even rescue you when they were sitting outside my doorstep!"

"Why are you doing this?" Sybil asked. "Is this really about your brother—about Johannes?"

Gustav scratched his scalp, then brushed several errant hairs from his face. "In part," he said, shifting in his seat. He leaned in closer, resting his elbows on his knees. "To be honest, I always lived in the shadow of my brother."

"Gustav . . ." Hedda began, but his raised palm quickly stopped her.

"Quiet, woman. Even though these bastards don't deserve answers, I'll give it to them if I wish." He reached into his tunic, produced his bottle of laudanum, and raised it to his mouth.

But nothing came out.

"Dammit." He stared at the empty bottle, then with a quick jerk tossed it out the window. It clinked against a passing tree.

Agitated, Gustav continued talking. "Yes, always in the shadow of my brother." He paused, thinking about a distant memory. "My father, Ludwig, always put my brother before me. Father saw me as a nuisance. He saw Johannes as an heir. In my father's eyes, I was emotional and erratic, while my brother was cold and ruthless—perfect qualities for a politician." Motioning his head out the window, probably at the bottle he'd just thrown out, he added, "*That* probably didn't help father's opinion of me."

Sneering, he folded his hands on his lap. "Johannes was arrogant, but under my father's tutelage he became a weapon against my family's political rivals. Once, a man argued with my father about a land dispute. Next day—without my father asking him to—my brother built a stone wall to separate the land in question. My brother told the man, in open parliament, that if the man crossed the boundary, his house would be used for the stones to build the wall higher.

"In short, Johannes threatened to destroy the man's land. Instead of being punished for his brashness, my brother became feared and respected."

"You were jealous of him?" Dieter said.

Gustav scoffed. "I wouldn't expect a rodent like you to understand the powers of fear and respect." Then he shook his head. "Call it what you will. I was angry that Johannes was getting lauded, and I was getting forgotten. As the first son, he had every right to my father's power and position, once my father died.

"But now, my brother is dead, and my father is still alive. Doesn't it make sense that I would be next in line? Father doesn't see it that way. I won't get his blessing until I earn his respect. Bringing you two devils to him will show me in a new light. I will be the avenger of my brother's death. My father will sing a new ditty once he sees the length I've gone to find you two."

"Does your father know you're here in England?" Dieter asked.

Gustav shook his head again. "I am not a bounty hunter, but you were easy to find. I couldn't take action while you were in Queen Elizabeth's court, but out here in the country is different. Your capture will be a pleasant surprise for my father—he's currently overseeing some witch-hunt in a town I can't bother to remember the name of."

"And what if you father doesn't give you the recognition you think you deserve?" Dieter asked.

Gustav narrowed his eyes on the priest. "He will, fool."

A loud knock came from the roof of the carriage, startling Sybil. A face leaned in from the window, upside-down. It was

Kevan. His brown hair rustled in the wind.

"We have company, my lord. A horseman on our rear."

Gustav stammered. "What in God's name," he muttered. He leaned over Hedda and stuck his head out the window. "Should we kill him?"

"If you'd like, my lord. Or would you care to see what he wants first?" Kevan asked.

Gustav scratched his ear. "Not particularly."

"Very well, my lord."

Sybil stuck her head out the window opposite Gustav.

Her eyes bulged and she shrieked. "Don't!"

Her head jolted back inside. She looked at Gustav with pleading eyes. "You can't!"

"And why can't I?" Gustav asked, crossing his arms over his chest.

Dieter wrinkled his nose at Sybil. "Who is it, Beele?"

"It's Martin! With our child!"

"You say you've followed us this entire time? How is it only now that we've seen you?" Gustav asked, his pistol aimed at Martin's chest.

Martin nestled young Peter in his arms, shielding the toddler from Gustav's gun. "Wheel tracks are not hard to follow, my lord. I merely decided to stay out of sight until I realized where you were headed."

"Where is it you presume we're headed, boy?"

"To the sea."

Gustav sighed. "Very perceptive." He turned to Sybil. "I suppose I was wrong about the allegiance you gained from your friends. This is quite . . . remarkable." He turned back to Martin. "So, boy, why shouldn't I just kill you where you stand?"

Martin stammered. "P-please, sire, this baby belongs with his mother. Are you so heartless that you wouldn't allow them to be together? Even in Sybil's most dire time?"

Gustav paused. Then he laughed. "Even if I agreed, you've given me no reason to spare *you*." He pointed at Sybil. "And as for the child, do you think I have *any* care for this whore's feelings? Or her tainted offspring? She's supposed to be suffering, you fool—she's my *prisoner.*"

"You can take me with you, sire. I will be your prisoner as well. Willingly."

Gustav's neck jerked. He fixed Hedda with a perplexed look, then swung back to the boy. "That still doesn't give me a reason to let you live."

"He's a fugitive as well!" Sybil blurted.

Gustav's eyes widened, his mouth curved up. "You do all this for this woman, and she betrays you so easily. Ha! What loyalty. What is your charge, boy?"

Martin scratched the back of his neck with his free hand. Peter wiggled in his arm. "Murder," he muttered.

"Say again? I didn't hear you."

"I killed my father."

Gustav clapped his hands. "Ah, patricide! Egregious." He rubbed his chin, studying Martin's shaggy appearance.

Sybil started to speak. "He—"

"I don't care what he did," Gustav said. Then he thought more on it. "But perhaps he will fetch a nice bounty in the Netherlands. I hear the Dutch slave trade is going strong." He eyed Martin head to toe. "And you seem to be a fit young man."

Martin cocked his head. "A . . . *slave*, my lord?"

"I have no use for you in Germany. Now give the baby to its mother and put your hands behind your back so Kevan here can tie them. Or I'll just have him run you through and we'll toss you in the next ditch, just like my empty bottle."

Martin complied.

As the sun peeked over the horizon, coloring the fringes of the sky with gray and blue streaks, the carriage rolled into town. Yarmouth was a quaint seaside village, its western shore abutting the River Yare.

Gustav had no time for pleasantries, tired as he was, so he simply restocked his purse with three bottles of laudanum, then slept for several hours at a local inn while Kevan and Paul watched the prisoners.

When he woke, a light rain had started to fall.

Stepping out from the awning of the inn, the rain streaks felt like linen curtains tickling his face. Of course, that may have had something to do with his early-morning laudanum haze.

After rallying Hedda, his soldiers, and his prisoners, he led the group to the docks. The overpowering reek of fish guts and salt made him gag, his insides even more upset than usual. He couldn't wait to be rid of England entirely.

He walked up to the boat docked in front of them, called the *Willow Wisp*—misspelled, Gustav mentally noted. This was the small vessel Gustav had commissioned to sail them away. Addressing the one-toothed captain eyeing him from its deck, he said, "I trust we've given you ample time to prepare for our voyage?"

"Huh?" The crusty old man's eyes were bloodshot and his beard was crusted with something disgusting. It looked like he'd been at sea for months, and hadn't washed the entire time.

Gustav sighed at the man's inexpressible intellect. "Are we ready?" he asked flatly.

"Ah, right-o, lordling. We is." The stench of the man's breath wafted all the way to Gustav on the dock.

Gustav turned his head. "Then let us not dawdle any longer."

"Huh?"

Gustav spit through clenched teeth. "Let's go, goddammit."

"Ah," the captain grinned. "Right-o. Let's."

The party of eight—Gustav, Hedda, Sybil, Dieter, Martin, Kevan, Paul, and young Peter—boarded the rickety old trading vessel. Along with Captain Jergen and his six shipmates, the ship was crowded, but seemed seaworthy enough to at least get them across the North Sea.

By mid-afternoon, the wind had cooperated, skimming them along at full sail, Captain Jergen looking every bit the seaman at the helm, his foot propped up on a stool. Even his raggedy hair and beard had taken on a somewhat majestic quality in the gusting wind.

After a while, the captain gestured toward Dieter, Sybil, and Martin, huddled near the rear of the boat by Gustav's two soldiers. "Saw ya brought pris'ners," he said, trying to make light chatter with Gustav.

"Yes," Gustav said with a firm nod, not wanting to continue the banter.

"Why bring the whelp?"

Gustav glanced at Sybil, holding her child close to her chest. He breathed in the crisp air.

"Dying woman's last wishes," he replied.

CHAPTER SEVENTEEN

ROWAINE

The *Lion's Pride* drifted along the North Sea. At the helm, Rowaine squinted from the blinding sunlight, unable to see the wool tradeship she'd been pursuing.

She shook her head, frustrated. If she couldn't locate the ship, it would be the first time her navigational skills had failed her. She was certain they'd been following the correct path— assuming she'd been given correct coordinates from Amsterdam.

They'd been searching for almost a week. The crew was getting antsy but she didn't want to give up. If the crew saw her fail at this very first pursuit under her command, it would seriously undermine, if not destroy, her leadership.

She knew she was stubborn—*I get it from my father*—but at some point she'd have to let it go and move on to other prey.

She motioned to the man stationed atop the lookout mast, but the man shrugged.

Daxton lingered beside her. He whispered, "The men won't think any less of you if we give up the chase, Row."

But Rowaine knew better. "They'll see me as less of a captain. They already do—I see it in their eyes."

"Can't win all the time, *captain*," Dax muttered, pushing out the last word with extra emphasis.

"Where's Dominic? I'd like to speak with him."

"Haven't seen him all day. Maybe he's locked in his room." The carpenter shuffled his feet nervously, trying to be careful with his words. "You know . . . a first mate who spends all day in his cabin isn't a great asset to the rest of the crew and—"

"I know that, Dax." She turned to the carpenter. Sweat from the sun seemed to oil his bald head, casting a bright white reflection off his skull.

Rowaine put a hand on Daxton's shoulder, then wandered away, down the stairwell below deck. As she walked through the tight corridors she felt the stares from some of the crew. Even a few leers. But she trudged along to Dominic's quarters.

She rapped on the door, but heard no response.

"Dom," she said, "I need your help. Or guidance. I'm . . . not sure what I need, but I need to talk to you."

Still nothing.

Creasing her brow, she tried the handle. It rotated, surprising her, as Dominic always kept his door locked when he wanted to be alone.

The small room was empty. Dominic's cot was nicely drawn up. Clearly no one had slept there in days.

"Dominic?" Rowaine called out, feeling foolish. She checked behind the door, then turned to leave. From the corner of her eyes, something caught her attention. She walked to the small wooden nightstand by the bed, picking up a crumpled piece of paper.

Rowaine felt slightly embarrassed at her nosiness, but unfolded it anyway. As she scanned the scribbled writing, her bottom lip began trembling.

For Rowaine—

I am sorry I could not be stronger. My mind has been awry since the torment Captain Galager put me through. No amount of ale seems to ease my anguish. If I were like you, I know I could have rallied back. But I am weak. And I am alone. If you are reading this, please do not come searching for me. It is too late. I made my decision while in Amsterdam, and I know you may never understand, and for that I am sorry. Perhaps I will be able to explain everything to you one day, when I see you again at the bottom of the deep blue. Until then, know that I love you. I always have.

Your favorite cabin boy,
Dom

She was barely aware of the hot tears rolling down her cheeks. She stared at the note, then re-read it. By the second reading her shock had set in.

Twisting her face, she tried to piece the puzzle together. She knew Dominic had come with her when they left Amsterdam. He was in bad shape, but he *did* board the *Pride*.

Where could he have gone?

She left the room—the crumpled letter still gripped in her hand—refusing to believe what her heart told her.

She rushed to the mess hall and called out, "Who here has seen First Mate Baker?"

There were three men at a table. They collectively shook their heads, eyeing each other. One of them asked, "Dominic?"

Rowaine nodded. "Yes. Dominic Baker," her voice now frantic.

"Haven't seen him all trip, captain. Figured he was locked away somewhere."

Rowaine left the hall, proceeding to the adjoining room where she asked the same question, and received the same response.

She scurried up the stairs to the deck. *If he left, there's only one way to do it safely.*

Jogging to the stern, she eyed the compartment housing the lifeboat, expecting it to be gone.

But it was still there.

Seeing Rowaine run to the back of the boat, Daxton rushed over. "Captain, is there a problem?"

Rowaine let the piece of paper slip from her hand. It floated to the ground like a leaf. Her mind raced, but she couldn't hold a thought. Suddenly the weight of the world was heavy on her shoulders and she felt dizzy.

She couldn't control her tears. "He's . . . he's gone," she whispered.

Daxton put his hand on Rowaine's shoulder. "Who's gone, Row? What are you talking about?"

Rowaine's knees grew weak. They buckled and she swooned. Daxton caught her, gently laying her down on the deck. He leaned across her, picking up the piece of paper and reading it.

"Shit," he said, his head sinking.

Rowaine let the sun beat on her brow, blinding her. But she wouldn't close her eyes. *Let the sun blind me,* she thought. *So I can't see what is true.*

She spoke softly. "I should have known, Dax. It's my fault. I should have noticed something was wrong when he apologized to me at Dolly's. It seemed so strange then."

"He apologized? For what?"

"For not being . . . strong enough."

Daxton put his hand on Rowaine's forehead. Members of the crew started crowding, curious to see what was wrong with their captain.

Daxton screamed at them, shooing them away. "Get out of here, you scoundrels! All of you! Get back to your positions!"

He looked down at Rowaine. Sweat dripped from his forehead and landed on her face as he spoke. "My condolences, Row. This is terrible. Poor lad probably sank himself in the ocean in the middle of the night, when no one would notice him missing."

Finally, Rowaine closed her eyes. The familiar oranges and yellows and greens beat against her eyelids. She felt the wetness on her eyelashes, on her eyes, on her cheeks. *He was so young . . . but so damaged.*

A bell rang out.

Daxton snapped to. He ran his hand along Rowaine's curly red hair, then jumped up, facing the main mast, where the bell was.

"Captain! We have company! A ship's on the rise!" the shout called.

"Can you take care of it, Dax?" Rowaine asked.

Daxton cleared his throat. "Row, you'll have time to mourn your loss. We all will. But your crew needs to see their captain. It's the first ship we've seen in a week—the first impression these youngsters will get of you."

He held out a strong hand.

Rowaine struggled, choking on her own spit. She took Daxton's hand and he pulled her up. She coughed and wiped the tears with her sleeve. "You're right," she said, stern but weak. Strutting toward the aft of the ship, she drew her cutlass. Its steel glistened in the sun. She raised it to the sky.

"Man the cannons, boys! Train them on the ship! Let's see

what these bastards have to give us! Charlie, get those ropes and ladders ready. Jerome, get your needles and saws set—let's see if they want blood."

She could hear the crew cheering, but it all seemed hollow to her, like it was coming from beneath the sea.

The target boat was small—much smaller than the *Pride*—with a blue and yellow flag.

Daxton moved alongside Rowaine. "By the wood and shape of the hull," he said, "I'd say it's from the English coast. Looks like a simple junk. Could be our fateful wool trader."

Rowaine steadied her breath. "The tradeship we're after is supposed to fly the yellow, red, and blue of Holland."

The junk stopped dead in the water, apparently fearful of the approaching raiders and the cannons aimed at its sails. The possibility of a violent death was always a powerful threat on the open water.

"I'm not afraid to use these cannons!" Rowaine called out as the *Pride* closed in.

A man cowered near the main mast of the junk, his hands high in the sky. "We're but simple traders, madame! We mean ya no harm!"

"Same can't be said about us, friend!" she yelled, her fiery hair blowing in the wind. "We're coming aboard! If you try to stop us or hide anything, you'll be the first one to feel the sting of my blade!"

It didn't take long for the pirates of the *Lion's Pride* to set ledges and ladders to the other boat. Rowaine was the first to cross, still holding her cutlass as she edged her way over the plank-bridge.

The captain of the other ship wore a proper captain's hat, with tufts of gray sticking out from the brim. His face was bright red.

Rowaine pointed her cutlass at the man. "Your name, sir?"

The man removed his hat and held it to his chest. "Jergen, m'lady. This here be the *Willow Wisp*."

"I am Captain Rowaine Donnelly of the *Lion's Pride*."

Fifteen of her hardest men surrounded her. Even the boys who'd just recently joined her crew made themselves seem dirtier and angrier by painting their faces and teeth with charcoal.

Jergen's eyebrows raised. Rowaine wasn't sure whether it was because the man was looking at a female captain, or because he was aware of the *Pride*'s reputation. Or both.

"What are you transporting, Captain Jergen?"

Jergen smiled meekly. Obviously he wasn't accustomed to being addressed as "Captain." The few teeth he had were brown from rot. "Dyes an' pris'ners, m'lady. Dyes an' pris'ners."

"Are you the captor, or the dye-merchant?"

"The second one, m'lady."

Rowaine hawked phlegm on the floorboards. "The next question is very important, Captain Jergen." She paused. "Are you going to make this more difficult than it has to be?"

Jergen shook his head profusely. "By Gods, no! What's mine's yours, m'lady. M'wares be mostly insured. But if ya could spare a few teeny things for us to get back to shore, I'd be 'bliged."

Rowaine eyed the dingy captain. "I'll see what I can do, Jergen." She faced her crew of smiling faces. "First thing we do, gentlemen, is separate the traders from the prisoners. Daxton, I'll leave you in charge of that. The others, search below deck for the wares that Captain Jergen is holding."

The bodies swarmed past Rowaine, their boots thumping against the wooden floor. She sheathed her sword and crossed her arms over her chest. She watched the men work.

A woman's voice cried out. It came from the back of the boat, where a woman was being separated from her baby.

Rowaine stormed to the end of the ship and held out her hands. She leered at a man in a ragged robe, who appeared more like a priest than a prisoner, and a scruffy young lad standing behind him. The priestly man held the hand of the girl who had cried out—younger than Rowaine but still a woman, fiercely latched onto her child.

A tall, handsome man with a head of thick, blond hair pulled a sword from its sheath, stepping in front of another woman, this one wearing spectacles.

Instead of pulling her cutlass, Rowaine drew her pistol from the back of her waistband. She held the gun on the tall man and pulled back the matchlock. "Careful there, stranger," she said flatly.

Two men beside the blond man—soldier types—had their hands on their weapons.

Rowaine's eyes drifted to the two soldiers. "If one of you moves any closer to your weapon, the man you're charged with protecting gets a bullet through his nose."

"You're making a mistake, my lady," the tall man said in choppy English. "These four here are my prisoners." He motioned with the edge of his blade at the priestly man, the scruffy lad, the woman, and the baby.

Rowaine chuckled. "You're holding a baby prisoner?"

The man scoffed. "Allow me to introduce myself, my lady. My name is Gustav—"

"Don't care what your name is. Explain yourself." Rowaine kept her gun aimed at the man's face. All around her, she could hear her crew loudly rummaging through the ship's possessions and tossing things aside. Daxton came to stand behind her.

The man with the gun aimed at his nose continued speaking. "I'm taking these two prisoners to Germany, my lady. They are fugitives. The young lad, he's also a fugitive, and I'm selling him as a slave."

"What did they do?"

Gustav cocked his head. "Pardon?"

"What did the woman and the priest do?"

"They killed my brother. And the young man there killed his own father. These are frightful people, my lady."

Rowaine pursed her lips.

"It's not true, madame!" the young woman with the baby shrieked. "We were just living our lives decently, and this man stole us away. Please help us!"

"He burned my church to the ground," the priestly man added softly.

Rowaine shooed away the soldier trying to take the baby from the woman. "Give the whelp here."

"N-no! Anything but that. Please, I beg of you." The woman was frantic, gripping her baby tighter. The child was now crying.

Rowaine sighed and put her gun away, which caused Daxton

to draw his own gun and point it at the tall man with the blond hair—the apparent captor.

"You're some kind of bounty hunter . . . Gustav, is it?" Rowaine asked.

The man narrowed his eyes. "I am merely trying to avenge the death of my brother, my lady."

"I can understand that," Rowaine said, frowning. She wagged her fingers in the direction of the woman. "What is your name, lass?"

"Sybil."

"Sybil, if you want me to help you, give me your baby. She doesn't deserve to be part of this."

Sybil sniffled. "My child is a boy."

Rowaine kept wagging her fingers. "Give the boy here."

"What are you going to do with him?"

"I simply want to look at him."

Sybil hesitated for a long moment. Finally, she handed her baby to Rowaine.

Rowaine cradled the child, beaming at the boy's innocent face and deep blue eyes. For some reason, the boy's face reminded Rowaine of Dominic, and it nearly brought tears to her eyes.

"What are you planning to do, my lady?" Gustav asked. "What is the meaning of this?"

"Shut your mouth." Rowaine shot steely eyes at the man. She grinned back at the baby. "What's the babe's name?"

Sybil wiped tears from her eyes. "Peter, my lady."

"Hello, Peter," Rowaine said in her best baby voice. The child whined and closed his eyes, clawing with small fingers at the bulge of Rowaine's breasts.

"Sometimes we call him Little Sieghart, though," Sybil said, smiling down at her child.

A jolt went through Rowaine's head. She imagined she hadn't heard correctly.

A moment of quiet followed. Only the sound of hooting pirates filled the sky.

"Your child's name is Peter Sieghart?" Rowaine asked, eyes aghast.

Sybil nodded.

"After whom?"

Sybil glanced at the priest by her side. "Dieter and I named him after my father, Peter Griswold, who was murdered unjustly."

"The child's surname—where does that hail from?"

"Er, well, it comes from a friend of ours, a man who saved our lives. His name was Georg Sieghart." Sybil scratched her head. "Why do you ask, my lady?"

Rowaine's heart pounded in her stomach. She nearly dropped the baby. For a long moment, she was silent, her eyes glazed over.

"My lady?" Sybil asked again.

Finally, Rowaine snapped to and refocused on Sybil and spoke.

"I've been searching for him for ten years. Georg Sieghart is my father."

PART II

Baying of the Hounds

CHAPTER EIGHTEEN

SYBIL

Sybil hiked her dress to her knees, grabbing the hems in both hands. She took a long step from the railing of the *Willow Wisp* to the railing of the *Lion's Pride*. Dieter held her arm to steady her. Teetering, she fell into his chest with a gasp.

"I have you," Dieter whispered in her ear, clutching her close.

Sybil looked over her shoulder. Martin held out a bundled Peter with steady hands from the edge of the *Wisp*. The baby was silent, unaware that, for just a moment, he was held over a twenty-foot drop to dark waters below.

Sybil snatched Peter in her arms and Dieter helped Martin board the *Pride*. The newcomers were given dark looks by the pirates on board, the worst from a bearded man with a shiny bald head who introduced himself as Daxton Wallace, the ship's carpenter.

Rowaine stood at Sybil's side, sword in hand. When Gustav Koehler moved to step toward the deck of the *Pride*, Rowaine held her sword at the tall man's throat.

"Not you," she said.

Gustav's neck jerked back. "Excuse me?"

"You're not boarding my ship."

A breeze blew Gustav's blond hair across his face. He stammered. "B-but these are my prisoners! It's my legal right to stay with them until I transport them to Germany."

Rowaine shook her head. "Your legal right ended when you sailed into the middle of the North Sea, Herr Koehler. Your delivery ends here, I'm afraid."

Sybil and Dieter shared a look, but said nothing.

Gustav gave an icy stare over Rowaine's shoulder to the

priest and his wife. Through tight lips he said, "Captain, you can't do this."

Daxton stepped beside Rowaine. "Try her," he said, folding his thick arms over his chest. A dozen other crewmen crowded the ship's helm, all leering at Gustav and Hedda.

Gustav spun toward his two guards, his expression demanding they do something. But Kevan and Paul wore blank looks on their faces.

Kevan, the dark-haired one, leaned toward Gustav's ear. "We're sorely outnumbered, my lord. I don't fancy getting my blood spilled on the decks of this shoddy boat. I presume I speak for Paul, too, when I say that."

The blond soldier nodded earnestly.

Gustav clenched his fists and let out a low growl. "Damn you, lady."

"Careful with your words, sir," Rowaine said flatly, her lip curling upward. "They can get you killed out here."

Looking past Rowaine at Dieter and Sybil, Gustav growled, "This isn't over, you devils."

Rowaine ignored the comment and pushed her ship away from the *Willow Wisp* with her foot. Her eyes remained locked on Gustav's until the space between the two vessels reduced Gustav's face to a tiny speck in the distance.

She turned and, resting her hand on Sybil's shoulder, set her gaze on Daxton. "Guide the ship back to port, Dax."

"Already?" the carpenter said. "We've been out less than a week."

"I'll make it up to you." She faced Sybil. "Follow me to my room. I want you to tell me about my father."

Back in Rowaine's cabin, Sybil sat next to her on the bed, while Dieter perched himself in the corner, his hands folded on his lap.

"He was a courageous man," Sybil said. "He saved both my life and Dieter's when we were wrongfully jailed. He also helped us escape Bedburg and the tyranny there. A battle was raging at the time, so we slipped away with relative quiet, captain."

Sybil couldn't help but stare at the young captain. With her flaming crimson hair, her piercing green eyes, and her leather shirt and pants, she struck an imposing figure.

"Where did you go?" Rowaine asked.

"Georg told us to head for the Dutch coast, so we did. I was bulging at the belly with Peter by the time my father's trial ended." Sybil peered at her sleeping child resting peacefully at the head of the captain's bed. "I never saw my father again, but I heard he was framed, labeled, and indicted as the Werewolf of Bedburg before they killed him. We had to leave the city immediately. And, once again, we have Georg to thank for that."

Rowaine smiled softly. "He must have really loved you two."

"He said we reminded him of a life he once had . . . one that he wanted us to carry on for him."

Rowaine sniffed, her gaze drifting away toward the cabin door.

Dieter cleared his throat and shifted his weight. "The last time I saw Georg, captain, he was surrounded by four soldiers. It looked dire. The soldiers were under the employ of Gustav's brother, Johannes von Bergheim." Dieter's eyes dipped to the floor. "I-I'm sorry, my lady, I thought you deserved to know."

Something caught in the back of Rowaine's throat. She coughed. "Please, you may call me Rowaine, or Row." She picked at her hands. "And even that is somewhat of an untruth."

Sybil cocked her head. "How so?"

"I was born Catriona, daughter to Agnes and Marcus Donnelly." She stared off. "My mother used to call me Cat. I don't know why—she hated cats."

"Marcus Donnelly?" Sybil said. "So Georg was not your father?"

"Not by blood," Rowaine said, shaking her head. "My mother was Irish, transplanted to Germany. My father was a captain in the Welsh army. A terrible man. He beat my mother. And hated me." Rowaine twisted in her seat uncomfortably.

Sybil could tell it was difficult for Rowaine to speak of her past. She likely hadn't done so in a long time. If ever. Sybil gave her a warm, kind smile, then gently touched her knee.

"Georg was fighting for the Duke of Parma at the time," Rowaine continued, "Alexander Farnese. His company came to my village. Since my father was a Welsh captain, he was clearly Georg's enemy. My father took my mother hostage—trying to save his own skin, of course." She paused, then finished. "And with one well-aimed arrow, Georg killed him."

For several moments the room grew silent. Then, Rowaine added, "Georg was always an expert with a bow . . . and I remember feeling a weight of relief when I watched my father die. His eyes never closed, the shock on his face frozen." Rowaine faced Sybil. "Does that make me a bad person?"

Dieter answered. "God will forgive you, Rowaine. You saw a man die—a man who hurt your mother. It is a natural feeling."

Rowaine leaned forward, stooping her head. "Georg took us in. At first I was reluctant. I loathed him, if I'm being honest. He was crude, dirty—I could barely understand him. I believe my mother felt the same way. But he grew on us. Without question my mother fell in love with him. As did I, coming to love him as the father I felt I never had. He was kind, affable, sometimes even funny . . ."

Sybil grinned. "He did have a way with words . . . even when he didn't use the right ones."

Rowaine smiled as she thought about that, then turned serious again. "Eventually, Georg had to return to his soldierly duties. We were poor. By that time, my mother was pregnant with my baby brother. I was fourteen years old. It was the last time I saw Georg." Rowaine's voice cracked. She eyed the floorboards as she cleared her throat and set her jaw.

"The killer came less than two months later, while Georg was gone. We were living in the house Georg provided for us, a small place, but secluded away from anyone else. We had fields of wheat, barley, and potatoes. I always wondered what brought the killer to our house. Was he there to avenge my father's death? A Welsh soldier, perhaps? Was he there for Georg, to finish a vendetta after finally finding where he lived? I don't know."

Rowaine paused and closed her eyes. It took her a long time to continue. She finally drew in a deep breath and her body shivered. "I was away in the fields when I heard the scream. The killer never saw me." Her voice grew dark. "But I saw him."

A thick silence filled the room again, until Sybil heard a small sob. She turned, but Rowaine's curly locks hid her face.

"I-I'm sorry that we've upset you," Sybil whispered. She put her hand on Rowaine's back, feeling the strong muscles spasm beneath the thick leather shirt.

Rowaine shook her hair loose. "It's not that," she said, wiping her face. "All this talk of death has reminded me of a dear friend. That's all."

"I'm very sorry," Sybil repeated. She felt a kindred spirit to this poor woman.

"Dominic was so lost," Rowaine mumbled, mostly to herself. "He killed himself this morning, leaving me a damned note in his stead." She snorted, lifting her head. Tears streaked her fair cheeks.

Neither Sybil nor Dieter said anything. Sybil knew how painful yet necessary grief was. No one else could really diminish it. She'd gone through it when she'd lost her father, then her brother. And with a wound so fresh, she knew no words of comfort would help.

That night, Sybil sat on a bench with her head on the ship's railing. She searched the black sea, listless and calm as it beat against the boat. The wind swept through her hair and she felt free again.

She stared up at the tiny silver stars twinkling above her. She focused on the North Star—the one her father told her to always follow if she were lost. She'd thought it was something fathers said to their children, but now—in the vast open ocean—it seemed a real and honest message. It was the brightest star in the sky.

Saved again. She exhaled deeply. *When am I going to be able to do that for myself? Whether it's Georg or Dieter or Rowaine, I've always relied on others to help me. Is that wrong? From here on out I must contribute to my own saving. But not for me.* She smiled at Peter beside her, wiggling on the bench, wrapped in his little blanket.

I will save myself for his sake. So he may have what I never did—a mother.

She heard footsteps approaching and craned her neck. Expecting Dieter, she smiled.

But it was the bald carpenter, Daxton Wallace. He sauntered over, hands behind his back. "I don't know how you talked Captain Row into going back to Amsterdam, but you must have a strong way about you, my lady," he said.

"Your captain and I have past acquaintances, my lord."

Daxton laughed. "I'm no lord, missus. You can call me Dax."

"Does everyone here have a name that someone else has given them?"

Daxton grinned. "Are you telling me you don't?"

Sybil's cheeks flushed. In a small voice she said, "It's Beele."

After a moment Daxton spoke again. "I'll tell you a secret, my lady." He leaned in close, whispering, "Daxton isn't my real name, either. It's John."

Sybil's eyes widened. Then she burst out laughing—a sweet, infectious laugh that started Daxton chuckling as well.

They laughed so hard Sybil's sides began hurting. Daxton coughed and spit over the railing, the yellow phlegm disappearing into the black void. He sat down next to Sybil. When he caught his breath, he said, "I was hoping you could do me a favor, Beele."

Hearing him use her nickname made her smile.

Daxton ran a palm over his bald, sweaty head. "I was wondering if you could talk to Row for me . . ."

Sybil leaned in. "About?"

"Well, now that we're out a first mate—"

"Dominic, yes?"

Daxton paused. Then, like a dam breaking open, his verbal barrage spilled out in one big flood of words. "I wanted to see if you could talk her into giving me a go at it. With the new vacancy, and Rowaine grieving in her room—which I understand—but the men need direction, you see. I've been on the boat the longest, my lady, always by her side, even before she was captain." He stopped and took a breath. His face swelled red from speaking so fast. But he wasn't done. "Dominic was a good man, don't get me wrong about that, but I figure you women are good at talkin' to each other and—"

Sybil placed her hand on his shoulder, which stopped him cold. "Don't worry that shiny head of yours, John. I'll speak with her."

He leaned back, satisfied, then his eyes scanned suspiciously from side to side. "You can't call me that, my lady. Please. I would lose all credibility here."

Sybil chuckled again. She pushed up from the bench and cradled Peter in her arms. "I enjoy your company, Mister Wallace. I hope we may have more conversations in the future."

Daxton bowed his head in mock formality. "I'm forever at your service, Lady Nicolaus."

Sybil made her way below deck. The corridors and rooms were eerily quiet. She knocked on Rowaine's door.

"Who is it?" came the response.

"It's Sybil, captain." Then, explaining, "I'm here on behalf of Mister Wallace."

She heard a groan, but Rowaine said, "Come in."

When Sybil poked her head in, she saw that Rowaine had barely moved since the afternoon. She was still in the same position—on the edge of her bed, head bent low.

Sybil stepped in closer. She noticed the captain eyeing something in her hand with deep interest. A piece of paper with a drawing on it.

Sybil creased her brows. "What's that you have there? A portrait of Georg?"

Rowaine shook her head. "Remember how I told you that my mother's killer didn't see me, but I saw him?"

Sybil nodded.

Rowaine held up the paper.

Sybil fidgeted with her hands. "It may not be my place," she said, "but why would you keep something like that, my lady?"

"I drew a picture of him so I would never forget his face. I've committed it to memory, but I like to keep my memory fresh. When I'm feeling sad, I look at the picture so I can blot out my sadness with anger. And hope. You may not understand."

Sybil nodded slowly. "I believe I do." She held out her hand. "May I?"

Rowaine swept her red hair out of her eyes and hesitated. Eventually, she handed the paper to Sybil. "I've sworn to find him some day. It's probably made me what I am today— vengeful, and always near the sea so every corner of the world is open to me." Rowaine chuckled to herself.

Sybil looked at the drawing and tilted her head, not sure she was seeing right. She suddenly felt faint. Everything grew blurry. Though Rowaine was speaking, her words seemed to fade away.

"M-my lady," Sybil stammered. Rowaine noticed her expression and stopped talking.

"I think I know this person," Sybil muttered weakly, looking up from the picture. Her eyes drilled into Rowaine's. "No . . . I'm *positive* I know this person. I recognize this face."

Rowaine met Sybil's stare, her eyes blazing with hellfire.

Sybil continued. "This man was a friend of your father— with Georg. A good friend, actually."

"Who is it, Sybil?" Rowaine asked. "Tell me! I've been hunting that face since I lost my family."

Sybil swallowed hard. Her heart fluttered. *That mustache . . . those eyes.* "He's the chief investigator of Bedburg. His name is Heinrich Franz."

Rowaine bolted off the bed and snatched the paper away. "Bedburg, you say?"

Sybil nodded.

Rowaine looked down at the picture one more time, then stormed out of the room. Over her shoulder she yelled back, "Then we've found our next destination."

CHAPTER NINETEEN

HUGO

The group was gathered in front of Bedburg Castle. In all, there was Hugo, Ulrich, and eight others. And one dog.

To Hugo's right stood Ulrich, Grayson (the bodyguard), Arne (the young tracker), and Tomas (Hugo's sword trainer). To his left stood Severin and four others Hugo didn't know—three men and a woman who were tasked with assisting the witch-hunts in Trier. Ulrich's group would be escorting them.

As Hugo gazed up at the castle, out of the corner of his eye he leered at Severin.

Even with his bruises and scar, he still looks so smug.

Though Severin was a year older, Hugo thought he'd probably never outgrow his hawkish, angular features.

He'll always have the appearance of an untrustworthy ferret.

Ulrich referred to members of the group by first name only. "Herr Samuel," he said to the one Hugo knew only by reputation as the head inquisitor, "I trust you have the paperwork that will prove your profession once you arrive in Trier?"

Samuel was middle-aged, with dirty blond hair to his shoulders and gaunt cheeks that actually enhanced his good lucks—much too handsome, in Hugo's opinion, to be the man who sentenced people to their fiery deaths.

Samuel nodded at Ulrich's question.

"Why do you ask?" the woman next to Samuel asked, wrapping her skeletal arm around Samuel's waist. She had high cheekbones, substantial hair that rested on top of her head like a roll of dough, half-lidded eyes that made her look perpetually tired, and the voice of a hyena. Hugo assumed she and Samuel were married.

Ulrich rubbed the back of his head. "Why do I ask?" He huffed. "If you run into any highwaymen or bandits on the road, Frau Tabea, it might help to clarify who you are. Less likely to get killed that way."

Tabea put a hand to her mouth and gasped.

The remaining two men in the group were Gregor and Klemens.

Gregor was Samuel's secretary. Pudgy and a bit older than Samuel, his round belly resembled a soft apple. Hugo guessed he lacked the ambition or charisma of the handsome inquisitor necessary to excel on his own in that profession.

Klemens was closer in age to Hugo, with soft features and a lute slung across his back. Besides being a musician, his role in the group was as Inquisitor Samuel's cook. To Hugo, he seemed sad, like he was pining over some young lover he'd left behind in Bedburg. Then again, most musicians Hugo knew carried that same forlorn look.

Rounding out the group, sitting quietly by Klemens' right foot, was Mord, a panting bronze-and-black Shepherd dog with a lolling purple tongue and pointy, white-tipped ears. The dog immediately took to Hugo, and Hugo felt the same toward Mord, crouching down and scratching behind the dog's ears, Mord returning the favor with a slobbery lick to Hugo's face.

Addressing Inquisitor Samuel's wife, Ulrich said, "The trek is more than one hundred miles, Frau Tabea, through poor roads, woods, and hills. If you aren't prepared for the hike, or the possible danger, it is my advice that you stay behind."

Tabea quickly shook her head, wobbling her hair bun on top. "I won't leave my husband behind, not when there's treachery afoot. I shall aid him in outing the witches, in God's name."

More likely you want to keep an eye on him so he doesn't lay a tender hand on any of those witches, thought Hugo.

"Besides," Tabea said, tilting her chin, "I have the carriage."

And while that was technically true, with the massive quantity of luggage she'd brought, it was a small miracle her husband could even fit in the carriage with her, much less anyone else. And judging from the harried expression on Samuel's face whenever his wife started chattering, if he had a say in the matter he probably would have chosen to ride a horse like the rest of the group, rather than spend the whole trip crammed in there with his wife.

Surveying the colorful assortment of characters before him, Ulrich said, "If you're lucky, you'll make it to Trier within the week."

"And if w're unlucky?" asked Grayson.

Ulrich shrugged. "You won't make it at all."

Grayson and Tomas chuckled, but Tabea once again blanched—a look she seemed quite comfortable with.

Their horses were packed and ready. A brilliant morning sun began its ascent up to a cloudless sky.

Before mounting, Ulrich pulled Hugo aside. "Since I won't be journeying with you, I want you to follow Tomas' lead. Whatever he says or does, you do."

"You already told me that," Hugo said. "I will, Ulrich."

"Good," he said, patting Hugo on the shoulder. He started to walk away.

"I still don't understand why Severin has to come," Hugo yelled out, stopping Ulrich in his tracks. Slowly, Ulrich turned toward him.

"Did he steal your woman?"

Hugo furrowed his brow. "W-well . . . no."

"Did he get you arrested?"

Hugo shook his head. "But he certainly could have been a better help."

"The only thing he's guilty of, boy, is trying to steal your precious ring. The same ring that *you* stole to begin with. He's a thief—has been all his life. What do you expect from him?"

Hugo frowned.

Ulrich gave him a weak smile. "Maybe you can learn to forgive and forget. Maybe he will, too. God knows you'll have plenty of time to do it."

It was mid-afternoon by the time the group got under way. As they left Bedburg, it was clear that spring had arrived—the town's stench of mud, sweat, and leather replaced by the almost dizzying scents of crisp, fresh pine.

A murder of crows cawed overhead. When Hugo looked back to the gravelly road, Klemens the cook rode up beside him. He bounced on his horse like a boy unused to travel—quite a detriment for a supposed minstrel.

Hugo eyed Klemens' white knuckles on the reins. "Loosen your hold. You'll anger your horse, and he won't be afraid to buck you if you treat him like a caged animal."

Klemens smiled wide and bright, like he wasn't accustomed to being talked to—even if just to be reprimanded. He tried loosening his hold on the reins but nearly took a tumble, causing his dog, Mord, to growl at the horse.

"Careful with your hound, too," Hugo said. "He'll frighten the horse."

In truth, Hugo didn't know what he was talking about. He had no real experience traveling, never having ventured more than a stone's throw from Bedburg or his home to the south. He wasn't sure if his advice was sound, but at least it was better than listening to the verbal abuse passing between Tabea and her husband in the carriage.

As the party rode past Hugo's former family estate, vivid memories flashed through his mind of his life not so long ago: the horse-shaped doll his sister had carved for him when he was young; the two of them running through the fields or sneaking about and eavesdropping on their father.

But then he thought of what had happened to his father, and to Sybil, and the pain forced him to turn away from the abandoned estate.

Better to forget it altogether. All it ever brought me was misery.

"I noticed Mord took a liking to you," Klemens said, interrupting Hugo's thoughts, his voice sweet and friendly.

His own memories still lingering, Hugo faced Klemens blankly, unsure what the boy had said. Then, without a word, he rode ahead to join Tomas at the front of the group.

When Hugo had moved up behind Tomas, Tomas said, "I saw that we passed your house."

It astounded Hugo how Tomas could know he was behind

him without even turning around.

Hugo came up alongside him as Tomas continued speaking. "My adolescence brings back painful memories as well."

"I don't mind it," Hugo lied.

Tomas chuckled. "Then why did you ride up here?"

"To get away from those yammering fools back there." Hugo thrust his thumb over his shoulder.

"Get used to them. They'll be with us for a while."

Hugo said nothing. Instead, he delayed, struggling to find the right words. Finally, he said, "What happened to you, Tomas?"

The soldier glanced at him, his blue eyes fierce. "What are you talking about?"

Hugo moved a hand from his reins and rubbed the back of his neck. "When I was a boy, I remember you leading me away from my home, taking me to the jail to see my father. That was the last time I spoke to him. You were working for Heinrich Franz then—that bastard investigator."

"He *was* a bastard," Tomas said with a nod. "But I still don't understand your question."

Hugo hesitated. "Well . . . it seemed you had good work as a soldier. A respectable profession. You were the right-hand man to the chief investigator of Bedburg. You were garbed in Bedburg's colors. Where did all that go?"

"All that went away with Heinrich Franz. Simple as that."

Hugo could hear the disappointment in Tomas' tone. *He was abandoned too . . . he feels the same grief I feel.*

"What brought you to leading these sorry folk?" Hugo asked, realizing too late the impertinence of his question.

Tomas didn't take offense. "I've always been good at this. I escorted folk before I met Heinrich. I didn't go anywhere—I just came back. In fact, I first escorted Heinrich when he came to Bedburg. We were both young then."

"Why did he leave you?" Hugo asked.

Tomas eyed the boy. "If you're prying to get a better understanding of your own circumstances, you're searching the wrong place. Our lives are nothing alike."

"But we had the same thing happen to us. We were both abandoned by those we love."

Tomas laughed. "You are sorely mistaken, boy. I never loved Heinrich Franz. In fact, I was happy he was gone. I didn't agree with most of his methods."

He elaborated. "Grief is different for everybody, Hugo. Of course I felt betrayed when Heinrich moved on, but what was I to do? Wallow? I've never advocated self-pity. I couldn't let myself be downtrodden. So I became a freelance guard, as I had done before. It was really nothing more than that."

A silence lingered as both men stared straight ahead. Hugo didn't believe the mercenary. *People might react to grief differently, but we all still feel it.*

Tomas cleared his throat. "I knew a boy who was born to evil parents," he began. "The father gave the boy to drunken friends who molested and beat him regularly. The mother finally killed the father, then drank herself to death. When the boy was orphaned out, his new parents gave him a pup, not much different than that Shepherd hound back there. But those parents were killed in a robbery, the boy left for dead. He was found by a couple, and this third set of parents seemed right and true.

"But then they killed his dog—burned it alive. Said the boy couldn't have any ties to his old life. Slowly these heinous people became worse than any of the boy's former parents. Yet they were the most pious of the bunch, respected in their community. The boy grew up not knowing what love was. He was misled, harmed, neglected. But did the boy let himself waste away, or be victim to his own misfortune?"

Tomas stopped his story. Hugo's mouth was agape, eager to hear more. When it became apparent Tomas wanted an answer, Hugo uttered, "No."

"No," Tomas echoed. "You see, Hugo, sometimes you have to grab life by the reins when it tries to buck you off. Sometimes you have to take what you want."

"What did he do?" Hugo asked. "How did he recover from all that pain?"

"Well . . . he became Bedburg's torturer and executioner. He became Ulrich."

CHAPTER TWENTY

GUSTAV

Gustav paced fore to aft on the deck of the *Willow Wisp*, his boots creaking on the rickety floorboards with each step. His mind wouldn't focus and he felt flustered. It was partly from overindulging his laudanum, but also from the indignity of losing his prisoners to the pirates. A warm sensation pulsed behind his eyes. He tried blinking it away, but that just made him look even more like a crazed and confused drunkard.

"So . . . damn . . . close," he muttered to himself.

Hedda took off her spectacles and massaged the bridge of her nose. "You should get some rest, Gustav. You're in no state to—"

"I won't hear it!" Gustav yelled, gawking at the grooves and holes in the wooden floor. He tried to avoid stepping on the uneven parts, and ended up hopping about, which only added to his crazed appearance.

Kevan and Paul sat at the end of the boat, looking everywhere but at Gustav, trying hard to avoid invoking his glare. Kevan fiddled with his boots; Paul stared off the gunwale at the black water. Hedda kept glancing at the two, trying to get them to lend a hand in dealing with Gustav, but it was a hopeless endeavor.

"I won't let them slip away—can't let them slip away. They *will* face the end of noose, even if it's the last thing I witness." Gustav trembled violently. He stopped in place, putting his hands on his hips.

"You're focusing too much on the small things," Hedda said, nodding and agreeing with herself. "Remember that Sybil and Dieter Nicolaus are a means to an end. If the last thing you see is their swinging corpses, you've let them beat you."

"My father . . ." Gustav said suddenly. "You may be right, woman, but the only way I see myself on that seat is if I bring those swine to my father's feet. It's the only way."

"I'm sure there are other ways to win Ludwig's approval, Gustav."

"It's the only way," Gustav repeated a third time.

Captain Jergen poked his head up from the stairwell, his eyes nearly shut, his appearance even grimier than usual. "Could ya shut it for a coupl'a hours there, lordling?" he said, eye-level with Gustav's boots. "After today's adventures, me men and meself need us some real quiet time."

Gustav felt like kicking the man in the face, or at least kicking something, hard. But having enough trouble just staying upright, he instead yelled, "Quiet your tongue, you rogue!"

Jergen jerked back. "Hey, I ain't the one who robbed us, *sir*. So don't go spoutin' off on me. Listen to your lady love and give it a rest for the night."

The captain's head disappeared, his loud footsteps fading as he stomped back down the stairs.

"Wait!" Gustav said. The footsteps stopped. "Where will we be going tomorrow? When will we reach Amsterdam?"

A loud chuckle echoed from the bottom of the steps, bouncing off the walls. "Amsterdam?" Jergen called out. "We ain't headin' there, lordling. I got nothin' to sell—you seen the bastards that fleeced us. They took all my goods! What am I gon' trade, the rottin' floorboards?"

Anger swelled in Gustav's chest. "Then where will we go?"

"Back to the island, I s'pose."

"You can't do that!" Gustav whined, stepping toward the stairs. He gazed down at the captain.

"Course I can. It's my ship."

"I paid you to bring me to Amsterdam!"

Jergen shrugged. "I didn't see us gettin' robbed. Wasn't in the itiner'y. We'll go back, restock, be back to 'Dam in a week's time." He smiled crookedly. "I won't even charge ya again. How's that?"

Gustav growled. "I don't feel you're taking this seriously, Captain Jergen."

Jergen stepped onto the lowest step, peering up at Gustav. He sneered. "Course I is. Ya think I *wanted* to get pinched? No. But it happens—even to the great Captain Jergen."

Hedda rolled her eyes.

"Now stop your damn poundin' and let me sleep," the captain finished. He spun around and headed down the narrow corridor to his room.

Gustav faced Hedda. "That soggy sea rat is going to cost me even more time!"

"More time? For what, Gustav?"

"To catch up to the priest and the girl!"

Hedda frowned. "You still plan on pursuing them?"

Gustav wagged his head vigorously. "Of course I do—but I can't waste any more time being stuck in the middle of the sea."

"Well, you heard the captain, Gustav. We aren't going to get anything done tonight. Why don't you put away the brown bottle and sleep?"

For a moment, it seemed that Gustav might finally relent. But that moment passed, replaced by a new wildness in his eyes. He leered at Hedda with that lustful, laudanum-riddled look she so despised. "Fine, woman, I will. But you're coming with me."

Hedda squirmed and pushed Gustav's hairy arms away from her face. She was on her back, her dress hiked to her hips, trying to hold her breath. A sickly sweet stench emanated from Gustav's naked body, not quite like booze, but not natural, either—the smell of a frenzied soul trapped in a vicious and lewd haze. And Hedda wanted no part of it.

With every thrust of Gustav's hips, Hedda sought refuge elsewhere, focusing her thoughts on a soothing place far from reality.

She dreamed of one day being strong enough to distance herself from this humiliating existence, to live her own quiet life. But the fact was, Gustav was a handsome man with endless prospects. The more he moved up the ladder of life, the more Hedda did, too. She'd come from a dark place and a poor family.

Any vertical movements Gustav took were big steps for her. Even if she had to put up with his disgusting habits and desires.

Gustav groaned. The sweat dripped from his face onto Hedda's breasts and neck. Finally, after what seemed like forever, he flexed his body, grabbed Hedda tightly by the waist and, with a silent gasp, crumpled into a slick, foul-smelling mass and rolled off her to the side of the bed.

Hedda took quick, short breaths. As her heard pounded, her hands rummaged near her knees, smoothing down her dress. Closing her eyes, she pulled the straps of her top back onto her shoulders, then reached over to the nightstand for her spectacles. Her breathing began to slow, as did her racing heart.

Quietly, she put on her glasses and faced Gustav. He was already snoring, his face mashed into the pillow.

She surveyed his naked body. His strong shoulders, his toned waist, his backside. Then, with a sigh, she gently covered him with the single blanket and closed her eyes.

She silently prayed for a long break before Gustav's next vile episode of debauchery occurred. Though she knew better. She'd made her choices, at least for now.

She opened her eyes and looked down toward the end of the bed. Gustav's half-empty bottle sat there on a stool. For a moment she contemplated pushing it over with her foot—the satisfying sound of the bottle crashing into a million pieces.

But she quickly came to her senses. She knew Gustav wasn't beyond hitting a woman. She also knew his state of mind, how he felt it his *right* to have his drug at will. Maybe some day, when life was less hectic and he didn't need to rely on that bottle, he'd become a kinder person.

But that day was not tonight, and Hedda fell asleep before she could dwell on it further, her spectacles still on her face.

Gustav awoke in a cold sweat. He knew he'd been dreaming—a terrible dream, something that made little sense. But before he could put it back together, the memory dissipated like the morning fog. So he looked around, trying to gauge his surroundings.

He was on a bed, naked, facedown. He rolled over. And there was Hedda. Curled up, still clothed, breathing lightly.

Did we . . . he arched his brows. *We must have. Lucille can never find out. If she does, that will be the end of us both.*

Gustav was married. And like most men he knew, he was terrified of his wife. She was wealthier than he, with far more political influence. Which was embarrassing. And all the more reason he needed Sybil and Dieter to hang. The boost to his dignity and image would be immense.

He had no regrets about his adultery. He did not love his wife. And he presumed she didn't love him, either. Their marriage was one of necessity. There was no love lost.

On the other hand, Gustav truly did love Hedda. Or at least loved the idea of being in love with her. And he hoped she felt likewise. *She followed me across the North Sea. That must say something. Or does it? Did she follow me because she felt forced?*

He couldn't remember how he'd gotten downstairs. He hoped Hedda had something to do with it and not his two soldiers, Kevan or Paul. That would be another blow to his pride, one he'd have to reconcile with them first thing in the morning.

Is it morning yet?

His eyes moved to the tiny window at the far end of the bed. *Still dark outside. Good.*

He sighed. Then an epiphany struck his brain like lightning. He remembered his dream. He remembered what must be done.

Amsterdam . . .

He got up from the bed, as slowly as possible to avoid waking Hedda. He searched for his clothes, his mind fuzzy and aching. As he put on his clothes, they stuck to his clammy body.

In bare feet he padded to the door, then tiptoed down the hallway.

The vessel was silent. Eerily so.

He moved deliberately, with practiced quiet. There was a job to be done. When he came to the door, he stopped for a moment, breathing in and out three times. Then he quietly pushed it open, leaning in slowly until his eyes adapted.

A large form lay in the bed in the corner of the small room. Silently, Gustav inched across the room, stubbing his toe on something, then cursing under his breath before stopping near the side of the bed.

The snoring form on the bed rolled over, onto its back, eyes still closed.

Gustav gazed down upon Captain Jergen, his face and beard glimmering dark blue from the first remnants of light through the window.

Gustav leaned in close, close enough to smell the rot from Jergen's foul breath. Then he reached down to his hip with one hand while placing his other firmly over Jergen's mouth.

Jergen's eyes blinked open a few times. His brow creased, confused, as he started to wake.

Slowly but with firm pressure, Gustav slid the knife across Jergen's neck, making sure to cut cleanly below the beard, through the veins, tendons, and cartilage.

As Jergen realized his fate, his eyes blinked furiously. He let out a wet groan, then his body writhed for a moment as his warm blood sprayed outward, then spilled through Gustav's hand, down his fingers, and began puddling around the captain's chest.

"Shh," Gustav whispered, staring straight into Jergen's fading eyes. He watched them turn from dark blue to stone cold gray as the captain's life ended.

When Gustav was sure the man was gone, he leaned back and wiped off the blade on Jergen's undershirt, then returned it to his waist sheath. He gazed at the lifeless eyes of the captain for a moment as the blood continued pooling onto the sheets, turning them black.

Before Gustav turned away, a modicum of decency prevailed. He reached over and closed the man's eyes.

The six men working for Captain Jergen all slept in a large, single room below deck. As the morning took hold, they were awakened by the clicking sounds of matchlocks and the sulfuric smell of gunpowder.

Kevan and Paul paralleled the doorway, their arquebuses aimed at two of the men.

Gustav stood between his soldiers, arms folded across his broad chest. He waited for the men—dressed only in their undergarments—to gather enough wakefulness and fear, before speaking. Then he said, cheerfully, "Good morning, gentlemen."

No one answered. One man gulped loudly. Another, the lone sentry from the night before, sat near the door, neatly bound with rope.

"Where's the captain?" one man asked, feigning bravery.

Since Gustav had discarded his blood-drenched shirt, the answer was not yet obvious.

"Captain Jergen is currently sleeping where he's always loved best—his natural habitat."

Gustav waited for the men to say something—to complain, to yell, to cry—but to his dismay they stayed quiet.

He frowned. "Unfortunately, Jergen did not want to bring me to Amsterdam, after I *paid* him to do so. Since he could not uphold his end of the bargain, he had to go."

"You killed him?"

Gustav bobbed his head from shoulder to shoulder. "Killed is such a strong word, isn't it?" He felt in an oddly chipper mood, considering the headache that pounded behind his temples. His frown morphed into a scowl. "Since I could not open his mind, I opened his throat instead."

Another silence followed, Gustav eyeing each man one by one.

"What happens now?" one of them finally asked.

"What happens now is entirely up to you, sir. Do you want to join your captain?"

The man shook his head.

"Then I guess we're all in agreement. We'll be sailing to Amsterdam." Before leaving the room, he added, "My secretary made breakfast. You should thank her."

CHAPTER TWENTY-ONE

ROWAINE

Rowaine's eyes were wide. "You're telling me that the man who killed my mother . . . was a *friend* of my *father?*"

"More like acquaintances, captain." Dieter shook his hands, trying to ease Rowaine's anger. "I doubt Georg had any inkling as to the evil Heinrich had done."

Rowaine had grown increasingly agitated since learning the name behind the face she'd carried with her all this time. For ten years she'd tried to match a name to that face. And now, suddenly knowing, it was almost too much to bear.

She thought of how fate had led her to this life-changing discovery.

Here is a group of strangers, floating in the middle of the North Sea, and they just happen to know my father . . . and my mother's killer.

Rowaine had spent the entire night locked in her room, peppering Sybil and Dieter with questions, forcing them to relive their uncomfortable time in Heinrich Franz's presence. She had wanted to know everything about her late father. But, first, about her mother's killer.

"He was a rotten man, obsessed with finding the supposed werewolf that haunted our town," Sybil said, frowning. "I never trusted him, but never imagined that *he* could be . . ." Her eyes grew big and she fell silent. A moment later, the tears started rolling down her cheeks. She wiped them away as quickly as they fell. "I promised myself to never weep again over things like this, but I guess I can't even keep a promise to *myself.*"

Dieter ran a hand up and down Sybil's slumped back. "There's no shame in your tears, my love."

"My father . . ." Sybil said through short breaths, "Dorothea, Josephine, Margreth, all those people killed. For what?" She looked at Dieter, as if he might know the answers.

Dieter frowned. "We may never know, Beele."

"Could it really have all been a charade? Why did my father have to be the whipping boy? I don't understand Heinrich's motivations, if what you say about him is true, Row."

"Neither do I," Dieter added.

Rowaine scowled. Even though she'd been through a similar tragedy as Sybil—losing her parents—she couldn't help but pity the poor girl. But watching Sybil weep only hardened her resolve.

She can cry her tears, but I am a fighter. I will get to the bottom of this. Even if these two can't help me.

But she knew that, as much as Sybil and Dieter might weigh her down, they could also be invaluable tools. To a point. She would need them to show her Bedburg—to get the lay of the land, to learn the ways of its people.

But they're fugitives. They said as much. Can they really help me?

"There was another man whom your father was friends with for a time," Sybil said, scrunching her nose. "He was a large, stout man with a red beard and Irish accent. He wore an eye-patch, which set him apart from most others."

Rowaine arched one brow.

"One day, he disappeared. If you could find him, maybe you could find more about your father."

"What was this man's name?" Rowaine asked.

Sybil snapped her fingers, thinking.

Dieter spoke for her. "Konrad," he said with a nod. "I saw him at Mass with Georg every so often. They did seem close."

Rowaine threw her head back and laughed. It was a dark laugh. "Konrad Donnelly was my mother's brother. My uncle. And he never helped my mother from my father, even when she was beaten. I'll never forgive him for that. We had nothing to do with him. I don't have a clue why he would associate himself with Georg, unless he was trying to spy on the man."

Rowaine moved from the edge of her bed to the window, staring out as both Sybil and Dieter watched her. The moon waned, turning the sky pale and gray. "Perhaps he felt guilty for letting my mother suffer all those years," Rowaine said.

"Maybe he was trying to atone for his actions," Dieter added.

Rowaine scratched her head. "He'll be of no use to me, even if we find him."

"We?" Sybil asked sheepishly.

Still gazing out the window, Rowaine said, "We'll be docking in Amsterdam by the time the sun rises. I'll need your help to guide me to Bedburg."

"But, captain, we are fugitives there," Dieter said.

"So you told me," Rowaine replied.

Ever since she'd lost her family and had been forced to live on her own, Rowaine was ever the opportunist. She'd found success beyond her wildest dreams doing things she'd never thought herself capable of. She'd done awful things, but that had only built her resilience. And made her the person she was today: the captain of the *Lion's Pride*.

Rowaine turned to the couple, folding her arms over her chest.

"I'm sorry . . . but this isn't a request. I will force you to guide me to Bedburg, if I must. But I don't want to have to. Remember, I didn't become captain of the *Pride* by letting things go easily."

A few hours later, the *Pride* was safely harbored at the docks. It had taken them less than a week to arrive, to the grumbling of most of the crew. As they disembarked from the ship, Rowaine took the lead, striding quickly across the dock. Dieter, Sybil, and Martin were barely able to keep up with her, while the rest of the crew straggled behind.

"I have a quick errand I must take care of," Rowaine said, not stopping to look at her tagalongs. "Then we'll be off. I'd like to be on the road before sundown."

"We'll be traveling in the dark?" Dieter asked.

Rowaine nodded. "I'll be sure to arrange the horses. It'll be the best time to travel without alerting any undesirables."

Sybil glanced over her shoulder. "What about your crew? Do

you imagine they'll agree to follow you all the way to Germany?"

Rowaine stopped short. Sybil almost ran into her. The captain glared at the young woman. "You let me worry about my crew, girl."

Sybil dipped her gaze and swallowed hard.

A voice called out from behind. "Captain, can't we drop these folks off and get back out there?" It was Daxton, his comment raising discerning grumbles from nearby crewmen. "We're all itching for the water," he said. "When I said we'd like to see land more often, I didn't mean like this . . ."

"I told you I'd make it up to you, Dax. Don't question my actions."

That instantly silenced him.

The crew of twenty pushed through the dockhands and sailors and merchants along the shore to make their way up the hill to Dolly's. When they reached the tavern, Rowaine was the first to enter, her eyes wandering around the main room.

But the only thing familiar was the stench of stale booze. The place was nearly vacant. Granted, the day had just begun, but Rowaine expected to see more faces she recognized.

Perhaps my expectations were set too high after my last visit here.

Dolly stood behind the bar, the only familiar face to Rowaine. When their eyes met, Dolly's lit up. "Back so soon! I knew you couldn't do without me, lass!"

The big woman waddled around the bar and rushed to Rowaine, wrapping her in a tight hug. Feeling Rowaine's muscled back, she said, "Oh, you're as wound up as my patrons, girl. What's got you fussed?" She pushed Rowaine out to arm's-length, studying her face with eyes caked in thick black makeup.

"I learned some unsettling news at sea, Doll. But it's nothing." Rowaine turned, trying to keep her feelings to herself, as she always did.

"Well, you know I don't believe that for a cold second. But I won't pry. Prying ain't what I do."

Except that prying was *exactly* what Dolly did. It is what made her such a successful business owner. But Rowaine was in no mood to enlighten her at the moment.

"Have you seen Mia?" Rowaine asked, her eyes darting

around the empty tables, finally landing on the back stairs at the far end of the tavern.

Without making eye contact, Dolly hesitated, then shook her head, wobbling her fat chins. "Not since last night, my dear."

Rowaine scowled. She was good at reading people. The way Dolly spoke, taking too long with her words, speaking in a high voice . . .

But Dolly would only lie to Rowaine for a good reason. "Doll . . ." she said slowly.

The big woman twirled around and sashayed back to her bar. "I guess you'll have to come back another time, lass. I don't know what to tell you. I just don't know."

Rowaine's blood began to boil. She understood. Her mind started racing. Too many things were happening too fast. Dominic's death, the discovery of Sybil and Heinrich, her arrival back in Amsterdam, the information about her mother's killer. Suddenly she lunged toward the stairs, racing around the tables through clouds of tobacco smoke.

When Daxton tried to follow, she held up her hand. He stopped in his tracks. His captain had spoken.

She continued climbing the stairs alone, her boots stomping louder with each step. At the top, she waited for a moment, listening.

At first she didn't hear anything.

But then . . . she did.

A whimper.

Rowaine sped toward the nearest door—not running, but not walking. She put her ear to it and heard the whimper again, this time louder. Then a moan.

She tried the door but it was locked.

She stepped back, braced herself, then kicked it with a violent grunt. The lock disintegrated and wood splinters exploded across the room, freezing in place the two bodies in bed.

Don't let it be . . .

But it was. Mia's shocked head popped up from beneath the sheets, her eyes wide with panic.

Rowaine didn't even notice the other person. She didn't care.

Her eyes focused only on Mia's amber, terrified face.

"Row!" Mia gasped, holding the sheets high to her neck. "What in God's good graces are you doing here?"

The man lying next to her smirked, eyeing Rowaine, then Mia. "The two of you?" he said.

Rowaine pulled her pistol from the back of her trousers and aimed it squarely at the tented sheet above the man's crotch.

The man screeched and rolled to his side. As if that would do any good. Then he jumped from the bed and ran like a rabbit for the door, his socks the only thing clothing his flabby white body.

"Goddammit," Rowaine said under her breath, still holding the gun.

Mia's eyes remained fixed on the gun, until Rowaine realized she was still pointing it at her and returned it to her holster.

After a moment, Mia said, "What do you mean, 'Goddammit'? You haven't answered me. What the hell are you doing back so soon?"

"Something's come up," Rowaine muttered, eyes sinking to the ground.

Mia jumped from the bed and put her hands on her naked hips. "Well, you can't be angry with me. You can't do that."

"I can't?"

"You know what I do, Row!"

At that moment, Daxton burst into the room. He eyed the splintered door, then glanced quickly at Mia's body. His cheeks flushed, his mouth gaped, and he quickly lowered his stare to the floor. "J-just wanted to make sure everything was all right. I heard a loud . . . bang." His stare remained fixed to a spot in front of his feet as he spoke.

"Get out!" Rowaine shouted.

The red-faced carpenter stammered and took another quick glimpse at Mia's gorgeous, naked body before exiting the room without another word.

When Rowaine turned back to Mia, she was putting on her tunic. Rowaine's eyes couldn't help taking in her sheer beauty, her bare, dark legs, from foot to hip, smooth as a well-oiled wheel. She stuttered. "I-I found someone who recognized the face in my picture."

Mia's mouth fell open. "You did? That's great news! Isn't it?"

"That's why I'm back."

Mia stepped toward Rowaine and reached out. "Come now, Row, let's celebrate. You know I cared nothing for that man . . ."

Rowaine stepped back. Her heart sank as she gazed into Mia's pouting eyes. "I can't," she said, unconvincingly. "I have things to take care of."

Mia scowled. "Rubbish, Row. If you didn't want to see me, why'd you walk up those steps?"

"I'm . . . not sure." Rowaine suddenly felt dizzy. Her adrenaline was wearing off, replaced by that lethargic aftershock that often came after raiding a ship.

She looked into Mia's eyes. "Come with me this time," she said abruptly, her eyes pleading.

But Mia wasn't ready. "Dammit, Row. Nothing has changed with you. I can't. Papa still isn't dead! You've only been gone a week!"

Rowaine clenched and unclenched her fists. She ground her teeth until her jaw hurt.

This will never work. She can never love me the way I love her.

"What's that look in your eye, Row? I know that look." Mia pressed forward another step.

Again, Rowaine retreated. "I've . . . I've got to go," she said. And with that, she rushed from the room, her steps echoing down the stairs.

She couldn't stay in Dolly's tavern for another moment. She walked outside and gazed up at the sky, thinking of the past few days. Of Dominic, which brought tears to her eyes. And Mia, which brought a different kind of sorrow.

Perhaps I should have given Dominic a chance. Maybe that could have saved him? Maybe it was my fault.

She didn't normally think that way—people's lives were their own, to do with as they saw fit.

But I know he loved me. I saw it in his eyes.

Someone cleared a throat behind her. She spun around. Dieter and Sybil stood there, waiting patiently.

"Why are you two following me?"

"I'm sorry about your . . . friend, Captain Donnelly," Dieter said.

Rowaine grunted. "I don't need your pity, priest. Life goes on. Why are you here?"

"We're waiting to see what you're going to do with us," Sybil said.

She certainly speaks more directly than her husband. Maybe she has more gall and strength in those thin bones than I gave her credit for.

"The day is yours, Sybil," Rowaine said, looking up at the sky again. "Like I said, we leave at twilight. I can't go back in there, but you can do—"

She looked down to finish her sentence but no one was there. Sybil and Dieter had already scurried back ino the tavern.

She sighed, then directed her attention to the street and businesses around her. At the corner of the tavern building she noticed Martin standing there against the wall, staring back at her. She yelled out to him, "What is it, boy?"

Martin's face lit up, but he couldn't seem to speak.

Maybe he's simple.

She walked toward him. "Well? Say it."

Martin tried to stand tall, but was still a head shorter than Rowaine. His fingers fiddled and twisted at his stomach.

Rowaine put her hands on her hips.

Martin stuttered, then blurted, "You're very pretty, like a summer rose! I'm sure you'll find someone special!"

And with that, the boy fled back into the tavern.

Rowaine smiled to herself and shook her head. Despite her pent up anger, she blushed.

Two hours later, Daxton met Rowaine at another tavern not far from Dolly's. Unfortunately, Dolly had noticed Rowaine slip into the competitor's business and had scowled at her, slapping a towel in her hands and cracking it like a whip, before waddling back into her place.

Rowaine knew she'd have to explain her behavior to Dolly,

but another time.

"If this is about earlier, Row," Daxton began, "I-I'm sorry—I saw nothing. I just wanted to make sure you were safe—"

Rowaine held out her hand, stopping his apology. She closed her eyes. "This isn't about that. I forgive you."

An awkward silence followed, until a waitress came to their table. "Would you like some food in ya?" she asked, but Rowaine promptly waved her off.

Rowaine reached into her pocket and fingered a small brass pin. She pulled it out, but kept it hidden. "I'm going on my own journey, Daxton. I'm sure you noticed. I'm sorry for being so flustered. That wasn't very . . . good of your captain."

Daxton massaged his temples. "Well, I'm not sure I can get everyone to come along, but I'll round up some of the boys. The loyal ones—they'll come with us."

Rowaine shook her head. "I presumed you might say something like that, and that's why I know my decision is right. That isn't what I want from you, Dax."

Daxton arched his eyebrows.

Propping her elbow on the table, Rowaine revealed the pin to Daxton. It was a roaring lion's head.

Daxton stared at it like a hungry boy seeing his first meal in days.

Before Daxton could say anything, Rowaine leaned in, grabbed his grimy shirt, and stuck the pin through. She grazed skin while trying to close it, causing Daxton to wince, but he made no complaint.

Once in place, she smiled at him. "I told you I'd make it up to you, Dax. Now I have."

"What are you on about, Row?"

She chuckled. "Take good care of the *Pride* and the boys, my daft friend. Their future is in your hands, *Captain* Wallace."

CHAPTER TWENTY-TWO

SYBIL

Sybil sat on an uneven bench in Dolly's, kicking her legs out, watching Little Sieghart run around. Every time the lopsided leg of the bench knocked onto the stone floor, Peter's eyes would shoot over, big and wide, and his dimples would show on his confused face.

Sybil looked across the room where Dieter sat talking to Dolly behind the bar. Sybil assumed the subject was likely religious, judging from the serious expressions on both their faces.

Even when he isn't practicing his faith, God is beside him.

It seemed Dieter was becoming more outspoken about his faith the closer they got to Bedburg, as if the town were a religious beacon beckoning him.

Shouting from the back of the tavern drew Sybil's attention. Rowaine and her lady friend stood at the front of the stairs in the midst of a heated argument.

This is the company I keep . . . an easily amused toddler, a religious zealot of a husband, and a vengeful woman angrier than the stormy sea.

Her eyes moved to the door, where Martin sat next to the crackling fire, entranced with the argument Rowaine and her woman were having.

And an adolescent boy allured by the vengeful woman . . .

Sybil stood from the bench, the wooden leg knocking on the stone, causing Peter to turn once again. She tousled his hair, then walked over to Martin. "Will you watch Peter for me, Martin?"

Martin's eyes never left the scene developing between Rowaine and Mia. Sybil glanced over just as the two women apparently decided to make up with a huge hug. She turned back to Martin and waved her hand up and down in front of his preoccupied face. "Hello there?"

Martin blinked. "I'm sorry Beele, I was . . . distracted."

"Is that right?" she said with a smirk.

"What did you want?"

"Make sure Peter stays safe, will you?" She glanced toward Dieter at the bar. "I've got something I need to do."

"Always," Martin said, focusing again on Rowaine and Mia. Their passionate embrace had evolved into an even more passionate kiss. Martin's eyes bulged wide.

Sybil sighed. "You like that woman, eh?" she asked. "You can't seem to take your eyes off her."

Martin finally looked at Sybil. "I think I'm going to be alone forever."

Taken aback, Sybil kneeled next to him, putting her hand on his shoulder. "Why would you say that?"

"That woman's so pretty, but she doesn't even notice me."

"It's not that she doesn't notice you, Martin, it's that she has certain . . . other interests."

"Is it because I'm too young?"

"No," Sybil scoffed, watching Mia grab Rowaine by the arm and yank her up the stairs like a ragdoll. "You could be the most handsome man in Amsterdam and, sadly, she wouldn't notice you. At least not the way you'd want. But don't sulk. We'll find you someone. I prom—"

Sybil cut herself off. *No promises.*

She squeezed Martin's arm, then stood up.

She pressed her wrinkled dress and walked to the bar. Standing behind Dieter, she waited a moment for him to notice her, but he kept preaching to Dolly. She cleared her throat.

And got the desired result.

Dieter turned around, eyebrows raised. "Oh, Beele, we were just talking about you. I was mentioning how—"

"May I see you for a moment, my love? Privately?"

"O-of course. Is something wrong?"

She grabbed his arm and pulled him from his stool, across the room, to the stairs. Then, as Mia had done with Rowaine, forced him to follow her up.

"What's the matter?" Dieter asked, stumbling to keep pace.

Sybil leaned down toward his ear. "We haven't had any time alone since we left England, Dieter," she whispered. "And we probably won't for quite some time once we get on the road."

Suddenly Dieter stopped stumbling. With a big smile on his face, he marched the rest of the way up, arm-in-arm with his sweetheart.

Once they were alone in one of Dolly's small rooms, Dieter closed the door and turned. Sybil stood facing him, already snapping the dress-straps from her shoulders. She let her dress fall, her smile broadening, her eyes piercing his soul.

When Dieter realized he'd been holding his breath, he quietly exhaled, her exquisite nakedness too much to bear.

Sybil held her arms out, guiding him to the bed. Sitting on the edge, she tenderly removed his clothes, then took his hands, laid back across the sheets, and gently pulled him on top of her.

After that, everything dissolved into a blur of passion, fury, and ecstasy. Their breathing grew rapid together, as did their beating hearts. Caught in each other's gaze, they could have been together for minutes, or days. All sense of time evaporated as the two lovers melted into blissful unity.

When it was over, there was a long silence as they lay next to each other. Sybil ran a single finger down Dieter's arm.

When one of them finally spoke, it was Dieter. His comment took Sybil by surprise. "I was thinking we might try to run. While we have the chance."

Sybil's gliding finger stopped. "Run? From what?"

"From Rowaine, Beele. Don't you see we're still prisoners, just with a different captor? She might not be trying to kill us, but she has her own motives. Remember that we're fugitives in Bedburg. I want to help her, believe me. But it isn't safe. We have to think of Peter."

Sybil propped herself on her side, resting her weight on her elbow. "Aren't you tired of running, Dieter? I am. We've been running since we had Peter. Look where it's gotten us. We're right where we started—even when we haven't been *running*, we've been fleeing."

"You would follow her to Bedburg? Where we might be arrested and tried?"

"That was years ago." Sybil flopped her head down on the pillow. "Maybe they've forgotten about us. Bishop Solomon is no longer there."

Dieter snorted. "The new bishop is Balthasar Schreib. Those people don't forget, Beele. Not when you're the daughter of a supposed killer. If we go, we're walking right into the den of the beast. It just seems foolish. Especially with all the talk I've been hearing of witch-hunts."

"Then we'll be fools together. I want to help Rowaine. I want to uncover what's really going on in Bedburg. I want to clear my father's name. No one else is going to do it. I mean, Heinrich Franz . . . a killer? We could be investigators ourselves. Doesn't that excite you—a little bit—hunting the hunter?"

"It sounds exciting for all the wrong reasons, my love. It sounds dangerous."

"What do you imagine Georg would say to that? Don't you want to learn what happened to him?"

"You're starting to sound like Rowaine." Dieter sighed. He knew he was losing the argument. Still, he had to try. "Georg would tell us to live our lives. He would be the *last* person to advise us to return to Bedburg."

Sybil bit her bottom lip. "Well, like I said, I want to help Rowaine. And that's what I'll do. I hope you'll join me." She narrowed her eyes at him, knowing what his choice would be.

Dieter coughed or chuckled—Sybil wasn't sure which.

"You know I go where you go, my love," he answered. "For better or for worse. It's always been that way, and always will."

Rowaine embraced Daxton once again. Then she pushed him back and smiled into his eyes. "You're a much more fitting captain that I would ever be, Dax." She squeezed his arms.

"I doubt that, Row. I just hope I can get these boys from one end of the sea to the other without sinking the ship. Or starting a mutiny!"

Rowaine playfully shoved him. "I'm sure of it, you big bastard. Now get out there and raise some hell."

"Now *that*, my captain, I can do."

He gave Rowaine a final salute, to which Rowaine responded in kind. Then he stepped onto the wooden docks to begin preparing for departure. They'd likely be in port for another day or two before leaving, since so much needed to be done.

Rowaine watched as the newly-annointed Captain Daxton Wallace directed his crewmen back and forth from the deck to the shore, reloading gear, rigging the sails.

Sybil came up alongside Rowaine. "You really trust that man, don't you, Row?" Sybil asked, not realizing she'd used her nickname.

"More than any of those other scoundrels," Rowaine replied. "Even when I doubted his allegiance, he stayed loyal. There's something to be said about that. As long as he does right by his crew, he'll be a great captain."

Sybil watched the sun sink into the western horizon. The water flashed emerald green as the last sliver disappeared beneath the waves. "Is your friend coming with us?" she asked, noticing that Mia wasn't around.

Rowaine shook her head. Though she'd tried, she couldn't hide the sadness in her voice. "I wish she were."

Sybil put her hand on Rowaine's shoulder, but quickly moved it away. "I'm sorry, Rowaine."

Rowaine turned to her, her bright green eyes clear with resolve. "We've got a hundred-forty miles to cover, so we'd better get to it. But please, I think I'll let 'Rowaine' die with her captaincy. From here on, please call me Catriona, or Cat, if you'd like. If I'm going to ever find my father, I want to spread a name he'd recognize."

Sybil smiled, but with a heavy heart. While she admired Rowaine's—or Catriona's—hope and confidence, she feared that when she last saw Georg Sieghart, it might very well have been the last time she'd *ever* see him.

CHAPTER TWENTY-THREE

HUGO

For three days the caravan bumped along Germany's trade roads, passing travelers and merchants along the way, over wooded hillsides, through stinking marshes that dried into yellow flatlands, and whichever way they needed to detour to keep the carriage's wheels turning.

On the first day, Hugo kept mainly to himself, awed by the wideness of the world outside his Bedburg bubble. The air was crisper, the pines finer, the hills bigger. He saw animals he'd never seen before, homeless souls on foot clothed in rags, and others on horses and in carriages dressed like royalty.

His eyes regularly strayed to Severin, whose expression never seemed to change—what Hugo saw as spiteful jealousy. Spiteful, Hugo assumed, for having to travel with Hugo in the first place. Jealous, probably because by the second day Hugo had formed a quick friendship with Klemens, the group's cook and minstrel. And since Severin wasn't treated as an adult by the others, he pretty much kept to himself. Which was fine with Hugo.

The only time they ventured even close to each other was when forced to sit at the fire during meals.

As for Hugo's new friend, Klemens, they were both close to the same age and, as such, had several things in common, including their love for new adventure and their constant adolescent struggles to meet young women.

One big difference, though, was their respective upbringings. While Hugo had basically raised himself when his family abandoned him, Klemens remained close with his kin.

"A brother that I rarely see," Klemens explained one night at the campfire, "is fighting for the Spanish right now. I miss him. And then there's another brother I see too often and can't seem to get away from," he said, jokingly. On this particular night, their meal was over and Klemens, sitting cross-legged on the ground, was plucking his lute. He was quite good at it, brightening the darkness with his magical tones. "There's a song somewhere in there, I'm sure," he said, gazing off at the wispy flames of the fire.

As Klemens played, no one in the group paid much attention, except for Hugo and of course Klemens' faithful companion, Mord, who always seemed to mellow and scoot in a little closer whenever he heard his master's lute.

Hugo liked the boy for his easy attitude, his aptitude with both a skillet and musical instrument—things completely foreign to Hugo—and for his dog with whom Hugo had already sealed a special bond. In fact, he'd often find Mord stepping on his heels, trying to get him to throw something to fetch. And most times Hugo would oblige and the dog would happily bound off, almost always returning a few minutes later with tail wagging and ears flapping and the treasured item safely secured in his mouth.

The other three members of the group—Inquisitor Samuel, his wife Tabea, and Secretary Gregor—made small talk amongst themselves, but stayed away from the others. They were stingy, uptight folk, unused to traveling, especially with youngsters, riffraf, and dogs. So they griped constantly, especially Tabea, who never stopped haranguing her Samuel, to the chagrin of everyone else in the caravan.

Often, the others would hear Tabea bark out obscenities through the carriage curtains, to the point where Hugo almost felt sorry for Samuel.

Until he reminded himself what an inquisitor's job was.

During the days, the young tracker Arne would ride ahead, then return hours later with useful news of what lay ahead. Sometimes he'd scout merchants on the road; sometimes he'd see highwaymen and bandits and warn Tomas of the upcoming danger so Tomas could guide the caravan down a different route, out of harm's way. It was an efficient means of travel and, for the most part, kept them out of danger.

*   *   *

On their third day, the sun shone brightly as the caravan made its way through a thinly wooded copse of pine and birch trees. Tomas sat at the driver's seat, reins in hand, eyes searching the flat road ahead. Klemens and Hugo were bantering near the back of the caravan; Mord, as always, by their side. Grayson and Severin both flanked the group, eyes peering into the trees. Samuel and Tabea—the precious human cargo—were tucked away in the coach, blinds pulled to shield them from the sun and the lower life forms around them.

About thirty yards off, the trees shivered. Tomas knew the breeze wasn't strong enough to cause that. He instantly reached for his sword, as did Grayson and Severin.

But it was just Arne, popping through the foliage, streaks of mud and grass acting as his camouflage. The young man approached the horses, putting his hand on one of their manes.

"Any trouble ahead?" Tomas asked, moving away from his sword.

Arne shook his head, his face emotionless and unreadable—fine traits for a tracker. Shielding his eyes from the sun, he said, "I reckon we have three more hours of daylight. What say you, Gray?"

The older man drew in his green cloak and stepped in from his position alongside the carriage. He frowned. "Why do you ask?"

Arne smirked. "There's a rowdy cottage up ahead. I believe it's a traveler's tavern. We could stop in for the night—actually have some beds to sleep on."

Tomas weighed the options, shifting his head side to side. "I'm sure the inquisitors would like that."

On cue, the handsome face of Inquisitor Samuel poked out of the carriage's drawn blinds. "A rest-stop, you say, boy?"

At hearing the word "boy," Arne's lips curled downward. "Yes, my lord," he answered flatly. "You could say that."

"How many people are in this place, Arne?" Tomas asked.

"At least ten. It's big, though. I'm sure there'd be enough room for all of us."

Tomas looked over his shoulder at the carriage. "I'm not worried about the roominess, but I'd like to keep these people's identities private."

"Why?" Hugo asked, walking alongside the carriage.

"I doubt they'd be well-liked if people knew who they were—especially a group of sauced-up travelers. Who knows who those people are. One of them could be a spy ready to warn bandits lying in wait up ahead."

Grayson chuckled, scratching his peppery beard. "I think you're giving the drunks too much credit, my friend."

Tomas shrugged. "I still vote no."

Severin came into view, eyebrows arched. "Vote, you say?"

"I don't run a dictatorship, nephew. We can all have a say."

As Tomas prepared for a vote, Tabea's sunken face popped through the carriage window over Samuel's. From the outside, it looked like their heads might belong to the same body.

"I won't have a vote," she said in her shrill voice.

All eyes converged on the hyena-woman, unsure what she meant. Tomas began to speak, then thought better and closed his mouth.

Tabea pushed the curtain back all the way, nudging her chin pompously toward the sky like she were the Queen of England. "The 'vote' is decided. I'll be sleeping in a bed tonight, sir. I won't spend another night in a tent."

Tomas spoke softly. "Frau Tabea, for your safety—"

But the woman was already shaking her head. "I won't have it, *sir*. Bring us to the tavern."

Arne wasn't exaggerating. "Rowdy" definitely described the place. The second Hugo stepped inside, the familiar stench of body-heat, booze, and tobacco nearly crushed him.

Reminds me of Bedburg, he thought.

Rather than being put off by the boisterous scene and sour smells, the familiarity actually comforted him. Even at his relatively young age, he'd already seen his share of brothels and taverns, and they all smelled and looked the same.

Grayson also wore a wide smile, for the first time in a while. Almost like he'd found his way home.

Tomas was the only one with his guard up, eyes scanning the big room, searching for danger.

The tavern was a large, two-story cottage, nestled behind a cloister of trees. Built from brick and thatch and stone, it bordered the woods.

"This is where the bandits, fools, and thieves must go," Klemens whispered, walking past Hugo and tugging Mord on a leash behind him. The dog didn't look happy—leashed and frightened by all the people, his tail was stretched straight out like an arrow as he snorted through thick pockets of smoke.

Drunken travelers eager to get drunker occupied four of the tables, as scantily-clad women paced around them, eager for their money. Every so often one of the wenches would latch onto a target and scurry upstairs with him.

Hugo wondered where the women came from—the nearest city was many miles away. *Were they dragged from the forest, or plucked right off the road?*

Still, despite the debauchery and loudness, it was a homey, inviting atmosphere to most of the men from the caravan.

"Can I get a beer, Tomas?" Hugo asked his designated mentor.

Tomas chuckled. "I'm not your father, Hue. I reckon if you can make it to the bar, you can order yourself a drink. The staff don't seem like the scrupulous type." He motioned toward the bar where a heavy-breasted woman was pouring two different bottles of liquor directly into the mouths of two raucous young men, spilling it down their necks and shirts.

Taking a seat next to a hooded fellow, Hugo ordered a mug of ale. He glanced over at the man but couldn't see his features. A few seconds later, the familiar twang of Klemens' lute glided softly through the room's noisy chaos. Hugo turned to see his friend at the other end of the tavern by the hearth, instrument in hand and trusty dog patiently resting by his feet.

As Klemens fingered the strings, the effect was magical, gradually calming the room until the music became the prominent sound.

"Isn't he worried someone might wreck his instrument?" Hugo asked as Tomas came to sit next to him.

Tomas leaned back against the bar and spread his arms out. "I'm sure Klem figures the opportunity outweighs the risk. There's money to be made here for someone with his skills."

Hugo watched as the mostly drunken crowd collectively focused on the young musician. One man mumbled out a request for a certain ballad, but Klemens was already deep into his own selection. His head was bent low, his scruffy hair flowing with the rhythm, his fingers moving faster and faster until they became a mesmerizing blur.

As the audience quieted even further, the orange-tinged smoke from the hearth cast an eerie glow across Klemens' image, adding even more fire to his blazing performance.

At that moment Hugo realized that he was watching a true artist. His friend was better than "good." He was a master at his craft.

As Klemens' crescendo built to a frenzy, he maintained it for the proper interval before abruptly stopping, his fingers frozen above the strings like a statue.

The ensuing silence was deafening.

And suddenly the crowd broke into spontaneous applause and cheers.

"Come on, boy, enough showing off! Play us something!" a man shouted, hands cupped to his mouth.

Klemens smirked. Then his middle finger plucked a single string, the warm sound resonating across the bar. His other fingers started moving, and a slow mixture of chords emerged. A few seconds later his voice joined in, softly at first, then building to a richer, more confident tone—high in pitch, yet not shrill. Firm and pretty.

There once was a young lass,
Who could have held kingdoms in her grasp.

The men hollered, a few pounded their mugs on the tables. Klemens was playing to the crowd, the subject matter perfect.

Broken dreams, damsels, and chivalry, Hugo thought.

Klemens sang on.

So light was her kind laugh,
So fair was her skin of gold.

But her soul had another plan,
And from her queenly fate this girl ran,
For she loved a poor and lonely man,
And her heart could not be sold.

"That bitch!" a man yelled, drawing a few laughs. One of the tavern women standing behind the man smacked him on the back of the head, drawing more laughter.

Her father tried to stop her,
By forcing her on someone proper,
'You can't marry this pauper!
My daughter won't be so bold!'

Klemens' fingers rose up the neck of the lute as he strummed and sang the final lyrics:

But her heart outweighed her soul,
And though his skin resembled coal,
The poor man made her whole,
And so together they grew old.

The furious strumming became a living thing—the music gasped and grew into another crescendo, this one even more transfixing than the last. The crowd marveled until the final notes slowed, then stopped.

Klemens looked up and smiled. "At least . . . that's how the story's told," he said, brushing through one final flurry of notes.

The entire bar broke into cheers, shouts, and whistles.

One of the prettier ladies crept up behind Klemens and grabbed his arm, trying to pull him upstairs, but he fended her off and instead began another tune.

This one perked Hugo's ears. It seemed familiar. Not the melody, but the words.

It was about a man—a legend, actually—by the name of

Sieghart the Savage.

Hugo had heard that name uttered around Bedburg. He was sure of it. Something about a ghost, a beast-slayer, a hero.

But in Klemens' song the man was a murderer.

Hugo listened carefully to the lyrics. The man's brother was killed in a war, which drove Sieghart the Savage insane. He then went on a killing spree, first murdering his family, then going after young women.

The song ended by identifying this Sieghart the Savage as the Werewolf of Bedburg.

When Klemens stopped singing, a man yelled out, "Peter Stubbe was the werewolf, you fool!" Then other patrons began shouting out other comments.

Hugo's eyes danced around the room. The crowd was becoming unruly, the song causing considerable disagreement.

"Not Peter Stubbe—Peter Griswold!" another man argued. "They were two different men!"

Hugo looked at Tomas, who simply shrugged.

Soon, two of the shouters were engaged in a fistfight, crashing through several tables. Klemens' eyes bulged. He searched for the pretty girl who had touched his arm earlier, but she'd disappeared.

The hooded man seated next to Hugo quietly rose and moved toward Klemens. In a slow, booming voice he spoke. "The Savage was neither of those men. But he *did* kill his brother."

A fourth man piped in. "Why in God's name would he do that, you fool? They fought together—did everything together!"

The hooded man said, "Maybe he was a coward. Perhaps he still held a savage spirit in his heart."

The other man leered drunkenly at the hooded man, then laughed. "You talk like you know the man, beggar! Well *I did* know the man. I can tell you he never did that."

The hooded man looked at the drunk with serious eyes. "I don't suppose anyone ever really knew the man, my friend. For how can you know anyone when you don't even know yourself?" He then drew something from his pocket and handed it to Klemens.

A coin.

As Klemens looked down at it, the man said, "For your song . . . about the priest and the girl. I liked that one." Then he turned and walked toward the door.

Klemens cocked his head, eyeing the man's back as he walked away. "I never sang about a priest, sir. But thank you for your generosity."

The hooded man stopped and turned back around. His mouth formed an unsettling smile. "My mistake. Many thanks, regardless."

And then he was gone.

"I knew this was a bad idea," Tomas said in a low voice, "bringing the inquisitors to this place. I'd better go check on them." He stumbled up and headed for the stairs.

Hugo nodded absently, his mind elsewhere. Out of the corner of his eye he caught Klemens ascending the stairs with one of the girls, and Tomas not far behind. But his gaze remained fixed toward the front door. There was something strangely familiar about the hooded man—the way he spoke, the way he carried himself.

But he couldn't put his finger on it. He shuddered. *Probably just my fuzzy brain from the alcohol,* he reasoned.

Finally, he looked away, focusing on one of the bar wenches nearby.

Which did the trick.

He quickly forgot all about the strange turn of events—his immediate base needs taking priority.

CHAPTER TWENTY-FOUR

GUSTAV

It hadn't taken much persuading for Captain Jergen's salty crewmen to convert to Gustav's cause.

A little coin and a little savage violence do wonders convincing desperate men.

The down side to that, of course, was worrying that one of the crew might learn a little too well from Gustav's actions and slit his throat in the dead of night. He'd just have to remain vigilant, as a man in his position tended to be.

Gustav moored the *Willow Wisp* into a neglected cove, away from the tradeships and galleons stationed in the Port of Amsterdam. Earlier, while guiding the ship into port, he'd noticed the blood-red hull and leonine flag of the *Lion's Pride* glaring back at him. So he had steered clear.

His heart raced as the *Wisp* quietly passed by the *Pride*, which fortunately was too busy being restocked for anyone to notice his boat's arrival.

Finding the *Pride* in port gave him high hopes. It meant that Captain Rowaine, that bitch, was not far off. And wherever she was, so were the main objects of his hunt: Sybil and Dieter.

Scanning the docks, he saw no wild red hair blazing back at him. Which was unfortunate, but not alarming. The captain's striking mane would make her easy to spot once his real search began onshore. *If I have to scour this entire town, through every slum and nook to find them, I will.*

Once securely berthed, Gustav, Hedda, and the six crewmen quickly melted into the crowds of traders and merchants, invisible to anyone who might otherwise recognize them. As Gustav strolled through the throngs of passersby, he passed the shiny bald head of the *Pride's* carpenter—Daxton, Rowaine had called him—barking orders to his men. Another sign that the captain couldn't be far off.

When they'd cleared the harbor, Gustav asked, "Kevan, Paul, do you know this place well?"

Amsterdam was a sprawling city, laden with canals and waterways and bridges. Gustav had only been there once before, when he'd first sailed to England in hot pursuit of Sybil and Dieter Nicolaus.

Kevan parted a slip of dark hair from his eyes. "I know it well enough to know where pirates like Captain Donnelly might go, my lord."

Meanwhile, Paul was swiveling his neck around, eyes wide open, taking in all the sights and sounds like a bewildered child. The fair-haired soldier had obviously never experienced the goings-on of such a big, vibrant city, and it was clearly overwhelming him.

Gustav put a hand on Kevan's shoulder. "Good. Take two of Jergen's men and search the eastern part of town. Offer a ten-ducat reward to anyone with information regarding Rowaine Donnelly's whereabouts. If she's as renowned as she thinks she is, someone will come forth."

Kevan gave a small salute, then departed with two men in his wake. Gustav then set Paul off in the opposite direction with two more men.

Hedda stepped up beside Gustav. "What do you plan to do if the crew of the *Lion's Pride* catch wind of your inquiry?" she asked, pushing her spectacles to the bridge of her nose.

Gustav shrugged. "If the price is right, perhaps one of them will help me."

"Or maybe ambush and hang you, Gustav."

Gustav scowled. "Has anyone ever told you that you'd be much prettier if you weren't so negative, my dear?"

Gustav sat in the dim tavern, his third mug of ale—with a few drops of laudanum—in front of him. His feet hung casually out the side of the bench. He leaned back. His head felt foggy. The high anticipation of his search had now given way to a cloudy, drug- and alcohol-induced calm.

He'd been imbibing at the tavern for two hours, waiting for his men to return. Hedda sat across from him, studying her big book on botanical merits, science, and God.

Finally, Kevan walked in. He sat down next to Gustav. He was edgy, his fingers fiddling. He waited to speak.

Gustav took another long swallow of ale, set the mug back down, then turned slowly toward the soldier. "Kevan, do you have something to say?"

Kevan nodded. "I believe I've met a man who is willing to help you, my lord. He says you must act quick if you want to catch the *Pride* before it sets off."

Gustav gripped the seat of his bench, leaned back slowly, and swiveled side to side, cracking his back. When he was done, he said softly, "I think I'd like to meet this man."

"What if it's a trap?" Hedda asked without glancing up from her book.

With a snort, Gustav stood. "I suppose we'll see, Hedda. If you'd like to stay here and finish your reading, you're more than welcome."

Hedda's finger followed the page she read until it reached the bottom-right corner, then she slammed the book shut. "No, I'll go. I'd like to see this. Where are we to meet this man, Kevan?"

"At a tavern, my lady. Where else?"

The three set off toward the western section of town, back by the docks. A sense of anxiousness crept up Gustav's spine as he stepped closer to the docks.

They crossed a bridge overlooking brilliant turquoise waters where a large narrowboat was gliding gracefully under the archway.

Gustav took no notice.

They walked by a brothel with a large, blonde woman standing in the doorway. As they passed her, she put her hands to her hips and sneered. They proceeded down the street, then crossed over to where a small, rundown structure stood, dingy and uninviting.

They went inside. The place was dark and almost empty, save for two men drinking at the far end of the bar.

The men glanced at the new arrivals, then went back to their drinks. Convinced they posed no danger, Gustav took a seat at a table well away from the bar. Hedda joined him while Kevan lurked nearby, eyes darting about. When the bartender appeared by their table, Gustav ordered drinks for the three of them.

A few minutes later, a large shadow stepped through the doorway, blocking the sunlight. Due to the glare Gustav could only make out a wide silhouette, until the man stepped into the room. His face was gristly, with a short-cropped beard, and he wore a large overcoat that swept to the ground. Another younger man—with a pretty face, strong arms, and big ears—followed him inside.

"Gustav Koehler?" the first man bellowed.

Gustav stared expectedly at the man.

"Name's Adrian Coswell," the man said in a gruff voice. "This young man here is Alfred Eckstein." He looked around the room before continuing. "Your man says there's a reward for finding Rowaine Donnelly." His tone soured when he uttered the captain's name.

Gustav motioned to the other side of the table. "Please, Herr Coswell, take a seat."

"I want to see the reward."

"If your information checks out, sir, you will." Gustav narrowed his eyes.

Kevan stepped forward timidly. "Herr Coswell says he sailed with Captain Donnelly, my lord."

"Herr Coswell can speak for himself," Gustav said.

The big man took a seat across from Gustav. Gustav motioned the bartender for an ale for his guest which arrived seconds later. The man took a swig, then said, "I was Captain Galager's first mate. So, yes, I sailed with the bitch."

"Captain Galager?" Gustav asked.

"My captain before the bitch. She cut off his cock."

Several long seconds of silence followed.

Then Gustav spoke. "Sounds dramatic," he said, casually scratching his neck. "And you weren't fond of her for that?"

Adrian chuckled sharply, then coughed and spit phlegm on the floor. "She should've killed me when she had the chance."

"When is the last time you saw Frau Donnelly?"

"Couple days ago, right over there," Adrian pointed past Gustav toward the bigger building across the way where they'd passed the fat lady standing outside. "That's Dolly's, Rowaine's regular haunt. We'd normally be meeting there, but I worry someone there might try to cut off my cock, too."

"A fair concern," Gustav said with a nod.

Another figure stepped into the tavern. All eyes spun around. A woman, thin with wide hips, walked toward their table. She was tanned, with a pretty but tired-looking face. "Word goes you're lookin' for Rowaine Donnelly," the girl said.

"Who told you that?" Gustav asked.

The girl folded her arms over her ample chest. "At least three different people, sir. It's not much of a secret around here."

After giving Hedda an evil look, Gustav turned back to the girl, who was probably no older than twenty. "And who are you, my lady?"

"I'm Mia."

"What can you tell me about Rowaine Donnelly?"

Mia frowned, her nose twitching. "That she broke my heart."

Gustav peered at Hedda again, whose eyes widened, magnified further by her spectacles. Kevan murmured something under his breath.

"I don't trust you, woman." It had come from Alfred Eckstein, the man who accompanied Adrian Coswell into the bar. Adrian looked up at his companion, standing next to the girl, then back at the girl.

"Aye," Adrian agreed.

With hard eyes aimed at Gustav, Mia said, "I know how Rowaine thinks. She's a vengeful woman. She'll be searching for her father, Georg Sieghart. I don't know where she'd go to find him—she wouldn't tell me after our final argument." She looked around at the others, then back at Gustav. "But I will be more of an asset when you *do* find her than any of these vagrants, sir."

Gustav pondered that. He rubbed his clean-shaven chin with

197

the heel of his palm. After a moment, he asked, "Who *would* know where Rowaine Donnelly might have gone off to?"

Adrian Coswell drummed the tabletop with his fingers, then cleared his throat. "As first mate of the *Pride*, one of my duties was knowing all the crew—where they came from, who they were, and, most importantly, where they lived." He paused for effect, then with a grin continued. "The man you'll want to talk to is named Daxton Wallace. Former carpenter while I was aboard. Became first mate, I believe. He was Rowaine's right-hand man during her mutiny. Bastard stole my position and gave me a good bump on the head. I've been keeping an eye on the two of them from the shadows."

Mia said, "He ain't the first mate anymore. Rowaine made him captain after she left the ship. She apparently had more important plans to attend to in the country." Her tone implied those plans hadn't included her.

"What can you tell me about this Wallace fellow, Herr Coswell?" Gustav asked.

"First, I want guarantees that you'll pay my men—ten in all. You'll have to dwell quick on it, for I doubt Daxton plans on staying in port much longer." Adrian shifted in his seat, folding his hands on his belly.

Gustav glanced at Hedda. The secretary opened her book, ran her finger down a few lines. "We can manage those expenses."

"There you have it," Gustav said, throwing his arms out wide. "You're lucky that I'm a wealthy man."

After shaking on the bargain, Adrian clasped his hands together on the tabletop. "I saw the bald-headed scoundrel recruiting more men before he set off to port—young men, able-bodied, with moldable minds."

"What does that mean to me?" Gustav asked.

"It means he's planning to be out at sea for quite some time, where you'd never catch him." Adrian raised his index finger. "But, I have an idea to stop him. As I said, I know where the man's family lives. He has a wife and young daughter stowed away on a farm outside town."

Gustav's face darkened. "I don't kill young girls . . ."

"I'm sure you've done worse, Herr Koehler. But you mistake my meaning."

Gustav nodded slowly. A plan began forming in his fuzzy mind, building gradually, until a faraway look overcame him. The others continued talking, until Adrian paused.

"Gustav, are you listening?"

After a beat, Gustav broke through his trance. "Yes, yes, I understand your meaning now. You say you know where they live? Well, let's pay them a visit, shall we? We have no time to waste."

As Gustav's coterie made their way out of Amsterdam, the sun gently nudged the horizon, causing the sky to shine pink and orange, creating a brilliant skyline behind them.

As the sun continued its descent, the colors darkened to pale blue, then deep purple. The farmlands east of the city came into view. *With any luck, Daxton and his crew will wait for the morning before sailing off—not at twilight.*

But Gustav wasn't sure. After all, these were pirates, who lived, pillaged, and fought by the cover of darkness. But he was already committed to his plan. He had a healthy crew with him: six former tradesmen who'd worked for the late Captain Jergen, plus Adrian, Alfred, Mia, and Hedda.

Adrian pointed out a small farm in the distance, smoke wafting through a hole in its roof. Confidently, the group approached the front door. Gustav knocked hard.

After a moment, the door started to open and Gustav put his foot in the way and pushed firmly.

With a yelp, a woman retreated back, a young girl by her side. Instinctively, the woman placed her hand atop the little girl's head. The woman had short brown hair, a pretty face, and was clearly pregnant. The girl, also brown-haired, was maybe ten years old.

Gustav stared down at the woman. "You are Daxton Wallace's wife?"

"Who the hell are you?" she snarled, clearly scared but

putting on a good face.

Adrian popped out from behind Gustav, smiling wide. His green overcoat billowed in the wind, knocking against the door. "Hello, Darlene. Remember me?"

The woman gripped her daughter, pulling her closer. "Coswell," she spat. "Who are your friends?"

"Never mind them," Adrian said. He stepped past Gustav and headed into the small living room. Gustav followed with Hedda close behind. The rest of the crew remained outside.

Closing the door, Gustav crouched low, eye-level with the little girl. "You must be Abigail. My name is Gustav Koehler. I'm your father's friend."

"Don't speak to her," Darlene said. "I've never heard Daxton mention your name." Her eyes turned to the big man beside Gustav. "But I definitely know Coswell here. What is it you boys want? We want no trouble."

"Nor do we," Gustav said. He paced the room, noticing the holes and rotting floorboards. "For a carpenter, you'd assume Daxton would care more about his own house. This place is a pit."

"He's been busy," Darlene replied. "We've had rain and storms since he's been gone. Brought part of the roof down."

Gustav sighed. "You mean you haven't seen him since he's been back in port?"

Darlene opened her mouth to say something, then closed it. She looked down at her daughter. "You lie," she muttered. "He would see me."

Gustav shrugged. "Family secrets aren't my concern, woman. The fact is, he's been in Amsterdam going on near a week. He'll probably be gone by morning. Who knows when you'll see him again . . ."

He let the words sink in, trying to drive a wedge between the woman and her husband. It must have worked. She shook her head slowly. "He's always cared more about that ship and that navigator woman than he has us. Whatever you say won't make me hate the man, though."

"You're a better person than I," Gustav answered. "But haven't you heard? The woman you speak of is no longer the navigator of the ship. Rowaine Donnelly killed the captain and took the role for her own."

Darlene said, "It's not my business. We're simple folk."

Adrian took a seat on a bench by the door. Stretching his arms out, he said, "Rowaine Donnelly passed on the captaincy to her second-in-command."

"That boy Dominic, you mean?" Darlene asked.

Gustav shook his head. "No, woman. Your husband is now captain of the *Lion's Pride*. Maybe he wanted to save the surprise. Think of all you could buy with his new station in life."

"Papa is the leader, mother?" Abigail looked up at her mother with big, watery eyes.

Darlene rubbed her daughter's head, silencing her.

Gustav noticed something by his foot. He leaned over and picked it up, keeping eye-level with the girl. It was a doll, shaped like a small girl, made from hemp rope and yellow curlings.

The girl ducked away from her mother's hand. "That's Franny," she said, reaching for it.

Gustav flashed a grin, then wiggled the doll in his hand. Abigail giggled. He lumbered up to his full height with the doll still in his hand. Staring down at Darlene, he said, "If you want to reap the benefits of your husband's new title, you'll cooperate with me. Do that and you and your daughter will be safe. So will Daxton."

"What do you want?"

"Information."

"I know nothing of what he does. He leaves his business in the sea when he comes home."

Gustav ignored the woman's comments. "We have a large company of men outside. I'm afraid they will have to stay here until we return. And you will need to remain indoors. But only until we can persuade your husband to help us." He smiled at the little girl. "And as I've promised, all of you will remain safe."

Darlene put her hands over her daughter's ears. "What guarantees do I have that you won't harm Abby?"

Gustav wiggled the doll in his hands again. He said, "You have my word." He crouched down again. "I'm going to borrow Franny, Abigail. Is that all right?"

The girl's lower lip trembled, but she nodded.

When Gustav got back outside, he turned to Adrian and said, "We need to gather your pirates." Next, he faced Mia and said, "You'll stay here with the men from Jergen's ship. They should be docile enough. Make sure those two inside stay safe. I won't have their harm on my conscience. Do you understand?"

Flustered, Mia said, "What do I do if the men get . . . rowdy?"

Gustav leered at her. "Service them yourself, whore. You should be used to it." He stormed away, walking over to Kevan and Paul, who were standing by the six men he'd chosen to stay. He leaned in close to his two soldiers.

"If I don't return by sun-up," he said, "kill both girls inside and burn the house to the ground."

CHAPTER TWENTY-FIVE

ROWAINE

Rowaine's party was closing in on Bedburg. They'd cut into Germany near Venlo, a municipal city and stronghold in the southeastern Netherlands that sat near the Dutch and German border.

Rowaine had purchased horses for all of them in Amsterdam, allowing them to cover ground quicker. It was the reason they'd reached Venlo in just over three days—a hundred miles from their starting point in Amsterdam.

It had not escaped Rowaine what a strange group she led: a pirate, a priest, a farmer's daughter, a bastard, and a toddler. But she was used to that—being "different"—and not caring. She'd been that way since she was young, when she'd become a bastard herself.

She had no concern whether the people she befriended were considered good or bad. She relied on her gut to discover her acquaintances' strengths and weaknesses, like she had with her shipmates and the co-conspirators of her mutiny.

Unfortunately I was wrong about one of them . . .

So far her gut told her that Dieter Nicolaus was strong-willed but weak-boned. *His greatest strength is his love for family and God. His greatest weakness is his love for family and God. This makes him easily exploitable.*

On the other hand, Sybil Nicolaus was stronger than her husband. She'd lost more. Rowaine could relate to that. She was fiery, too, like Rowaine. However, where Rowaine wanted to find her lost family and exact revenge, it seemed Sybil wanted to escape from those things and leave her past behind. *But through the walls at Dolly's I overheard her speaking with her husband, and her agreeing to come along when she could have fled into the night shows courage and resilience.*

As for Martin Achterberg, Rowaine hadn't been able to get a good read on him yet. He was apparently a bastard, had lost his family, and murdered his own father. The latter fact alone gave Rowaine pause. *But he's loyal to Dieter and Sybil, so he can stay with us. For now. It's also plain that he's wildly infatuated with me, which may prove useful.*

Lastly, there was the baby, Peter Sieghart. Though clearly too young to analyze anything, it was his very existence that was the catalyst for this entire search.

And in Rowaine's mind, that's exactly what this journey was. On one hand, a search and rescue mission—to find her father. On the other, a search and destroy mission—to eliminate Heinrich Franz.

Sybil's voice called out, interrupting her thoughts. "Ulrich. That was his name."

"Pardon?"

Sybil rode a brown mare and had Peter in a pack attached to her torso. The little boy squirmed, his legs sticking out from the bottom of the pack. "You asked who Heinrich and Georg might have both known. Bedburg's executioner was a man named Ulrich. He hurt Dieter when we were both jailed, until Georg came and rescued us."

Defensively, Dieter said, "I was fine . . . he only pulled my fingernails from my hand. It looked worse than it was."

"I heard your screams, Dieter," Martin offered, riding up behind them.

Dieter scowled. "I didn't ask your opinion."

Martin smirked. "Well, he didn't lay a hand on me the entire month I was in that stinking cell, so he must have not liked you."

"Enough, both of you." Rowaine rolled her eyes. *They're like quarreling children.* She turned back to Sybil. "You say my father knew the torturer?"

"Possibly. Georg smashed Ulrich over the head and saved Dieter from further torture. I don't know if they were acquainted before that. But I *do* know that Heinrich Franz spent many days in the jailhouse. It seemed to be his headquarters."

Rowaine rubbed her chin, contemplating. "I'd have guessed

the chief investigator of Bedburg would reside in Castle Bedburg. Unless he was trying to avoid that place . . ."

"I suppose it's possible," Sybil said.

"He could have been at odds with Werner, the little lord of the town," Dieter said.

"We can find out." Rowaine yanked the reins of her black steed, pulling him away from an overturned log. "Until we do, our assumptions are hearsay." As Venlo's structures shrank in the distance, she asked, "Who else might Heinrich have known? I'd like to have a plan before we arrive."

Silence passed, only the cawing of crows disrupting their thoughts.

A few moments later, Dieter said, "He knew Solomon, the former bishop. But they disliked each other."

Rowaine smiled. "The enemy of my enemy is my friend."

Dieter raised his shoulders. "True, but Solomon was excommunicated after his careless inquisition and investigation, though Heinrich *did* help escort the bishop's replacement to Bedburg."

"Wait," Rowaine said, stopping her horse. "You're telling me the bishop of Bedburg was shunned and banished, but the investigator was rewarded . . . for the same investigation? "

Dieter and Sybil both nodded.

"Don't you two find that odd?"

The husband and wife glanced at each other.

Rowaine sighed. "Who was Solomon's replacement?"

"A Jesuit by the name of Balthasar Schreib," Dieter said. "He came from Cologne, and was bishop in Solomon's wake. He's well-known and respected, and a formidable foe to Solomon. I hardly knew him, but he seemed a strong force."

Hiding from the castle and the lord? Conducting business with an outsider? I'm sensing a pattern here. How could Dieter and Sybil be so blind not to see it?

"Was Heinrich Franz born in Bedburg?" Rowaine asked.

"I'm not sure," Dieter said. "Why?"

"I'd like to find out, first thing we do."

"Why, Catriona?" Sybil asked, echoing her husband.

"It seems to me that Heinrich Franz may have had

motivations coming from outside of Bedburg. If he stayed away from Lord Werner, cozied up with the town's *executioner*, for God's sake, and helped overthrow the town's bishop, that all leads me to believe he was receiving orders from someone disassociated with the town itself."

Dieter waved his hands in the air rapidly, wobbling in his saddle. "Hold on. I don't know if he purposefully did *all* of that. He could have just been in the right place at the right time. Could be coincidence."

Rowaine clicked her tongue. "I don't believe in coincidence, Herr Nicolaus. It sounds more likely to me that some power-hungry man behind a mask is pulling the strings and trying to influence the whole masquerade. Maybe someone wants to keep the Protestants at bay—maybe for strategic or political purposes. And Heinrich Franz is that man's puppet."

"Investigator Franz never struck me as a puppet, Cat," Sybil said.

Rowaine's ideas were bubbling over now, and she ignored Sybil's remark. To both of them she asked, "Can you imagine someone who might want to sway popular opinion, but without anyone knowing he was doing so?"

After several long seconds of silence, a voice called out.

"Archbishop Ernst, elector of Cologne."

Everyone spun toward the voice.

It was Martin.

"My father talked about Archbishop Ernst often. I also heard Bishop Solomon talk about him when I was Solomon's . . . altar boy. I never met the archbishop, but I know who he was."

At least someone's paying attention.

"And who was he, Martin?"

"My father hated him, but the bishop idolized him. If there was anything Solomon could do to win the archbishop's favor, he'd do it. I imagine that's why Solomon was so angry when Balthasar Schreib arrived. As far as my father, well . . ." the young man trailed off, looking down at the grass and scratching the back of his neck. "He worked with the Protestants, after all, so he was more inclined to agree with Archbishop Gebhard."

"Gebhard was the one deposed by Ernst?" Rowaine asked,

making sure to get her facts straight.

Martin nodded.

Rowaine patted the neck of her horse. The stallion breathed softly, whipping its head in a circle. "We may need to speak with Archbishop Ernst, then."

Dieter chuckled. "You'd never get an audience with him. He's an elector of the Holy Roman Empire, for Christ's sake." He squinted up at the sky and said, "Forgive me."

"No, you're right," Rowaine said. "But if he's employing Heinrich Franz, I want to know. Actually, we may not even need him. We can work around him."

"How so, Cat?" Sybil asked.

"By being sharp-witted, my dear girl. Clever and sneaky." She winked at Sybil. "Two things I'm very good at."

CHAPTER TWENTY-SIX

SYBIL

At twilight, the company reached the western gate of Bedburg. A chill swept through the town as the sky darkened, almost making the group's arrival seem ominous.

As Sybil rode through the gate, memories flooded back. Her last time in Bedburg she'd been fleeing for her life. Now she was returning to uncover mysteries she'd tried to forget for the past two-and-a-half years.

Dieter had killed a man here, forty yards from the very gate she'd just passed. Now Johannes' older brother was in pursuit, probably still riding on their heels.

Still in the lead, Rowaine glanced back over her shoulder. "This place is foreign to me," she said. "Where do we go from here?"

"I reckon we find a warm place to bed, get started in the morning," Dieter said. "If we're lucky, we'll be able to hide ourselves away without alerting the town of our presence."

"What are the chances of that?" Sybil asked off-handedly. "I feel as though we're *already* being watched." She added, "I hate this place," as she watched the shuttered windows of every house they passed. Even though it was spring, winter still seemed to cling to Bedburg, dripping damp and wet from the windows, roofs, even the ground.

"This place was once your home, Beele," Martin reminded her.

Sybil shrugged. "That fact doesn't change how I feel."

The group dismounted, opting to lead their horses in by foot rather than raise unnecessary awareness of their arrival.

"The town's tavern will likely be bustling on a cold night like tonight," Dieter said. "It's on the eastern side of town, down this road."

"I could use some whiskey to warm my blood," Rowaine said. "That's where we'll go."

Sybil put her hands on her hips. "Not an inn?"

"You can go sleep if you'd like. But I'd prefer to make my presence known. The quicker I find news about my father and my family's killer, the quicker we can leave."

With a sigh, Sybil followed Rowaine.

They made their way to a stable near the center of town, close to the inn. They put up their horses, and Rowaine paid the man to make sure nothing ill befell the steeds. Then she marched toward a building with an orange glow coming from the windows.

Two guards holding spears passed them by. Sybil looked down, avoiding the men's gaze.

Suddenly she felt a presence and looked up quickly. Someone from the other side of the road bumped into her. Startled, she exclaimed, "Pardon me," but the hooded figure kept walking.

Rowaine spun around and grabbed the fleeing person by the hood, pulling back hard.

The hood came off and the person turned. It was a young woman, hardly more than a girl by the look of her pale cheeks and big eyes. Her eyes weren't naturally big, but were made so from Rowaine's sudden grab.

"Hey!" Rowaine snarled, keeping hold of the girl's hood.

"E-excuse me," the girl said, trying to squirm away.

"Ava!" a male voice called out from behind.

Everyone but Rowaine turned toward the voice. If it were meant as a diversion, it fooled everyone but her. Rowaine's eyes remained fixed on the girl.

"Give the lady back her purse," Rowaine demanded through gritted teeth.

Sybil felt around her waist, where she usually kept a small pouch of coins. Indeed, it was missing.

A large young man—the mystery voice they'd heard—popped into view from beside a building. "Let her go, you bitch!"

Rowaine was in no mood. She reached into her waistband and pulled her pistol, pointing it squarely at the approaching boy. He raised his hands and took a step back.

"I said give my friend back her purse, girl." Rowaine clicked back the matchlock. Sybil gasped.

The two guards they'd recently passed, hearing the disturbance, had returned. At seeing the drawn pistol, one of them pointed his spear at Rowaine. "What's going on here?" he demanded.

Rowaine kept her eyes trained on the de-hooded girl. "I'll tell you, once this—"

"This man tried to rob us," another voice called out.

All eyes faced Martin Achterberg, baby Peter wiggling in his arms.

Martin was pointing to the bulky young man, whose arms remained raised due to Rowaine's pistol still aimed at his face.

"W-what?" the boy said.

Martin kept pointing at the boy. "This man did it. He tried to pawn the goods off to the girl." Though he pointed at the boy and spoke to the guards, his eyes remained fixed on the girl.

Sybil noticed the girl was staring back at Martin, too.

"Not the girl?" one of the guards asked.

Martin shook his head.

The guards stepped toward the boy, their spearheads aimed at him. The boy, hands still raised, looked from side to side—two spears pointing from his right, a pistol from his left.

One of the guards said, "Let's go, boy. You need a talk with Old Ulrich."

Sybil winced at the mention of that name.

"You liar!" the boy shouted, but the two guards grabbed his arms and started dragging him off. Rowaine lowered her weapon but kept hold of the girl's hood.

"Ava, tell them!" the boy shouted.

The girl stuttered as the boy was dragged off. She muttered, "Karstan . . ." under her breath. When she took a step forward, she was tugged back by her hood.

"The purse," Rowaine said.

The girl handed it back.

"Consider yourself lucky, girl, and get out of our sight." Rowaine waved her gun at the girl, who took off running the opposite way.

When she was gone, all eyes circled back to Martin.

"You want to tell us what that was about?" Dieter asked.

Martin watched the ground and stayed quiet for the rest of the walk to the tavern.

Sybil, Dieter, and Rowaine sat at a roundtable near the bar. The tavern stank of the usual smells, so Martin sat away from the stench of smoke and booze, and held Peter.

After guzzling her mug, Rowaine wiped her mouth with the side of her sleeve and asked, "What's wrong with the boy?"

"Never mind him," Dieter said, waving off Martin's odd behavior. He drummed the table with his fingers, then said, "I've been thinking about tomorrow. I think we should avoid contact with Bishop Balthasar. At worst, he could arrest us and have us tried for our original crimes—and I don't mean being branded Protestants, I mean being indicted for murder."

Sybil said, "We have to assume that by morning he will know of our arrival. What do you imagine he'll do? He could still pursue us."

"True," Dieter said, "but if we steer clear of him, perhaps he'll forget about us. There's no reason for us to make a . . . scene."

Dieter's eyes looked past Sybil.

Rowaine had grabbed a passing bar wench and wrestled the scantily-clad woman onto her lap. Rowaine's face rested on the woman's bosom. She started kissing the dark-haired girl.

Sybil sighed. Trying to ignore Rowaine's escapade, she faced Dieter. "What else do you have in mind?"

Dieter continued gawking at Rowaine and the other woman. Hoots and hollers were coming from other bar patrons. Sybil snapped her fingers in front of Dieter's face. Shaking his head, he said, "Er, well, I'd like to see the church records. See who was killed by the supposed werewolf."

"Balthasar is the keeper of those records," Sybil said.

"Yes, but I think I can skirt around him. Speak directly with Sister Salome."

Sybil's eyes narrowed. "That woman was in love with you, Dieter, and you broke her heart. You figure she'd actually *help* us? I think she'd more likely turn us in!"

Dieter raised a single finger. "I'll use her admiration for me to our advantage, Beele. Besides, she knew Georg better than Balthasar ever did. And Heinrich. She heard me give Georg confession."

The wench's face shot up, her face covered in Rowaine's sticky saliva. "Did you say Georg and Heinrich?"

Rowaine cocked her head. "You know them?"

The girl ran a finger under Rowaine's chin and smiled alluringly. "I wouldn't know one name from the other, but together, sure I do."

"In what capacity?" Rowaine asked.

"Huh?" A blank look.

Rowaine groaned. "How did you know them?"

The girl pushed her dark hair from her face. "Georg Sieghart you're talkin', right? His brother was one of my best customers."

Rowaine nearly pushed the girl from her lap. She clenched her jaw. "Who are you, girl?"

"Name's Aellin."

"And what was Georg's brother called?"

The girl tapped a finger to her chin, narrowing her eyes. "Eh, I recall it started with a 'C'—Conway, Connor, something like that."

"Konrad?"

Aellin's eyes brightened. "That was it."

"And what happened to Konrad, madame?" Sybil asked.

"Well, he stopped coming 'round on account of him dying and all." She pushed herself from Rowaine's lap, straightened her skirts, and cleared her throat. "You all should talk to Claus if you want to know Georg and Konrad better. That's where they stayed. At the inn, I mean. When they weren't here, they were there."

Rowaine jumped from her stool. Sybil and Dieter followed.

"Where you going, mermaid?" Aellin asked, groping at Rowaine as she walked off.

Rowaine slapped the girl's bottom. "To the inn of course, my dear. But don't worry that pretty face—I'll be back. And you'd better be waiting."

The inn was a small, cozy place in the shadow of bigger buildings, tucked away from most passersby. Unless you knew where to look, you'd never find it.

An old man sat on a stool behind a desk, snoring, head slumped to his chest.

Rowaine pounded on the desk, and the man woke with a start and a gasp.

"Jesus, woman, you trying to kill an old man? 'Cause that's how you do it." Even in alarm, his wrinkled face seemed jolly.

"We're looking for a man named Claus, sir," Sybil said softly, stepping next to Rowaine and using a bit more diplomacy.

"What the hell do you want with me?" he asked, a smile forming as he eyed the two women. "Or am I still dreaming? Haven't had two beautiful things like yourselves calling my name in . . . well, forever, now that I think on it."

Sybil blushed, but Rowaine frowned.

"We've heard you know a man named Georg Sieghart," Rowaine said.

The affable look on the man's face instantly disappeared. He sucked his lips together, his eyes darting from Sybil to Rowaine. "I haven't heard *that* name in a time. What do you want with Georg?"

Rowaine slammed her palms on the desk. "Y-you mean you know where he is?"

Claus shook his head. "You mistake my meaning, lass. What I'm saying is, how did two pretty things like you come to hear that name? By all accounts, the man's a savage heathen."

Sybil folded her arms over her chest. "That's not true."

"Georg Sieghart was my father, old man," Rowaine said, this time a bit more civilly. "So will you talk to me?"

Claus appeared even more surprised than when first startled awake. "By God," he said, leaning in closer and gazing into Rowaine's face. "But you look . . . nothing alike."

"My name is Catriona Donnelly. He was not my father by blood, rather by ward—he rescued my mother from—"

"Yes, yes, I remember now," Claus said, wagging a hand at Rowaine. "He rescued a pretty young Irish thing while fighting with Alexander Farnese."

"Where's Martin?" Dieter stood at the doorway, inspecting the small interior. He held Peter, but Martin was nowhere in sight.

Sybil put a hand up, quieting him. Her eyes remained locked on Claus—like Rowaine's were—eager to hear his next words.

"H-how in the name of the Blessed Virgin do you know all that, old man?" Rowaine asked.

Claus flashed a grin that belied his age. "Because I was with him when he rescued that girl." He closed his eyes. "I was Georg Sieghart's superior in the Spanish Army, my dear. They used to call me captain, a time ago."

Rowaine smiled. "They used to call me that, too."

Claus matched Rowaine's grin. "Seems we have a few things in common, Catriona. You may not look like him, but you sure *sound* like the man I knew."

"What can you tell me of him, captain? How did he die?"

Claus cleared his throat. "First of all, my dear, I don't believe Georg Sieghart is dead. No corpse found!" He made a snorting sound, dipping his hand in the air like that proved his point. "Secondly—" Claus stopped himself, pointing a finger to the ceiling, closing his eyes again, then opening them, his expression bright and cheery.

"Say, would you like some tea before I begin? I knew the man for years and have stories that could take the entire night. And I make a cup so mean it'll sober up a wild boar."

He grinned. "Worked for your father, at least."

CHAPTER TWENTY-SEVEN

HUGO

After their pleasant stay at the travelers' lodge, Tomas and Hugo's group set off for Trier in the dark hours of the morning. They journeyed for two more days, barely stopping to rest. Frau Tabea complained the whole way, much to the dismay of everyone else.

"My mind isn't as nimble as it used to be," Tomas told Grayson from the front of the carriage. "I believe I'm turning into you, Gray. I can't heal from a hard night of drink like I used to."

Grayson chuckled, tightening his grip on the reins of the two horses. "I don't know what you're talking about," the older mercenary said, "I feel as sprightly as an elf."

From the side of the carriage, Hugo listened, bouncing atop his steed as it expertly navigated the rough terrain. Throughout most of the day the sun showed little mercy, beating down on the riders with such intensity that it was a constant battle to keep the sweat from their eyes. They used anything available—pieces of clothing, bare arms, the sides of their hat—to wipe themselves off. Mord seemed to fare the worst, his tongue hanging out the side of his mouth almost to the ground as he scampered along, trying to keep up.

"It's too hot!" Tabea screamed from inside the carriage, as if one of her escorts could change the climate.

Hugo agreed with the woman, but would never admit it. Instead, he conversed with Klemens. "You have quite a talent with the lute," he said. "Those songs you played were wonderful."

"Thank you. My mother taught me to pluck when I was a young whelp. Told me that if I couldn't find honest work, I could always learn to swindle the drunks with song. The young minstrel flashed a grin.

"She sounds like a wise woman."

"She was."

They made small talk for a while, until they started up a steep incline which, in the brutal heat, made conversation nearly impossible. Hugo prayed they'd finally stop for a break and a meal when they reached the top.

"Not much farther," Tomas said, reading Hugo's thoughts. "The other side of this mountain is more forgiving, I promise."

"Because it's downhill?" Klemens joked.

"That, and more trees."

Hugo wiped his forehead again, wondering how Tomas knew about the other side of the mountain. *Has he been on this trail before? This far from Bedburg?*

Eventually the long climb started to level off.

The carriage creaked along the narrow pathway, the horses snorting and panting. When they came to a clearing, Tomas called for a much-needed break. Hugo sighed. *At last.* Clumps of bushes and small trees dotted the outskirts of the clearing.

"Are we stopped?" came the shrill voice from within the carriage. "Why are we stopping? Ask them why we're stopping, Samuel."

She complains when we're moving. She complains when we're not.

Hugo dismounted, then found a rock to sit on. Mord panted over to join him. Klemens followed, sitting on the ground, his back propped against the rock. Hugo gently scratched the top of Mord's head as the dog tried to find a comfortable spot to rest.

"At least we don't have to hear complaints from you, boy," Hugo told the dog. Mord finally plopped between him and Klemens, apparently too hot for play or small talk.

Despite the heat and exhaustion, Tomas stayed in charge, setting out a circle of stones near the center of the clearing, gathering and arranging dry kindling in a neat pile, then searching about for a good stone to start a fire. "We're less than a day out, my friends," he said, his voice strangely grim.

Hugo noticed the peculiar look Tomas and Grayson shared for just a moment. Something seemed off.

Arne, the tracker, walked in from the brush, pushing between two bushes to make his appearance. He confirmed to Tomas that the coast was clear, not a soul in sight, and sat down next to the kindling.

By the time Tomas was ready to start the fire, the sun had mercifully begun to set, quickly disappearing behind the rock walls.

Secretary Gregor stepped out of the carriage and leaned against it, blinking at his fingers as he counted something in his head. Inquisitor Samuel came out next, yawned and stretched, then quickly waddled toward a bush while unbuckling his belt.

Hugo heard the steady stream that followed, the inquisitor sighing in relief with his back to the travelers.

Curiously, Grayson circled around Hugo, heading toward the same bush Samuel occupied.

Odd, Hugo thought, watching Grayson move quietly toward Samuel. *There's plenty of room to piss around here . . .*

Suddenly Samuel's long sigh contorted to a chilling groan. Hugo swiveled around just as Samuel's head slumped to his chest, bright red liquid replacing the yellow urine stream running down his legs.

Casually, Grayson walked away, back toward the carriage. Hugo noticed the glint of sunlight reflecting off a steel, bloody knife Grayson held in his hand.

Samuel collapsed into his puddle of piss and blood.

Hugo sat dumbfounded, then turned to Klemens to see if he'd seen the same thing. But before he got the chance, a blood-curdling scream echoed from inside the carriage.

"W-what?" Hugo gasped, reeling toward the sound. The answer was obvious; the white curtains shielding the inside of the carriage were now splattered with blood.

The door flew open and Frau Tabea tumbled out, hitting the ground with a thud. She began crawling, wailing, a brown, sickening mixture of blood and dirt trailing behind her.

Tomas stepped out from the carriage, sword in hand.

With panic in his eyes, Secretary Gregor—who'd been leaning against the side of the carriage—took off running. But Arne blocked his way. Gregor winced as he ran into the boy.

217

Arne, snarling wickedly, pulled back his arm as Gregor slid from the boy's grasp and crumpled to the ground holding his chest.

At the same moment, Hugo heard fast footsteps. It was Klemens, no longer beside him, running for his life toward the brush, his lute bouncing on his back, his dog chasing after him.

"Get him!" Grayson shouted. "Don't let the boy run!"

Hugo's shock froze him in place. The gruesome scene and how quickly it unfolded literally paralyzed him. He tried staggering to his feet, but couldn't move his legs—much less grasp what was happening.

Severin bounded past Hugo, shouldering him out of the way. Drawing a pistol from his waist, he leveled it at the running boy twenty paces away.

Severin fired.

Acrid smoke filled the air.

"No!" Hugo yelled.

An instant later, Klemens' hands and legs flailed as he pitched face-first onto the ground, dirt billowing around him. His lute bounced once on his back, then cracked as it struck the ground—an image and sound Hugo would never forget.

Hugo turned in time to see Tomas plunge his sword into the still-moaning Tabea. With his boot on the woman's back, he brutally twisted the blade, then pushed off with his foot, springing the sword free.

Holstering his gun, Severin took out a knife and walked toward Klemens' collapsed body, where Mord sat whining.

"No, please!" Hugo cried again. "Not the dog!"

Tomas appeared beside Hugo. "That's enough, nephew."

Severin glared at Hugo, then stopped.

The massacre was over.

In all, it had taken less than two minutes to slaughter four souls.

Hugo finally found his words. "W-what? Why?" His mouth was dry, his head spun.

Tomas faced Grayson. He motioned at the bush where Inquisitor Samuel lay slumped over. "Find his paperwork."

Grayson obliged, leaning over the body and rummaging inside the man's tunic. Finally, he let out an "Aha" and pulled a few pieces of crumpled parchment from Samuel's clothes.

"It's something that needed to be done," Tomas said, resting his hand on Hugo's shoulder.

Hugo shoved it away. He looked into Tomas' eyes. It was like seeing a stranger for the first time. "You just killed the people we were ordered to protect and escort! What in God's name are we doing, Tomas?"

Ignoring the question, Tomas sheathed his sword and took the papers from Grayson. "Your services are no longer needed, my friend," he told Grayson. "Nor are yours, Arne. Your payments await you near Trier."

"Very well," Grayson said with a curt bow. Arne followed the motion.

Tomas read the papers, then said, "It looks like Tabea was not on the docket, so we're in luck. We will not need to find another woman in her place." He looked at Tabea's corpse and shook his head. "I tried to get her to stay home—told her it'd be dangerous, but the damn woman never chose to listen."

Severin chuckled.

Still reading the paperwork, Tomas pointed at himself. "It seems myself and Inquisitor Samuel were of a near age—" he said, his tone as if he'd just finished a lunch of bread and wine.

"He was prettier," Grayson interjected.

"—I'll be taking his place as 'inquisitor.' Until we reach Trier, you'll speak to me only as Samuel, or Inquisitor, or My Lord, so we can get accustomed to the names."

Hugo just stood there, still in shock, staring off into nothing.

Tomas tucked the letters into his tunic. "It's simple, Hue. We were paid to escort these people. But we were paid *more* to make sure they never arrived in Trier."

"For what cause? Who paid us?"

Tomas shrugged. "I assume so we can be ordered around by the lord inquisitor of Trier. Simply put, we have been paid to be his puppets. I know no one wants to be a puppet, but that's the nature of this life, boy. We work for the highest bidder, and do his or her handiwork. In this case, it was murdering and assuming the identities of these fine folk."

Tomas spread his arms out at the carnage around him:

Samuel slumped over a bush in a pool of blood and piss; Tabea with a silent scream plastered on her gaunt face, a trail of red behind her; Gregor, a knife sticking in his heart; and Klemens, face-first in the dirt.

With stunned eyes, Hugo surveyed the scene. "This is madness. What would Ulrich say about this?"

Tomas leaned his head back like he'd been struck. "Ulrich? It was his idea, boy. There's wealth to be made in Trier. We assume these people's positions and take the money they're owed for the executions they're in charge of. Our 'superiors' get to kill the people they want killed, everyone walks away happy." He scratched his forehead and looked around. "Well, almost everyone."

He continued. "I know this is sour, Hugo. But we are paid to do ugly things. You said you wanted to learn what we do. Well, here you go. If you can't live this life, I'll understand. But you need to tell me now."

"What do *I* get to do?" Severin asked excitedly.

Tomas eyed Hugo one more time, then turned to Severin. "Since you're a bit older than Hugo, and because the boy doesn't seem ready, I suppose you'll be the inquisitor's assistant."

Severin frowned. "I have to be a secretary?"

"Play your hand right and you could ascend the ranks, I'm sure. Hugo, it says there's a cook on this entry list, so I suppose that's what you'll be. You'll take Klemens' place. It's all right that you can't play the lute—I think the thing broke on his fall anyway."

How much of a fool I was to think I could trust these people, Hugo thought, shaking his head. *Ulrich and Tomas both . . .*

Tomas clapped his hands. "Come now, boys. Get the bodies off the mountain. We're less than a day from Trier. There are witches that need killing."

CHAPTER TWENTY-EIGHT

GUSTAV

Gustav and his group made their way into Amsterdam while the moon still brightened the purple-black sky. Adrian Coswell and Alfred Eckstein were at his sides, Hedda shuffled along a bit behind, and the other eight of Adrian's crew brought up the rear

Glancing at the two men beside him, their contrasting demeanors were striking: Adrian, edgy and wired; Alfred, much more at ease. But at least both were focused and serious.

Nevertheless, Gustav had some concern about where Adrian and his crew had come from. As prior shipmates on the *Lion's Pride*, they'd rebuked Rowaine Donnelly's mutiny and fled with First Mate Coswell upon arriving in Amsterdam. They were thus loyalists of the ship's original leader, the late (and mutilated, so he'd heard) Captain Galager. As such, they likely felt cheated at the sudden death of their captain, and the loot they were owed.

Perhaps I should have brought Jergen's men with me—men who don't have a vested interest in this parlay.

Gustav reached into his tunic and took a sip from his brown bottle to ease his nerves.

Or maybe I can use this vitriol for my benefit . . .

Addressing his two aides, Gustav said, "Remember, I want this to go smoothly."

"If the bastards are still there . . ." Adrian growled.

"Do I have your oath that you won't start a firefight, Herr Coswell?" Gustav asked.

"My *oath*? Only people I'm giving an oath to are my women and God. I don't make promises I can't keep, Koehler."

Alfred leaned into Gustav and whispered, "I'll try to keep the hound from baying."

Gustav patted the ex-rigger on his shoulder. "I'd appreciate this going without any spilled blood. Threats should be enough to win the day."

"Indeed, but Coswell has always been a man of action first, talk later."

"Well, try your best."

"Using the right words, we should be fine."

They trekked through a richly decorated shopping district, a less-crowded town square, and over three bridges. The canals were dotted with boats, even at the late hour.

Love never sleeps, Gustav thought, distractedly, as he glanced at a passing boat. Then he looked at Adrian's angry face. *And neither does hate, apparently . . .*

As they made their way to the docks, Gustav scanned the area carefully. The stench of salt, birdshit, and fish wafted in the air. He pinched his nose. He hated that waterfront smell, and the laudanum only heightened his senses, making the odor worse.

His eyes passed over different banners and flags belonging to tradeships and galleons, until they lit upon the distinctive flag of the *Lion's Pride*—the red lion and gold coin—flapping in the wind.

Adrian noticed the ship as Gustav did and quickened his stride down the rickety plank leading to it, forcing Gustav to hurry his pace to keep up. Even when Gustav reached out and grabbed Adrian's arm to slow him down, the anxious first mate shoved it away.

Frustrated, Gustav stopped walking. "If you want the rest of your money, you'll let me do the talking, Herr Coswell. I know emotions run high, but this is neither the time nor place to start a brawl."

Adrian froze. His eyes twitched. "By all means, *my lord.*" With a dramatic wave he gestured for Gustav to take the lead. Storming past him, Gustav pushed Adrian's fluttering coat out of the way.

As they approached the ship, Gustav spotted a small man on the boat ramp, straining to push a rolling chest on board. Gustav recognized him from his first encounter with Rowaine.

"Mister Penderwick," he bellowed, his intimidating crew pausing behind him. On the ship's deck, boots ground to a halt as the men onboard poked their heads out over the railing. Passersby on the dock gave Gustav and his entourage a wide berth.

With a loud thud, Jerome Penderwick dropped his wooden chest on the ramp. "Y-yes?" the surgeon said.

"Do you remember me? I'd like to speak to your captain. Tell him Gustav Koehler would like to talk with him."

"Talk? About what? We're j-just getting ready to d-depart."

Adrian pulled a pistol from his belt and aimed it at the man. "Get your skinny hide on that ship and get the damn captain, man, before I blow the few teeth you have left out the back of your skull."

His words worked. Jerome scurried up the ramp without another word.

They waited for nearly five minutes at the bottom of the ramp. Gustav tried to formulate the speech he'd give when the captain arrived. But when Captain Daxton Wallace did finally appear, his plans were dashed.

Daxton stood at the ship's railing, one foot hoisted on top of a barrel, his arms folded across his chest, with about ten other sailors circled around him in support.

Before any words were spoken, things quickly escalated. Most of Gustav's men drew their guns. Daxton's crew did the same.

A classic standoff.

"The hell do you want, Herr Koehler?" Daxton shouted. "And Adrian Coswell, you louse, you have a heavy pair to be showing yourself here."

Gustav heard Adrian gritting his teeth.

"How does it feel to be a traitor, you weasel?" Adrian shouted back, his hand resting on the butt of his gun, still tucked in his waistband.

Daxton spread his arms out wide. "I feel like a captain," he chuckled. Some of his men laughed nervously alongside him.

"Galager had it coming," he continued. "Anyone could see that. He was sinking the ship by just being on it." Several of his crewmen nodded.

Adrian seethed, but Gustav put a hand in front of him

before he could do anything foolish.

"You seem to have climbed the ladder quickly, Herr Wallace," Gustav told the captain. "From carpenter to first mate to captain in, what, the span of a week?"

Daxton shrugged. "I s'pose I'm blessed to be a friend of Rowaine Donnelly." He reached into his shirt, drawing the immediate sound of clicking matchlocks from Gustav's men. But he brought out a pipe, ignoring the weapons pointed at him. Casually, he packed it with tobacco, lit it, then sucked in several heavy drags. Smoke dribbled out his nose and mouth.

He's enjoying this, Gustav thought.

Perhaps I can change that.

After exhaling a large cloud of smoke, Daxton said, "Now, state your business. You nearly stopped poor Jerome's heart, sneaking up on him like that. He's the one supposed to be fixing rotten hearts, not busting his own. So say your peace or begone, before my men lose their patience."

"It's regarding Rowaine Donnelly."

"Oh?"

Gustav nodded. "Where is she?"

Daxton drew on his pipe again. The smoke came out in puffs as he chuckled. "Avoiding you, I imagine."

"You won't tell me where she might be, or where she's going?"

Daxton stroked his chin. "See no reason to."

"Is this reason enough?" Gustav reached into his shirt—drawing a new set of matchlock clicks from the men onboard—and pulled out the raggedy doll, holding it up for all to see.

The men on the ship let out a collective gasp, as if Gustav were holding the head of his enemy.

The pipe in Daxton's mouth clanked to the deck. A shipmate whispered in his ear, but Daxton pushed him away. Trying to maintain his composure, Daxton asked coyly, "What's that you got there, Herr Koehler?"

"You know what this is, Captain Wallace."

"And where'd you get it?"

"You know that, too." He wiggled the doll in his hand. The yellow hair curlings flopped in the wind.

Daxton drew his pistol and aimed it directly at Gustav's face. He spoke slowly, decisively. "You could have made that thing, or stolen it from a shop."

Unfazed, Gustav said, "Her name is Franny."

And just like that, the fight left Daxton's face, his eyes widening, his shoulders slumping. "What have you done with my family, you fucking mongrel? God preserve you, if you've hurt them—"

"Your wife and daughter are fine, captain. I have them holed up for a bit until I receive the information I require. They are mere bargaining chips. Nothing more. Don't take it personally."

Daxton growled. "What guarantees do I have that they're safe?"

"My word."

"Your word is as useful as rat-piss."

"Then rat-piss will have to do. If I'm injured or killed . . ." Gustav didn't need to finish the sentence. He cleared his throat. "Now that we've gotten the pleasantries out of the way, tell me where Rowaine Donnelly is."

Daxton slammed his gun down on the railing, a loud *crack* echoing across the dock. "Forgive me, Row," he muttered, peering down at the floorboards.

"I can't hear you," Gustav said, cupping his ear with his hand.

"She went to Bedburg, Germany." Daxton raised his eyes from the deck's floor and scowled at the two men beside Gustav. "You actually put yourself in this evil man's company, Adrian? Alfred? You heartless bastards."

Bedburg. I should have guessed.

"Should we make him lead us to her, Gustav?" It was Hedda, leaning in to whisper in his ear.

Gustav swayed his neck back. "He probably doesn't know that much. I'd be worried he'd slit our throats as we slept." He turned back to Daxton.

"Where is she going from there? Why Bedburg?"

"She thinks that's where her family's killer is. She's following the farmer's daughter and the priest." Daxton bent down to pick up his pipe. "No idea where she'd go from there. You'll have to

225

ask her."

"I intend to," Gustav answered, spinning around and pushing back through his men as he left.

"W-wait, where are you going? What about my family?"

Gustav stopped, his back still to Daxton. "I left very specific instructions, Captain Wallace. As long as I returned before the light of day, they would remain unharmed." He turned toward Daxton and smiled. "So I'm sure you understand the need for me to return to your house before dawn." He turned away, then thought of something else. "Follow me and they both die. Do you understand?"

Reluctantly, Daxton nodded.

"It's been a pleasure, and congratulations again on becoming captain. I'm sure you'll make a fine one."

As Gustav turned to leave, he dropped Franny from his hand. The doll bounced once on the dock, then slowly rolled into the sea. It wasn't long after Gustav and his team left that the doll had sunk to the bottom.

By the time Gustav arrived back at the Wallace estate, the first glimmers of pink were already peeking up the horizon. Yet the house still stood, neither burned nor razed. He scowled at being disobeyed.

But what caused his scowl to deepen was how strangely empty the surroundings were. As he approached the dwelling, Mia and Kevan and Paul walked out to meet him.

"Jergen's men all left about an hour after you did," Mia explained. "Said they weren't getting paid enough to kill women and children. Said it was Satan's work."

Gustav frowned. He'd lost six men. But men he hadn't trusted anyway. He walked through the front door and looked around. The house was as empty as the outside. Darlene and Abigail were gone.

"Where are they?" he yelled.

Mia put her hands on her hips. "I let them flee once the men left. You had the doll—proof of your hostages—you didn't need them anymore. They didn't need to be harmed."

"And what if things hadn't gone as planned? They could have been valuable."

Mia shrugged. "It seems everything worked out."

"Where'd they go?"

"Didn't ask. Besides, I'm not killing women or children either, Gustav."

"Need I remind you that two of the people we're hunting are also women—one of them your lover?" Gustav said.

Mia whisked past Gustav out the door. "Should we get going? Don't we have better places to be than this sorry estate?"

Gustav watched her walk.

She's right.

Time to head into the belly of the beast—where my brother was murdered.

CHAPTER TWENTY-NINE

ROWAINE

The monolithic gray structure loomed high in the dreary morning light. Bedburg's jailhouse cast a long shadow over Rowaine as she lingered in front, surveying the main gate's security measures.

Which, surprisingly, was lacking. Apart from the building itself, there were no guards, no sentries, no one to stop her entry.

If a man were to escape his cell, he could easily saunter out this gate and be free. Not a very efficient means of captivity. Unless of course no one ever left one's cell, nor saw sunlight, nor saw the justice of a real trial.

She gazed down the empty road where, earlier, she and her two "captives" had parted ways. Hopefully Sybil and Dieter wouldn't abandon her now that they were on their own.

Surely, she thought, *they too want to see this to its end. They've come this far with me.*

Rowaine took a deep breath, then slowly exhaled. *Will this be where my questions are finally answered?*

She involuntarily shuddered from the morning chill, then strode onward toward the front entrance.

The gate was heavy but unlocked. Inside, a staircase led her deeper into the bowels of the dismal prison.

The steps were stone, damp, and grimy. The pitter-patter of water dripping from the ceiling sent a shiver down her spine, the liquid trickling down each step and pooling at the bottom. She doubted the place had ever seen repair since its original construction.

At the bottom of the stairs, a man with a scarred face sat in a chair against the wall, half-hidden by shadow, next to a closed door. His legs were crossed and he appeared to be sleeping with his eyes open. A torch protruded out from the wall, partially illuminating the gruesome scar on his face.

The man glared at her, his eyes unblinking.

Could he be dead?

After a long pause—each watching the other—the man's forehead wrinkled as he tried to raise eyebrows that weren't there. "It's been some time since a beautiful woman stepped foot in this place. Am I dreaming?"

"That's the second time in as many days I've heard that," Rowaine answered, confidently, without hesitation—the only way she knew to act. Now was not the time to show weakness.

A man like this no doubt preys on that.

The man smiled, the scar on his cheek sliding up with his lips. "What is it you need, Frau . . ."

"Donnelly," Rowaine said, giving a curt bow. "My name is Catriona Donnelly. I've heard you knew my father." No sense in skirting the issue. A jailhouse was no place for small talk, unless at the torturer's behest.

"Donnelly, you say." The man scratched his chin. "I haven't had a ginger-bearded man as a prisoner in some time. I am Ulrich. Who was your father, Catriona Donnelly?"

"His name was Georg Sieghart."

Ulrich visibly tensed.

"I've also heard you were acquainted with Heinrich Franz," she added.

Ulrich rose from his chair with surprising agility and stormed toward Rowaine, who stood tall, not backing away even though her heart raced.

"I knew Heinrich more than I knew your father, girl," he said, slowly pacing around and behind her. "But I haven't seen either in some time, so I'm afraid you've come to the wrong place. The last time I saw Georg Sieghart, he gave me a good contusion on the head. And helped two prisoners escape."

Rowaine's shoulders tightened. She knew those two prisoners.

"But for his rudeness, I hardly knew the man," Ulrich said, stopping behind her. She refused to turn, instead staring at his empty chair. "I'm guessing you know all of that," he continued.

"I'm also guessing you know the two prisoners he helped free. And that they're somewhere in town right now."

At that, Rowaine turned. "What will you do about them?"

Ulrich smiled. "Nothing. It's none of my business, though it is foolish for them to have returned. But since they became fugitives based on hearsay and a wrongful investigation, I have no claim of indictment against either . . ."

He paused. Then, to prove he wasn't bluffing, he slowly spoke their names. "Sybil Griswold and Dieter Nicolaus . . . are of no concern to me."

Rowaine nodded. "They're both of the Nicolaus family now."

"Good for them. As far as I'm concerned, they're safe in Bedburg until Bishop Schreib says otherwise. In actuality, I feel for the girl. I put Peter Griswold through much misery and pain. Had I known the facts—that he was an innocent man—I might not have taken such satisfaction in watching him suffer. In the end, it was all for show." He shrugged.

Rowaine crossed her arms. "I'll tell Sybil you said as much."

Ulrich chuckled, his tone dark. "If you know your father isn't here, what are you *really* doing in Bedburg, Catriona Donnelly?"

"Searching for the Werewolf of Bedburg."

"Join the pack."

"I have a drawing here, something I penned when I was young. A picture of the man who killed my mother and brother. Sybil already identified the man for me."

Ulrich extended his hand. "May I see it?"

Rowaine reached into her jerkin, then held the picture up for Ulrich to see. He slowly exhaled, trying to remain expressionless, though Rowaine immediately noticed his subtle change of expression.

"It *does* look a bit like him," Ulrich said. "You either are quite an artist, Catriona Donnelly, or you have quite a healthy imagination."

"Have you seen him?" Rowaine asked, carefully folding the paper before slipping it back in her jacket.

"Not in over two years."

"Where might he have gone?"

"No idea. Anything I say would be pure conjecture."

"If you had to guess?"

Ulrich scratched his scarred cheek. "Somewhere far from here, possibly to do another man's bidding, or to rest on his laurels. He was never my friend, merely a business associate. He ordered me around. But he *was* a friend to your father. How that must sting. Knowing your father was best friends with his wife's—your mother's—murderer."

Rowaine felt a wave of heat reach her ears. The man was frustrating and knew which buttons to push. But, then again, as the resident torturer, it was no wonder he was well versed in such tactics.

"There are other people who might know more about Heinrich Franz's whereabouts," Ulrich said at last, possibly sensing her building anger.

She arched her brow, waiting for more.

"Balthasar Schreib, our bishop, might be one." Ulrich wagged a finger. "But that's playing a dangerous game, is it not? Speak with him and he might decide to arrest and try your friends. Are you willing to risk their lives to get the answers you seek?"

"Why would Bishop Schreib know anything about Heinrich Franz?"

Ulrich shrugged. "Like I said, Catriona Donnelly . . . pure conjecture. But he is a man who seems to know things."

Rowaine bit her lip, tasting the coppery flavor seep down her throat. *This man's off-handed riddles are getting me nowhere.*

"What can you tell me about the werewolf?" she asked.

Ulrich strolled back to his seat. "All I can tell you about the Werewolf of Bedburg is who he killed. From there, you'll have to make your own way."

"If you could give me that information, I'd be in your debt."

"It's the least I could do for a poor orphan girl. Consider it recompense for losing your mother and brother . . .

"And for whatever happened to your father."

*   *   *

Back in the tavern, Rowaine had been at a corner table for the past two hours, reading through the list of names Ulrich had given her.

When Sybil and Dieter arrived, they pushed their way back to Rowaine's table. Hearing them approach, Rowaine looked up, then blinked a few times to shake off her blurring vision. Immediately, she noticed the papers Dieter was carrying.

"What's that?" she asked.

Dieter grinned, dropping the yellow parchment pages on the table. "Church records. Names. Lots of names. With plenty of details."

Rowaine motioned for them to sit. Aellin brought over two mugs of ale as they scooted in their chairs. She winked at Rowaine before sashaying away, and Rowaine's eyes followed her hips back to the bar.

Dieter sipped his drink, then motioned to the papers. "All the deceased folk in Bedburg, going back twenty years—since the murders began, and a little before."

Rowaine raised her brows. "How'd you manage that?"

Dieter leaned closer. "Using Sister Salome's undying love for me."

Sybil rolled her eyes. "He stole them."

Rowaine chuckled, more shocked than anything. "That's not very Godly of you, Herr Nicolaus. Thou shalt not steal?"

Dieter pointed a finger, suddenly serious. "Wrong," he said. "It's for a good cause. I promised Him I'd return them when we're done." He nodded, pleased with himself. He picked up one of the pages and began reading. "Now we just need to decipher what they might mean." He motioned to the papers in front of Rowaine. "What do you have there?"

It was Rowaine's turn to smile. "Something that might help shorten our search. These are the names of the people supposedly killed by the Werewolf of Bedburg. Eighteen in all. In dark detail. *How, when, where.* I'm shocked the torturer kept such records."

Dieter slapped his hands on the tabletop. "Excellent! Now we can link the names on this list with the names on your list."

God knows it's never that easy, Rowaine thought.

To be as thorough as possible, each of them assumed a different task. Dieter combed through his list of Bedburg's deceased for the past two decades, first looking to see if anything interesting stood out. Rowaine continued reviewing her list of eighteen murder victims to familiarize herself with the killer's methods. And when each of them would finish a page, they'd hand it over to Sybil who then began circling names common to both lists.

Dieter was impressed with the level of detail the church had maintained for the town's dead.

"Not only do they list dates of death, and their backgrounds, and when they moved to Bedburg, but they even have a sidebar with possible affiliations for each person."

Nearly all the victims on Rowaine's pages were female, killed in the countryside in terribly gruesome ways. At some point, Rowaine began reading aloud.

"Helga, seventy-three years aged, killed seventeen of August, 1575. Found naked, throat torn, in the lowlands near the Peringsmaar Lake. Possible Waldensian." Rowaine drank a sip of ale. "She must have been one of the early victims." She continued with another passage. "Gretchin, eighteen years aged, found near the northern woods in the hills, third of October, 1580. Stomach opened, suspected unborn child missing." At that, Sybil nearly gagged.

When Rowaine got to one of the more recent names, she stopped, squinting at the entry for a while. "This is odd. It shows my . . ." she cleared her throat. "It shows my uncle as a victim. Konrad Brühl." The other two looked up.

"I mean, first, he doesn't really fit the killer's pattern—being a man—except for his throat being torn out. And then, it lists his place of death as 'unknown.'"

At that moment, Aellin happened to set down three more mugs of ale and, overhearing the conversation, said, "Ain't no secret where your uncle was found, girl." The three of them stared up at her. "At least not to anyone who lives here. I'm guessing the jailer wanted to save himself the embarrassment."

"What do you mean, Aellin," asked Sybil.

The wench put her hands on her hips. "Konrad was found

in a tunnel beneath the jailhouse."

Sybil's mouth dropped. "Why didn't you tell us that when you mentioned him last night?"

"Figured you already knew. Everyone knows. Some say it's a secret underground passage."

"Leading where?" Dieter asked.

"Hell should I know? I ain't no explorer, priest—and it ain't none of my business." She sauntered away, again drawing Rowaine's attention for a brief moment.

"Cat, what do you think?" Sybil asked.

Rowaine's eyes veered from Aellin's alluring backside to Sybil. "I think we're getting closer to the truth. But before we're forced to ask Balthasar Schreib any questions, let's see what this tunnel is all about."

CHAPTER THIRTY

SYBIL

The opening to the underground tunnel was exactly where Aellin said it would be. Just after dark, Rowaine, Sybil, and Dieter had snuck around to the back of the jailhouse to see if Aellin's information about the killing under the jail might prove useful.

Before leaving, Sybil had once again entrusted her son Peter with Claus, the jolly old man whom she'd quickly come to trust and respect.

"Do you suppose the jailers know of this?" Rowaine asked, staring down the black fissure. Old rocks and refuse surrounded the sunken crevice, partially hiding it from view.

"If it's common news that your Uncle Konrad was found dead down there," Sybil said, "how could they not?"

"Why would they not cover it over?" Dieter wondered aloud.

"There must be a reason for keeping it open," Sybil said.

They descended down the shaky ladder that rested against the lip of the crevice, Dieter going first. Once the three were gathered at the base of the ladder, they waited for their eyes to adjust. Except for a small perimeter of diffused moonlight filtering down from the opening above, everything around them was pitch-black. Fortunately, Dieter noticed an unlit torch resting against the wall near the ladder, and Rowaine found a suitable rock nearby and used her knife to spark it.

With Rowaine in the lead with the torch, they proceeded down the only pathway.

The tunnel had the rank odor of a catacomb—stale and pungent. Water droplets from the concave ceiling occasionally trickled on their heads as they moved along single-file. After a while the tunnel widened, allowing them to travel abreast of each other.

If this place is *a catacomb, it's much bigger and goes much farther than I imagined,* Sybil thought.

At one point, the path split into a three-way fork, with two narrower walkways branching left and right while the wider one in the middle continued straight. They chose to continue straight because it seemed to be the main corridor and, thus, the best chance to find something important.

Every so often they'd pass another small walkway snaking left or right, which led Sybil to wonder what these underground routes were really for. "If this tunnel follows the breadth of Bedburg—" she began, but Rowaine was already nodding and continued her thought.

"It would be an easy way to travel through the city without notice."

"And perfect for a killer," Dieter added.

Eventually, the main passage turned muddy, the ground wet and more difficult to walk on. They crunched along the soggy gravel until they came to another ladder, this one more decrepit than the first. Three feet past the ladder, their passageway dead-ended. As Sybil sloshed her way to the ladder, she abruptly raised her hand, quieting the others.

They heard voices. From above.

Sybil grabbed hold of the ladder and slowly began climbing. With each step the thing wobbled in the mushy soil, forcing the other two to hold its sides to keep it steady. When Sybil reached the top, an iron grate blocked her path. She tried pushing it and felt the dirt begin to give, but she couldn't budge it further.

"It will move, but I'm not strong enough," she murmured, climbing back down.

Dieter volunteered to try, but Rowaine took the lead. Wedging the torch into a large crack in the wall by the ladder, she climbed to the top, then gently began wiggling the grate while applying upward pressure. For several minutes she kept at it, trying to be as quiet as possible, until it finally began to dislodge.

Mud and debris spilled onto her face. She turned her head

and spat out the grime, then managed to raise the grate high enough to slide it to the side. She poked her head through the clearing, then leaned back down.

"It opens into a dark room," she whispered to the others.

Sybil and Dieter both waved her on, so she climbed up the rest of the way and disappeared through the hole.

A moment later she reappeared, on her stomach with her head hanging over the edge, motioning for the others to climb up. As they did, she helped each one off the ladder and into the room.

It was a storage area of some sort, musty, dark, and cold. Enough light seeped through the bottom crack of a door on the far side for them to make out bags of wheat and moldy crates of fruit scattered about.

Quietly, they made their way to the door. Sybil gently turned the knob. It opened. She peeked out.

To her left, a woman with white hair—holding a knife—was leaning over a table, chopping carrots, her back to Sybil. Flickering torchlight lit the room. A younger girl dressed in a maid's gown stood next to the woman, facing in Sybil's direction. When Sybil materialized from the shadows, the younger girl recoiled, then tugged the older woman's dress.

The older woman turned slowly, still holding her carrot knife. Surprisingly, she didn't seem startled. Instead, she calmly turned to the younger girl and, with eyes fixed on Sybil, said, "We're fine for tonight, Isabel. Run along now."

Isabel stared at the woman in the shadows, now joined by two more strangers. "Should I alert the guards?" she asked in a squeaky voice.

The old woman shook her head. "No. Just get some rest. We have a big day tomorrow."

Isabel's dark curls bobbed on her shoulders as she left through a side door. In unison, Sybil, Dieter, and Rowaine stepped closer to the white-haired lady.

"How may I help you?" the woman asked evenly. She followed Sybil's eyes to the knife she held. "Oh, pardon me." She set it down on the table.

Wasting no time, Rowaine stepped out from behind Sybil

and unfolded the picture from her pocket. "We mean you no harm, my lady. We're seeking this man. Do you know him, perhaps?"

The woman's eyes creased near the edges. Sybil sensed a certain sadness overtake her. Then the woman's face contorted and her eyes grew moist. She looked up from the picture.

"What is your name, young lady?" she asked Rowaine.

"I am Catriona Donnelly, and this man—"

But Sybil put her hand on Rowaine's shoulder, stopping her, then stepped forward. It was the look in the woman's eyes that Sybil read. She spoke softly to her.

"He's a friend of ours, and we're earnestly trying to find him. You know him, don't you?"

The woman blinked several times. "Of course I know Heinrich. Or should I call him Herr Franz now? Or 'my lord?'" She chuckled to herself.

Rowaine shared a look with Sybil, unsure of the woman's meaning.

"I am Sybil Griswold," Sybil said, using her given surname for the first time in years. It felt odd saying it.

The woman frowned. "Ah, the Griswold girl. I was sad to hear of your father."

Sybil arched her brow. "You knew my father? Who are you?"

"I'm just a simple old kitchen-maid, my lady. My name is Odela. And no, I did not know your father personally, but I weep for any man who leaves children orphaned." For a "kitchen-maid," Odela's voice bespoke wisdom and education.

"Do you know where Heinrich is, Odela?" Sybil asked.

"I do not. I have not seen poor Heiny in some time." The sadness overtook her again, her eyes dipping downward.

Heiny?

"What was Herr Franz to you, if you don't mind my asking?"

Odela studied the three faces, then zeroed in on Dieter. "Who is your handsome friend?"

Dieter stepped forward. "My name is Dieter Nicolaus. I was once a priest here—"

"I know who you are," Odela said.

"How do you know so much?" Sybil asked. Clearly, this woman was more than a simple staff-lady. Sybil looked around the room. "And . . . where are we, exactly?"

Odela chuckled sweetly again. "Why, you're in Castle Bedburg of course, my dear."

Sybil tried to mask her surprise.

"And to answer your question—what was I to Heinrich? . . . I suppose I was a great many things to him. I've known him since he was a boy, so I might be considered his godmother. Though I doubt he would agree with that."

"Why?" Rowaine asked.

Odela sat on the bench near the table. She motioned for her company to join her. They did.

"We had a falling out, you could say."

"What was he like?" Sybil asked. "Heinrich. As a boy."

Odela let out another soft snicker. "If I had to choose a word? . . . Wild." She paused. "Rambunctious. Different from the rest. His mother died when he was young. But he was still old enough to feel the pain." She shook her head slowly, her eyes staring off. "And I just couldn't stand to see the boy suffer, so—"

"You took him in?" Rowaine ventured.

Odela nodded. "He loved nature, playing in the woods," she said, smiling, thinking of the memory. "One time I went to find him in the woods. When I heard him laughing, my heart soared. But when I found him, I was shocked."

The trio waited, leaning forward.

"He was surrounded by wolves."

Sybil gave a small gasp.

"Oh, don't worry yourself, my dear. It was not like you think. He had *befriended* them! Can you believe it? He was throwing a stick, playing fetch with them. It was astounding." She got a dreamy look. "I do miss those days," she mumbled. Then her face tightened and she refocused on the group. "But he grew up so strangely. I don't know why."

"What do you mean, my lady?" asked Rowaine.

Odela clasped her hands together and rested them in her lap. "I don't know if I should be telling you this. But since you say

239

you're friends . . ." She bent forward conspiratorially.

"I would often catch him . . . *dressing up.*"

"Dressing up?"

Odela shifted in her seat. "Sometimes he would wear his mother's old stockings and heels. When he learned to knit, I wondered what he was making. Until one day I saw him wearing the dress he'd knitted."

Sybil leaned her head back. *What a strange, strange thing,* she thought. *But why?*

"I don't know why," Odela said, reading Sybil's mind. She giggled. "Judging by the looks on your faces, I'd say it's as strange to you as it was to me. But I still loved the boy like a son. Perhaps he was confused."

"Maybe it was guilt," Rowaine added.

Odela frowned. "Guilt? Over what?" Her face softened and she waved her hand. "No, no, my dear, that wouldn't come 'til later."

"How do you mean?" Sybil asked.

"Oh my . . . Heiny would be so angry if he knew I was saying all this." She smiled and shook her head. "I haven't seen him for so long, and I do miss his company. It feels good to reminisce."

Sybil smiled as warmly as she could.

Odela continued reminiscing. "He worked the kitchens with the women as he grew. Until Count Adolf must have seen his potential. He was a smart, smart boy, after all. He was my little helper, and it was sad to see him go."

"Where did he go?" Rowaine asked.

But Dieter had another question first. "Count Adolf? Do you mean the Protestant general who served in Gebhard Truchsess' army? The man who ruled here before Lord Werner?"

"Ah, so the priest has found his words. No, this was before all that—before the talks of war and such. I don't know in what capacity Heiny worked for Adolf, but I didn't like it. I saw him change. He became a bitter young man. It pained me to see . . ." she trailed off, remaining quiet for a long moment, as if mentally reliving the past. Finally, she clapped her hands on her knees and sighed.

"Believe it or not, I was one of Count Adolf's favorites for a time. But as I grew older, I presume the lord lost interest in me."

Her candor surprised Sybil. Odela continued.

"I was ousted from Adolf's court. And became bitter, I must admit. Then Heinrich left . . . for Cologne, I believe. And suddenly, I became the head mistress of the kitchens. To this day I don't know what strings Heiny pulled, but I'm certain it was his doing."

Rowaine nodded. "He cared for you, like a son to a mother."

"Yes, my dear, he did. But that became something more. Oh, this is so embarrassing." Her cheeks flushed like a shy schoolgirl's. "My, how you three have really opened the floodgates!"

Sybil had other questions, though. "When Heinrich went to Cologne, my lady, was Gebhard the archbishop at the time?"

Odela thought about that. "No, no, it was the Catholic man. Ernst? But why does that matter?" She tapped her foot, yearning to return to her love story. "I loved that boy like a son, but when he returned from Cologne, he was a man. He had an edge about him—I'm sure he must have gotten it from Rolf. It was very . . . alluring."

Sybil waited, but couldn't hold her tongue. "So, did you . . ."

Odela sighed, nodding. "We became lovers. It was meant to be. I know I was almost twenty years his senior, but we were star-struck." Then, like a storm cloud darkening a picture-perfect day, her expression changed. She tensed her thin white eyebrows. "After spending more time with him, I started noticing odd behavior." She fidgeted with her fingers. "He would sneak away at night. One night, oh, I shouldn't be saying this, but he returned, hands covered in"—she leaned forward—"*blood*. I later learned he'd shared a meal with his wolves!" Her eyes grew big as she searched the faces of her company. "I know. Quite bizarre!"

"You did nothing of it?" Rowaine asked, a bit of a bite behind her words.

"What was I to do? I was smitten. But the behavior got stranger. Until I could tell he was . . . detached. Something was off." She glanced at the floor. "Very off," she said, refocusing back on Sybil. "When I told him I was with child, well, that's when he told me his secret. Believe me, I too thought I was too old to have a child."

Pregnant?

Sybil nearly blurted it out. Then something caught her eye. On Odela's hand. She was fiddling with a ring, absently twisting it around her finger. Sybil recognized it. She'd recognize it anywhere, as she used to fight over it with her friend.

That ring belonged to Dorothea Gabler. Sybil's best friend—the girl whose death incited the search for the Werewolf of Bedburg.

Rowaine broke through Sybil's thoughts. "What secret, Odela?"

The old lady wagged her finger. "No, no, I won't betray him or gossip any more than I already have. You'll have to ask Rolf about that. However, I will say that he became a very severe man. I started to lose the passion I once had for him. When he took the baby, well, I couldn't forgive him for that."

"*Took* the baby?" Rowaine's eyebrows rose so high her forehead lines almost merged together. "What do you mean?"

With a slight shrug, Odela said, "I don't know what happened to that babe. I can say that it tore us apart, though. Heinrich eventually told me—very cryptically, I might add—that he could not allow his own bloodline to continue. Can you believe that? He considered it the one noble thing he'd ever done in his life, getting rid of that baby. I still don't know what he meant by it—but then again, I never tried to understand Heinrich Franz. I just loved him. Even at the end."

Sybil was still gazing at the ring. "And you haven't seen him since?"

"Oh, he'd come to visit every so often. But now? No, I haven't seen him in some time. It saddens me, of course, but life goes on. Besides, the event with the child happened fifteen years ago."

Despite the time interval, Sybil could see the permanent hurt in the poor woman's eyes. She placed her hand on Odela's knee. "I'm sorry for your loss, Lady Odela. I know what it's like to lose a parent. I cannot even imagine the depth of pain for a mother to lose her child."

Odela's frown remained for several seconds before she perked herself up. "I haven't been called 'Lady Odela' in years, girl. You warm an old maid's heart."

Sybil smiled, genuinely. *How could a man raised by this woman have ended up so . . . tragically?*

Odela sighed and said, "My, I feel like I've been rambling for hours! It really must be time for bed. I have enjoyed your visit, my dears, but if you want to know more, I think you'd better ask Rolf."

"You keep mentioning him," Rowaine said. "Who is this Rolf?"

"You don't know Rolf Anders? Why, he's the steward of Heinrich's estates, of course."

"Heinrich's estates?" Sybil asked. Her heart started to race.

"It's less than half a day's ride east from here, between Bedburg and Cologne. I always hoped that once Heinrich received that estate from Adolf, he would allow me to share it with him. But alas, I doubt I'd let myself be seen in a frivolous place like that. I'm sure it was just the idle fancy of a torn lover."

"You don't suppose Heinrich would be at his estate?" Rowaine asked, rising from the bench.

"No, no." Odela shook her head. "Like I said, my dear, he was a wild boy. I don't think he could stand to live in such a glamorous villa, not with the vast countryside out there, always calling his name."

Dieter stood. Sybil clasped Odela's hands in her own, feeling the ring beneath her palm. "Thank you, Odela, you have been a delight. It's time we allowed you to get some rest. But be assured, you've given us hope to find our . . . friend."

Odela grinned, showing teeth for the first time, yellow and crooked—a stark contrast to her clear, smooth face. She gave the trio her well-wishes, then, as they turned to depart, asked, "Where are you going? The door's that way," and pointed behind her, where Isabel had scurried off earlier.

Sybil smiled. "If it's all the same to you, Lady Odela, we'll just leave the way we came."

CHAPTER THIRTY-ONE

HUGO

Hugo tossed and turned in the dirt and gravel, unable to sleep. Every time the weight of exhaustion forced his eyelids closed, he jolted awake to the sound of Grayson's shouting.

Don't let the boy run!

The image of his friend crashing lifelessly to the ground face-first, the heartbreaking sound of his lute cracking open, wouldn't stop playing in his mind.

Sweat rolled down his face. His eyes fluttered. He hyperventilated, feeling hot and cold at the same time.

Don't let the boy run!

He knew the day would haunt him forever. So many dead people. At the hands of his *acquaintances* no less! His *travel companions!*

The thought sickened him. It was not something he could drink away, or that time would heal.

He sat up. They'd never left the area where the killings had occurred, Tomas deciding it was best to get a fresh start down the mountain in the morning.

He surveyed the camp. It was eerily quiet. Everyone sleeping, or dead. Almost like nothing had happened. Even the bodies were gone. Before going to bed, Grayson and Arne had thrown them off the cliff. So except for the carriage there was no reminder, no physical evidence, of the brutal atrocity that had taken place just hours before.

These men truly are slaves to the highest bidder. Paid pawns.

Well, not me. I will never be another man's tool.

With sleep futile, Hugo rose to his feet. He stretched, looked to the sky, then quietly padded around the snoring bodies sleeping next to him and walked to the side of the cliff.

He looked down, inching his toes closer to the edge, again flashing on what he knew was down there somewhere, thrown away like garbage, likely being torn to pieces by scavengers.

A sudden move would mean certain death as his body bounced down the craggy rocks. But he didn't care.

He closed his eyes. The image and sound of his friend's grisly death replayed in his mind yet again.

Though I've never given him much credence, today's work was most certainly the work of the Devil. I'm a fool to have believed I could trust Tomas and Ulrich. How can I trust people I hardly know? I thought I could trust them just like I thought I could trust Sybil and Ava . . .

I can trust no one.

His eyes took in the vast vista around him. Even in the dead of night, it was a glorious spectacle—rows of treetops in perfect harmony, rolling hills blanketing the land all the way to the horizon. And all of it illuminated by the soft glow of the moon and stars.

A scenario played in his head, of him falling off the edge, embracing the rocks below—maybe it would ease the chaos in his mind.

The sound of gentle footsteps brought him back to reality.

He didn't need to turn to feel the presence behind him.

To his surprise, Severin stepped beside him, gazing along with him at the majestic scenery.

"A beautiful sight," Severin said in a low voice.

Hugo said nothing.

"Did you ever imagine we would see a sight like that, living in Bedburg?"

"No."

"I suppose we weren't really *living* in Bedburg, were we?" Severin added wryly.

"Whatever we were doing in Bedburg was much better than what we did today."

Severin turned to Hugo. "What *we* did? If I remember correctly, you merely stood there."

Hugo felt his ears get hot. "You're right, Sev. I didn't want to kill the minstrel. He didn't deserve it. None of those people did."

Severin scoffed. "We all deserve it, Hue. We're highwaymen, robbers, bandits . . . we'll never be right to those people. We'll always be outcasts. Don't you see that?"

"We can change."

"Yes, we can change. But that won't change who we are, or how the aristocrats and nobles see us. But now, going into Trier with new identities and new lives, we really *can* change our fate. We can become something we've never had a chance to become before."

Hugo met Severin's gaze. "And what will we become, Severin? We are a gang of liars and killers."

Severin frowned, his beaked nose moving inches from Hugo—a hawk ready to descend on its prey. "We can become whatever we want to be. That's the beauty of it. If those people had to die to let me change my destiny, then so be it. I'd gladly do it again."

Hugo exhaled. "That's where we differ. You are able to do barbaric things to further yourself. I am not."

"That's because I'm strong and know what I want. You are weak." Severin scowled. "Why do you think Tomas made me inquisitor's assistant, and you the cook?"

"Because you're older. And his nephew."

Severin clicked his tongue. "No, it's because you are not ready. I doubt you ever will be. You can't fault me for being ambitious, Hue. Once, I thought you were too, that we weren't much different. But now I see that we are."

"Thank God."

The wind bit at Hugo. Shivering, he tucked his hands in his pockets. That's when he felt the ring he'd stolen for Ava, cold against his palm. He'd never had the chance to give it back to her after rescuing her from jail. Just when he was about to, he'd caught her and Karstan embracing.

But Severin was right. Back then, they weren't so different from each other. Maybe in temperament. But they'd both wanted to impress the girl, pilfer the biggest catch, find the lost treasure.

We were bandit-brothers.

As Tomas said, sometimes you have to take what you want.
And we did. Together.

Hugo scratched his brow. "That day in the town square, when we were doing the Bird Coup . . . do you remember?"

Severin cocked his head. Hesitant, he said, "What about it?"

"Right before the guards came upon us, I searched for our Owl—*you*. But he was nowhere to be found. Where were you, Severin? You were supposed to alert us."

Severin's shoulders went stiff. "I don't know. I didn't see the guard, Hue."

"Maybe you wanted us to be captured. Maybe your ambition outweighed your loyalty."

Severin twisted his face. "That makes no sense. Why would I want to split up the group? We had a good thing going."

"Because you loved Ava, and you wanted her for yourself."

"If I loved that foolish girl, why would I want to see her arrested?"

"So you could free her and be the hero. Isn't that why you tried to steal this?" He pulled the ring out of his pocket.

Severin's eyes widened as he stared at it, the emerald reflecting off the moonlight. He raised his eyes up to Hugo's. "You have quite an imagination, Hugo. But you're wrong. I didn't want your little girl. I gave up on her, like I gave up on you."

"And that's what shows *your* weakness, Sev. Your lack of loyalty—your short-sightedness. You may have ambition, but you'll betray everyone you know to reach your end."

Severin opened his mouth to speak, but no words came out. Finally, he said, "That's a hell of a thing to say, Hugo. I carried all three of you on my back for months! I deserved to be the leader of our pack. I was the oldest and most experienced."

"And the weakest link in the chain, Sev. But I forgive you, as I'm sure Kars and Ava did. You never were one of *us*. Maybe you were just better than us."

"Maybe I was. Maybe I still am."

"Well, here's your reward." He lifted his hand, the ring still resting in the middle of his palm. "You want it, don't you? Of course you do."

"It doesn't mean as much to me now as it once did."

"Nor to me," Hugo said through clenched teeth, his mind flashing to Ava and Karstan again. "Take it anyway . . . as a celebration gift for becoming the new inquisitor's assistant."

Severin chuckled. "I'm simply a glorified secretary, Hue . . . not really worthy of a celebration."

"I know that. But you heard Tomas. You could move up the ranks." He held his hand forward, until Severin could resist no longer.

He took the ring.

"Well, thank you, I guess . . ."

He brought it close to his face, holding it up to the moonlight between his thumb and forefinger.

As he was admiring its green brilliance, Hugo pushed him off the cliff.

Sometimes you have to take what you want.

He wondered whether Severin kept hold of the ring all the way down.

Hugo awoke feeling resolute, though a bit sleep deprived. The sun was not yet up, nor were the others in the group. He folded his blanket, then started a fire in the cooking pit. By the first hint of morning light he'd made breakfast for everyone.

Which was not really so difficult considering there were just four of them left—Hugo, Tomas, Grayson, and Arne.

Tomas woke up to the smell of scrambled eggs nearby. He groaned pleasantly and blinked his eyes open. Hugo was standing over him with a plate in his hand.

"Hugo?" Tomas blinked rapidly, sitting up and taking the food.

"We'll want to have breakfast if we're to get to Trier."

Hearing their voices, Grayson and Arne got up and joined them by the fire.

For the next fifteen minutes everyone ate in sleepy silence. No one spoke of what had taken place the day before. Hugo wasn't even sure if the group had noticed Severin's absence yet.

When the breakfast was finished, Grayson stretched, then began readying the horses. Arne joined him. Tomas stood up and, after scratching his scalp, surveyed the campsite. After scanning the area for a few minutes, in an odd tone he finally asked, "Where's Severin? Has anyone seen my nephew?"

No one answered.

Grayson and Arne both shrugged as they finished with their horses.

When Tomas' eyes landed on Hugo, they stayed there.

He knows.

But instead of shrinking under the weight of Tomas' stare, Hugo stood tall, staring back at him with equal intensity, thinking back on some of the reasons why Severin got what he deserved: He'd betrayed their gang early on; he'd tried to steal Ava's ring, and Ava herself; he'd murdered innocent, sweet Klemens; he'd attempted to take Hugo's place within Tomas' group.

With cold eyes that Tomas had never seen before, Hugo spoke in a steady voice.

"You told me I wasn't ready to be the inquisitor's assistant, Tomas. But I believe you were mistaken."

CHAPTER THIRTY-TWO

GUSTAV

Gustav's crew rode into Bedburg just after sundown, the unrelenting wind making the horses snort and shiver. There were fifteen of them in all—Gustav, Hedda, Mia, Adrian Coswell, Alfred Eckstein, Kevan, Paul, and eight other pirates. After leaving Daxton Wallace's house in the Dutch countryside, they'd been riding hard for nearly three days.

Gustav felt certain that, after traveling hundreds of miles on land and sea to get to this point, his mission would finally succeed here. He knew he'd find Dieter and Sybil, though he wasn't sure if it was a true premonition or just the laudanum.

And how fitting it would be to finally bring them down in the same town where they'd killed his brother Johannes.

"Now let's find them!" he instructed his party. "They won't be in plain sight, that much is certain."

"How can you be so sure they haven't left already?" Hedda asked. She sat behind Gustav on the back of his horse with her arms wrapped around his waist.

"I can feel it." He turned sideways. "Can't you, my dear? It's in the air."

Overhearing him, Adrian Coswell grunted. "All I feel is the cold against my bones. I say we head to the nearest brothel and continue the search tomorrow."

"No!" Gustav spat. "We haven't come this far to sleep. Not yet."

The horses ambled along the road, which meandered through a slummy, filthy part of the city. All except Adrian rode two to a horse—eight steeds in all—forcing the peasants and merchants to step aside as they filled the width of the road. People eyed them, but said nothing.

Alfred, with Mia saddled behind him, came alongside Gustav. He nudged his chin toward a white church on the hill up ahead. "Dieter Nicolaus was a priest. Maybe he'd go there first."

Gustav hesitated. "If he's a Protestant traitor, they might not take a liking to him. On the other hand, it's worth checking. A fine observation, Herr Eckstein."

Alfred smiled. His big ears twitched.

They climbed the hill and gathered in front of the church. Gustav dismounted and the others followed. Ordering his men to stay put, he strode up to the stained-glass door, taking just Hedda with him.

They entered, stopping a few feet inside the doorway.

Rows of pews lined both sides of the nave; a large statue of Christ's crucifixion stood behind the pulpit at the very front. A stout woman with a veil over her head was sweeping the floor by the first row of pews. Gustav swaggered down the center aisle toward her. The woman kept her eyes down until Gustav was directly in front of her, then she peered up from her broom.

Towering over her, Gustav said, "Sister, my name is Gustav Koehler. I am looking for a small group of people. It's my belief that you may be familiar with one of the them."

The woman cocked her head, staying silent.

"What is your name, lady?" Hedda asked, walking up beside Gustav.

"I am Sister Salome, my lord and lady. Who is it you're seeking?"

"His name is Dieter Nicolaus. He used to be a priest here."

The nun tried to hide her surprise, but Gustav read her easily. "I know of the man, but have not seen him since he was excommunicated from this church. That was more than two years ago."

Gustav stared into the woman's eyes for several moments. "You're lying," he said flatly. "Perhaps you are confused," he sighed, pulling his pistol from his waistband and pointing it at Sister Salome's face. "Where is Dieter Nicolaus?" he enunciated clearly.

Salome took a step back, but did not appear scared.

"Gustav!" Hedda cried out. "She's a lady of Christ, and this is a house of God!" She put a hand on his shoulder. "Have some control!"

But Gustav was not one to be told what to do, especially by a woman, especially with the laudanum fortifying him. He'd have no qualms splattering the brains of anyone defying him at this point, "lady of Christ" or not.

Through tightened lips, and with the gun barrel poised inches from the nun's left eyebrow, he spoke slowly. "I have a legitimate decree stating my intent to arrest that man. And his wife. My father, Ludwig von Bergheim, signed the papers. I'm sure you know of his influence and power, sister. If you value your station in life, you will tell me what I need to know."

"My station in life is as a woman of God, Herr Koehler. You're going to have to bring your decree to Bishop Balthasar, but he does not stay here most nights. He is in Castle Bedburg. That is all I can tell you." Then, as if to mock him, she gave a curt bow before calmly returning to her sweeping.

Gustav growled, realizing he was getting nowhere. *They could be getting further and further away with every minute I waste.*

Holstering his gun, he spun on his heels and stormed back out through the front door, striding quickly to his horse, Hedda hurrying along to catch up.

Shortly after, they reached Castle Bedburg. The brick-and-stone structure had been built with four spires pillared on each corner, like four giant exclamation marks punctuating its importance. Crossing over a short bridge above the River Erft, Gustav approached the guards at the front gate.

After flashing his paperwork, he and his intimidating gang were granted immediate entry.

Once inside, Bishop Balthasar Schreib met them at the door, ushering Gustav and Hedda into the main room. The rest of the group loitered about outside. The bishop was a short man, with a round belly and red, oval face. If not for his white bishop's dressage, he may have been mistaken for a common drunk.

The bishop greeted them cheerily. "You are Gustav Koehler, son of Ludwig von Bergheim, I presume?"

Gustav grunted and nodded. *He already knows my name?*

Raising one eyebrow, Gustav glanced around the room. It

was essentially bare, with simple wooden stools, nondescript tapestries and windows, and a small table with a carafe of wine and unadorned cups sitting on top.

The bishop, noticing Gustav's inspection of the room, explained. "Once the prior lord here was deposed, I took the liberty of relieving the castle of its frivolities. When a town can barely survive on its own merits, it's a bit disingenuous to parade excessive accoutrements around, no?"

I'm sure the gold and silver are either hoarded in the basement or clinking in your pockets, Gustav thought, sneering.

"Quite," Gustav said. "I imagine you know why I am here."

The bishop nodded and reached out a hand. "Your letter of intent, please."

Gustav handed it to him.

When the bishop finished reading, he folded the paper and returned it to Gustav. Then he slowly shook his head, forming a smile that showed no pleasure. "While it may be true that Dieter Nicolaus and Sybil Griswold are both fugitives of a crime, albeit long-past, and traitors to the true Christian faith, I'm afraid I can't help you. The crimes they committed are hearsay at best, and, at worst, unfounded. And more to the point, they were both pardoned when it was discovered that the investigation leading to the Werewolf of Bedburg was tainted."

"Tainted?" Hedda asked. "By whom? The former bishop?"

"Indeed, my lady. By Bishop Solomon. You are familiar with Bedburg's history?"

"I am from Bergheim, Your Grace. As is Gustav here. We are your neighbors." She nodded, as if that explained it. "I do find it odd, however, that you have no lord in this town?"

"We've not had a lord for over two years, yes." The bishop sighed. "Archbishop Ernst would have it that way."

"But Ernst is in Cologne," Gustav said, "and you are here. Why do you let him control you?"

Bishop Schreib chuckled, but, again, there was no humor in it. "The archbishop controls everything in this principality, sir. That includes your own town—and your father."

"So, you fancy yourself a statesman and a nobleman?"

"I am merely a humble servant of God, my lord," the bishop

said coolly, bowing his head. "Until we've found a suitable replacement for Lord Werner, I aid the town in fiscal matters. However, I am also the ecclesiastic head of Bedburg—not a political head. That would be the archbishop-elector."

"Then you won't help us?" Gustav said.

Balthasar said, "How can I give you answers I do not have? I have no idea where those two are. Last I heard, they'd escaped to England. I gave it no more thought after that, and, quite frankly, had not given them a moment's musing until you came into town today speaking their names."

"This is ridiculous," Gustav muttered. *It's like they're all trying to hide the priest. But why?*

Without further exchange, Gustav left, Hedda again scurrying along to keep up. Once outside, he took another swig of his laudanum, then announced to the pirates, "It seems we'll find no help here, boys."

"We'll reconvene tomorrow, Gustav, once we have rest and food," replied Adrian, no longer asking for permission. "I'll take my men to the brothel, where I'm sure they'll make themselves at home. Will you join us?"

Feeling a new wave of drug-induced electricity engulf his body, he gazed lustfully at Hedda. "No, I've no need for whores or drink," he said. "Hedda and I will go to the town inn."

"I'll go with you," Mia said.

"No, you won't," Gustav answered quickly. "You'll join the boys. You'll fit in better at the brothel. We'll meet at the tavern in the morning. "

Mia's icy glare followed Gustav as he and Hedda rode off.

The inn was near the slums in the eastern district, not far from the tavern. Gustav and Hedda both dismounted, tied off their horse, then walked to the entrance, nearly tripping over a homeless couple camouflaged against the brown wooden wall.

Inside, the lobby was warm and cozy. A hearth-fire blazing in the corner added to the ambience. An old man sat behind a desk, his head slumped. In his arms a small toddler wiggled and whined.

Gustav's boots thudded loudly against the wooden floor as he trudged toward the desk. The old man's eyes blinked open. Though bloodshot and blurry, his smile was welcoming.

"One room, clerk," Gustav said with a grunt. He yawned and stretched, longing to be upstairs and inside Hedda.

The old man tapped the desk with his fingers and pointed to a sign that indicated the price of the room.

Gustav finished stretching, then flipped a coin onto the desk. The old man gave him a key, and Gustav turned to leave.

Then he did a double-take, spinning back around to the old man and the child.

His throat caught in his chest. "It can't be," he muttered.

Hedda gave him a curious look. Gustav nudged his chin forward, but Hedda was still confused. Then she followed his eyes and realized they were not on the man, but on the boy. Her eyes widened.

"Fine boy you have there," Gustav said, resting his hands palm-down on the desk.

The clerk softened immediately. "My grandson."

Gustav flashed a smile. "And what a precious thing he must be to you."

Gustav could scarcely believe his good fortune. He recognized the child. The same one Martin Achterberg had brought with him earlier. The same curly hair—there was no doubt about it. This boy had been on the *Willow Wisp* and the *Lion's Pride*.

Practically handed to him on a silver platter, this was Dieter and Sybil's son.

CHAPTER THIRTY-THREE

ROWAINE

The estate of Heinrich Franz was located on a large, secluded plot of land not far from the eastern side of Bedburg. To get there, Rowaine, Sybil, and Dieter traveled most of the night through winding, heavily wooded trails that blocked out what little moonlight there was.

Riding up to the main structure, Rowaine wasn't quite ready for what she saw. For several moments she just sat there on her horse, frozen in place, marveling at the sheer opulence before her. Even in the dark, it was stunning. Its immense size, its gothic style with twisting spires, vaulted roofs, and flying buttresses arching into an enormous dome in the center. She could only imagine what it might look like during the day.

Dotting the perimeter of the monolithic main structure— which more resembled a cathedral than someone's living quarters—were several bridges and a handful of small, much newer stone houses that looked strangely out of place when contrasted against the gothic mansion they surrounded.

A large black gate blocked entrance to the main quarters, but creaked open when Rowaine nudged it. Once inside the courtyard, the horses hoofed their way along a tiled roadway bordered by perfectly aligned, towering bushes on both sides.

And the closer they got to the main structure, the more foreboding it seemed.

Somewhere in the distance, a crow cawed, then planted itself on a single leafless tree. It gazed at Rowaine as she passed and, even in the darkness, its black beak and yellow eyes set on her like a living nightmare.

"He couldn't have picked a more frightening house for himself," Sybil whispered from the back of Dieter's horse.

"It does seem fitting," Dieter muttered.

Eventually, they reached the grand entrance.

They tied off their horses as close as possible to the large double-door fronting the building, just in case a quick exit was required. The massive door handles were in the shape of two snarling wolf-heads.

Since the place looked dark and uninhabited, rather than knocking, Rowaine simply pushed in on one of the handles. And as with the front gate, the door swung open. She gulped, took one last look back at her two companions, then entered. Sybil and Dieter followed.

It was surprisingly bright inside, the main foyer lit by torches on all sides. A far cry from the desolate view from outside. They walked down a red-carpeted hallway, passing several stairways that led to darker places they couldn't see. Murals, paintings, and tapestries adorned the walls.

"Hello?" Rowaine called out, her voice echoing through the huge, domed space.

To their right, a man poked his head out from behind a door. He was small, with a long white beard, a bald head, and beady little eyes. He wore a simple brown tunic that swept to the ground, hiding his legs and feet. In his hands he held what appeared to be a bleeding piece of uncooked meat.

Rowaine's eyes immediately focused on the large chunk of meat.

"Guests?" the man squeaked in a high voice. "We have guests! Oh my, Beauregard, we have guests!"

Another man leaned over the upstairs railing, equally exuberant. He wore a white suit and slacks and came running down the stairs, nearly tripping several times on his way.

"Hello, travelers," the bearded one with the meat said, shuffling toward them. "This is Beauregard, butler of House Charmagne." He pointed to the other man in white.

"My name is Catriona Donnelly. This is Sybil and Dieter Nicolaus. You must be Rolf Anders?"

The bearded man smiled, showing two perfect rows of tiny white teeth. "I must be."

"We are looking for Heinrich Franz."

Rolf Anders' smile evaporated. "I'm afraid you won't find him here. However, this is his house." He stretched his arms out to show them they'd come to the right place. "Did he invite you here?"

"Er, no," Rowaine stammered. "We were made aware of this place by the Lady Odela."

Rolf coughed, which became a laugh. "The *Lady* Odela, eh? How is that senile old crone?" He didn't wait for an answer. "Come, come, I was going to feed the hounds," he said, beckoning them with the dripping meat. "We can talk while we walk."

After sharing a bewildered look, the trio followed Rolf through the doorway and down another long, red-carpeted hallway lit by more wall torches.

The trio stayed far back from Rolf as they walked. Rowaine tried to gauge his demeanor.

"Come now, I won't bite," Rolf called over his shoulder, flashing his tiny white teeth.

I'm not so sure of that, Rowaine thought.

Moving up alongside the man, Rowaine asked, "What is your capacity here, Lord Rolf?"

The old man chuckled as he shuffled along. "I am the steward of Herr Franz's estate, my dear. Beauregard and I watch after this place in his absence. But as a steward, please, do not refer to me as 'lord.' Rolf will suffice."

"How do you know Heinrich?"

"I suppose I should be asking you the same question."

"We are friends of his," Rowaine replied.

Rolf laughed at that. They rounded a corner in the hallway. The path seemed much the same as the last, like they were navigating through a labyrinth.

"Is that what you told Odela?" he asked.

Rowaine scrunched her brow but said nothing.

"My dear," Rolf said, elaborating, "Heinrich Franz has no friends. He'd be the first to tell you that."

Our secret is out, Rowaine thought.

"If you're here to kill him, that's no matter. I suppose he's brought many people a life of agony." Rolf opened a door at the end of the hall. "But I have no idea where he is. I haven't seen Herr Franz in months."

They entered a small room, then headed down a stone staircase, the temperature growing noticeably colder. A few dozen steps later, they descended into a basement, or cellar, or possibly a dungeon. Unlike the grandeur above them, the walls here were grimy and the air stale and damp—sufficiently unpleasant enough to make the three visitors instantly leery.

"How did you come to know Herr Franz, Rolf?" Dieter asked, looking around nervously.

"I taught him how to inflict that agony, good sir."

The three shared another look.

Rolf led them to a barred gate. Rowaine took a closer look and realized it was actually a cage. Rolf wedged the piece of meat between the steel grids and flung it into the enclosure. It slapped to the ground as dark forms emerged from the shadows.

Crossing his arms over his chest, Rolf watched the forms attack the piece of meat. "I was a one-time acquaintance of Ernst of Bavaria," he explained, obviously enjoying the feeding spectacle before him. "We met through him."

As the creatures devoured the food, Rowaine realized they weren't hounds at all. They were wolves. Four of them, growling and nipping each other as they fought for the meat.

"The Archbishop of Cologne?" Rowaine asked, staring wide-eyed at the raging beasts.

Rolf leaned his forehead inches from the cage. "They're beautiful, aren't they? So majestic in their wildness . . . Yet they actually turn quite docile when Heinrich is near."

Rowaine couldn't believe she'd heard correctly. "These are Heinrich's . . . pets?"

One wolf snapped at another, then grabbed a chunk of the meat and retreated to a dark corner.

"Indeed. He took two of his favorites with him the last time he was here. That was . . . maybe six months ago."

Dieter, also with eyes locked onto the feasting frenzy, asked, "What do you mean, you 'taught him how to inflict that agony,' Rolf?"

The old man sighed. The original chunk of meat now gone,

each animal peacefully chewed remnants in separate corners. Rolf looked away and faced Dieter. "He was an obsessive investigator. I can only imagine the hardships he brought upon his interests."

Rowaine tilted her head. "But that's not all you mean, is it, Rolf?"

Again Rolf sighed, his gaze turning severe. "I only speak of these things because I am no longer a part of that life. But you are a clever lass, and you are correct. I taught Heinrich the noble, diplomatic ways of . . ." he waved his hands in the air, contemplating the right word. "Politics."

"What does that mean?" asked Rowaine.

"Diplomacy, disguise, inspection," Rolf said, rattling the words off as if they meant nothing. "And the darker arts involved in those things—espionage, assassinations, and the like."

"You taught him all those things?" Dieter asked, taken aback.

"You have to understand . . . when he was sent to me as a young man by the archbishop, he was a wild, unpredictable knave."

"I'm afraid to say it," replied Dieter, "but he was an unpredictable man even past his youth."

"That may be true." Rolf shrugged, wiping his hands on his tunic. "I tried my best." He started walking back toward the steps. "Come, my friends, it is chilly down here. I'll have Beauregard prepare us supper."

They climbed back up to the grander sections of the mansion. On their way, Rowaine nixed the dinner invitation. "That won't be necessary, sir."

She glanced behind, realizing for the first time that Sybil hadn't spoken a word. The girl's face was stricken, ghost white and pale.

"We won't be staying," Rowaine added.

Rolf frowned. "That's a shame."

"But before we go, please continue your fascinating tale. I wish to know all you can tell us about Heinrich Franz."

With his signature chuckle, Rolf nodded. "It is quite

fascinating, isn't it? I plan to write a memoir and release it upon my death." He smirked, adding, "Since releasing anything before then would likely result in my somewhat *premature* demise." Another chuckle, this time followed with a wink.

They made their way into the main foyer, where Beauregard waited, as stiff as a statue, arms tucked behind him.

"When Heinrich came to me," Rolf continued, "he was an agent for Count Adolf of Bedburg. At the time, Bedburg was a Protestant stronghold, and Adolf answered to Archbishop Gebhard of Cologne. Of course, once Archbishop Ernst defeated and deposed Gebhard, he replaced Adolf with his own Catholic man, Lord Werner.

"Heinrich wanted no part of this, however, as he was never a religious man. When working for Count Adolf, he never cared much for his Protestant master."

"Is that why he so easily switched sides to the Catholics and Archbishop Ernst?" Rowaine asked.

"You are quick, my dear. And correct. Plus, Heinrich wanted to help that dear old girl, Odela, who was quite a beauty at the time, if I may say." He ambled to another room near the back of the hall. As he walked, he rubbed his hands across his stomach while talking. "He learned who the enemies of his enemies were. Namely, I showed him who the archbishop hated in parliament, and in the aristocracy. It was Heinrich's task to do something about those folk."

"By whatever means necessary?" Dieter asked, reaching into his tunic.

Rolf stopped and turned. "Indeed, young man. What is that you have there?"

Dieter pulled out a piece of rolled parchment. "Perhaps you recognize some of these names?" Unrolling it, he handed it to Rolf.

Rolf searched his pockets, found a pair of large spectacles, and fastened them carefully over his ears. "Let's see," he said, running his finger down the list. "Achterberg, Tomlin, Rickenbock, Gabler . . ." He muttered a few more names under his breath, nodding as he went. "I recognize many of these," he said. "If I can recall—and it's been a long time—these families were associated with the Waldensians."

Rowaine looked at him blankly. "The Waldensians?"

Rolf sucked his lower lip while he kept reading the paper. "Yes, yes, a precursor to the Protestants, if you will. But surely you noticed that by these records?"

Dieter stepped forward. "I did," he said. "Many of them are *accused* of being Waldensians."

Rolf looked up at Dieter. "These families would have been associated with Lord Adolf at the time."

"Many of the women and children of those families were found murdered, Herr Rolf," Dieter said. "Can you explain that?"

They'd entered a large dining room. Rolf took a seat at the head of a long, circular table. His company sat around him, waiting for an answer.

Rolf sighed. "That is a shame, but I'm sure you can figure it out." The cryptic answer angered Rowaine. Rolf clapped his hands and shouted, "Beauregard, supper!"

Rowaine opened her mouth to lash out, and to remind Rolf they were not staying for supper, but Dieter stopped her with a hand on her arm, then continued his questioning. "What good would these children's deaths be to Archbishop Ernst?"

Rolf chuckled. "I'm sure they'd be of great value, young man."

Great value . . . The words hit Rowaine hard. "If they were all part of a secret group," she said, "these Waldensians, as you call them, they would all have words against Archbishop Ernst? And in turn, they'd support Archbishop Gebhard?"

Beauregard appeared through a swinging door, holding a large tray with four steaming bowls of soup. One by one he placed a bowl in front of each guest, and Rolf, while everyone waited in silence. Rolf thanked the butler, who then disappeared.

While the host slurped his soup, head down, Dieter broke the silence.

"Would they have any power, though? Weren't these families peasants and farmers?" he asked.

"Don't believe all you see, Herr Nicolaus. Sometimes the weakest man holds the strongest hand."

That made Rowaine think of her last card game aboard the *Lion's Pride,* gambling with Daxton and Alfred and Jerome. *In some games, the power is in the Ace. In others, Deuces hold sway.*

"Hold sway," she thought, and then . . .

"That's it!" Rowaine exclaimed. "The families would want to vote to sway popular opinion away from the Catholics. By putting a Protestant archbishop on the electoral seat."

Rolf clapped his hands together.

Dieter suddenly saw the grim reality of it all. "And getting rid of these men's daughters and wives would . . . frighten the other families against that?"

"A powerful tactic, fear," Rolf said.

"These deaths," Dieter continued, his outrage growing, "would have been to scare other families from helping Protestants gain a majority, or a following?"

Sybil stood up quickly, fury in her eyes. "Dorothea died so that her family wouldn't vote for a Protestant leader?" The first words she'd spoken since arriving.

"Not just *her* family, my dear." Rolf paused from his soup, his spoon halfway to his mouth. "It has a domino effect, fear does. Scare one man with the death of his neighbor, and what will the man think?"

"My family is next . . ." Dieter whispered, staring at Sybil.

Rolf slurped down the rest of his soup. "I think you have the crux of it."

Silence ensued. The untouched soups in front of Rolf's guests grew cold.

"But Odela said Heinrich received this estate from Count Adolf," Dieter finally said. "And I assumed it was for doing his—and the Protestant's—bidding."

"Odela is senile, young man. I already said as much. Heinrich gained this estate for his work with Archbishop Ernst. The surrounding buildings of this estate, however, were imported from France after his more recent successful investigations and rewards."

"He was a double agent," Dieter stated, not as a question. "Working in Count Adolf's castle, but secretly swaying the votes in Ernst's favor. He worked against the Protestants while staying in their home."

Rolf, realizing his guests weren't interested in eating, moved his own empty soup bowl out of the way, then reached over and slid the soup in front of Dieter down in its place. Without looking up, he immediately began slurping it.

"Odela knew all of this?" Rowaine asked. "This is what drew Heinrich to madness and murdering his own offspring—killing these folk?"

Rolf furrowed his brow and coughed up some soup spittle. "Drew *Heinrich* to madness? No, no, Frau Donnelly, you have that the wrong way. What drew Heinrich to madness was his own child being taken from him."

Dieter scratched his scalp. "But Odela said . . ."

Rolf was chuckling. "I think that old crone put you through a spin, my friend. If it wasn't for what Odela did, I'm sure she'd be sitting in this seat right now, as steward of this house. Heinrich loved that woman, for whatever reason. Until she betrayed him."

Rowaine's mind raced. "You mean the baby? Heinrich didn't kill his baby?"

"Of course not, foolish girl. Odela took that baby, and Heinrich could never forgive her. I'm surprised he didn't kill *her*. I would have."

"How could that sweet old woman kill an innocent baby—tainted bloodline or not?" Sybil asked meekly.

"Are none of you listening?" Rolf's voice rose an octave, the first time he'd seemed flustered. "Odela killed no one. She took the whelp, yes. But she gave it to some poor family who was wailing over the loss of their stillborn. I could never tell Heinrich that, of course, that his bastard child was still alive. Could you imagine the wrath that man would dispense upon the poor, unsuspecting family of that orphan?"

"Where is the baby now?" Rowaine asked urgently.

"Well, it's certainly not a baby any longer," Rolf snorted. "Only Odela knows where that bastard went. You'll have to ask her."

"I intend to," Rowaine said, rising from her seat. With a curt nod to her host, she headed for the front door. Dieter and Sybil followed. A few strides from the table, she spun around. "Your knowledge is much appreciated, Rolf Anders. I won't forget you."

"Nor I you," the old man said, clasping his hands at the table and pushing his bowl away. "Good luck in finding what you're so desperately searching for."

At that, Rowaine stared into the man's eyes. "One last question, if I may, sir."

Rolf gazed at her expectedly.

"Did Heinrich ever mention a man named Georg Sieghart?"

Rolf chuckled. "Of course, my dear. Georg Sieghart first came here about two years ago. He had some nasty wounds that I helped him with. When he was better, he took off into the shadows."

"Have you seen him since?"

Rolf clicked his tongue. "I have. No more than six months ago."

CHAPTER THIRTY-FOUR

SYBIL

By the time the trio was on their horses headed back to Bedburg, it was early morning and still dark.

"We must speak with Odela and get the truth out of her," Rowaine said, setting a much faster pace back than their trip there. After hearing that her father was alive as of six months ago, her determination had reached new heights.

"I'd like to gather my son first," Sybil told her. "I've not seen him in nearly two days."

They traveled through the woods, along the northern bank of Lake Peringsmaar, which circled the main road leading back to town.

Thoughts swirled through Sybil's mind as she bumped along on the back of Dieter's steed, gripping his waist for dear life. She had learned much in the past day, from both Odela and Rolf. She still wondered who these elderly people had once been.

Could these be the only folk that Heinrich Franz ever truly cared for? They both seem to know so much about him . . . how he was raised, how he came to become the man he is. But neither knows where to find him? I find that hard to believe.

On the other hand, if Georg is still alive, as Rolf says, where could he be hiding? If he stayed at Heinrich's estate to heal and recover, where is he now? Could he be in those trees, peering at us, watching us from afar? And could he possibly know of Heinrich's dark secrets?

She had recognized the ring Odela wore when they first spoke. The one that had belonged to Dorothea Gabler. Of that, Sybil was sure.

Does that mean Heinrich would go to Odela, secretly, and give the woman trophies of his conquests? If Odela knew what was happening, does that put her in the same league as that evil man? All of those deaths, those poor girls, just for the sake of scaring the Protestants away from voicing their opinions. It just doesn't make sense. But if true, then perhaps Heinrich Franz isn't the real evil one here, but rather Archbishop Ernst of Cologne. I must speak to this "holy man."

As the group crested over the last hill before Bedburg, the town's low rooftops came into view. The sun was just rising. From afar, the town seemed cramped, the buildings closing in on one another, with few roads in between. And the farmlands on both sides—flat and green and spanning off in both directions as far as the eye could see—made the town itself look smaller than it really was.

It looks so peaceful and quaint. Hardly the place where so many gruesome murders occurred.

As Sybil's group began their descent down the hill, they noticed a carriage led by two black horses headed their way. As it neared the trio, the horses leading the carriage slowed their pace to pass to the left of Sybil's group. The carriage's windows were drawn open and, as it passed, Sybil glanced over, then did a double-take.

Odela's little white head turned toward her. They locked eyes for a moment and time seemed to freeze. Sybil's face drained of color as the carriage continued on.

Sybil yanked on Dieter's tunic. "That's her!" she cried.

Rowaine tightened her reins, halting her horse in its tracks. "What did you say?"

"Odela was in that carriage!"

Without a word, Rowaine grunted, then kicked the flanks of her mare, wheeled around, and raced off. She tucked her head low against her horse's neck.

"What are you doing?" Sybil called out, as Dieter circled around and followed Rowaine.

"Catching her!" Rowaine screamed, pulling out her pistol.

As Sybil and Dieter kept a safe distance behind the carriage, Rowaine made a wide sweep, riding past it to the top of the hill and dipping out of sight. When the coach and horses finally reached the summit, Rowaine was standing in the middle of the road, left hand on her hip, right hand pointing her pistol squarely at the driver.

The driver gasped and nearly lost the reins. Once he'd brought the carriage to a stop, his hands shot up in the air.

Dieter came up alongside the coach, Sybil peeking over his shoulder.

"W-what's this all about?" the driver asked. He was young, scared, and obviously not paid enough to argue with a pistol-wielding, crazed-looking firebrand like Rowaine.

Rowaine's leather jerkin creaked and her boots thumped as she ambled toward the carriage door. "I wish to speak to your guest, boy." The young man remained silent, nervously nodding, his hands still straight up.

Sybil could hear Odela's groan as Rowaine approached. Sybil jumped from her horse and joined Rowaine, if only to make sure she didn't shoot the poor woman in her fury. After all, she *was* the daughter of Georg Sieghart—a man with ballads written about his savagery.

"You lied to us, Odela," Rowaine began, resting one foot atop the carriage's side-stair, her gun at her side. Sybil put her hand on Rowaine's shoulder, but the redhead shrugged her away.

"About what, my dear?" Odela said, her voice sweet and helpless.

"You knew Heinrich Franz was killing people for his lord. Brutalizing poor women and children. And you did nothing!"

Odela folded her hands on her lap, calm as could be. "You must have met with Rolf. How is that sour old weasel?"

Rowaine growled. "Dammit, woman, don't bring—"

"We did meet with Rolf," Sybil interjected, stepping into view of Odela. "He told us Heinrich's secret, the one you wished not to betray. And now that we know, you must tell us where he is."

Odela raised an eyebrow. "Or what?" she smirked. "I suppose you'll have to kill me, girl." She nodded toward Rowaine's gun. "Go on. I've lived a full life."

Sybil gave Rowaine a hard stare and frowned. Rowaine hesitated, then snorted and put her gun away.

Sybil turned back to Odela. "Tell us where Heinrich's child is, then," she said, her tone conciliatory.

"Now *that* I truly don't know. I stopped watching him."

"We know that Heinrich didn't take the baby away," Rowaine said. "We know that whole tale—about that being the most noble thing he ever did—was a complete lie. A fabrication. And we were fools to believe you. *You* took the baby, once you learned Heinrich was a murderer. You took the whelp and you gave it to some poor family."

"We know you're lying, Lady Odela," Sybil added. "No mother ever stops watching her children."

Odela chuckled. "Oh? And where is your child, Sybil Griswold?"

Sybil's words caught in her throat. *How does she know about Peter? How does she know I even have a child?*

A stiff silence ensued until Odela finally sighed.

"What would you do with that knowledge?" she asked. "What good would it do to know whom the child is, or whom he belongs to?"

Sybil had to admit it was a reasonable question. She hadn't really thought that far ahead. And she doubted Rowaine had either.

She studied Rowaine's face.

Perhaps she plans to take the child to draw Heinrich out of hiding . . .

But if Heinrich isn't even aware of where his child was taken, how would he recognize the child fifteen years later?

"We aren't leaving until you tell us where the child is," Rowaine said, more calmly but with resolve.

Odela considered it for a moment, then seemed to make a decision to herself and threw her hands up in the air. "Then you're in luck—we aren't too far. If you promise not to harm the child, I will show you the house where I left him as a pup."

Rowaine and Sybil shared a look, then nodded to each other, reaching a silent agreement.

"And one more condition," Odela said, noticing the nod. "You have to promise to then let me go."

Rowaine narrowed her eyes. "Go where?" she asked.

Odela tilted her chin. "That's none of your concern, young lady."

Probably to warn Heinrich of his pursuers.

"We promise," Sybil said.

Reluctantly, Rowaine agreed. "Fine."

Odela punched the ceiling of the carriage with her small hand. "Rodrigo, turn left at the bottom of this hill. We're changing course."

The driver glared down at Sybil, Rowaine, and Dieter, as if to say, *How could you bully such a sweet old woman?*

They followed the carriage to the bottom of the hill, then down a side trail off to the left.

"What *do* you plan to do with the child?" Sybil asked Rowaine while the three of them kept pace behind the carriage.

"I haven't decided yet. It would make a great hostage though."

Dieter creased his forehead. "We can't stoop as low as the man we're chasing, Catriona. It isn't right."

Rowaine spat on the ground. "That *man* almost got my father killed—God knows he probably tried. And that *man* murdered countless innocent women and children to satisfy a master and God he doesn't believe in. So don't tell me what is and isn't right."

"You're letting revenge cloud your mind," Dieter said softly, his words reminding Sybil why she loved him so much. He looked down at his horse's flanks. "I did it once, and I've never forgiven myself."

They followed the coach for another thirty minutes. When they reached the top of another small foothill, Odela knocked on the coach's ceiling again and the carriage stopped.

Rowaine and Sybil dismounted and walked to the side of the coach. Sybil peered in, then held her hand out to help the old woman out.

Odela took Sybil's hand and slowly navigated her way down the three steps. "Thank you, my dear."

With both women beside her, Odela walked to the end of the path, then pointed to a structure at the bottom of the hill. "That's the house where I left my child—mine and Heinrich's."

When no one spoke, Odela continued. "When I took the babe in my arms, I could feel his little heart beating so fast. I don't know what I planned to do with him, I only knew I had to get him away from Heinrich. As I was traveling away from

Bedburg, I noticed a gathering of folk. I'd happened upon a funeral.

"I remember thinking to myself, 'This must be fate.' A poor woman was wailing, holding the cold body of her stillborn child. I hid away until night, and when the family awoke the next morning, they awoke to a miracle: a swaddled babe at their doorstep. My child.

"I wept as I returned to Heinrich. I told him the child had died during the night, of a chill, but I could see that he didn't believe me. He forsook me. I later learned that the mother of that stillborn child died of a shattered heart."

Rowaine turned to see Sybil trembling, her eyes moist and wide, as she stared down at the house. She touched Sybil's shoulder, whispering, "Are you all right?"

But Sybil was not all right. Hearing Odela's story, seeing this house from this distance, had hit Sybil like a sword in the gut.

"I-it's . . . impossible," she muttered.

She was looking at her own house. The house of her youth, where she'd tilled the soil during the sweltering summer days. Where she'd listened behind closed doors to her father's conversations. Where she'd danced around the roses, trying to catch butterflies.

Dieter put a steadying hand around her waist and pulled her close.

"I'm afraid so, Sybil Griswold," Odela said. "This is why you were better off not knowing."

All the things Sybil had done at that house, and most of the years she'd grown up, she'd never been alone.

She'd always had . . .

Hugo.

They were on their way back to Bedburg.

They'd left Odela and her driver on the hillside, unharmed and free to continue their journey.

Sybil's head was slumped numbly against Dieter's back, while jumbled thoughts raced through her mind. Of her brother Hugo.

The brother she loved. The brother she'd vowed to return for, but never had.

The brother I grew up loving . . . is the son of . . . a murderer? A monster? Why did father never tell me? He'd say 'to protect me'—but from what? I could have taken it. But could Hugo?

So many questions, so many confusing new facts and old memories mixed together. Her only refuge was to think how much she just wanted to hurry back and hold her *own* child in her arms. To never leave him again. Not for a day, an hour, a single minute.

Her precious Peter.

They made excellent time returning to Bedburg, reaching the town's southern gate just as the morning sun slipped behind dark storm clouds and the wind shifted.

They headed straight for Claus' inn.

As they moved through the town, an odd feeling overtook Sybil in the pit of her stomach. She lifted her head from Dieter's back. It felt like she was being watched. An ominous darkness enveloped her.

Perhaps it was a mother's instinct. Or just the weather turning brisk.

Something wasn't right.

Nearing the inn, a gut-wrenching terror welled up inside her. She clutched her chest and gasped.

Men surrounded the inn. Evil, vile men. Men she recognized.

Gustav Koehler's men.

In the middle of the pack, waltzing through the door of Claus' inn, was Gustav Koehler himself.

When he saw Sybil, Dieter, and Rowaine, he smiled cruelly.

And then Sybil saw it.

In Gustav's arms. Asleep.

Her child.

Her precious Peter.

PART III

Thrown to the Wolves

CHAPTER THIRTY-FIVE

HUGO

Hugo's tongue stuck to the roof of his mouth as he swallowed. The veins in his throat were taut, and his body shook.

Tomas stood in front of him, looking down the length of his sword, aimed at the boy's throat. A bead of sweat dripped down Hugo's forehead, landing on the tip of the blade.

Tomas clenched his jaw, the bones near his ears bulging. "I never thought you had the capacity for such treachery, Hugo Griswold."

It was the first time he'd called Hugo by his full name, which at any other time would have elated the young man. Unfortunately, in his current predicament, it only frightened him to his core.

Trying to maintain his composure, Hugo locked eyes with Tomas. "I could say the same about you, Tomas Reiner, and anyone you associate with."

"You came to *us*—to Ulrich, you fool. What did you expect from the scarred executioner, a life of happiness and rainbows?"

"I expected to learn how to be a man. I expected to learn a valuable trade. And I did, from both of you."

"You just hoped you'd never have to use the things we taught you."

Hugo glanced away. "That was my hope."

Tomas bit his bottom lip. "What am I going to tell that boy's mother—my sister? I may have never enjoyed Severin's company, God knows he was a thorn in my side, but that didn't give you the right . . ."

The image of Severin cascading down the cliffside replayed in Hugo's mind. Yet despite what he'd done, despite Tomas' piercing eyes debating his fate at that very moment, he felt no remorse. And that emptiness sickened him. He should feel *something* for the man who, for better or worse, he'd lived with, shared adventures with, and had known for years.

Have I really changed so much, in so little time? Ulrich, Tomas, Severin, Ava, Karstan—how have I let them turn me into this . . . savage? These don't feel like my thoughts . . . they feel planted.

Still, he had not lost all of himself, yet. Because he still felt something—whatever shred of empathy still lingered inside him—for the others, the ones he knew least—Klemens, Gregor, even Tabea and Samuel—and their senseless slaughter.

"Severin's better off where he is," Hugo said flatly. "His is a case of ambition far outweighing ability." Hugo knew he spoke rash and blunt, but didn't care. Suddenly the idea of joining Severin at the bottom of that cliff didn't sound so horrible.

Tomas' eyes widened. He'd expected Hugo to grovel for his life. Instead, the young man remained resolute, unbending, strong. And Tomas couldn't help but respect the boy for it.

Maybe that's what saved Hugo's life that day.

Or maybe it was Grayson, who strolled up to them and, putting his hands out in surrender, tried to defuse the situation in his own unique way.

"You could take his head from his neck and roll it down the bluff to join your nephew, Tomas—"

"I hear an alternative idea bubbling behind your words, Gray," Tomas said, his sword still poised against the boy's throat.

"But before you make any final decisions, remember that the inquisitors' paperwork expects an inquisitor's *assistant* to arrive in Trier, too. Arne and I won't be joining you, so—"

Arne approached them. "He's all you've got, is what Gray's saying."

"I could kill him and leave this forsaken hill and just return to Bedburg. There's plenty of work there—the money in Trier isn't important to me."

Grayson snorted. "Well, we all know *that's* hogwash, Tom. If it wasn't important to you, would you have carried out the murders? I doubt it."

Hugo saw Tomas' eyes soften, ever so slightly.

"I can never trust him again," Tomas said, still trying to justify jamming his sword through Hugo's neck.

Grayson glared at Hugo. "If he can do what you claim he did to Severin, it goes without saying that he can do a hell of a lot worse to those folk in Trier. Perhaps he'll fit right in. Maybe this is just what that place needs: a young savage willing to kill the innocent to set that place right."

"The innocent?" Tomas said, glancing at Grayson.

Grayson shrugged. "Alls I know is that he'll make the diocese a hefty sum of gold. And maybe you, too." He motioned toward the cliff. "He's clearly got no conscience. A rotten soul. Look at him."

Hugo remained motionless, trying to minimize the chances of Tomas accidentally slicing him open with a sudden twitch.

Grayson continued. "The burnings in Trier—I hear there're hundreds of 'em. Biggest witch-hunt ever. You really think they're *all* witches? Or a power grab from the old bishops and clergy?"

Arne chimed in. "I hear nobles and judges and priests are even being swept into the frenzy. No one's safe." He looked from Tomas to Grayson. "There's a reason Ulrich sent us there—or whoever paid Ulrich. The money is ripe."

Grayson nodded. "The other job me and Arne're taking in Trier, we're supposed to haul in a gaggle of hags and find reasons they need to die, so their wineries and fields can be confiscated. You fancy that's all by chance? No, Tom, it's hunting season in the diocese. Everyone is trying to make their coin, get their share of the kill." He nudged his chin toward Hugo. "I think this boy's got the grains to do what's needed. He's proven that."

Tomas grunted. He tapped his forefinger on the guard of his sword, then finally let it drop point-first toward the ground.

Hugo let out a sigh.

"I've heard similar tales," Tomas said, turning to Grayson. "Ulrich wasn't happy about it when he told me. There was a time when judgment came by way of a traveling executioner—a horseman of death, like Ulrich. But he complained that now, this inquisition comes from priests riding carriages bought with the souls of the hapless. They ride over roads paved with blood."

"Blood money," Grayson said, nodding.

Tomas scowled. "They kill heretics to build roads and mansions from the wealth they take. They sell indulgences to buy their horses and gold crosses and fineries."

"You're saying you don't want some of that blood-and-soul money?" Grayson asked with a glimmer of a smile. He put a hand on Tomas' shoulder.

Tomas stomped his feet. Then smirked. "Let's go get us a share of the kill," he said, walking away from Hugo who, somewhat surprisingly, was still very much alive.

They arrived in the countryside of Trier a few hours later. At first blush, the land looked green and fertile, reborn from the night's spring showers. But a closer inspection revealed the multiple plumes of thick black smoke rising off in the distance from the surrounding villages of the diocese.

Not the burning of buildings, but of people . . .

There was a time when Trier was one of the most prosperous regions in the Holy Roman Empire. And the current archbishop, Prince-Elector Johann von Schönenberg, still held one of the most powerful seats in the Empire. But rather than use his power for good, he oversaw one of the most destructive massacres the region had ever known.

Hugo had done his learning while on the road to Trier. He knew what to expect, especially after the brutal deaths of his fellow travelers. The event on the mountainside validated what was to come and Hugo knew it. He could feel it. He could see it. The thick tendrils of smoke in the distance bearing witness to it.

As the setting sun fashioned the polluted air into a flaming orange sky, Tomas and his men followed the Moselle River into the valley. They passed a small village with a large wooden cross stuck in the ground near its entrance. A man was vigilantly guarding it, white gowns over his plate mail, every bit the Knight Templar.

Grayson called to the man. "What's this town?"

"Naurath."

Grayson's eyes gleamed. "Ah, Arne my boy, it seems we're at the right place! Tomas, I suppose this is where we part ways."

Tomas surveyed the village of Naurath below them. Mostly small dwellings, hovels, and sheds. A tiny town, surely no more than a few hundred inhabitants. "This is where you go?"

Grayson grinned. "We follow the coin, my friend. But I have a feeling we'll see you again."

The two mercenaries embraced, then Tomas tousled Arne's hair. Grayson simply gave a stiff nod to Hugo, but said nothing.

As the two walked away, Hugo felt a sense of dread. Grayson had saved his life—of that there was no doubt. And now he was gone, leaving Hugo with no protection . . . nor words of wisdom.

He was now at the sole mercy of Tomas.

Hopefully time will heal our wounds.

Though I have a feeling time won't heal this wound until either me or Tomas is good and buried.

When Tomas and Hugo arrived in Trier, the sparkling stars brightened its rooftops, casting an inviting glow. The city was large, but not quite a metropolis. Situated between sandstone hills and the banks of the Moselle, it was in the heart of the region's wine country.

Hugo dared not speak when they entered Trier's northern gates. He waited for issue from Tomas. As they made their way through the streets, Hugo took in the sights, sounds, and smells of the city. Half-naked women clawed and dragged their hands across him as he walked by. A man flew out of a tavern, landing in the mud. A grimy beggar lifted his cup and begged for coins. Another beggar did the same. Then another.

So many penniless souls.

Trier was unlike anything he'd ever seen. He'd never been to a place so big. So many smells invaded his senses, mostly foul and stinking, but others he couldn't really place. Yet despite the outward appearance of raging festivities around him, Hugo saw through the façade. Trier was hurting, its people in dire need of aid. The city was crumbling.

"Come, boy," Tomas urged, watching Hugo fall behind, slowed by the constant grappling of harlots in the night. "Remember who you are," he whispered angrily. "You are not a sightseer. You are Inquisitor Assistant Gregor."

Hugo nodded.

"And who am I?"

"Inquisitor Samuel, my lord." Hugo hadn't meant to call Tomas 'my lord,' but it slipped out.

As they moved on, Hugo saw another thing he'd never forget: Three tall crosses had been erected in the square they passed. And behind those stood three more. And even more behind those.

But unlike when they'd passed Naurath, these crosses were not empty.

The burned shells and skeletal remains of victims and heretics were nailed to each, as if a warning to visitors entering the city. Hugo could smell the rank, rotting skin and flesh. Flies buzzed noisily about the carcasses.

Hugo gulped. "Where are we going?" he finally asked, realizing that Tomas seemed to know the lay of the land.

"To find the suffragan bishop, Peter Binsfeld. He started this witch-circus. Maybe then we'll meet our commissioner. Keep up and don't turn your head too much." He nodded toward the crosses. "Lest you want to end up like those poor souls."

CHAPTER THIRTY-SIX

GUSTAV

Keenly aware he now had their full attention, Gustav made a show of smiling at the sleeping boy in his arms. As Sybil, Dieter, and Rowaine looked on, he tickled the child awake by gently stroking his chin, then set him down on the ground. The toddler wobbled on uneasy feet, with Gustav's soldiers, Adrian and Alfred, standing on both sides of him, while the rest of Gustav's pirates formed a protective circle around them all. His other key aides, Kevan and Paul, remained inside the inn watching the old innkeeper.

From inside his guarded circle, Gustav eyed Sybil, Dieter, and Rowaine, one by one. He didn't care much about the redheaded one, though he was aware of the immense hatred Adrian, standing to his left, held for the woman who had unceremoniously dispatched and mutilated his former captain.

But Gustav's ire was squarely directed at Sybil and Dieter, his brother's murderers. And now, after many grueling days of hard travel, his efforts had finally paid off. He'd found them!

Sweeter still, he now held all the cards—in the shape of the tiny toddler wandering around in front of him.

Gustav wasn't a religious man, but he thanked the stars for his good fortune in coming upon the child by sheer happenstance. Old man Claus had refused to say where the trio had gone—even with a gun pointed at him. But Gustav knew it was only a matter of time before the boy's parents returned for their precious little one.

And here they were.

Gustav caressed the wooden butt of his brother's pistol, which he always kept close for such an occasion.

With the delicious laudanum coursing through his veins, plus a healthy dose of adrenaline, his eyes grew wild.

Noticing his crazed expression, Hedda crept up beside him. "Be reasonable," she said in a low voice, eyeing the child as she spoke.

But Gustav pushed her away, sending her back inside the inn. He kept a hard stare on the two people he'd worked so hard to find, deciding then and there that one way or the other he would not leave without taking what he came for: Either they'd come peacefully or their blood would spill on the street.

Sudden shadows darkened his view. At first he assumed it was Adrian's men closing around him, or possibly even his drugs intensifying his senses. But when he glanced over, he saw that four of the town's guards had arrived to investigate the situation. Standing about ten paces back from Gustav's circle of protectors, they stood several paces apart from each other to cover as wide an area as possible.

Apparently news traveled fast in these parts.

Gustav wasn't too concerned. His crew vastly outnumbered these four Bedburg defenders.

But one of them in particular stood out to Gustav—the largest one, with a deep scar on his face. Two things about him drew Gustav's attention: the grisly nature of the scar running down the man's cheek, visible even from ten paces away, and the enormous arquebus rifle he held at his side. As Gustav looked away, refocusing on the toddler in front of him, the scarred man swung the huge weapon around, clutching it in both hands, though not yet aiming it. As Gustav glanced back up, the man spoke.

"Frau Aellin from the tavern told me some rowdy men were set at the inn, refusing to leave until a certain couple arrived," he said with authority.

Gustav forced a smile, then said, "Seems you've found us." He motioned toward Sybil and Dieter. "There's the couple we're here for. If they agree to come with us, we'll be on our way, no harm done."

"To go with you is to go with death," Dieter said.

Gustav yawned. "I have the paperwork that validates my arresting these two, if you'd like to see it, Herr . . ."

"Ulrich," the guard replied. "There was a time when I ripped the fingernails off that man's hands," he said, nodding toward Dieter. "But they were exonerated for their crimes. Therefore your paperwork must be illegitimate."

"Not true, Herr Ulrich. The papers are signed by Baron Ludwig von Bergheim—my father, and—"

"We're not in Bergheim," Ulrich said firmly. "Your father's jurisdiction doesn't extend to Bedburg. I'm going to ask you to hand over your weapons or else quit my city. There are ales and whores aplenty here, but if you start trouble, I'll be forced to respond in kind."

Although Ulrich was an imposing figure, Gustav still sneered at the man. *Why does he speak so confidently when he knows he's outnumbered?*

"We've already had our taste of your whores," Adrian said from Gustav's side. "We found them lacking."

"That's a shame." Ulrich tightened his grip on his arquebus, narrowing his eyes.

Dieter quietly moved Sybil behind him. They both fixated on their child, who began waddling their way. Gustav stepped in front of the child, blocking his route. Sybil gasped.

Rowaine had her hand hidden behind her, fingering her pistol.

From his periphery, Gustav felt the presence of two hooded figures creeping in close from the other direction. His eyes darted to them but he didn't recognize either. Then he realized they were the beggars from the night before—the ones who'd been sitting against the inn's wall—the ones he'd nearly tripped over.

To the beggars he said, "Leave here, knaves," and leaned down, trying to look beneath their hoods.

A gurgling sound—then a cough—made Gustav spin around toward Alfred, his soldier to the right. Alfred wore a strange face, eyes askew, the point of a dagger sticking through the front of his neck. Blood trailed down his mouth and chin, as Mia held his forehead firmly from behind, sawing her way through his neck. "For betraying Rowaine's mutiny," she whispered in the dying man's ear.

Sputtering, Gustav lifted his gun at Mia.

Chaos erupted all around him.

From all directions bodies sprang into action. Grunts and shrieks filled the night air—weapons engaging.

Mia, her arms and clothes covered in blood, ran toward Sybil, Dieter, and Rowaine. The pirates nearest to Gustav aimed their weapons at the guardsmen, while others stood dumbfounded, unsure where to direct their wrath.

Utilizing the turmoil, one of the hooded beggars leaned in and swept the toddler off his feet.

"Peter!" Sybil yelled from a distance, seeing her son snatched by the beggar. The beggar's hood flew from his head as he ran, his homeless friend a pace behind.

As Sybil helplessly watched the unhooded beggar holding her boy scurry toward the inn, she realized it wasn't an old beggar, but a young man. A young man she knew well.

Martin Achterberg darted inside the inn with Peter safely in his grasp.

But Gustav had no time to think about Martin and the toddler. With a roar he raised his gun at Ulrich. But Ulrich already had his arquebus leveled squarely at Gustav. At the last instant, Gustav ducked behind one of his pirates.

Ulrich's blast blew a hole through the pirate's side as the pirate's gun wildly fired into the air, smoke wafting from the barrel of his weapon.

Rowaine ran to Mia, grateful that her true colors had shone despite their earlier conflicts. Amid the chaos, the two embraced.

The two guards with Ulrich engaged Gustav's pirates. One of the pirates took a guard with him, both falling on each other's swords and rolling in the mud.

Just then the inn's door flew open and the two guards Gustav had left inside, Kevan and Paul, came stumbling out backward as old man Claus chased after them with a fire poker.

Another volley of gunshots exploded—more carnage and screams followed.

One pirate grabbed at his own leg, frantically searching for his foot in the mud while his stump bled out.

Abruptly ending their embrace, Rowaine pushed Mia aside

and pulled out her pistol as two pirates headed in their direction, one of them the former first mate, Adrian Coswell.

Dieter stepped in front of Sybil to shield her from the bloodshed. He had no weapon. The two pirates split up—Adrian heading toward Rowaine, while the other pirate approached Dieter and grinned sadistically, exposing three yellow teeth, then pulled a curved dagger from his belt.

Dieter growled and charged the man.

The pirate easily sidestepped Dieter, stabbed into his arm, then dragged his dagger straight across, opening a nasty, gaping wound. Blood spurted in pulses and Dieter crumbled to his knees, wailing in pain.

Sybil covered her mouth and shrieked as the pirate crept behind Dieter for the kill, readying himself to slit the man's throat.

Sybil charged forward and screamed like a banshee. Confused, the pirate craned his neck just as Sybil barreled into her own husband, which in turn shoved the pirates legs out from under him, sending all three of them sprawling in the mud.

Back near the inn's front door, Claus—with surprising speed for his age—finally connected with one of his targets, sticking Paul in the neck with his fire poker and bringing him to the ground. The old innkeeper quickly moved on to Kevan, who was so astonished by the old man's abilities, he momentarily froze, mouth agape in utter shock at his fallen brother. With a mighty swing of his bloody poker worthy of a man half his age, Claus bashed in the left side of Kevan's skull cleanly from ear to crown.

Rowaine stepped in front of Mia to block an attack from Adrian Coswell, but Adrian already had his pistol drawn. Realizing it was too late to aim her own weapon, she closed her eyes as Adrian's gun erupted.

But Rowaine felt no pain.

Blinking her eyes open, she saw Mia fall to the ground in front of her, face-first, a thin line of smoke rippling from her back. She had sidestepped Rowaine and taken the bullet intended for her lover.

Looking down at Mia's contorted face, rage consumed

Rowaine. She quickly aimed and fired her pistol at Adrian before he could reload. But her fury caused her hand to tremble, distorting her shot, and Adrian rocked back on his heels as the bullet landed in his shoulder.

Meanwhile, in the mud, the pirate was straddling Sybil and choking the life from her. Dieter managed to crawl toward his wife but his bleeding arm failed him and he fell back down in the mud.

Rowaine's eyes shifted to the pirate atop Sybil. She only had one bullet left in her gun, and Adrian—despite his shattered shoulder—was nearly done reloading his own.

Sybil's face was turning purple, gagging and choking against the strength of the pirate's hands.

Rowaine hesitated, unsure which target to use her final bullet on—the pirate choking Sybil, or Adrian.

She fired.

The back of the pirate's skull exploded in a pink mist and he fell off Sybil, who coughed and crawled away on her elbows, bits of brain and skull scattered through her hair and torso. Dieter rolled onto his back and clutched his bloody arm, closing his eyes and shaking from the pain.

Rowaine swiveled to face Adrian. Adrian grinned, set his feet in the mud, and aimed his reloaded pistol at her.

A gunshot went off. Rowaine jumped and Adrian's eyes rolled to the back of his head. He fell backward, a large black hole smoking from his forehead.

Rowaine turned.

Daxton Wallace stood behind her, arm and gun extended. He lowered it. "Something you should have done the first moment you became captain, Row," he said, nodding his bald head toward Adrian's still body.

"Dax!" Rowaine screamed.

Daxton said, "I had to tell him where you were going, Row. I'm sorry. He had my family hostage—"

But Rowaine was already on her knees, cradling Mia.

The smoke started to dissipate from the battlefield, but the screaming dragged on.

Ulrich was the only one of the three guards still alive.

Covered in blood that wasn't his own, he was swinging an axe in circles as he backed away from two advancing pirates.

By now, the rest of Daxton's shipmates had flooded the melee and taken control of the situation. They ran past Ulrich, aiming guns and swords at their former crewmen, until the rest of Gustav's men dropped their weapons and threw their hands in the air.

Tears rolled down Rowaine's cheeks as she caressed Mia's head.

"W-why were you with them, Mia? Why did you come out here?" Rowaine asked through choking sobs.

"I-I wanted to make sure you w-were . . . okay . . . my love." Blood trickled down the corner of her mouth. She swallowed painfully. "You always wanted . . . me . . . to join you . . . yes?"

Rowaine struggled to smile. "I love you, Mia." She wiped her eyes with her forearm.

"D-don't worry, Row. I can't feel a thing." Mia shuddered.

Snot and tears poured from Rowaine, her bottom lip trembling. She wanted to say more but Mia had stopped blinking.

"Mia?"

The girl's murky gray eyes ceased their trembling, then saw nothing.

Rowaine bent down and gently rested her forehead against Mia's.

The battle around them had ended. In the background Daxton barked orders to his men. "Tie those bastards up!" he screamed. "No, you fool, not that one. Just the ones alive!" He pointed where Dieter lay in the mud. "Jerome, get over there, patch up the priest. See if the captain's woman is still alive."

"Yes, s-s-sir."

Dieter mumbled to himself.

As the smoke cleared, the aftermath of the fierce fight took shape. At least half the pirates lay dead or dying. Kevan, Paul, Alfred, and Adrian were sprawled motionless in puddles of their own blood.

Jerome, the ship's surgeon, went to check Mia, but Rowaine pushed him away. He scooted to Dieter, who mumbled something again.

"What was that, s-s-son?" Jerome asked, bending in closer.

"S-s-s . . ." He took in a breath. "Son!" he cried out, his eyes still shut. "Where is my son, dammit? And my wife! Where is Sybil?"

A grimy, hooded boy approached.

"Peter is safe, Dieter," Martin said, holding the young boy's right hand while Ava, his new friend, held the boy's left. "Your son is safe," Martin repeated. He straightened and peered around, surveying the entire field, eyes quickly darting from one wounded man to the next.

"But where's Sybil?" Martin asked.

"She was right . . . beside me," Dieter said, huffing, trying to stay conscious.

All Martin saw next to Dieter was a pirate with half his head gone. Then he noticed the imprint of a second body in the mud, along with the telltale skidding marks of a person being dragged.

"How's he to pay us?" a man in the distance yelled out. His hands were bound behind his back.

Ulrich slapped the man hard across the face as the pirate tried to open his mouth to speak again.

"What's that?" Ulrich teased.

Another pirate called out. "Where'd that dandy bastard go?"

The bound pirates were being forced to sit next to each other, at the feet of Ulrich and Claus.

Martin kept scanning the field, shaking his head.

That's when he realized what the pirates were trying to say.

Gustav was gone.

And so was Sybil.

CHAPTER THIRTY-SEVEN

ROWAINE

Rowaine leaned over, her lips twisting in disgust. The wound on Dieter's arm bled like a rushing river. It was a jagged cut from under his forearm near his wrist to the fleshy part of his arm near his elbow. He lay on his back on a table in Claus' inn, ruining the innkeeper's white tablecloth.

The room was full: Rowaine, Claus, and Daxton stood over the injured priest, while Jerome, the surgeon, sat beside him, prodding and examining the wound. Martin was also there, near the door, shielding Ava's eyes with his hands and keeping careful watch over Peter, who slept soundly on the ground near Claus' desk.

"Seems it was done with a rusty knife," Daxton said aloud, to no one in particular.

Jerome coughed. His spectacles hung precariously near the end of his nose as he poked at the wound to gauge Dieter's pain threshold.

"I need s-s-s—" Jerome began, then stopped mid-stutter and growled in frustration. Daxton patted him on the back.

"Stitching," the surgeon said at last. "I need stitching to staunch the bleeding a-and something to keep it from f-festering." He thought for a moment. "If we can find some bee-ee-ees wax"—his face bobbed up and down as he tried to say the word—"we could mix it with peroxide and make s-some s-sort of s-salve." He rubbed his forefinger with his thumb to clarify his meaning.

"Don't imagine we'll find beeswax nearby, not at this late hour," Daxton answered.

Claus disappeared into another room, returning with a roll of thread. "I don't have stitching, but perhaps you can thread this through the wound to close it. At least until we can get him to a proper doctor."

Jerome leveled his eyes at the old innkeeper. "I *am* a proper doctor, s-s-sir."

"Of course, no disrespect intended, Mister Penderwick," Claus said, bowing his head.

Jerome nudged Daxton. "Hold him down." He poured a bit of rum onto the wound. Dieter howled. Daxton latched onto the priest's arms as Dieter shivered and writhed.

Jerome handed the rum bottle to his patient, who snatched it and took a hearty swig. He gritted his teeth, then Jerome pierced his skin with a needle and started to sew the wound.

"I trust you have it from here, Jerome," Rowaine said, heading for the door.

"Where are you going?" Daxton asked, tightening his grip on Dieter to stop him from another bout of spasms.

"To find out where Gustav took Sybil."

"You're positive he took her?"

"It's the only reasonable explanation, Dax. Sybil wouldn't run off on her own without her husband and son."

Dieter lifted his head, his eyes glassy. "I'm going with you," he told Rowaine.

Rowaine hesitated. "Where?"

"To find my wife." He grimaced as Jerome continued threading his wound.

Rowaine shared a look with Daxton, who shook his head slightly. The doctor turned toward her and did the same.

"That's not a good idea," Rowaine said. "But I promise I'll find her. I brought you two into this. You have my word that I'll find a solution out."

"I can help," Dieter mumbled, sucking his upper lip.

Rowaine respected the man's resolve and regretted what she had to say next. "You'd only slow me down, Dieter. I can ride faster without you, fight better without having to look over my shoulder to make sure you're still alive. That wound will only worsen with travel. You know that."

Dieter opened his mouth to say something, but then just groaned, dropping his head back down. "Bring my wife back alive, woman," he said firmly.

As Rowaine started to leave, she heard Daxton ask the surgeon, "Still need me?"

A moment later, Daxton was beside Rowaine, outside. "*I* won't slow you down," he said.

Rowaine frowned. "What reason do you have to rescue Sybil? You don't even know the girl."

With an icy glare, Daxton said, "That's not right, Row. You're correct, I don't know the girl well. But Gustav Koehler held my wife and daughter hostage. He menaced my home. Only reason they managed to escape was thanks to your poor lady friend over there." He pointed to where Mia lay with a white sheet over her body.

Rowaine glanced over, fighting back tears. Her eyes looked downward.

"I'm . . . sorry," Daxton muttered.

Rowaine flicked her red mane from her face. "No, you're right. You have a claim on Gustav, same as me. But if you want him, you'll have to wait your turn."

"Deal," Daxton said, putting out his hand. They shook on it.

"What will you do with your crew from the *Pride*?" she asked. "They'll grow restless away from the sea."

Daxton scratched the back of his neck. "Let them. Storms have plagued the waters, so they could use a time away from the ship. The men will come back rejuvenated."

Rowaine nodded. "Very well. There's one more thing I need to do," she said, heading around the side of the inn.

Ulrich was sitting on a barrel near the far wall, flicking the blade of his axe while gazing menacingly at the pirates bound beside him. Rowaine strutted past, stopping in front of the woman sitting on a bench by the pirates. She was small and shivering, though her hands were not tied. She was the one Rowaine had seen almost constantly by Gustav's side.

"You, girl," Rowaine said harshly, "are going to tell me where your master went."

"He isn't my master," Hedda said, pushing up her spectacles, then tightening her arms around her body.

"Master, lord, lover . . . I don't care what he is. I'll kill you unless you tell me what I ask. We've wasted enough time. In my eyes, you're just as evil as he." Rowaine lifted her foot and jammed it down on the bench with a *thud*. The girl jumped. Rowaine rested her elbows on her knee, ogling the girl. *A pretty thing. Close to my age, too. In other circumstances, I wouldn't mind taking her for a frolic . . .*

Hedda recoiled. "I've never killed a man."

Rowaine searched her face. "Your eyes tell me you're lying, girl, but that's not why you're as guilty as him. It's because you never tried to stop him. Did his attractiveness sweep you off your feet? Were you just too cowardly to ever find your voice?"

Tears welled in Hedda's eyes. "I was originally employed as his father's secretary. Then Ludwig, his father, forced me to be his mistress and, before long, pushed me off on his son, Gustav."

"I don't pity you," Rowaine assured her.

"I'm not asking for your pity. If I disobeyed Gustav, he surely would have killed me."

"Perhaps you deserve it."

Hedda opened her mouth, then closed it. She met Rowaine's gaze. "Maybe you're right. I've seen him do terrible things." She paused, considering what to say next, then continued. "But there's one thing he's especially been hellbent on doing—bringing that priest and the girl to his father. That's where he'll be going, to find his father. He knows that if he brings one, the other will follow."

"I don't intend to allow Dieter to follow. Where is this Ludwig, Gustav's father?"

"In Trier, a city south of—"

"I know where it is."

Hedda gulped. "Baron Ludwig is overseeing an inquisition in the area."

Rowaine scoffed. "How noble of him."

"The witch-hunt has been going on for years. I did my research on the area and its inhabitants," Hedda said. "They're doing awful things to people down there. I heard that, in one village, they slew every female in the village, save one woman. Then moved on to the next village to do the same."

Daxton stood behind Rowaine, shaking his head. "Bloodthirsty savages."

"The rich prosper on the deaths of the weak and indefensible," Rowaine said. "Nothing new."

At that, Hedda shook her head. "Not just the weak! I've heard that no one is safe from the executioner's axe, not even noblemen and aristocrats."

"Sounds like chaos," Rowaine said, sighing. "We'd better get moving."

As Rowaine and Daxton headed back toward the front door of the inn, Hedda's voice rang out. "How do you intend to find them?"

Without turning, Rowaine said, "I was the best navigator in the North Sea. My father was—or is—a famed tracker and huntsman. I'm sure we'll manage."

Inside the inn, she glanced over at Martin and Ava leaning against the wall, arms wrapped around each other.

"They grew close quickly," Rowaine remarked. Daxton didn't reply.

Jerome followed the two to a corner of the room. "His wound is d-dire, captain."

"I'm not your captain any longer, Jerome."

The surgeon smiled, his few teeth protruding randomly from his gums. "F-force of habit. Anyway, his arm may have to be amp-amp-amput . . ." he sighed. "Cut off."

"There's nothing I can do for him. I leave it to you. Better to save his life with one arm than let it fester and kill him."

The surgeon nodded.

Rowaine glanced at the old innkeeper still hunched over Dieter. "But I'm sure Claus won't want him staying forever. Can you find him suitable arrangements?"

"*I* will," a voice called from the doorway. It was Martin. "I'll watch over him and Little Sieghart."

Rowaine walked to him, looking him up and down, then offered a dramatic bow and smiled. "Very well, sir, I leave his safety in your capable hands." She clutched his shoulder, then abruptly leaned forward and kissed him on the cheek.

Martin's pink face boiled red. He stammered, then quietly

plopped back down next to Ava, wide-eyed and weak-kneed. Ava whispered something in his ear and scuffed his head.

Rowaine stared at each friendly face in the room—Martin and Ava, Claus, Jerome, and finally Dieter.

"Stay safe, my friends," she said.

Then she and Daxton left the inn and headed for the stables.

"Wait! Let me go with you!" It was Hedda. "I want to see this through."

Rowaine looked back at the girl now standing in front of the inn's door. Since Ulrich hadn't joined her, Rowaine assumed she was not officially under arrest. She narrowed her eyes at the woman.

"I don't trust you," she said, "so I won't let you come with us. But I won't stop you from following our trail, either. Just remember, Trier's a fair distance from here, so if you don't keep up, you'll make a decent meal for the wolves."

Hedda's face went pale.

Rowaine spun back around and continued walking, navigating her way around puddles of blood-stained mud, abandoned weapons, and dead bodies. As she passed the covered body of Mia, her bottom lip trembled, but she kept her head bowed to hide her tears.

Farewell my love. May you finally find peace from this wretched world.

CHAPTER THIRTY-EIGHT

SYBIL

Somewhere in a dark void, Sybil crept toward a small foothill. Dressed in nothing but a white gown, the blackness seemed to envelop her thin body. A single, leafless tree sat on the hill, darker than black. Fog swirled through the tree. As she drew closer to the tree, she saw forms on the hill. A crow circled and landed on the tree's top branch, clutching the limb with its talons. A wolf padded along and rested on its haunches next to the trunk. It gazed up at the moon, then its eyes moved to the crow. It licked its watering lips. As Sybil approached the base of the hill, the wolf tilted its head toward her and their eyes met— the wolf's reflecting brilliant orbs of yellow. Slowly, the creature bore its fangs, sharp white teeth glistening in the darkness. Sybil let out a scream, but no sound escaped.

Sybil awoke with a start, her heart pounding.

She had no idea where she was, her nightmare clouding her reality. She felt the wind blowing through her hair, so she knew she was outside. Her throat was dry, her lips raw. She tried moving her hands, but realized her wrists were stuck together. She tried wiggling her arms, but they chafed against a rope.

From the force of the wind, she knew she was moving fast. Then she realized she was on a horse, her hands tied to the reins. Though she couldn't remember how she'd gotten there.

Her head ached. She felt hot breath on her neck and sucked in sharply.

Gustav was behind her on the same saddle, his warm body pressed into hers. His arms were extended over her shoulders, gripping the loop of the reins, spurring the horse onward.

She blinked through the darkness and saw trees whirling by on both sides. They were on a dark trail, only the moon and stars illuminating their path.

"What's going on?" she croaked, barely recognizing her own voice.

"I have you, girl," Gustav whispered in her ear.

She shuddered. She couldn't see his smirk, but felt it.

Slowly, she began piecing together the night's events.

We were standing against Gustav and his men, I remember that. Then Ulrich and the guards came from the shadows. Someone died. Mia! After she killed a man. Then everything went crazy.

Someone had my child. Gustav? No . . . he'd already set Peter on the ground. Someone else snatched him.

Martin! And that thief-girl?

And I remember Dieter . . . trying to save me.

Dieter!

"What happened to my husband?" she called out.

"Last I saw, he was rolling in the mud, nursing a nasty cut, covered in blood."

Sybil wanted to cry, but the wind kept her eyes dry. She choked on her own scratchy throat. "Is he alive?"

Gustav said nothing, but she felt his body move. A shrug, perhaps.

"And my son?"

"Your little friend took him. I don't know where."

"Where are we going?"

"To the place I've been trying to take you for weeks. Trier. Where my father is."

"What's in Trier, besides your father?"

Gustav chuckled. "Your imminent death, girl. And my imminent glory."

Sybil clenched her jaw. "Dieter will come for me. Or Rowaine—"

"I'm hoping so."

"You won't get away with this."

Gustav gripped the reins tighter. "You may have friends in Bedburg, where you've lived your life. But you have no such support in Trier. Nothing awaits you there besides a trial in front of bloodthirsty inquisitors, and the cross you'll burn on."

Despite her best efforts, Sybil's teeth began to chatter. Her body shivered. The wind was cold, but her despair colder.

Gustav speaks true. I have nothing in Trier, no one to protect me. What can I do? If Dieter is injured, how can he rescue me?

I once told myself I'd do my own rescuing, but how can I, strapped to this damned horse?

As if reading her thoughts, Gustav said, "You can plan your escape all you want, but you'll always reach a dead end, girl. I lost a lot of good men trying to capture you and, now that I have, I will not be denied."

"You didn't care about those men."

Gustav laughed. "Well, perhaps you're right."

"You only care for yourself."

"And Hedda. It's a shame she wasn't quick enough—maybe she could have joined us. But she'd only slow us down. I suppose they will hang her." He shrugged. "She had her uses." His voice was grim but edged with lustful memories.

"Is she your lover?" Sybil couldn't have cared less, but knew she had to keep Gustav talking. And not thinking. The more he talked, the more time she had to design her own plan.

"In some ways, she was," Gustav said. He sighed. "She's my father's spy. Once I bring you to him, I'll get to enjoy the things I've been owed all my life. Maybe you did me a favor, killing my brother, because I am now next in line."

Sybil frowned. "I didn't kill Johannes. Though I should have, after what he did to me."

Gustav nodded to himself. "For a moment, I did wonder if that whelp of yours belonged to Johannes—"

"My son is Dieter's."

Gustav steered the horse around a wide bend in the road. "It's no matter. All that matters is that your husband and perhaps your redheaded friend follow you to Trier. Once that happens . . ." he made a sound like he was ripping paper, "I win, and you and they . . . lose."

"What is your father giving you for bringing us to him? Wealth? Land?"

"Those, I'm sure. But also something much more valuable. A seat!"

"A seat?"

296

"In the parliament at Cologne, my dear. You are my ticket to true nobility."

Sybil stayed quiet for a while, the wind and horse hooves the only sounds she heard.

So avenging his brother's death was never his motive. It was always purely selfish. I should have known.

"Are you guaranteed this position? What if your father doesn't follow through with his promise?"

"He'll have no choice."

"Everyone has a choice, Gustav."

"You don't." At that moment, Sybil couldn't argue with that. "But I'll play your little game," he said, clearing his throat. "If my father doesn't give me the position I desire, then I'll just have to take it from him."

Sybil winced. "You'd kill your own father to further your ambition? It's no wonder everything went to your brother. Your father must have never trusted you."

A low growl reverberated behind her. She knew she'd gone too far.

"You know nothing of the Koehler family, whore. Now quiet your tongue and ready yourself for your final days. Pray, or do whatever it is you Godly folk do."

Sybil opened her mouth to speak again, but felt a sudden heat near the back of her head. Her sight went unfocused, the edges of her vision closed in.

Then darkness took her.

CHAPTER THIRTY-NINE

HUGO

"Trier is the oldest city in Germany, Herr Samuel."

Bishop Binsfeld, his hands clasped behind his back, was speaking with Tomas as they—and Hugo behind them—walked down a lavish hallway adorned with timeless relics and paintings from the early Roman times. "It wields great power within the Holy Roman Empire," the bishop explained. "Here in Trier, Archbishop Schönenberg sits on one of the most influential seats in the electorate."

"But why this sudden outbreak of witches plaguing the diocese?" Tomas asked.

Bishop Peter Binsfeld was a white-haired man with a stooped back and a soft voice. To Hugo, he didn't look at all like the bloodthirsty witch-hunter he'd been made out to be. But Hugo had also learned that looks were often deceiving—Tomas being the perfect example: His mentor looked nothing like the merciless killer Hugo knew him to be.

The bishop had yet to answer Tomas' question. They headed toward double-doors engraved with a language Hugo didn't recognize.

The bishop eyed Tomas. "You hail from . . ."

"Cologne, Your Grace. My assistant and I oversaw trials in Bedburg at the request of Archbishop Ernst. We were then sent here."

Hugo was impressed with how easily Tomas had fallen into his new role as "Inquisitor Samuel," though still a bit apprehensive about playing his own part as Samuel's assistant, "Gregor."

"Right." Binsfeld cleared his throat. "Balthasar Schreib, he leads God's glory in Bedburg, correct?"

Tomas nodded.

Binsfeld gazed up at the vaulted ceiling and tapped his chin. "He is a fine man—a Jesuit, as I remember, and a very holy bishop. I'm sure he has brought the faith back to the region."

Hugo pursed his lips. *He helped kill my father, which brought back faith, I suppose.*

They came to the double-door and waited. A man of Bishop Binsfeld's stature would never consider opening, or even knocking on, a door in front of him—he'd expect it to be opened for him.

Which is what happened. The door opened and two guards reared back their heads to salute the bishop as he walked by.

Ignoring them, the bishop continued. "While the blessed return of the faith may be the case in Cologne and Bedburg, Trier is unfortunately in turmoil. Protestants, Jews, and witches have berated us for some time. For those reasons, the archbishop saw fit to separate the three groups, and called upon me for that task. Witchcraft, superstition, and dangerous dealings have robbed the people of Trier of their livelihoods."

They were in a vast hall lit by golden crosses and elegant ornaments. Doors leading to smaller rooms lined both sides of the hall.

"The study I'd like you to see is in the third room on the left. Perhaps it will help you gain some understanding of how we do things in Trier, Herr Samuel."

"Yes, Your Grace," Tomas said, bowing his head.

"Lord Inquisitor Adalbert will be in that room, overseeing a trial."

Hugo opened the door—not wanting to wait for entry—and the trio entered the room. It was a courtroom, of sorts, though it more resembled a prayer-room in a cathedral.

Except here, the law—at least as set forth by the powers-that-be—is what is prayed to, not God.

From what Hugo had heard, secular law and God's law was one and the same in Trier.

Bishop Binsfeld moved to a back row and sat alongside other spectators. Hugo followed, then Tomas.

A young woman and her daughter stood in the middle of the

room, boxed in by several metal bars. Three men were seated at a dais on a raised platform at the front of the room.

Hugo immediately recognized the older man on the left.

That man has been in my house before! I recognize that smirk and gaunt face.

Ludwig von Bergheim, father of the man who hurt Sybil . . . Johannes.

Hugo didn't recognize the man on the right—a bald gentleman, older than Ludwig on the left, with a large crucifix hanging from his neck. His eyelids were so puffy they practically hid his eyes, making it impossible to tell if he was asleep or just listening through closed eyes.

The man in the middle was a whole different matter. He wore a mask—a plain white one, nothing sinister-looking, just a way to hide his identity. He was tall and thin, but the mask gave him an unnerving quality that sent a chill down Hugo's spine.

"Why does that man mask his face?" Hugo whispered to the bishop.

Binsfeld leaned over. "The inquisitors in Trier face hard rebuke from the many people they prosecute. None more so than that man, Lord Inquisitor Adalbert. It is to hide his face from possible retribution."

Though Hugo longed to learn from his mentors, this revelation gave him pause. *We are to be so hated in this city from the commonfolk that we'll be forced to wear masks?*

Tomas whispered in Hugo's ear, out of earshot of the bishop, "Does he hide from men . . . or does he hide from God?"

Hugo almost smirked, but kept his face expressionless, taking in the spectacle before him.

The masked inquisitor spoke, his voice high and slightly muffled. "Catherine and Anne Bartholomew, we've heard your testimony. We've heard the evidence against you both. You claim to have not stolen the cattle from Herr Armistad." He motioned to a man Hugo hadn't noticed, a rugged peasant-looking type sitting across from the two girls. The man held a shaggy cap in his hands. "And yet, Frau Catherine, the brown-spotted cattle just magically appeared in your shed? So it must have leaped over the barbed fencing of Armistad's pasture—the same barbed fencing that is taller than a man?'"

Several in the crowd chuckled at such an absurdity.

The masked man continued. "But the mysterious disappearance of Herr Armistad's cattle was not the dark omen that brought you before this council. This would not have been a matter for these courts if it weren't for your past association with others charged with sorcery." The inquisitor cleared his throat and readjusted his mask. "What was most telling and disturbing was the sudden death of Herr Armistad's daughter, following the disappearance of his cattle. And the doll found in your daughter's hands, marked with pinpricks that corresponded with the pockmarks on Armistad's poor girl's body . . ." he trailed off, shaking his head.

"These are damnable things!" he screamed. Then, softening his tone like a seasoned actor, asked, "Have you anything more to say for yourself?"

The woman held her daughter's small hand and stared at the ground. She huffed and everything seemed to leave her—her dignity, her posture, her hope. "Preserve my daughter. Please, I beg of you."

The inquisitor was unmoved. "I'm afraid only God can preserve your daughter, Frau Catherine, for even *she* cited witchcraft when asked by the prosecution. Your own daughter exposed you!"

"She's four years old!" Catherine cried. "Children will say anything!"

Lord Inquisitor Adalbert peered to his left, then right. As he did, Hugo noticed his black hair beneath the mask. "Let us vote, shall we? If guilty, state 'yay'—if innocent, 'nay.' "

Baron Ludwig von Bergheim raised his hand. "Yay."

Somewhat surprisingly, the older piest on the other side was less convinced, explaining he hadn't seen enough evidence to convict the daughter—just the mother—so he voted 'nay.'

Hugo heard an audible scowl from under Lord Adalbert's mask.

The priest's timid sentencing is probably what Tomas and I are here to replace, Hugo realized.

Adalbert raised his hand last, said 'yay,' then slammed down his cudgel. "Then it's settled. I sentence you and your daughter to death for witchcraft and sorcery, to be executed on the morrow."

The woman grabbed her daughter in a heavy embrace and howled. Unfazed, Lord Adalbert rose calmly—as if he'd just gotten up from the dinner table—and walked off.

"The daughter dies too?" Hugo asked, shocked. "She's only four . . ."

Bishop Binsfeld snorted. "Did you not hear the testimony I heard, young Gregor? And the evidence against them? Open your ears. She is as faulty as the mother, and all but killed that farmer's poor daughter." Binsfeld rose. "Come. I'll now present you to the lord inquisitor and be on my way."

Tomas and Hugo followed the bishop down the hallway into another room.

The masked inquisitor stood alone in the room, turned away from them, his mask in his hand. When Bishop Binsfeld cleared his throat, the mask went back on.

"Lord Adalbert, may I present to you Inquisitor Samuel and his assistant, Gregor." The bishop waved his hand out in a flourish. At the same moment, the door opened and Ludwig von Bergheim entered the room.

Adalbert gave Ludwig a quick glance before turning to Hugo. Even through his mask, Hugo could see his eyes narrow. "You seem young," Adalbert said. "You are the two I sent for, from Ernst, correct?"

"We are, my lord," Tomas said, bowing.

Bishop Binsfeld smiled, wrinkles forming. "If that's all, I will leave you." And with that, the old bishop shuffled from the room. Hugo was still staring at the lord inquisitor. He wore an immaculate suit, sharply tailored to his body, without question the most expensive outfit Hugo had ever seen on a man.

Adalbert's eyes fixed on Tomas. Finally, trying to break the awkwardness, Tomas said, "It has been a long journey to meet you, my lord. The bishop was telling us about the problem plaguing Trier—"

"*Problems*, Herr Samuel. Plural. Archbishop Schönenberg has allowed me any means necessary to dispose of these *problems* that have caused his country to go astray."

From the other side of the room, Ludwig added, "The Protestants, the Jews, and the witches," raising three fingers as he spoke. He leaned against a bookcase, his legs leisurely crossed at the ankles.

"Indeed, Baron Ludwig," Adalbert said. "We confiscate the lands of the plowman, and the wineries of the vintner, who we find guilty of treason, or for abetting witches, Protestants, and Jews." Through the mask, Hugo saw the man smile. "Systematically, we are ridding Trier of its blasphemers."

Tomas cleared his throat, nodding slowly. "And, er, how many—if I may ask—how many of these peopl—blasphemers have you ridded since these trials began, my lord?"

The room grew silent as Adalbert stared up at the ceiling. Then he nodded. "Ninety-eight and two hundred in the five years since the trials began."

Nearly three hundred people? Hugo almost gasped.

"And we are not done," Adalbert said.

This man is proud *of the ruination he's caused . . .*

Adalbert straightened up and walked behind the desk. "Though we've seen recent outbreaks of unruliness and sadism from the peasants, Bishop Binsfeld keeps them in check. This is a holy endeavor, after all. We are purging the infected from God's earth."

"It is holy to kill so many, my lord?" Hugo dared to ask. "What did they do?"

Tomas gave Hugo a hard stare. "Quiet your tongue, Hu—*Gregor.*" He smiled at Adalbert. "Please, excuse my unruly scribe. He's good with numbers and tallies but otherwise a bit . . . scatter-brained."

"If this is what it takes to bring Trier back into God's favor, then, yes, it is a holy endeavor to extinguish so many," Adalbert replied, ignoring Hugo's slight.

"Amen," Ludwig called from the other side of the room.

Adalbert went on. "What did they do, you ask? Well, every case is different—but perhaps it is best to ask Bishop Binsfeld about the origins of this plague. He's been here longer than I. He is also the one who created the Classification of Demons, as it were."

"The Classification of Demons, my lord?" Tomas asked.

Adalbert tilted his head. "Don't tell me you haven't heard of it, inquisitor?"

Tomas stammered. His hands began to shake. "N-no, no, of course I have. But I did not know it was penned by such a man."

"*I* haven't heard of it, my lord," Hugo blurted out, trying to divert the masked inquisitor's attention from further scrutiny of Tomas.

Adalbert squinted down at Hugo. Apparently deciding him worthy of a response, he explained. "Binsfeld realized the correlation between witches, their crimes, and the demons and devils who must be inhabiting their bodies. That woman and her daughter out there? Their crimes, for instance, were likely perpetrated from envy, which correlates with Leviathan. Lucifer controls pride, Asmodeus controls lust, Satan is wrath, Beelzebub is gluttony, Mammon is greed, and Belphegor is sloth. With this knowledge, we gain a better understanding of every individual witch we're dealing with."

Hugo was dumbstruck.

These poor souls are being tried for nothing more than superstitious words written by a fanatical priest!

His reaction, apparently, showed on his face.

"I see your skepticism, my young friend, but I figured you had dealt with this already in Cologne. If I may speak plainly," Adalbert held his hands out as if balancing a scale. "Religion is tradition, Herr Gregor. Witches are a threat to tradition. These evil folk are inhabited by devils. Devils who bring change . . . evolution . . . invention—"

"The very things tradition hates," Ludwig added, finishing Adalbert's sentence.

Adalbert glanced at the lord. "Quite, Herr Ludwig." He looked back at Hugo. "Until we can return Trier to the status quo—back to faithful tradition—we are all in danger. That is why I wear this mask. I have overseen hundreds of trials. If the peasants knew my face, they would surely retaliate at the sight of me."

Hugo crossed his arms. "Why can't *we* see your face, my

lord? We're on your side."

Adalbert chuckled. "Because I hardly know you. Prove to me that you can carry out my will—nay, God's will—and you'll learn my identity soon enough. That is a promise."

"I don't like promises," Hugo said flatly, remembering back when Sybil promised to return and his father promised to never abandon him.

Tomas stammered, again diverting attention from his young apprentice. "E-excuse my assistant. He is young and stupid."

But Adalbert was chuckling. He shook his head slowly at Ludwig. "I like this boy. Reminds me of all the mettle and audacity I once had."

Ludwig's lips formed a thin line. He glared at Hugo.

Adalbert addressed Tomas. "Now that you are here, Herr Samuel, I would like you to oversee a few small trials of your own. Bishop Binsfeld and myself will be there to aid you."

Tomas bowed. "Very well, my lord."

"Tomorrow," Adalbert added, "as a special treat, you can watch that demonic woman and her daughter burn."

Tomas glanced at Hugo before respectfully nodding.

"I look forward to . . . the opportunity . . . my lord."

CHAPTER FORTY

GUSTAV

They made the trip from Bedburg to Trier in three days instead of what normally would take five. In the process, Gustav had nearly ridden his horse to death, taking minimal stops for food and rest.

Admittedly, Gustav had enjoyed sharing his saddle with his lovely prisoner for most of the journey. But he knew that once they got to Trier that image would simply not do. He needed to project leadership. So, as they now approached the city's gates, they were on foot—Gustav in the lead, Sybil and their horse trudging along side-by-side behind him. Sybil's wrists were tied with a section of the horse's reins so Gustav could use the reins as a leash to pull both horse and captive through the streets of Trier.

As he led his horse and captive through town, Gustav took notice of the three days' worth of grime caked on his clothes and boots. It made him grimace, especially when several noblemen passed by wearing crisp, clean attire—in sharp contrast to the embarrassingly smelly, disheveled clothes he wore.

He decided that his very first item of business—well, after throwing Sybil to the wolves, of course—would be a steaming hot bath.

Except . . . maybe it would be best to wait until *after* bathing before presenting his prisoner to his father. All the better to make a good impression on the aristocrats he expected to meet.

Then again . . . the task at hand—delivering the witch to her well-deserved fate—did outweigh his personal hygiene . . . he supposed.

So, yes, dumping off his prisoner would come first, immediately followed by a nice long bath.

That decided, he began taking in the sights around him. And wasn't impressed. Having traveled extensively as his father's courier, he'd seen it all—from the dingiest cesspools of society to the most glamorous cityscapes of Germany.

And Trier fit somewhere in the middle.

They'd entered Trier through its northern gate, which was decidedly the ugliest part of town. Not at all fit for nobility. The brothels they passed stank of booze and unabashed lewdness. Plus, the women were hideous—nothing he'd ever pay for, no matter how hard they might try. A few of them even tried crowding around Sybil, but Gustav quickly tugged her away.

It didn't take long for him to realize he had no idea where he was—that he needed directions. Searching for a place to ask for help, they passed several fields with rows of life-sized crosses bearing human-shaped shells of black char on them.

A definite detractor to visitors.

Gustav's face brightened when he saw a passing patrol of guardsmen. He approached the five men—*does it really take that many to keep this place beggar-free?*—tapping one of them on the shoulder.

The guard turned to him with a sullen expression. Gustav smiled. The guard didn't. The other guards circled Gustav, frowns of suspicion on their faces.

"Excuse me, gentlemen, I am seeking the city jailhouse," Gustav said cheerfully, pulling Sybil close for emphasis—and to show off his prize.

"Which one?" the guard asked, inspecting Sybil head to toe.

Gustav raised an eyebrow. "This town has more than one jailhouse?"

The guard nodded. "On the archbishop's orders, we built us a new one. You'll find the . . . *nicer* jail in the south of town, near the Moselle's bend." He glanced at Sybil again. "But for a pretty slave like that, you're best suited to the dungeons, a quarter-mile down this road." He pointed down a street lined with brothels, taverns, and shabby inns. With a chuckle, he added, "Or you could simply unchain her here. I'm sure she'd bring some happy brothel-owner a nice bit of coin. Though she's a bit bony."

Sybil's face hardened. "I'm not a slave," she spat, eyeing the guard sharply. "Or a whore."

The guard snorted and went on his way with the rest of his group.

Gustav tugged Sybil along through the gritty streets of sin until they eventually reached a more auspicious neighborhood. The houses were white and the streets were clean. He loosened his hold on Sybil's reins a bit. After a small span of pleasant dwellings, he rounded a turn in the road and found himself back in the heart of the poor. He did his best to weave around the peasants and farmers, leering at anyone who stepped too close.

At one point, he saw an elderly woman heading straight for him, unaware, her head bent toward the ground. Though he tried to avoid her, he bumped her shoulder. The old lady bounced with a start and said, "Pardon me, young man."

Her hair was long and white and a partial veil covered her head. Sybil locked eyes with the woman. As Gustav dragged Sybil along, he noticed she remained fixed on the old lady.

He lost interest when the white-haired woman disappeared from view.

Finally, they arrived at the jail. And from the outside, it was everything the guard had described: grungy, old, decrepit. Gustav could only imagine how it must look inside.

The perfect place for this wench.

After cutting the reins and tying his horse, he led Sybil inside, the cut section of reins still wrapped around her wrists. Just past the door, an armed and armored soldier stopped him. The man was tall—almost as tall as Gustav—and held his hand near the hilt of his sword. "Who are you, and who is that?"

Gustav reached into his tunic, clinking his hand against his half-empty laudanum bottle, and located his crumpled paperwork. He presented it to the guard. "Gustav Koehler, son of Baron Ludwig Koehler von Bergheim. I am bringing you a prisoner. The rest of the details are in that paper."

Halfheartedly, the man glanced at the paper. His eyes twitched as he tried reading it. Gustav sighed.

Giving up on the paper, the guard looked up. "Bounty hunter?" he asked.

Gustav shook his head. "I've told you my credentials, good

sir."

"And the girl's charge?"

"A witch. I've transported her here from Bedburg, so that I may present her to my father. He is a current judge and barrister of the archbishop's."

At the mention of a witch, the guard stepped back. He handed the paper back to Gustav, turned, and left without another word. Gustav watched him approach another person, clearly his superior, and speak in hushed tones. A minute later he returned with his superior, a skinny man with a skinny robe and skinny spectacles.

"How is this woman touched by the Devil?" the man asked, nudging his spectacles.

"She's the daughter of the Werewolf of Bedburg. Among other things." Gustav hadn't quite figured out those "other things" yet, but he would in time. He'd been in such a rush to *get* Sybil to Trier that he hadn't concocted the exact wording of the charges against her—other than being related to a man executed for sorcery and cannibalism and murder.

Seemingly convinced, the superior nodded. "Van here will take the girl." He smiled. "And I will take you to your father."

"You are an inquisitor for the archbishop?"

The man bowed. "I am Inquisitor Frimont. Now, please follow me."

Gustav handed the reins to the armored guard and left with the skinny man, glancing one last time over his shoulder to make sure Sybil was being taken to the dungeons.

Walking down the street with Inquisitor Frimont to meet his father, they came to a two-story inn, which Gustav stopped at to clean up. While Frimont waited outside, Gustav oiled his blond hair, slicked it back, shined his boots, then ordered a fresh suit from the innkeeper, providing an extra gratuity for quick delivery.

Pleased with what he saw in the mirror, he straightened his jacket and returned outside to join Frimont.

The sun was beginning to set. They passed under the Porta Nigra, a brilliantly pillared city-gate that Frimont explained was built during Roman times. A short distance later, the Cathedral of Saint Peter came into view—a white-bricked monument to God of massive proportions, and, as Frimont described, the oldest cathedral in the country.

Just past the cathedral, Frimont stopped in front of a large complex of townhalls and courthouses, nearly rivaling in size the cathedral they'd just passed. At the bottom of a stone staircase leading up to the complex stood Gustav's father, Ludwig, arms crossed.

Gustav's heart fluttered. He hadn't seen his father in nearly a year. And even though his father had always been closer to Gustav's brother, Johannes, his brother was no longer around.

Finally, it's my *time.*

"Father! I come bearing terrific news," Gustav began, bowing low. He felt giddy, almost wishing he could sneak a quick shot of laudanum.

Ludwig peered down his beaked nose at his son. With a curt nod, he said, "Oh? And what, pray tell, Gustav, might that be?"

It pained Gustav to hear his forename, rather than "son," come from his father's lips, but he hid his disappointment.

Two men surrounded Baron Ludwig: a blond inquisitor who seemed strangely out of place in his robes, and a young assistant who couldn't have been more than fifteen years of age. Gustav ignored their disapproving stares.

"A witch, father! And a Protestant!" Gustav exclaimed.

"There are many witches and many Protestants in Trier, unfortunately," Ludwig calmly replied.

Gustav raised a finger. "None like this one." Glancing at his father's two companions, he said, "If we may speak in private, father?"

"I'm busy, Gustav. You may speak plainly here. Samuel and Gregor will stay. What am I to charge this woman you've brought me with?"

Gustav tightened his jaw. "She helped kill Johannes."

For a moment, Gustav thought he saw a hint of surprise play across his father's eyes. But it didn't last. "And you brought this woman to Trier for . . ."

"For your—no, for *our* benefit, father." He threw up his arms in frustration. "I figured it would be fitting to try her together. Also, now that she's in custody, that may well lure her husband here as well—the man physically responsible for killing Johannes! And I'm sure we can then get a confession from both of them—the witch *and* her murderous husband."

Ludwig donned a dark expression. "We won't be trying anyone together, *son*"—finally that word, and Gustav's heart jumped before quickly sinking—"though I appreciate you bringing the girl to my attention."

"F-father . . ." he murmured. "Why are you acting like this? I believed we could do this together. For Johannes."

Ludwig ignored Gustav's whining, his arms still crossed. "And what do *you* hope to gain from this, Gustav? What reward would you like?"

"This is the woman who would have married your other son. Your *favorite* son." Gustav's voice got lower, angrier. Ludwig raised a brow at his son's disrespectful tone. "I would like what you would have given Johannes, *father*." Gustav spat out the last word. Which apparently worked, for his father's demeanor softened, slightly.

Ludwig cleared his throat. "I know you would never bring this person to me charitably. You are like your brother in that reagrd. So, I ask again: What do you want, Gustav?"

Gustav had imagined this conversation many times over, and each time it had been far different from this. It angered him. After all this time, all this travel, all this hunting and searching and killing. He'd finally brought the white queen to the black king, on a silver platter . . .

And for this? To be treated like an insolent child? No differently than he'd always been treated by his father?

Gritting his teeth, Gustav said, "I want your place on the seat of parliament, old man."

Ludwig snorted. "There it is."

"I'm deserving of it."

"Are you?" Condescension reeked through the words.

"I will bring you the heads of the man and woman who

killed your son and my brother. *Then* you will see my worth. You are getting old, father. You can't wield your estate forever. You know that—who else would you bequeath it to?"

Ignoring his son's question, Ludwig said simply, "Your work here is done, Gustav. I will see the woman and determine if she is fit to stand trial, or if she is too far removed from God's grace for even that. You may watch from the pews, son, but you will not be sitting at the dais."

How I wish I had my poisons with me—even just a small dose.

For the first time in his life, Gustav felt like throttling his father.

Recognizing the wild look in his son's eyes, Ludwig discharged Gustav like a common servant. "Good day, son," then spun on his heels and marched up the steps with his two inquisitors in tow.

Watching his father walk away, for a moment Gustav felt paralyzed. But almost instantly that was replaced with a thunderous wave of roaring anger. He reached in his tunic and took a healthy chug from his laudanum bottle.

But this time it didn't quell his fury.

Gustav Koehler was now ready to take what was rightfully his.

CHAPTER FORTY-ONE

ROWAINE

Rowaine and Daxton arrived in Trier in the middle of the night.

Even so, the city was bustling with spirited activity.

Hedda was now riding with them. Halfway through their hasty exit from Bedburg—once Rowaine's nerves had settled from the battle at the inn—she'd agreed to allow Hedda to join them the rest of the way. She'd felt sorry watching the poor girl struggle to even start a fire. That, combined with Hedda's steadfast denials that she had anything to do with Gustav's plan to kidnap Sybil, had convinced Rowaine that Hedda deserved another chance at redemption.

During a meal break, Rowaine had asked Hedda, "What did you presume he was going to do, after trying to enslave those poor folk? If the *Lion's Pride* hadn't shown up to intercede the tradeship you were on, Sybil and Dieter would be dead right now." With a frown, she added, "Dieter still might be."

"I . . . don't know," Hedda said, taking off her spectacles to clean them. "I was simply supposed to keep watch on Gustav, by orders of his father."

All in all, to Rowaine, Hedda seemed harmless enough.

I don't know if I can attribute all of her misfortune to poor decisions, but I can't fault her for wanting to stay with her man . . . or her charge . . . whatever Gustav is to her.

Now, walking through Trier, they were in the midst of a wild celebration of some sort. A huge white cross was aflame, dazzling orange waves leaping and brightening their path. Daxton stopped to ask an incredibly drunk, tottering man what was going on.

"Showing our discon . . . disconten . . . we're *mad*, sir!" he hiccuped. "They can't keep killing our people without retribu-taliation!" Gripping a bottle of wine, he raised it high, waddling off to join his drunken friends.

"So, they aren't celebrating," Rowaine said. "They're . . . angry?" She scanned the streets—slobbering drunks, topless whores, she even saw a couple copulating against a barrel. It was difficult distinguishing between celebration and outrage.

"I guess that would explain the burning crosses," Daxton said, pointing at one ready to topple over on an unsuspecting group.

"I don't think they know what they want," Rowaine said, "or how to achieve it. They just want the killings to stop."

They hiked their way through the pandemonium, eventually coming to a quiet road. Rowaine sighed heavily, a worried look on her face.

Daxton noticed. "What's wrong?"

"N-no, it's just . . . I'm not eager to see Sybil's heartbreak when she notices Dieter isn't with us."

They kept walking. After a short silence, Daxton said, "It's for the best, Row."

"Call me Catriona, Dax. Rowaine Donnelly is dead."

Daxton chuckled. "Well, I'm not going to ask you to call me John." Rowaine stared at him blankly, so he elaborated. "In my mind, you're still my captain. Rowaine Donnelly will never die. So, just as my real name will never see the light of day, as far as I'm concerned, neither will yours."

They continued on quietly for a while, trying to gain their bearings in the foreign city. They refrained from asking several passing guards for directions to the jailhouse, lest they stick out in someone's mind.

Eventually, they rounded a bend where a monolithic structure loomed in the distance. As they neared it, they saw guards milling about, so assumed it was either a barracks or a jail.

They hid behind a wagon abandoned on the side of the road across from the structure. Rowaine watched for a while, until she saw several guards forcibly shoving a clearly tipsy man through the gate, convincing her this was definitely a jail.

Crouching by her side, Daxton asked, "Do you think Sybil's

in there?"

Rowaine drummed her fingers on the edge of the wagon. "It's our only hope. I have no idea where else she might be. But it's much more protected than the jailhouse in Bedburg. It's nearly the size of Amsterdam's jail."

Daxton thrust a thumb back toward the loud chaos they'd just come from. "And you wonder why?"

As she contemplated their next move, adrenaline coursed through she veins, just like whenever she bore down on an unsuspecting ship on the high seas. Then a feeling of dread engulfed her.

"If she's still alive . . ." she muttered.

Daxton leaned in. "What was that?"

Rowaine shook her head.

"Let's go to the nearest inn and plan our approach," Daxton said. "Nothing will be accomplished if we go in blind. It will just add three more bodies swinging from a rope."

"I agree with John," Hedda said, speaking for the first time. With a determined expression, Hedda was bent over, her hands on her knees like this was exactly the type of situation her analytical mind was made for.

At hearing his true name mentioned, Daxton gave the girl an icy glare. "Don't make me regret allowing you to come along."

Hedda visibly gulped.

Rowaine clenched her jaw. She knew Daxton and Hedda were right, but it wasn't easy staying put. Every fiber in her body wanted to charge ahead, slay the guards keeping watch, and save Sybil from certain doom.

If she's in there . . .

But just as quickly as it had surged, her adrenaline began to fade. Exhaustion was taking over. The swift pace of their trip from Bedburg had begun to show its effects on her mind and body. Her head ached and her vision blurred.

"Fine, we'll take refuge for the night, but only to plan things better. Sybil doesn't have much time—"

"They have to put her to trial before burning her, Row."

"And they couldn't have arrived much earlier than us," Hedda pointed out.

"I hope you're both right," Rowaine said, still not comfortable leaving despite her waning strength. Finally, she relented. Stepping from behind the wagon, she crept along the shadows, Daxton and Hedda close behind. When they were far enough away to avoid being seen by the guards, they moved onto the roadway to find an inn.

As they neared the boisterous protests, Rowaine's eyes caught the blur of the passing faces, peasants and drunkards moving in all directions. Suddenly something white and familiar caught her attention. Her face shot back around. Walking away was a small head with long white hair.

Odela?

She gasped, blinking rapidly. But the image was gone—evaporated into the crowd.

Had she imagined it?

She said nothing and continued on with her group. Several minutes later, they found an inn, a small place, but from the western window of the corner room the jail would still be in sight.

The clerk inside was delighted to greet three sober customers. Daxton approached his desk. "We'll take that corner room," he said, "the one that views west."

The clerk's smile faded. "That room is taken, my lord."

Without hesitation, Daxton pulled out his pistol, sighed, then told the women, "I'll be back shortly, ladies," and headed for the stairs.

"Don't hurt anyone, Dax," Rowaine called out, but he was already gone.

Two minutes later, a young naked couple came running down the stairs, clothes awkwardly held to shield their privates as they raced out the front door.

Daxton came back down with a wide grin on his face. "It's a shame," he said. "I had to break it up just as it was getting good."

Rowaine rolled her eyes.

Hedda said, "I'm retiring for the night, then. I'm exhausted." She started up the stairs, holding the railing tightly to guide her unsteady feet.

Rowaine wasn't ready to be cooped up in a room just yet, so she headed for the inn's front door. Daxton followed.

"Bring fresh sheets to the room," Rowaine called back to the clerk as she walked out the front door.

Once outside, the city seemed like a place on fire, though strangely fitting. Warm wind blew through Rowaine's hair, tangling around her face. Leaning against a barrel by the doorway, she closed her eyes.

"What's eating at you, Row?" Daxton asked, sidling up to her.

Eyes still closed, she said, "I want to rescue Sybil, of course, but I must remember the reasons I came here in the first place. Heinrich . . . My father . . . And I think I saw Odela heading into that crowd."

Daxton tilted his head. "The old lady you spoke of? Are you sure?"

Rowaine pondered for a moment. "If I can find Odela, I can find Heinrich. Of that I'm sure."

"Why can't we do both? Rescue Sybil *and* find Heinrich?"

She opened her eyes and stared at her friend. "This is a big town, Dax." She kicked at a rock on the ground. "What can we expect if we rescue Beele? The guards will be on us. We'll be recognized, sure as day, and I may never be able to get close enough to strike Heinrich again. Not if we rescue Sybil first . . ."

Daxton frowned. "You said it yourself, captain. She may not have much time."

Just then, the inn's door swung open and a face poked out. It was the innkeeper. With a troubled look, he said, "My lord, my lady, I spotted your friend climbing out the window when I went to put fresh sheets in your room." His head disappeared and the door slammed shut.

"Dammit," Daxton mumbled.

Rowaine chuckled, shaking her head.

But neither of them moved. They knew it was futile trying to catch Hedda.

Let her return to her abusive master. We have bigger things to do.

Daxton's face took a serious turn. "It sounds like you have a decision to make, captain. Luckily, you've always been pretty

317

good at that."

"Heinrich or Sybil? I hate that it's come to that."

A voice spoke flatly. "Perhaps I can help."

Rowaine nearly jumped out of her skin. She spun around, but only saw shadows. Squinting, she realized the voice had come from the alley next to the inn.

The speaker emerged from the dark.

Rowaine's heart raced. "It's . . . you."

A nod.

"H-have you been following me?" was all she could say.

Daxton glanced back and forth between the two of them.

"No, Catriona, I haven't been following you. I didn't know you lived. But I have been following someone *else* . . ."

CHAPTER FORTY-TWO

SYBIL

Sybil sat in her cell, her filthy dress chafing her knees and legs. She'd paced the small chamber until she felt herself going mad. She'd bitten the ends of her fingernails raw.

She'd been in a similar situation before, in another cell, in another town, so she thought she'd be able to cope with the loneliness better. But in Bedburg she'd had Dieter to comfort her. Here, there was no one.

Staring absently at the rocky stone wall, she tried to send her mind somewhere else. But the first thing that came to her almost brought her to tears.

Hugo, my dear brother.

She recalled what Odela had told her before the skirmish outside Claus' inn.

Could Hugo really be the son of that man—the son of Heinrich? The son of a slaughterer, a madman?

Why would father never tell me? Is it why he always put so much weight on my shoulders, to do right by the family, for our legacy, for our land? Because I was his true blood . . . while poor Hugo was just an afterthought?

But wasn't Hugo a family miracle? When Mother gave birth to a stillborn, then died? Hugo appeared! The only brother I've ever known. Could he possibly . . . know the truth?

No. It would have devastated him.

Or would it? Would he find relief from learning he was not the son of Peter Griswold?

If I ever see him again, what will I say? Will he think I deserted him because I knew the truth and didn't love him?

She shivered, shutting down those thoughts. There was nothing she could do, trapped here in this cage.

Who am I fooling . . .

They will kill me. I will die in this Godforsaken city.

Gustav is too clever to allow me to live. He will say anything to strengthen his future.

I can only hope Dieter and Peter will not see my burning corpse . . .

The isolation continued to churn up past memories.

Tears welled up again. Visions of the grisly battle in Bedburg rushed back to her.

So much blood, screaming, crying.

But I saw Martin escape with Peter. My son is safe—I trust Martin.

She looked through the bars to the empty cell across from her, half expecting to see Martin there, sitting in the shadows like he'd been when she was in the Bedburg prison.

Dieter was injured. Is he dead?

She gritted her teeth, slapping her fist into her thigh. She longed to do so much, see so much, to make sure everyone she loved was alive and safe. But she could do nothing.

With the darkness of her cell unchanging, she lost track of time. She was fed irregularly, so even that didn't help identify day from night.

Eventually, she heard the creaking of a door opening somewhere above her. Peering through the bars, she heard footsteps descending stairs. Boots echoing against the stone walls. Finally, a man stood just outside her cage. He grumbled to himself as he unlocked the cell, motioning for Sybil to follow.

"Where are we going?" she asked. But the man said nothing.

She was led by the arm through the hallway and up the stairs. Then through a back corridor which she wasn't sure was still underground or not. Then she climbed another set of stairs.

The sudden brightness blinded her. Sunlight! Showing through an open window at the top of a domed room.

As her eyes adjusted, she took in the scene. It was a courtroom, perhaps. Pews were lined up behind her with people seated. Scores of faces stared at her, some eager, some sad, some bored.

From the far back pew, Gustav Koehler stared at her, his arms crossed. Oddly, his expression wasn't what she expected. She thought he'd be gleeful, watching her delivered to her death sentence. Instead, he seemed troubled and upset.

She turned away. A guard led her to a small stand in the center of the room, facing a dais with three chairs on it. In the center chair sat a strange man wearing a white mask.

Sybil blinked hard. She recognized the other two faces on both sides of the masked man. To the left was Ludwig von Bergheim, the baron who tried to force her to marry his son, Johannes.

The catalyst to this whole mess of events.

On the right sat a man she recognized as Heinrich Franz's former right-hand man.

Tomas, I believe his name was.

And standing behind Tomas . . . Sybil gasped. It was't possible. But there he was. She blinked several times to make sure she saw correctly.

Hugo!

He stood without expression, like a statue, unblinking, his hands folded in front of him.

He looked so much . . . older. His face was still smooth, but his shaggy hair was longer. Most disturbing, his eyes no longer held their joyful innocence.

For a fleeting moment, Sybil saw his expression falter, a flash of . . . something . . . Regret? Sadness? Despair? Or was it her imagination? Whatever it was lingered for a second and then was gone. Replaced with a stone-cold indifference, as if she didn't exist.

Sybil wanted to say something, but two guards shoved her into the witness stand, boxing her in.

All eyes set upon her.

The man with the white mask peered down at a scroll and spoke, his voice muffled through the mask. "Sybil Griswold, you have been brought here from Bedburg on a bounty by Gustav Koehler."

Sybil heard Gustav snort behind her.

The man in the mask glared up at Gustav, cleared his throat, then continued. "You've been charged with sorcery, witchcraft, and murder. Witnesses will attest that you left Bedburg to flee your murderous crime and just punishment. You arrived in England, and under the protection of the queen joined a cult of

Protestant sympathizers called the 'Elizabeth's Strangers.' You lured a faithful Catholic man—a priest, no less—to the arms of the Lutheran heretics. And, perhaps worst of all, you are the daughter of the Werewolf of Bedburg."

Folks gasped from the pews, murmuring to themselves.

The man straightened his mask. "Gustav Koehler, please stand."

Sybil looked over her shoulder to see Gustav rise proudly, his arms still crossed over his chest.

"Where did you find this woman, Herr Koehler?"

"Among a small country-shire in Norfolk, England, lord inquisitor. She was attempting to teach the folk there the ways of Martin Luther—to pollute the minds of the children." Gustav exaggerated a hefty sigh. "I'm only saddened that I couldn't bring her away from Norfolk before her treachery had been inflicted on those innocent boys and girls."

The masked inquisitor looked to his side. A scribe sat in a corner, writing furiously. "Let the record make clear of Sybil Griswold's whereabouts prior to arriving in Trier. Herr Koehler, thank you."

Gustav sat. The inquisitor turned to his right. "Ludwig von Bergheim, how is this woman affiliated with your family?"

The baron leaned on the table and coughed. "She was to marry my eldest son. Although my family was in better standing, Johannes—my son—felt a liking to this woman." He spoke deliberately, as if trying to hold back tears. "I agreed to give the Griswolds land in exchange for cattle and pigs."

Sybil almost rolled her eyes.

"Did that marriage transpire?"

Ludwig shut his eyes. When they opened, they burned with a fire. He pointed at Sybil. "She and her Devil-driven husband killed my son in cold blood. And then fled Bedburg."

"I can attest to that," spoke Tomas, seated on the inquisitor's left. "I can attest to the woman fleeing Bedburg."

Sybil gazed at the man and saw Hugo's shoulders tighten.

Turning to Tomas, the inquisitor asked, "Oh, Herr Samuel, you know this woman?"

Tomas nodded. "I was under the employ of the chief

investigator of Bedburg at the time. She fled the town during the height of a battle with Count Adolf's Protestant army. At the time, she was imprisoned at the town jailhouse and under investigation."

"For?"

"For colluding with the Protestants, trying to raze the town, my lord. It was my master's belief that she had given pertinent information of our defenses to the enemy."

"Is that so?" the investigator said, scribbling something on his parchment. "I suppose we should add treason to the list, if that is the case."

"My lord, this is all extraneous." Gustav was on his feet again, pointing at Sybil. "This woman is the son of the Werewolf of Bedburg. That man's infernal blood runs through her veins. She is the daughter of that beast!"

"I heard that the Werewolf of Bedburg was never found . . . that there had been a mistake in the investigation!" one man yelled from the pews.

Sybil turned to see who'd spoken on her behalf, but didn't recognize the man.

"I heard the same," another man added.

A chatter of lowered voices began spreading through the courtroom.

"Silence!" the inquisitor boomed. "We have heard witnesses divulge her treason, her murder, and her devilish nature—marrying and breeding with a man of God. Her bloodline is irrelevant at this point. She has quite clearly strayed from God's grace, so I would now like to hear her defense. What do you say to us, Sybil Griswold. And, more importantly, what do you say to God?"

The brooding rage building inside Sybil blazed through her eyes. With a low, steady voice, she began.

"I have heard my name and the name of my family slandered for years. This is nothing new to me—I heard it in Bedburg, among the fields and streets. I've heard it in this courtroom. It's true, my husband and I eloped to England. We did so to escape persecution. For my husband's conversion, he would have hanged. For whom I was born to, I would have burned. So I say to you, gentlemen, what was I to do? I have killed no one, I have lured no one, and I have brought no ill to any man. But that makes no difference. I was seen as guilty before I stepped into this room. No level of defense will change that."

"You are guilty because God's truth has shone upon you!" Gustav yelled from the back of the courtroom.

Sybil spun around, staring daggers at the man. She thought she saw him momentarily cower at the face of her gaze, which gave her a small measure of satisfaction.

Since a little girl, Sybil had trod delicately when confronted with God's people. She was raised to fear them. Then she married one. A man she loved without hesitation, with all her heart. But scanning across the hard eyes of most of those in the courtroom, she suddenly realized where all the grief she'd suffered had come from. And in an astounding moment of clarity, it all made sense. Her misery, her constant persecution, her current situation—it had all derived from a single source. She turned back around to face her inquisitor.

"You ask what I say to God? I'll tell you, gentlemen. I say that God is a poison, masked as an antidote to suffering, fed to already-sick men. And once the venom is inside you, you need more to feel satiated." With a twisted snarl she pointed at each man on the dais—save her brother—one by one. "Then, like all sickness, it spreads like a plague to other innocent folk. Slowly eating away until you become a husk of false promises. And you die, empty and broken and weak from the poison. God is a poison," she repeated. "And priests are His alchemists and administers—the assassins of reason."

A hushed silence filled the room, as if everyone was holding their breath. Sybil inhaled loudly, then dipped her head, wiping spittle from her chin.

Out of the corner of her eye, she saw a frozen look of shock on her brother's face.

After several long moments of silence, the crowd seemed to come alive all at once, yelling, screaming, jeering, cursing the heretic she-devil before them.

Finally, when the cacophony reached a fevered pitch, the masked inquisitor stood and raised his arms.

"You are indeed a cursed witch, you succubus—tinged with Lucifer in your eyes! Take this woman away, guards. She'll burn on the morrow! Bring the biggest cross we have, and the wheel, and the rack!"

Sybil sat in her cell again, staring at the same wall, this time lost and despondent. All hope was gone. She was resigned to her fate. She wasn't ashamed of her outburst. It was something all of them probably believed at one time but never had the grit to say.

Though she couldn't help wondering . . . had she tried a different approach, might the result have been different?

She shook her head. *That would have never happened. One of the judges was the same man whose son Dieter killed! He alone would have persuaded the others.*

But why Tomas? Why was he so eager to curse me as well? He seemed like a reasonable man the few times I met him. Eager to please Heinrich, perhaps, but not vile.

I suppose he was paid to spout those lies.

She heard the creaking door somewhere above her open. Soft footsteps padded down the stairs, then across the hallway.

Hugo stood on the other side of her bars.

Sybil vaulted to her feet and lunged toward him.

"Hue!" she screamed.

"Why did you say all that, Beele? You doomed yourself."

Sybil clenched her eyes shut. Then she looked at him, her face twisted in anguish. "Are you angry with me?"

A million thoughts flashed through her mind—all the things she'd wanted to tell her dear brother for the past two-and-a-half years, now drifting away, replaced with heartache.

"Does it matter, Beele? I'm not the same person I was when you left me."

"I swear, my brother, I never meant to hurt you. I never meant to leave you or our father. I was swept away in—"

"You did hurt me. It may not have been your intent, but it happened. I had to grow up fast. We lost our home, Beele. We lost everything after father . . . I was so confused . . . I had no one. The one person I cared about, the one person I needed most, deserted me."

Tears were rolling down Hugo's soft cheeks. Sybil wanted to reach through the bars and wipe them away. But he was too far away, both physically and emotionally.

She began sobbing. "I'm sorry, Hue. You're right. My excuses are worthless."

He brushed away the droplets from his face. "Now I'm here, under false pretenses, and I have no idea who I can trust."

"You can trust me, Hue!"

He scoffed. "You'll be dead tomorrow!"

Sybil shrank back.

In a lowered voice, he said, "That time has come and gone, Beele. I just came to say goodbye. I can do nothing for you. I just don't understand why you doomed yourself with your own words."

"They would have killed me either way, Hue. You don't understand what's going on around us."

"You're right Beele, I don't understand. And unlike you, maybe I don't have to."

Sybil opened her mouth, hestitating. If this was the last time she'd ever see her brother, he deserved to know his true lineage.

But will that really help anything? What will he gain from knowing the truth? It would only confuse and sadden him more.

"What is it?" Hugo asked, tilting his head.

Sybil smiled warmly, wiping her face. "It's nothing, Hue. I'm simply admiring the man you've become. I'm . . . I'm so sorry I couldn't do more for you, my brother. That I wasn't there for you when you needed me."

Hugo started to say more, but then just clutched one of the steel bars. Sybil put her hand over his. They stood like that for a moment, regarding each other.

Then Hugo turned to leave.

"I love you, Hue. If there's one last thing I can promise you—a promise that I can keep . . . it is that I love you and always have and always will."

Hugo paused in his tracks, closed his eyes for a brief moment, then walked away.

*   *   *

Hours passed, but Sybil, lying on the floor, remained awake. Her eyes were closed and behind her lids she saw the red and green blending into the black. She began mentally checking off the names of those she loved, realizing her list was short.

Peter—both her son, and the father he was named after.

Dieter.

Hugo.

The four men in her life. The only ones that mattered.

Her mind raced through various scenarios. What if she'd never met Dieter? What if she'd tried to defend herself in court? What if she'd returned for her brother?

But as with all hypotheticals, it was a futile, depressing exercise, serving no purpose other than making her feel worse.

After a time, she heard the door at the top creak open again.

She jolted upright, her heart pounding, her vision fuzzy.

Is it already morning? Could the last of my time have passed that quickly?

Boots stomped down the stairs. Each new step spelled her doom.

As the bootsteps drew closer, the form of a large man appeared. Her body trembled and her heart seized in her chest.

Something landed at her feet with a plop.

A dark hood. More like a sack that might hold apples.

Her eyes moved up to the figure near the bars.

"Put that on, girl. It's time to go."

CHAPTER FORTY-THREE

HUGO

The day of Sybil Griswold's execution was a bright and crisp morning—a respite from the recent rains. The town square of Trier was crowded with throngs of eager and bloodthirsty citizens. Peasants, beggars, and nobles congregated together to witness their one common interest: the execution of the Daughter of the Beast.

Hugo's first thoughts were tinged with anger.

How could my sister have allowed herself to end up here? How could she let herself be caught? Is she so gullible as to believe any man with a golden coin?

He frowned. Staring out at the angry mob, he recognized the irony of his thoughts. Here he was, his dark robes covering his filthy jerkin and tunic, holding his leather-bound notebook to write down anything that Tomas demanded of him.

I am a fraud . . . I am the gullible one. What am I doing here?

Is there nothing I can do to save my own sister?

He took a seat and put his hands and head between his knees, trying to block out the thunderous crowd. As the morning dragged on, the mob swelled. Huge white crosses had been set up along the perimeter of the square to ward off any evil spirits that might attempt to intervene in the "justice" about to be carried out.

The conflicted thoughts in Hugo's mind intensified.

How can I just sit here while my sister burns?

I never bargained to be a witch-hunter.

All Hugo ever wanted was to distance himself from his old life, from his juvenile gang of thieves. To learn a trade—one that would give him honest work.

As an orphan and a thief, he had imagined that working the

jails might be suitable for his lifestyle. Which is how he met Ulrich—the man who'd tortured his father and sister years before.

What did I ever see in that bastard? How could I let him mold me?

Hugo took a deep breath, holding it in for a moment before blowing out hard.

But I sought him out—Ulrich.

And he warned me from the beginning that his was not a pleasant life. I should have heeded his warning.

Now I am here, staring into the wild eyes of madness itself.

What these people see as entertainment . . . is my sister, *dammit! Yet I am powerless and can do nothing.*

He looked to his right. Joining him on the raised platform was Tomas, Ludwig von Bergheim, Bishop Binsfeld, and a robed man who he assumed to be Archbishop Schönenberg—the mastermind of this fiasco.

Hugo seethed quietly at Ludwig, sitting so properly and primly, proud of his "accomplishments," watching the spectacle unfold before him.

A wooden white cross on top of a scaffold was wheeled out through the crowd and delivered to the middle of the square.

Hugo continued staring at Ludwig, who paid him no mind.

She had no one to defend her . . . not even her brother.

He closed his eyes and rubbed his temples, then his eyelids.

"What's the matter, boy?" Tomas asked, leaning over.

"What do you *think* is the matter?" Hugo said, speaking through his hands. "My sister is about to be burned before my eyes."

Tomas leaned back and arched a brow. "I thought you never cared for her? All I've heard from you is outrage at her abandonment of you."

Hugo finally looked up at Tomas with red-rimmed eyes. "It doesn't mean I wish her dead. She's my *sister.*"

Tomas put a hand on Hugo's knee. "You heard the testimony and evidence—"

"It was complete drivel. She never had a chance."

Tomas sighed. "Nonetheless, she isn't going to get out of this. If you'd spoken up during the testimony, our identities would have been revealed. *We* could be the ones tied to a cross right now."

"We deserve it," Hugo muttered. He remembered thinking a similar thought right before shoving Severin off the mountain. Try as he might to forget that night, it just wouldn't go away.

I'm as much a murderer as Ulrich or Tomas or Heinrich or Gustav or the Lord Inquisitor Adalbert.

And now I'm unable to even save my own kin . . .

He remembered a time when life was so simple.

Work the farms during the day, alongside father. Play in the fields when work was finished. Watch the sun set. Watch the moon rise. Eat and laugh at the dining table with father and Sybil.

Where did it all go wrong?

The crowd hushed as Lord Inquisitor Adalbert marched up the dais steps, parading forth like Jesus giving His Sermon on the Mount.

"We're here to witness the execution of Sybil Griswold, a young but powerful witch hailing from Bedburg. She is a murderer—"

Hollers and jeers erupted from the crowd.

"Satan's whore and succubus—"

People lifted rocks and heads of lettuce, shaking them.

"A traitor to Christianity—"

The jeers grew louder, fusing together like rumbling thunder.

Inquisitor Adalbert raised a finger to the sky, silencing the crowd. He knew his power and worked the stage masterfully.

"She is the Daughter of the Beast. For her transgressions, she must die." He faced the sky and clasped his hands together. "God, please cleanse this evil soul and forgive her trespasses. She will no longer stain your beloved earth with her darkness, so I ask that you admit her spirit to your side. Show her the path of forgiveness."

As he spoke, the crowd collectively raised their arms.

Hugo watched the mob grow frenzied and shook his head in disgust.

Like wolves in sheep's clothing . . .

He gazed across the obscene display—the "annointed" on the dais, the nobles and ladies below the platform, the hooded executioner next to the pile of kindling, the cross in the center.

A grand and genuinely evil play.

I am caught in the company of wolves.

And always have been.

His feet tapped the wooden floorboards. Tomas glanced at him, but Hugo did not look back. Once again the crowd parted like Moses at the Red Sea as two guards led a hooded figure in a white dress toward the cross.

The crowd hissed and booed, then started throwing their lettuce and rocks, forcing the guards to shield themselves with their hands.

Arms crossed, Lord Inquisitor Adalbert sat on his large, straight-backed chair like a king surveying the progress of his carnival.

Hugo could see the devilish grin beneath the man's mask.

"What will you do?" Tomas asked, noticing Hugo's shaking hands.

Hugo's head began swaying. "I can't let her die like this. She doesn't deserve it."

The guards led the hooded woman to the stairs in the center of the square. She did not struggle as Hugo had seen others do during previous executions.

She walked calmly, one foot in front of the other, up the stairs. She allowed her hands to be tied behind her back, then secured against the thick poll of the cross.

She's resigned to her death.

Hugo gritted his teeth and jumped from his chair. The others on the dais glanced over. Tomas tried to tug Hugo back down but Hugo shoved him away. His heart beat in his throat. The crowd's thunder was too loud for Hugo to hear whatever Tomas was trying to tell him.

With the woman securely fastened, the hooded executioner faced the dais and waited for a nod from the lord inquisitor and the archbishop.

In unison they both nodded.

The executioner took his lit torch and in a fluid motion flung the hood from the prisoner's head.

Cheers swept through the square.

Hugo covered his eyes with sweaty palms.

"She shows her true form!" a voice in the crowd bellowed.

"The crone is revealed!" chimed another.

Hugo peeked through his hands.

Surely his eyes had deceived him!

An old lady with long white hair stood on the scaffold, tied to the cross.

Hugo stared in disbelief.

The executioner bowed and moved the torch over the kindling.

Lord Inquisitor Adalbert leaped from his seat, both hands gripping the arms of his chair. "Wait! Hold that torch!" he screamed, but his voice wasn't loud enough through his mask to pierce the roar of the crowd.

The dry twigs and hay and wood burned and hissed black smoke as the structure exploded in a blaze, instantly surrounding the woman and the cross.

Hugo clutched the arms of his chair, his mouth open in shock as the flames licked at the old woman's feet.

When she caught fire, she did not scream.

Not at first. Not until the flames reached her long white hair.

And then she howled.

So intensely, so enduringly, with such acute agony, it completely hushed the crowd.

The cross blazed like a beacon. The old woman's blood-curdling cries lingered for an eternity, then faded into the smoke. The woman's body crumpled as it transformed into a glowing, hideous skeleton, frozen forever in a silent scream.

Hugo and Tomas exchanged a look, both wide-eyed and confused.

"W-what in God's name just happened?" Hugo asked in a low voice. "Where's Sybil?"

Tomas was focused elsewhere. "I'm not sure, but someone isn't pleased with the outcome . . ." he nudged his chin over his shoulder.

Hugo looked past Tomas. The center chair on the dais was empty.

The lord inquisitor of Trier was gone.

CHAPTER FORTY-FOUR

GUSTAV

Gustav's mouth dropped open when the veil came off, revealing an elderly woman he didn't recognize. Then he remembered. He *had* seen her before. The previous day, while leading Sybil to the dungeons.

As the crowd pushed into him, he tried to get away but was boxed in tightly. He elbowed a man in the head, eager to escape the violent show.

No one else had seen what Gustav saw. Everyone else had been focused on the roiling flames as they engulfed the woman's melting body.

But Gustav had seen Lord Inquisitor Adalbert jump from his seat, retreat from the dais, and run down the stairs.

Something was terribly wrong.

Gustav had no idea what it was, what was going on, how Sybil had been replaced with this old woman burning before him, and why the lord inquisitor had taken off.

All he knew was that he had to get away.

He raised his arms and spun the other way—the lone man in the crowd pushing against the grain. He reached out, roughly shouldering others aside. Finally, he was out of the madness.

As he moved farther away, a terrible premonition inched up his spine.

He headed for the nearby inn, next to which he'd stowed his stolen horse. Hedda would be at the inn. She didn't have the stomach to watch another human burn.

He hurried down the cobblestone road, picking up speed as he went, the unmistakable stench of burning wood and flesh wafting in the air. He turned a corner and cut through an alley, looking over his shoulder every few seconds. He felt like he was being watched. But that was impossible.

He came to the inn and burst through the door, startling the front desk clerk.

"Back so soon, sir?" the clerk said, but Gustav surged past and hurried up the stairs, two at a time. He rushed to the door and burst in, the sudden breach nearly knocking Hedda out of her chair. She'd been writing something on a piece of paper.

Probably a report to my father. Gustav grimaced.

"I could hear the screams from the window," Hedda said, repositioning herself on the chair. "Why are you not out celebrating with the rest of the townsfolk?" she asked, her tone condescending.

He reached into his tunic, found his bottle, and finished off the rest of the liquid.

Hedda shook her head in disgust. "That stuff will be the death of you."

"It calms my nerves, woman."

"It changes you, Gustav. It *has* changed you."

Gustav growled and swept past her. He'd purchased a new set of clothes prior to the execution. He started throwing his possessions in a bag.

"What are you doing?"

Stumbling against the edge of the bed, he hit his shin and groaned. The drug had already taken hold. He couldn't find the right words. "We have to go—have to get out of here. My father will never give me the things I deserve. Not until he's dead and buried."

Hedda tilted her head, watching him move in a frenzy. "You're paranoid, Gustav. Another side effect of that terrible—"

"Enough, woman!" Gustav thrust his finger at her. "I said we have to quit this place. Let's go. Pack your things."

Hedda shrugged. "I have nothing to pack."

Gustav dismissed her with a wave of his hand.

"And I'm not going with you."

Without pausing or turning, he said, "And why is that?"

"You know why. I must report to your father."

"And what will you tell him?" His hands were clenched, buried in the sheets of the bed.

"Only of the last few weeks I've traveled with you. Nothing that will come as a shock to you, Gustav."

He returned to the bag he was packing. "Will you tell him about Norfolk? About the taxman and our false identities?"

A long pause followed. He recalled that time in England. *If she mentions the taxman in her report, she'll have to add how she struck the man with a shovel. I never asked her to do that.* She *killed Timothy Davis. I only poisoned him.*

But I can't let my father learn those things.

He felt his eyes grow large, the drug piercing through his body stronger than ever before. Everything began to spin around him. He slapped himself, trying to shake the murderous rage from his mind.

Reaching into his waistband, he pulled out his knife and turned toward Hedda.

"I can't let you do that," he said, his face twisting into a manic snarl.

But Hedda was gone.

He'd been so focused on his own escape plan, he'd lost track of everything and now she'd vanished from the room like a ghost.

"That bitch," Gustav growled, running for the door. He raced to the stairs and peered down. The front door of the inn stood wide open.

"Where'd she go?" Gustav yelled down to the innkeeper.

"Out the door, sir. In a hurry."

Gustav punched his knife into the railing of the staircase, struggled to free it, then ran back to his room.

I'll get that bitch before she destroys my legitimacy! But for now, I must get out of here.

He closed his bag and dashed out of the inn, flicking a coin to the clerk on his way out. He headed for the stable, eager to leave the memory of Trier behind.

Gustav kicked the haunches of his mount and leaned into its neck, gripping the reins tightly. He'd left the northern gates of

Trier just as night fell, the moon already bright in the sky.

As he'd left the city, he'd heard people talking. Of the strange trial, of a witch morphing from young to old as she burned.

It had all happened so quickly. After the woman turned to ash, the archbishop dismissed the swelling crowd back to their homes, announcing the execution was over, then had descended the stairs and vanished.

It left a sour taste in the mouths of the townsfolk. People were confused. This was not like the executions they were accustomed to. There had been no post-burning celebrations. No long-winded, religious proclamations from those on the dais.

Gossip and doubt spread fast.

"The inquisitors are losing their edge and power."

"The inquisitors have lost the faith of the people."

"They kill for no reason—surely not for God."

"We're sick and tired of this. They rope us in with the entertainment, but all the while our crops are confiscated and our vineyards neglected."

"They wish to take everything from us. We're more destitute now than we were a year ago."

Things quickly snowballed and general upheaval took hold.

Gustav left town before things got too rebellious. He rode in the darkness, alone, down the main northern road on his way back to Bergheim, his home.

He'd be safe there.

As he rounded a curve, he slowed his horse to a trot. Trees started to close in on the road. Before long the canopies would block out the moonlight and stars.

He noticed something ahead. He blinked several times to make sure it was real. A carriage was blocking his path, sitting crossway in the middle of the road.

He debated whether to veer off and head into the woods, but knew it was just the drugs making him paranoid. It was only a carriage. He lightened his breathing and reined his horse to a stop.

Two guards came from around the side and approached Gustav.

"Name, sir?" one of them asked. He wore a leather jerkin, a helmet covering his eyes, and had an arquebus stuck in the dirt at his side.

"What's going on here?" Gustav asked.

"The Daughter of the Beast has escaped town. We're checking all roads leading out. So, what is your name, sir?"

Gustav straightened his back and puffed his chest out proudly. "I am Gustav Koehler, son of Baron Ludwig von Bergheim."

The guard shared a look with his comrade.

The carriage door opened and a man stepped down. He was tall and wore a white mask. Gustav's face paled.

"Ah, Herr Koehler," Lord Inquisitor Adalbert said through his mask. "Why are you leaving Trier?"

Gustav's heart hammered. He gulped and said, "Er, family matters I must attend to in Bergheim. I'm sure you understand."

Adalbert nodded. The mask on his face shifted awkwardly as his head moved. "Quite," he said, stepping forward. Gustav's horse snorted and took a step back.

After a momentary pause, Gustav said, "If that is all, my lord, I will be on my way. I ride in urgency."

Adalbert put his hand on the neck of Gustav's horse. "Before you do, I'll need to ask a few questions of you, Herr Koehler."

"Why is that?"

"Because you brought Sybil Griswold to this town. You were with her for the week prior to her arrival."

"And?"

"You might have information about her whereabouts."

"I swear I do not."

"You might know things about her that you don't realize, Herr Koehler. Please, join me in my carriage. It will only take a few moments."

Gustav swallowed hard.

What do I have to fear? I'm a nobleman of a respectable house. This man is a mercenary-for-hire. A sell-sword going from city to city acting like he owns the world.

He shook the fear from his mind.

"We will tether your horse to our carriage. You will be on your way expeditiously," Adalbert said, gesturing toward the carriage.

"Very well." Gustav dismounted and followed the inquisitor into the black coach.

Inside, they stared silently at each other, though Gustav could see little more than a phantom behind the mask. As much as he tried to appear confident, staring at that lifeless mask unnerved him. He couldn't tell whether the man inside was smiling, frowning, or plotting.

The wheels squeaked as the carriage began moving.

"W-where are we going?" Gustav stammered, looking frantically to his side. But curtains covered the windows.

"To my scribe, sir," Adalbert answered, folding his hands in his lap.

They traveled a short distance before the coach began bumping roughly. Gustav realized they'd driven off the road.

They continued a while further. Then the carriage stopped.

Adalbert stepped out and held his hand out for Gustav.

"Why must we go outside? We'll catch a chill," Gustav said.

Adalbert chuckled. "Please, follow me, Herr Koehler. It will only take a moment."

So Gustav followed. As casually as possible he eased his hand to the back of his waist and felt the comforting wood of his knife's hilt.

They were somewhere in the woods—surely far from civilization. The blooming trees overhead blocked the moon, save for a few tendrils of murky white. Finally, they came to a clearing. Gustav breathed easier.

The clearing rose to a small hill. At the top of the hill stood a lone tree. An odd-looking tree, leafless, with gnarled limbs and twisted branches. As they climbed the hill, Gustav's stomach sank.

A bird cawed in the distance. Gustav glanced up. The black outline of a large crow circled the tree.

Lord Inquisitor Adalbert stopped at the base of the tree. The crow landed on an upper branch.

Adalbert reached to his face and removed his mask. It fell to the ground.

Lord Inquisitor Adalbert was a black-haired, middle-aged man with a gaunt face and sunken cheeks. His wispy black mustache twitched in the breeze, his eyes gray and piercing.

"You don't know me, Herr Koehler," the man said, his voice much firmer without the mask. "But I am a friend of your father's." He ran his fingers over his mustache. "We did a bit of business in Bedburg together, when I was chief investigator for a time."

Gustav tilted his head. He reached behind him and gripped the knife in his belt. His eyes shot to his left, then his right as something rustled in the bushes.

Forms appeared, close to the ground—one, then two, then maybe more—blacker than the night sky or the crow in the tree.

What started as a soft buzzing noise grew to low growls. Small yellow dots shined from the black forms. Gustav pulled his knife from his belt.

The unmasked man's thin smile turned to a frown. His face hardened around the edges, and the years seemed to show.

"It is your fault she died," the man said. "You took the one thing I cared for in this world. If you'd never brought Sybil Griswold to this forsaken place, Odela would still be alive."

"There was nothing I could do! I didn't know that would happen!" Gustav shouted, faltering as he tried stepping back.

The forms closed in, snarling and snorting.

Gustav spun around.

"It is your fault she died, Gustav Koehler," the man repeated.

The black snarling shapes took form.

Wolves.

They leaped onto Gustav with a frenzy, claws and teeth ripping viciously.

Gustav tried to run, tried to swing his knife, but it was futile.

The wolves had no fear. They tore at his clothes and skin.

A giant maw latched onto his arm, driving him to the ground.

With pale, lifeless eyes, the lord inquisitor stared down at him, watching impassively as Gustav writhed and howled like the woman on the cross.

He could hear his own flesh ripping.

The last thing Gustav heard were the wolves howling back—
or it might have been the man controlling them.

And then everything went red.

CHAPTER FORTY-FIVE

As the hood was ripped from her head, Sybil sucked in her breath. She blinked a few times to gain her bearing. The night was calm. A soft breeze blew through her sticky hair. Someone was holding her by the elbow, leading her along a roadway.

She turned and there, off in the distance, was the northern gate of Trier.

She turned toward the person leading her and her face lit up. Rowaine smiled back.

She looked behind her and saw two more familiar faces grinning back at her. One of them was Daxton Wallace.

The other was Georg Sieghart, Rowaine's father.

"H-how?" was all Sybil could muster.

"My father says he was tailing Frau Odela for some time," Rowaine said.

Georg put a hand on Rowaine's shoulder. "You've done well, Beele, bringing Odela to Trier. She was a much bigger part of this story than you might realize. I learned of her while recovering in Rolf's—well, Heinrich's—estate two years ago."

"Odela?" Sybil asked. She had no idea the old woman had burned in her stead. "What of her?"

"I was waiting for her to lead me to Heinrich," Georg explained. "She appeared here once before, a few months ago. I didn't catch her with Heinrich, but I knew she'd be back." He glanced over his shoulder, making sure they weren't being followed. The road they were on was dark and winding—cut away from the main thoroughfare. "Keep your legs moving."

Sybil was still confused, but did as Georg instructed. Memories of Georg played in her mind. He hadn't changed much. His injured left arm seemed to work again, and he still had the rugged beard and tough look of a seasoned huntsman.

"I became a guard for the dungeons you were placed in, to

hide in plain sight, if you will." He chuckled. "I obviously didn't plan to see you in those dungeons. Perhaps it was fate. But I found Cat . . ." His lip trembled, his wet eyes glistened in the dark. "I had no idea she was alive. It's been a blessing ten years coming."

"You were waiting for Heinrich to play his hand?" Sybil asked.

Georg nodded. "It didn't take long for me to realize he was the lord inquisitor. How he came to that position, I have no idea. I suspect Archbishop Ernst had something to do with it."

"But wasn't Heinrich . . . your friend?"

Georg snorted. "He betrayed my trust and tried to blame me for the murders in Bedburg. Does that sound like a friend? When he vanished, my name remained tarnished."

"You *did* kill Uncle Konrad, father," Rowaine said flatly.

Georg pulled his beard and raised a finger. "True. Your uncle was a vengeful man, Cat. He blamed me for your mother's death . . . and for *yours*. He tried to kill me—I had to defend myself. I'm sorry." Though he didn't sound terribly sorry.

"When Odela arrived back in Trier, I knew my opportunity to act was soon," Georg continued. "Then I saw you thrown in the dungeons and figured I should help." He shrugged. "Catriona talked me into it."

Rowaine punched him in the shoulder. "He came to *us*, Beele. Popped out of the shadows, of course."

"How did you do it?" Sybil asked.

"I tracked Odela, found her in a dark alley, and took her. Then replaced you with the old hag during your execution walk. Simple."

"That poor woman," Sybil muttered. As her shock began wearing off, she remembered something vital. She stopped in her tracks. "We need to go back to Bedburg. My husband and my son are there."

Georg shook his head. "I can't condone that idea. If I know Heinrich, I know there's going to be a manhunt unlike anything we've seen before. You already have a title, Beele." He grinned, as if having such a title was something good.

"Oh? A two-time fugitive? A heretic? Succubus? Witch?

Traitor? . . . What are they calling me now?"

"The Daughter of the Beast. Quite ominous, though it does sound good off the tongue." He repeated it. "Almost makes you seem more terrible than you are," he joked with a wink. "Just by a bit."

"We're going to the *Lion's Pride*, my lady." Daxton spoke for the first time. The normally cheery captain didn't sound quite so at the moment. "We can hide away on the seas for a while, until things calm down."

And like Georg, Daxton also kept looking over his shoulder.

"But what about Dieter and Peter? And Martin?"

"They'll have to survive without us for a time," Rowaine said. She ran a hand down Sybil's shivering back. "They'll be fine, Beele," she added gently. "We need to keep you out of harm—"

"Shit. I hear something," Georg said. He and Daxton stopped and turned, while Rowaine and Sybil kept walking.

At first it sounded like the breeze rustling through the trees. Then more like creatures in the brush.

Then footsteps.

"Run!" Daxton shouted, pulling his pistol. Georg drew his trusty bow and both men faced the rear while backpedaling behind the women.

"Keep running!" Georg shouted to the women. "If you hear them close by, hide in the trees!" He waved them on.

Sybil could hear faraway voices as she broke into a sprint alongside Rowaine.

"There they are!" a voice called out.

Sybil glanced back and saw armed troops running through the darkness.

Georg let loose an arrow and turned to follow Rowaine and Sybil. Then Daxton's gun erupted and a muffled cry sounded in the distance.

Georg and Daxton continued behind the women, Georg turning every so often to launch an arrow back toward their pursuers while Daxton would reload his gun and do the same.

But the trackers were gaining, their banter growing louder.

"Get the witch!

"In the white dress!"

Realizing they couldn't outrun their pursuers, Daxton and Georg waited until the women had rounded a bend, then hid behind trees on opposite sides of the road.

The first man to reach them got a knife in the back from Georg. A second one, seeing his mate go down, crouched on one knee, aimed, and fired just as Daxton snuck up beside him, put his gun against the man's temple, and blew the other side of his head onto the roadway.

At the same instant, Georg heard a yelp from the women. Twisting around, he realized that the half-headless tracker Daxton had just killed had hit his mark before dying.

Rowaine was on the ground, face-first.

"Row!" Sybil cried, rushing to her friend's aid.

Rowaine groaned, her hand reaching behind to her lower back and coming away bloody.

Sybil grabbed Rowaine's other hand and tried to pull her along. "Get up, Row, please!"

"Keep running, dammit," Rowaine croaked. She somehow managed to pull her pistol from her waistband, remaining prone on her stomach. Sybil reluctantly moved off to hide behind a tree.

Daxton and Georg had dispatched two more approaching guards, but a third had gotten through and was charging down the road toward Rowaine.

As the only one of his group still standing, the attacker knew his best chance of survival was to simply run for his life. But his bloodlust got the better of him. He stopped and took aim at Rowaine's fallen body . . .

Just as Rowaine pushed off, rolled onto her back with a painful shriek and, clutching her weapon by her stomach, aimed and fired.

Before the man had a chance to get off his shot, his eyes bulged as his groin erupted in a red, thick cloud and he crumbled to the ground screaming. Georg rushed up to him and finished him off with a quick slice across the throat.

With all five hunters dead, Georg resheathed his knife, then scooped up his daughter and rushed on, carrying her like a baby.

"I told you—Rowaine Donnelly will never die!" Daxton cried out, running past Georg to take the lead. "Keep moving, come on! More bastards will be right behind!"

They fled down the road, Rowaine groaning in her father's arms, the four of them—the father, the daughter, the witch, and the captain—heading northwest toward the water, the *Lion's Pride,* and freedom.

EPILOGUE

$\mathbf{A}$ week later in Bedburg, Dieter watched from a window in Claus' inn as a parade marched by. He was on his back in bed, nestling his left arm—or what was left of it. Amputated at the elbow, it was rolled in a thick cushion of white bandage.

In his other arm he held his child. He kissed the boy's head.

Word had spread quickly through Bedburg of Sybil Griswold's "death." Dying at the stake in Trier, a proclaimed witch and traitor to the Holy Roman Empire.

Dieter's eyes were bloodshot from weeping. As he kept watch of the activities out his window, his heart suddenly tensed and his face blanched white.

There, in front of a large retinue of followers, rode Heinrich Franz. Perched on his horse like a hero, receiving a king's welcome.

Dieter breathed in sharply.

"What's wrong, Dieter?" Martin asked, sitting near Dieter's bed, holding Ava's hand. Ever since Ava had tried to steal from Sybil, the two had become close. When Karstan was jailed, Martin had followed Ava to her hideaway and had managed to convince her to join him and his friends, promising to eventually help her get out of Bedburg.

So far, he hadn't fulfilled that part of the bargain.

When Dieter didn't answer, Martin touched the priest's good arm. "I don't believe the rumors, and you shouldn't either," he said. "I won't believe Sybil is dead until I see her body for myself."

Dieter looked away from the window. "There won't *be* a body. She was burned alive, Martin."

"Have faith, sir," Ava said softly.

"Yes, Dieter," Martin said, squeezing his shoulder. "It

should come as second nature to you. If there was ever a time for faith . . . it is now."

Which is exactly what Dieter did; was all he could do; was all he knew how to do.

Keep the faith that his God wouldn't fail him—that his beloved wife was still alive.

Somewhere, somehow, some way.

Heinrich Franz met with Archbishop Ernst and Bishop Balthasar Schreib in Bedburg Castle. He brought Tomas Reiner and Hugo Griswold with him. As the witch-hunts and trials in Trier started to lose favor with the peasants, an exorbitant tax had been levied to continue in earnest the examinations, investigations, and eliminations of witches throughout the countryside.

But with that tax, the bloodthirsty zeal of the people began to wither.

Following this last debacle—with Sybil Griswold and the old hag who had taken her place—Archbishop Schönenberg had had enough.

And Heinrich had left Trier shortly after.

At the steps of his castle lobby, Archbishop Ernst embraced Heinrich, then held the investigator out at arm's-length, staring into his gray eyes. "You did a wonderful job in Trier, my friend."

Heinrich smiled wryly. "Lord Inquisitor Adalbert did a wonderful job, my lord."

Ernst chuckled. "Of course, of course." He winked. "What a wily fellow he was. Especially about a certain trial in particular."

Heinrich furrowed his brow, unsure of the archbishop's meaning.

"Odela Grendel," Balthasar Schreib explained, his chins wobbling as he beamed. "How did you do it?"

Heinrich's heart fluttered. "W-what do you mean?"

"We've been searching for that woman for ages, Herr Franz. You had to know," Ernst said. He leaned his head and rubbed his chin. "She was a major benefactor to the Protestants—one of their longest-lasting spies. Giving secrets to Gebhard and Calvinists across the land!"

"We never knew she was hiding right under our noses, in Bedburg . . . as a kitchen-maid, no less!" Balthasar added, resting his hands around his belly and laughing.

"Oh, yes . . . yes of course," Heinrich said, trying to keep his wits about him.

"Trying her as a witch and a traitor? And with such a public execution? Brilliant!" Ernst patted Heinrich on the back. "Let's see the Protestants rebound from *that!*"

"Merely doing as you ordered, my lord." Heinrich bowed.

Ernst spread his arms wide. "I've given you land and wealth for the terrific work you did here in Bedburg, so what else can I offer you?"

"I don't seek reward, my lord. I do this for the goodness of Catholicism," Heinrich lied.

Ernst waved that off. "Nonsense." His eyes darkened, and he shared a look with Bishop Schreib. "I do believe there's a vacant position in town."

Heinrich opened his mouth to protest. He didn't want a new job. He hated staying in one place for too long. He had wolves to raise, mouths to feed, an estate to look after.

How is old man Rolf doing, anyway? That old bastard will be happy to learn Odela is dead.

"Heinrich? What say you?" Ernst asked the investigator pointedly.

"I . . . I suppose that would be fine, my lord."

"Excuse me?" Ernst said flatly.

Heinrich hesitated, then bowed low. "It would be an honor, Your Grace."

Archbishop Ernst clapped his hands and put them on Heinrich's shoulders. "Would you like an alias again?"

The investigator paused. "I think not. My name will be fine," he said.

"Very well," Ernst said with a smile. "Then let me be the first to welcome you back home, Lord Heinrich Franz of Bedburg.

"It does have a nice ring to it . . . does it not?"

Fact Versus Fiction

Like Devil in the Countryside, this novel is based on true events in Germany between 1581 and 1593.

The Trier Witch Trials was perhaps the biggest series of witch trials in European history, and the largest mass executions in Europe during peace time. 368 people, the vast majority women, were confirmed killed, though others say the number exceeded 1,000. In two villages, the entire female population was exterminated save one female per village.

Everyone who was not real in the first book was also not real in this one. Rowaine and her entire crew (and ship) were made up. Same with Mia and Dolly, all of Hugo's friends—including his gang of thieves and the group of inquisitors traveling to Trier. Same with Odela, Rolf, and Heinrich's estate (House Charmagne).

The "Elizabeth's Strangers" in Norfolk was a real group of Protestants who fled to England to escape Catholic persecution. The individual Strangers in the novel, however, were fictionalized.

The suffragan bishop of Trier, Peter Binsfeld, was a real person and one of the prominent witch-hunters of his time. He also wrote about the "Classifications of Demons" in 1589.

A very real Archbishop Schönenberg was the prince-elector/archbishop of Trier during the witch trials, though I did take literary license about his possible association with Archbishop Ernst of Cologne.

Despite my literary liberties, I thought the Trier Witch Trials was a fascinating subject, and it just so happened to fit into the time period as a sequel to Devil, so I ran with it. I'm not sure what tragic historical event(s) will provide the backdrop for Book Three, but I'm sure I'll find one!

Thanks for reading!

About the Author

Cory Barclay lives in San Diego, California. He enjoys learning about serial killers, people burning, mass executions, and hopes the FBI doesn't one day look through his Google search history.

When he's not writing stories he's probably playing guitar, composing music, hanging with friends, or researching strange things to write about.

Subscribe to CoryBarclay.com for news on upcoming releases!